Defending Frequently Challenged
Young Adult Books

D0721756

CALGARY PUBLIC LIBRARY

APR   2017

Defending Frequently Challenged Young Adult Books

A HANDBOOK FOR LIBRARIANS AND EDUCATORS

❖   ❖   ❖

PAT R. SCALES

ROWMAN & LITTLEFIELD
Lanham • Boulder • New York • London

Published by Rowman & Littlefield
A wholly owned subsidary of The Rowman & Littlefield Publishing Group, Inc.
4501 Forbes Boulevard, Suite 200, Lanham, Maryland 20706
www.rowman.com

Unit A, Whitacre Mews, 26-34 Stannary Street, London SE11 4AB

Copyright © 2016 by Rowman & Littlefield

All rights reserved. No part of this book may be reproduced in any form or by any electronic or
mechanical means, including information storage and retrieval systems, without written permission
from the publisher, except by a reviewer who may quote passages in a review.

British Library Cataloguing in Publication Information Available

Library of Congress Cataloging-in-Publication Data Available

ISBN 978-1-4422-6431-1 (hardback: alk. paper)
ISBN 978-1-4422-6432-8 (paperback: alk. paper)
ISBN 978-1-4422-6433-5 (electronic)

∞™ The paper used in this publication meets the minimum requirements of American National
Standard for Information Sciences—Permanence of Paper for Printed Library Materials, ANSI/NISO
Z39.48-1992.

Printed in the United States of America

For Sandra Lott, my freshman English professor (1962–1963),
Alabama College (now the University of Montevallo):
In deep gratitude, for pointing the way and setting me free.

Contents

Preface

"There is more than one way to burn a book. And the world is full of people running around with lit matches."—Ray Bradbury, *Fahrenheit 451*

Young adult literature has been the target of censors since S. E. Hinton first presented *The Outsiders* to teenagers in 1967. It was the "gang culture" that caused parents and school administrators concern. Then along came Paul Zindel and *The Pigman* in 1968, and opposition to the novel mounted because the two main characters are "liars, cheaters, and stealers." They also curse, something some adults cannot accept in fiction for young adults. *The Chocolate War* by Robert Cormier came on the scene in 1974, and many adults became absolutely certain that the novel would cause teens to question authority. In 1975, *Forever* by Judy Blume was an overnight success with young adults, and the voices of censors became louder. This time the issue was a teenage girl's first sexual experience. And in 1977, Robert Lipsyte had boys and girls clamoring to read *One Fat Summer*, while their parents and teachers complained about the masturbation scene.

These writers gave birth to the genre of young adult literature, and teens took notice because suddenly they had books that dealt with adolescent concerns. A new wave of writers like Sherman Alexie, Laurie Halse Anderson, Chris Crutcher, John Green, Bette Greene, Ellen Hopkins, M. E. Kerr, and Walter Dean Myers began to write honest novels that deal with tough topics like drug and alcohol abuse, bullying and violence, date rape, incest, race relations, homosexuality, and mental illness. School and public libraries became a censorship battle zone, and the American Library Association's Office for Intellectual Freedom (OIF) began monitoring censorship cases and defending kids' right to read. The Freedom to Read Foundation (FTR), founded in 1969 as the legal defense arm for the American Library Association, has offered expert guidance and in some cases monetary aid to individuals and libraries in active censorship conflicts.

In 1982 Steven Pico, a high school junior, sued the Board of Education, Island Trees Union Free School District No. 26, when they removed nine books from the high school library. After a lengthy road to the Supreme Court, it was decided that "school officials cannot remove books from a library simply because they find the ideas objectionable." This remains the precedent case, and OIF, FTR, and other free speech organizations point to it when censorship battles develop. It was the Pico case that led four Olathe, Kansas, high school students to victory in 1995 when they sued the superintendent of schools after he removed *Annie on My Mind* by Nancy Garden, a book that had been on the library shelf for more than ten years. These important cases have given voice and courage to students throughout the nation to speak up for their right to read. In 2001 a student in Fairfax County, Virginia, spoke eloquently before a group of citizens about *The Pillars of the Earth* by Ken Follett and caused the superintendent to stand up to PABBIS (Parents against Bad Books in Schools) and retain the novel, along with a long list of other titles. The school district in Tucson, Arizona, shut down the Mexican American Studies program in 2011 and removed a number of books, including *Mexican WhiteBoy* by Matt de la Peña. An angry student invited de la Peña to speak at a rally, where he distributed copies of his book. When a school board member led the efforts to ban *The Miseducation of Cameron Post* by emily m. danforth from the ninth-grade summer reading list at Cape Henlopen High School in Delaware, a student wrote a convincing essay, sponsored by the National Coalition against Censorship, that ignited national attention and caused the school board to reconsider its decision. And in 2014–2015, Highland Park, Texas, students wore orange ribbons to signify their opposition to book banning efforts led by a group of citizens and some school board members.

According to data collected by the American Library Association's OIF, book challenges have actually decreased in libraries in recent years, but they have increased in the classroom. In the decade 2000–2009, school libraries had 1,639 challenges, classrooms had 1,811 challenges, and public libraries received 1,217 challenges. In 2014–2015, OIF recorded 311 challenges. Only two were published as young adult titles, but three were adult books commonly used in English classrooms. In 2013–2014, there were 307 reported challenges. Seven of the top ten were young adult titles. This was down from 2012–2013, when there were 465 reported challenges. Four of the top ten were young adult titles. Books being "sexually explicit" is the top complaint, followed by "offensive language," "unsuited for age group," "violence," "homosexuality," "occult," and "religious viewpoints." A complete report of the number of challenges, reasons for challenges, and the top ten most frequently challenged books by year is available at http://www.ala.org/bbooks/frequentlychallengedbooks/top10.

Not all challenges are reported, but a number of "free speech" organizations track censorship attempts through all types of media, including social media. The titles in this book are taken from the data collected by the American Library Association's OIF, the National Coalition against Censorship, Texas ACLU, National Council of Teachers of English, Comic Book Legal Defense Fund, and Oregon Intellectual Freedom Clearinghouse. A few titles in this book are reported in *Hit List for Young Adults 2: Frequently Challenged Books* (ALA, 2002) by Teri S. Lesesne and Rosemary Chance. They are included here because they continue to be challenged. Robert P. Doyle's *Banned Books: Challenging Our Freedom to Read, 2014 Edition* (ALA) and its supplements have been an invaluable tool in identifying the books that have been challenged or banned and the reasons why.

The Young Adult Library Services Association (YALSA) serves adolescents ages twelve–eighteen. For this reason, many of the challenges in this book have occurred in middle schools that typically serve students in the sixth through eighth grades. Some public libraries stop serving patrons in the children's room at age eleven. A concern of some parents is that books "appropriate for an eighteen-year-old" might not be "appropriate for a twelve-year-old." While this might be a valid concern, it is not up to the public library to determine age appropriateness. Parents and their teens must make that call.

Defending Frequently Challenged Young Adult Books: A Handbook for Librarians and Educators is a resource for librarians and teachers to use as they educate students, parents, and school and public library boards in understanding the risks involved when censorship is allowed. Fifty-four titles appear in alphabetical order and include a pertinent quote from the book. Bibliographic information for each entry is provided, including availability in paperback, e-book, and audio book. Phyllis Reynolds Naylor's "Alice" books and Lauren Myracle's "Internet Girls" are entered as series, but the titles are listed by date of publication. The first section for each entry focuses on specific challenges to the title, including when and where it was challenged, the reasons for the challenge, and the outcome if known. It is also noted when a title has appeared on OIF's Top 100 Most Frequently Challenged Books List and the Top Ten Most Frequently Challenged Books List for a specific year. The data does not reflect all of the challenges to a title. OIF pledges anonymity to schools and libraries if requested. There is a summary and a list of themes for each book and five or more open-ended questions to use when helping young adults understand the issues related to the challenges. The section titled "Resources for Responding to Challenges" includes review citations, quotes from reviewers, awards, and references to information about specific challenges. The section titled "Information about the Author" includes the author's website and sources for biographical information. It is followed by a section that lists bibliographic information for further reading about the book. YouTube interviews with the authors and patrons reading excerpts from the novels for Banned Books Week are examples of information provided in the final section, "Other Media Sources."

There are seven appendixes: A. Adult Books That Have Been Challenged or Banned in the High School Curriculum, B. Rankings of Young Adult Books on the Top 100 Banned/Challenged Books List of 2000–2009, C. Rankings of Young Adult Books on the Top 100 Most Frequently Challenged Books List of 1990–1999, D. Resources for Teaching Young Adults about the Freedom to Read, E. Professional Resources for Book Censorship and the Freedom to Read, F. Censorship and Teaching Ideas about the First Amendment, and G. Free Speech Organizations.

Censorship cases in schools and libraries are a moving target. By the time this book is published, there will be new challenges. It may be to earlier titles like *Forever* and *The Chocolate War*, or to books that deal with emerging social issues. For example, the news of mass shootings may cause people to question books that deal with violence; political chatter about foreign terrorism has already created fear among people who may begin to question teens reading anything related to Islam and the Muslim culture; and now that Caitlyn Jenner has been named runner-up to *Time*'s 2015 Person of the Year, the struggles of transgender teens are becoming more public. *I Am J* by Cris Beam, about a transgender teen who finds the courage to announce that "he" is a boy born with "girl" anatomy, has already received challenges and is included in this book.

No library or classroom is immune from censorship attempts. A book may be challenged, but retained when there is supportive information to defend it. Rarely is a book banned. Libraries are about choice, and no person has the right to block the reading choices of others, regardless of age. The National Council of Teachers of English strongly recommends that teachers offer reading choices to accommodate students' right to select books that satisfy their personal "sensitivities." There are always books that offend someone, but good book-selection policies for libraries and classrooms, which should include guidelines for dealing with challenges, is the best defense when the censor calls.

1

❖ ❖ ❖

The Absolutely True Diary of a Part-Time Indian

BY SHERMAN ALEXIE

New York: Little, Brown Books for Young Readers, 2007
Little, Brown E-book, 2007
Recorded Books Audio, 2008
Little, Brown Paperback, 2009

> "I wept because I was the only one who was brave and crazy enough to leave the rez.
> I was the only one with enough arrogance."

CHALLENGES: WHEN, WHY, AND WHERE

According to data collected by the American Library Association's Office for Intellectual Freedom, Alexie's novel was #1 on the Top Ten Most Frequently Challenged Books List in 2014–2015, #3 in 2013–2014, #2 in 2012–2013, #5 in 2011–2012, and #2 in 2010–2011. The reasons cited include "drugs/alcohol/smoking, offensive language, racism, sexually explicit, unsuited to age group."

2014–2015

The National Council of Teachers of English (NCTE) recorded a challenge for ninth-grade readers at a school in Virginia because of "language" and for sixth-grade readers in Iowa because it was "inappropriate for age."

2013–2014

The book was banned at Public School 114 (middle school) in Rockaway, Queens, New York, because the topic of "masturbation" isn't "appropriate for eleven-year-olds."

It was banned in the Meridian, Idaho, high school after a grandparent complained about "cursing and sexual references," and the book was ultimately removed from the high school reading list in all Idaho schools.

It was also challenged in Sweet Home, Oregon, for its "use of words not allowed by the student code of conduct" and "discussion of sexual matters." The school board voted to retain the book.

The novel was challenged because of "sexual content" at the League City Intermediate School in the Clear Creek, Texas, Independent School District. It was retained.

It was banned from the Jefferson County public schools in West Virginia because of the "graphic" content.

According to data collected by the NCTE, the novel was challenged at a high school in North Carolina because it "offends religious beliefs." The board voted to retain the book for grades 9 and up.

2012–2013

There were challenges to the novel as required reading in at least three freshmen English classes at the Westfield, New Jersey, high school because of "very sensitive material in the book, including excerpts on masturbation amongst other explicit sexual references, encouraging pornography, racism, religious irreverence, and strong language (including the f- and n-words)." The school board voted to retain the book.

The novel was challenged in the Geraldine, Montana, public schools as "inappropriate for classroom use because of sex and language." The status of the challenge is unknown.

It was also challenged but retained in the Springfield, Massachusetts, public schools after the Comic Book Legal Defense Fund aided in the defense.

2011–2012

The novel was challenged in the Richland, Washington, School District because of "coarse themes and language." It was later returned to the library shelves.

It was pulled from the Dade County, Georgia, library shelves and the required high school reading list because of complaints of "vulgarity, racism, and anti-Christian content."

It was also challenged at the Old Rochester Regional Junior High School in Mattapoisett, Massachusetts, as an eighth-grade English assignment.

2010–2011

The book was banned in the curriculum but retained in the library at the Newcastle Middle School in Newcastle, Wyoming. In the same year, the school board in Stockton, Missouri, voted to ban the book.

The novel was challenged at Helena High School in Montana, but the challenge was withdrawn under pressure from the Montana American Civil Liberties Union.

2009–2010

The novel was retained on the summer reading list at the Antioch, Illinois, high school despite objections from several parents who found the book "vulgar" and "racist."

2008–2009

A parent objected to the book in Crook County, Oregon, because of references to "masturbation." The book was removed from the library shelves.

THE STORY

Fourteen-year-old Arnold Spirit Jr. is caught between two worlds when he leaves the school on the Spokane Indian Reservation in Washington state to attend an all-white high school twenty-two miles away. Life on the reservation has been especially tough for him. He was born with "water on the brain," and his odd looks make him the ideal target of bullies. He knows that he must make drastic changes if he is to succeed. Grandmother Spirit encourages Arnold, and he is devastated when she is killed by a drunk driver.

There are times when Arnold's part-time life on the reservation and his part-time life in a school filled with spoiled rich kids collide. He faces prejudices against native Americans at school, and back home his status as a "traitor" makes him an outcast among his own people. Things turn around for him when he makes the high school basketball team, develops a crush on a popular white girl, and makes friends with a school geek who becomes his mentor.

Told in first person, Arnold's story contains sixty-five "comic-style" illustrations that add humor to the tragic parts of his story as he struggles to bridge two very different cultures.

Themes

❖ Bullying
❖ Courage
❖ Friendship
❖ Grief
❖ Home
❖ Hope
❖ Physical abuse
❖ Prejudice and bigotry
❖ Self-identity
❖ Substance abuse

TALKING WITH TEENS ABOUT THE ISSUES

Define prejudice and discuss the prejudices that the students at Reardon have toward native Americans on the nearby reservation. How does prejudice lead to bullying? Prejudices exist in every high school. What might students do to combat prejudice?

Analyze the title of the book. At what point in the novel does the meaning of "part-time" become obvious? Why is it so difficult for Arnold to be "part-time" in the two worlds in which he lives?

Explain how his struggles with identity are similar to what many teens face. How are they different? At what point does he gain a more positive sense of self?

Alexie opens a window for readers when he reveals the character of Junior and details his life on the reservation. What do you see? Why is it important to have an open mind when reading about other cultures, people, or environments that are different from yours?

A teen reviewer for *Voice of Youth Advocates* (August 1, 2007) calls the novel "funny and tragic." How does Alexie use humor to soften the "dark" side of Junior's life? Explain how the cartoon illustrations contribute to the novel. How do they expand the text?

This novel has been challenged and banned because of offensive language, drugs/alcohol/smoking, sex, and racism. How are these issues a very real part of Junior's life? Why is talking about these issues better than denying that they exist?

How is the novel about courage and hope? Focus on these themes and prepare a statement in defense of the novel.

CHALLENGED FOR SIMILAR REASONS

Aquado, Bill, ed. *Paint Me Like I Am: Teen Poems from WritersCorps.* New York: HarperTeen, an imprint of HarperCollins, 2003.

In 2009, the principal at the Landis Intermediate School in Vineland, New Jersey, removed two pages that included the poem "Diary of an Abusive Step-Father" after a thirteen-year-old Landis student's mother questioned its appropriateness. The thirty-one-line poem is peppered with profanity and details a violent relationship between an adult and child. San Francisco–based WritersCorps, an art organization linking writers with teens in urban areas to provide outlets for their experiences, produced the anthology.

Borland, Hal. *When the Legends Die*. New York: Random House Laurel Leaf, an imprint of Penguin Random House, 1984. (Original copyright 1963.)

In 1995, the novel was banned from the curriculum at Lincoln County high schools in Wyoming because a parent complained that this story about a Ute boy who struggles with identity contains "considerable obscenities."

Davis, Terry. *Vision Quest*. New York: Delacorte, an imprint of Penguin Random House, 1979.

This novel about a native American boy in Spokane, Washington, who trains to win the state wrestling championship was moved from the middle school to the high school in Bismarck, North Dakota, after a parent complained about "obscene passages." There are also recorded challenges in Wisconsin and Washington because of "profanity."

RESOURCES FOR RESPONDING TO CHALLENGES

What Reviewers Say

School Library Journal (September 1, 2007) recommends the book for grades 7–10 and says it "delivers a positive message in a low-key manner." Ian Chipman, the reviewer for *Booklist* (August 1, 2007), states that Alexie "doesn't pull any punches as he levels his eye at stereotypes both warranted and inapt." *Kirkus* (July 15, 2007) calls the novel an "achingly clear-eyed look at the realities of reservation life." *Publishers Weekly* (August 20, 2007) comments on the "dark humor" and the "jazzy syntax and Forney's witty cartoons." *Horn Book Magazine* (September 1, 2007) recommends the book for middle and high school and calls "Junior's spirit unquenchable and his style inimitable." Bruce Barcott, reviewer for the *New York Times Sunday Book Review* (November 11, 2007), calls the novel "a gem of a book." He praises Alexie by saying that this "may be his best work yet." The *Guardian* (October 3, 2008) praises the book and says, "It's humane, authentic and, most of all, it speaks."

Other Justification for Inclusion in Curricula and Library Collections
- 2010 California Young Reader Medal: Young Adult
- 2009 Delaware Diamonds Book Award: High School
- 2009 Great Lakes Great Book Award: Grades 9–12 (Michigan)
- 2008 ALA/YALSA Best Books List
- 2008 Boston Globe–Horn Book Award: Fiction
- 2008 Washington State Book Award
- 2007 National Book Award for Young People's Literature
- 2007 *New York Times* Notable Books: Children's Books
- 2007 *Publishers Weekly* Best Books of the Year List
- 2007 *Publishers Weekly* Best Children's Books List
- 2007 *School Library Journal* Best Books of the Year

Sources of Information about Challenges to the Novel

Bousquet, Mark. "Sherman Alexie: Censorship of Any Form Punishes Curiosity." Comic Book Legal Defense Fund, October 15, 2012. Accessed April 5, 2014. http://cbldf.org/2012/10/sherman-alexie-censorship-of-any-form-punishes-curiosity.

Connelly, Joel. "Sherman Alexie Novel Banned in Meridian, Idaho." Seattlepi.com, April 3, 2014. Accessed April 5, 2014. http://blog.seattlepi.com/seattlepolitics/2014/04/03/sherman-alexie-novel-banned-in-meridian-idaho/.

Flood, Alison. "Sherman Alexie's Young-Adult Book Banned in Idaho Schools." *Guardian*, April 8, 2014. Accessed June 1, 2015. http://www.theguardian.com/books/2014/apr/08/sherman-alexie-schools-ban-idaho-diary-part-time-indian-anti-christian.

"Sherman Alexie Talks to NCAC's the Write Stuff about Being Banned." National Coalition against Censorship (blog), February 19, 2013. Accessed March 31, 2014. http://ncacblog.wordpress.com/2013/02/19/sherman-alexie-talks-to-ncacs-the-write-stuff-about-being-banned/.

Staino, Rocco. "NCAC Honors YA Author Sherman Alexie as Defender of Free Speech." *School Library Journal*, November 13, 2013. Accessed April 25, 2015. http://www.slj.com/2013/11/industry-news/ncac-honors-ya-author-sherman-alexie-as-defender-of-free-speech/.

INFORMATION ABOUT THE AUTHOR AND ILLUSTRATOR

http://fallsapart.com (Alexie's official website)

"Ellen Forney." *Contemporary Authors Online*, 2014. Books and Authors. Gale.

"Sherman Alexie." *Contemporary Authors Online*, 2012. Books and Authors. Gale.

FURTHER READING ABOUT THE NOVEL

Alexie, Sherman. "Every Teen's Struggle." *Publishers Weekly* 255, issue 7 (February 18, 2008): 160.

Alexie, Sherman. "Fiction and Poetry Award Winner: The Absolutely True Diary of a Part-Time Indian" (speech). *Horn Book Magazine* 85, issue 1 (January/February 2009): 25–28.

Alexie, Sherman. "How to Fight Monsters." *Read* 57, issue 12 (February 8, 2008): 20–24.

Alexie, Sherman. "Why the Best Kids Books Are Written in Blood." *Wall Street Journal*, June 9, 2011. Accessed March 31, 2014. http://blogs.wsj.com/speakeasy/2011/06/09/why-the-best-kids-books-are-written-in-blood/.

Crandall, Bryan Ripley. "Adding a Disability Perspective When Reading Adolescent Literature: Sherman Alexie's *The Absolutely True Diary of a Part-Time Indian*." *Alan Review* 179, issue 2 (Winter 2009): 71–78.

Hunt, Jonathan. "Worth a Thousand Words." *Horn Book Magazine* 84, issue 4 (July/August 2008): 421–426.

Insenga, Angela. "Taking Cartoons as Seriously as Books: Using Images to Read Words in *The Absolutely True Diary of a Part-Time Indian*." *SIGNAL Journal* 35, issue 2 (Spring/Summer 2012): 18–26.

Macintyre, Pamela. "The Rise of the Illustrated Young Adult Novel: Challenges to Form and Ideology." *International Journal of the Book* 8, issue 1 (2011): 135–144.

Miller, Donna L. "Honoring Identity with Young Adult Novels." *Tribal College Journal* 24, issue 4 (Summer 2013): 28–30.

OTHER MEDIA SOURCES

http://www.c-span.org/video/?202083-3/book-discussion-absolutely-true-diary-parttime-indian. Posted November 3, 2007. Accessed April 5, 2014. Sherman Alexie speaks at the 2007 Texas Book Festival.

https://www.youtube.com/watch?v=LUs9Boyqqdc. Posted May 22, 2013. Accessed March 31, 2014. Sherman Alexie talks to the American Booksellers Foundation for Free Expression.

http://ncac.org/blog/sherman-alexie-discusses-book-banning-and-censorship/. Posted September 16, 2014. Accessed April 26, 2015. Sherman Alexie discusses book banning and censorship with the National Coalition against Censorship.

2

❖ ❖ ❖

The Alice Series

BY PHYLLIS REYNOLDS NAYLOR

New York: Atheneum, an imprint of Simon & Schuster, 1985–2013
Simon & Schuster Paperback, 1986–2014

"Just being alive embarrasses me."—*The Agony of Alice* (first in the series)

"When you've found the right one—when you see him, when you're with him—you'll feel like you're coming home."—*Now I'll Tell You Everything* (last in the series)

CHALLENGES: WHEN, WHY, AND WHERE

According to data collected by the American Library Association's Office for Intellectual Freedom, the Alice series was #14 on the 100 Most Frequently Challenged Books List of 1990–1999 and #2 on the Top 100 Banned/Challenged Books List of 2000–2009. In 2001–2002, the series was #7 on the Most Frequently Challenged Books List because of "sexual content" and for being "unsuited for age group." It was the second most challenged in 2002–2003 because of "homosexuality, sexually explicit scenes and unsuited to age group." In 2003–2004, the Alice series topped the American Library Association's Top Ten Most Frequently Challenged Books List because of "sexual content, offensive language and unsuited to age group." In 2006–2007, the series was named the third most challenged for "offensive language and sexually explicit scenes," and in 2011–2012 the series made #6 on the Top Ten Most Frequently Challenged Books List for "nudity, offensive language, and religious viewpoint." The American Library Association, the Texas American Civil Liberties Union (Texas ACLU), and the National Coalition against Censorship records the following specific challenges:

2013–2014

Intensively Alice was challenged at Buffalo Prairie Middle School in Buffalo, Missouri, because a grandmother, a teacher, and the principal felt the book was "pornographic and/or obscene." The book was retained after the American Library Association and the Missouri Library Association became involved.

Lovingly Alice was moved to the secondary campus in the Denton, Texas, Independent School District after it was challenged in the elementary school for "sexual content."

2010–2011

According to the Texas ACLU, *Alice on Her Way* was placed on a restricted shelf at Sealy Junior High School in the Sealy Independent School District because of "sexual content and nudity."

The Texas ACLU reports that *Alice on the Outside* was banned at Goliad Elementary School in the Eastland Independent School District because of "profanity, sexual content or nudity."

Dangerously Alice was banned in elementary schools, placed on restricted shelves in middle schools, and retained in high schools in the Beaumont, Texas, Independent School District. According to the Texas ACLU, the school district had issues with the "sexual content or nudity" in the book and felt it "offensive to religious sensitivities."

2008–2009

Alice on Her Way was challenged at the Icicle River Middle School Library in Leavenworth, Washington, because it was deemed "objectionable."

2006–2007

Alice Alone and *Patiently Alice* were moved from the Junior High School Library to the Senior High School Library in the Katy Texas, Independent School District because of "profanity and sexual content."

Reluctantly Alice was challenged in Wake County Schools, North Carolina, by parents who sought support from Called2Action, a Christian group that says its mission is to "promote and defend our shared family and social values."

2005–2006

Alice on the Outside was challenged but retained in the librarian's office at the Shelbyville East Middle School in Kentucky because the book is "too sexually explicit" for middle school students. The book is available with parental permission.

Lovingly Alice was challenged at the Quail Run Elementary School in the Paradise Valley, Arizona, Unified School District because it "contains highly inappropriate graphic sex content" and was permanently removed in 2011. It was also banned for "sexual content" at the Bens Branch Elementary School in the New Caney, Texas, Independent School District.

2003–2004

Alice the Brave was challenged in the Mesquite Pirrung Elementary School Library in Texas due to "sexual references."

2002–2003

Achingly Alice, *Alice in Lace*, and *The Grooming of Alice* were banned from the Webb City, Missouri, school library because the book "promotes homosexuality and discusses issues 'best left to parents.'" It was also banned at the middle school in the Lumberton, Texas, Independent School District because it is "sexually explicit." In the same school district, *Alice in Lace* was banned because it "promotes homosexuality."

2001–2002

Alice in Rapture, Sort Of was placed on a restricted shelf at the Tarver-Rendon Elementary School Library in the Mansfield, Texas, Independent School District because of "sexual content."

Alice on the Outside was banned from the Van Horn Junior High School in the Culberson County–Allamoore, Texas, Independent School District because of "sexual content." The novel was also placed on a restricted shelf at the middle school in the Lumberton, Texas, Independent School District because of "sexual content."

2000–2001

The Agony of Alice was challenged at the Franklin Sherman Elementary School Library and on the Fairfax County, Virginia, approved reading list. The book was retained in libraries but limited in its classroom use to small-group discussion and for girls only. The reasons were not cited.

1997–1998

All but Alice was restricted to students with parental permission at the Monroe Elementary School in Thorndike, Maine. The novel was removed in the same year from the elementary school libraries in the Rosemount–Apple Valley–Eagan Independent School District #196 in Minnesota because of a "brief passage in which the seventh-grade heroine discusses sexually oriented rock lyrics with her father and older brother."

Alice In-Between was removed from the Monroe, Connecticut, sixth-grade required reading list after some parents called attention to the book's "sexual content."

THE BOOKS

Alice McKinley lives with her widowed father and her older brother, Lester, in Silver Spring, Maryland, where her father is the manager of a music store. Since Alice's mother died when Alice was five, she isn't used to a female presence in her life, but now that she is growing up she finds that she has "girl" type questions that her father just can't answer. Aunt Sally, who lives in Chicago, is always available by telephone, but Aunt Sally proves too conservative for the "honest" answers that Alice needs. Alice is in the sixth grade in *The Agony of Alice*, the first book in the series. Her problems reflect her age: making friends and adjusting to a new school. *Alice in Rapture, Sort Of*, the second book, has Alice and her new best friends, Pamela and Elizabeth, getting their first boyfriends. As the girls grow, their questions and concerns become more complex. There are typical spats with friends, breakups with boyfriends, and issues related to curfews and social functions. As a high school student, Alice becomes aware of social issues and begins to ponder what she can do to make a difference. When her school becomes embroiled in a censorship case, Alice becomes passionate about free speech rights. She recognizes racial bigotry and wants to fix it. She sees bullying and wants to face the bully.

There are sad times as well. A friend is killed in a car accident; another is dealing with cancer and chemotherapy treatments. One friend faces an unwanted pregnancy; another has a shotgun wedding. The final book, *Now I'll Tell You Everything*, brings Alice's life full circle. At the beginning of the novel she is entering her freshman year at the University of Maryland, and by the last chapter Alice has turned sixty.

The Series

- ❖ *The Agony of Alice*, 1985
- ❖ *Alice in Rapture, Sort Of*, 1989
- ❖ *Reluctantly Alice*, 1991
- ❖ *All but Alice*, 1992
- ❖ *Alice in April*, 1993
- ❖ *Alice In-Between*, 1994
- ❖ *Alice the Brave*, 1995
- ❖ *Alice in Lace*, 1996
- ❖ *Outrageously Alice*, 1997
- ❖ *Achingly Alice*, 1998
- ❖ *Alice on the Outside*, 1999
- ❖ *The Grooming of Alice*, 2000
- ❖ *Alice Alone*, 2001
- ❖ *Simply Alice*, 2002
- ❖ *Starting with Alice*, 2002
- ❖ *Patiently Alice*, 2003
- ❖ *Alice in Blunderland*, 2004
- ❖ *Including Alice*, 2004
- ❖ *Alice on Her Way*, 2005
- ❖ *Alice in the Know*, 2006
- ❖ *Lovingly Alice*, 2006
- ❖ *Dangerously Alice*, 2007
- ❖ *Almost Alice*, 2008
- ❖ *Intensely Alice*, 2009
- ❖ *Alice in Charge*, 2010
- ❖ *I Like Him, He Likes Her*, 2010 (This multivolume edition contains *Alice Alone*, 2001; *Simply Alice*, 2002; and *Patiently Alice*, 2003.)
- ❖ *It's Not Like I Planned It This Way*, 2010 (This multivolume edition contains *Including Alice*, 2004; *Alice on Her Way*, 2005; and *Alice in the Know*, 2006.)
- ❖ *Incredibly Alice*, 2011
- ❖ *Alice on Board*, 2012
- ❖ *Now I'll Tell You Everything*, 2013

Themes

- ❖ Bullying
- ❖ Coming of age
- ❖ Dealing with death
- ❖ Family
- ❖ Friendship
- ❖ Racial bigotry
- ❖ Sex and sexual identity

TALKING WITH TEENS ABOUT THE ISSUES

Describe Alice's relationship with her father and brother. Why is she so eager to find a wife for her father? What is Lester's role in rearing Alice?

At what point does Alice realize that Aunt Sally is too conservative to answer some of her questions? Why does she feel more comfortable asking questions of her cousin, Carol? Why does every girl need someone to talk with about "girl" topics?

The Alice books have been challenged in school and public libraries because of sexual content. How are the books a good source of information for girls?

Discuss Alice's attitude toward sex. How does she have a healthier view than some of her classmates?

Many schools include sex education in the curriculum. Explain the rationale of a school board that votes to teach sex education but insists that fiction dealing with adolescents' curiosities about sex be removed from the shelves of the library.

Alice comes face to face with social issues that most adolescents witness in their schools: bullying, book censorship, homosexuality, drugs and alcohol use, and unwanted pregnancies. Why do these issues make some adults nervous? How does Alice deal with these issues? Explain how "not knowing" is more dangerous than "knowing" about these topics.

The Alice series is unique because Alice grows from a little girl to a grown woman. How has this unique approach contributed to some of the censorship cases? Explain how the series helps girls on their journey from girlhood to adulthood.

CHALLENGED FOR SIMILAR REASONS

Brashares, Ann. *Sisterhood of the Traveling Pants*. New York: Random House Children's Books, 2001.

This novel about four friends who deal with typical teen emotions was challenged in 2010 at Theisen Middle School in Fond du Lac, Wisconsin, because it's "sexually explicit and unsuitable to age group."

Drill, Esther. *Deal with It! A Whole New Approach to Your Body, Brain and Life as a gURL*. New York: Gallery Books, an imprint of Simon & Schuster, 1999.

In 2009–2010, this nonfiction work that contains information that all teenage girls need to know about their bodies, dealing with friends, confronting issues related to sex and sexuality, and all things about growing up was challenged but retained at the West Bend, Wisconsin, Community Memorial Library because a patron claimed the book was "pornographic and worse than an R-rated movie." There are also registered challenges in the Fayetteville, Arkansas, School District and the public library systems in Montgomery County, Texas, and Ocala, Florida.

Mackler, Carolyn. *Tangled*. New York: HarperCollins, 2009.

In 2011–2012, this novel about four teens whose lives become tangled on a vacation in the Caribbean was banned from the intermediate and middle school libraries in the Borger, Texas, Independent School District because of "sexual content and profanity."

RESOURCES FOR RESPONDING TO CHALLENGES

What Reviewers Say

In the *Booklist* (March 15, 1985) starred review, *The Agony of Alice*, the first in the series, is called "a wonderfully funny and touching story." The *Boston Globe* states the novel has "breezy dialogue and a solid story line." *School Library Journal* (January 1, 1986) states, "Alice's forthcoming fans will agonize with her and await her future adventures."

The Bulletin for the Center of Children's Books (May 1994) praises *Alice In-Between* for "energetic dialogue and sprightly episodes." The starred review calls the novel "fresh."

Publishers Weekly (May 1, 2000) says that Naylor, in *The Grooming of Alice*, "masterfully imparts physical, social, and emotional information while bringing readers to tears and laughter."

Kirkus reviews *Alice Alone* (May 1, 2001) and states that Alice "is blessed with a more loving family than many" and she continues to "get through the hard days as well as the good ones as best she can." The journal's review of *Incredibly Alice* (May 10, 2011) states, "As ever, Naylor-as-Alice fills the interstices with teachable moments."

The reviewer for *School Library Journal* (July 1, 2012) says of *Alice on Board*, "Avid Alice fans will want this next-to-last installment." *Voice of Youth Advocates* (June 1, 2012) calls the book "an enjoyable beach read for teens."

School Library Journal (June 1, 2010) states, "Alice is a wonderful role model" in *Alice in Charge*. Hazel Rochman, writing for *Booklist* (May 15, 2010), states, "Avoiding formulas, Naylor breaks new ground again." Rochman, who has reviewed a number of the Alice books for *Booklist* (April 1, 2007), calls *Dangerously Alice* "funny and honest." *School Library Journal* (August 1, 2007) calls the book "episodic."

Ann Kelly reviews *Now I'll Tell You Everything* in *Booklist* (August 2013) and states, "Naylor has given fans a gift: the chance to see how life unfolds for a beloved character."

Other Justification for Inclusion in Curricula and Library Collections

❖ *Alice in April*: 2011 IRA/CBC Children's Choices
❖ *Outrageously Alice*: 1998 ALA Best Books for Young Adults; 1998 *VOYA* Best Books for Young Adults
❖ *Alice in April*: 1994 ALA/YALSA Best Books for Reluctant Young Adult Readers
❖ *All but Alice*: 1993 ALA Notable Books for Children; 1993 IRA/CBC Children's Choices
❖ *All but Alice*: 1992 *School Library Journal* Best Books of the Year
❖ *Reluctantly Alice*: 1991 *School Library Journal* Best Book
❖ *Agony of Alice*: 1986 ALA/ALSC Notable Children's Books

Sources of Information about Challenges to the Novels

Bronson, Andrea. "Teens' Favorite Authors Face Book Bans." *We News*, October 22, 2007. Accessed March 8, 2014. http://womensenews.org/story/books/071022/teens-favorite-authors-face-book-bans#.UxthI9xOF4M.

Gounley, Thomas. "At Principal's Request, Buffalo Middle School to Consider Banning Novel." *News-Leader* (Springfield, Missouri), March 2, 2013. Accessed March 8, 2014. http://www.news-leader.com/article/20130302/NEWS01/303020053/Buffalo-Middle-School-book-ban.

Staino, Rocco. "Ellen Hopkins, Phyllis Reynolds Naylor, and Chris Finan Are Honored for Their Roles in Battling Literary Censorship." *School Library Journal*, November 19, 2012. Accessed March 8, 2014. http://www.slj.com/2012/11/events/ellen-hopkins-phyllis-reynolds-naylor-and-chris-finan-are-honored-for-their-roles-battling-literary-censorship/.

West, Mark. "Speaking of Censorship: An Interview with Phyllis Reynolds Naylor." *Journal of Youth Services in Libraries* (Winter 1997): 177–182.

INFORMATION ABOUT THE AUTHOR

http://alicemckinley.wordpress.com/. (Naylor's official "Alice" website)

Contemporary Authors Online, 2013. Books and Authors. Gale.

http://www.scholastic.com/teachers/contributor/phyllis-reynolds-naylor. Scholastic. Accessed March 8, 2014.

FURTHER READING ABOUT THE NOVELS

Busis, Hillary. "Phyllis Reynolds Naylor Talks Finishing the Alice Series—a 28-Book, 28-Year-Long Opus." *Entertainment Weekly*, October 15, 2015. Accessed December 14, 2015. http://www.ew.com/article/2013/10/15/phyllis-reynolds-naylor-alice-last-book.

Devereaux, Elizabeth. "An Appetite for Alice." *Publishers Weekly* 249, issue 39 (September 30, 2002): 26–27.

Flynn, Kitty. "Everygirl: Phyllis Reynolds Naylor's Alice." *Horn Book Magazine* 83, issue 5 (September/October 2007): 463–467.

Hesse, Monica. "Closing the Book on 'Alice.'" *Washington Post*, October 14, 2013.

Jones, Carolyn E. "For Adults Only? Searching for Subjectivity in Phyllis Reynolds Naylor's Alice Series." *Children's Literature Association Quarterly* (Spring 2005): 16–31.

Naylor, Phyllis Reynolds. "To Be Continued . . ." *Horn Book Magazine* 82, issue 1 (January/February 2006): 41–44.

Scales, Pat. "Because of Alice: Phyllis Reynolds Naylor's Alice Books." *Book Links*, a supplement of *Booklist* (June 2011): 14–17.

Winfrey, Kerry. "I'll Miss You, Alice McKinley." *Hello Giggles* (blog), October 26, 2013. Accessed December 14, 2015. http://hellogiggles.com/ill-miss-you-alice-mckinley/.

OTHER MEDIA SOURCES

http://www.readingrockets.org/books/interviews/naylor. Reading Rockets. Accessed July 11, 2015. In this video, Naylor reflects on her childhood and love of story.

https://www.youtube.com/watch?v=oYvJXVGa_2Q. Posted November 14, 2012. Accessed July 11, 2015. Phyllis Reynolds Naylor talks about attempts to censor her books.

https://www.youtube.com/watch?v=N1D3QvJtRUI. Posted December 6, 2012. Accessed July 11, 2015. Free Speech Matters talks with Phyllis Reynolds Naylor.

3

❖ ❖ ❖

Am I Blue? Coming Out from the Silence

BY MARION DANE BAUER, EDITOR

New York: HarperCollins, 1994
HarperCollins Trophy Paperback, 1995

"I have never met a bigot who was a reader as a child."

CHALLENGES: WHEN, WHY, AND WHERE

According to data collected by the American Library Association's Office for Intellectual Freedom, the book was #25 among the 100 Most Frequently Challenged Books List of 1990–1999. It ranked #18 on the Top 100 Banned/Challenged Books of 2000–2009.

2010–2011

According to the Texas American Civil Liberties Union, the book was challenged in all middle schools in the Fort Worth Independent School District because of "sexual content." It was retained.

2004–2005

A parent of an eighth-grader in Solon, Iowa, challenged the title short story by Bruce Coville because it "explores a boy's confusion with his sexual identity and the gay fairy godfather who helps him overcome homophobia at school."

2000–2001

The book was challenged at the middle and high school libraries in Fairfield, Iowa, because of the "graphic description of a sexual act between two girls." It was retained.

THE STORY

These sixteen short stories, all by well-known writers for young adults, deal with issues related to being a gay or lesbian teen, or living in a home with gay or lesbian parents. In the title story, "Am I Blue?" by Bruce Coville, Vince is bullied because he is gay. When his fairy godfather offers Vince three wishes, he wants all gays, and the guy who bullied him, to turn blue. M. E. Kerr writes about a girl who comes out to her grandmother in "We Might as Well All Be Strangers." In "Running" by Ellen Howard, a girl is kicked out of her home because she is gay, and in C. S. Adler's "Michael's Little Sister," a little girl learns that it is all right to be different. Some of the stories are funny and others are touching and heartbreaking. All of the stories are intended to "dispel myths and provide needed information."

Themes

- ❖ Bullying
- ❖ Coming of age
- ❖ Family
- ❖ Friends
- ❖ Homosexuality
- ❖ Tolerance

TALKING WITH TEENS ABOUT THE ISSUES

Discuss why those who want to ban the book have singled out Bruce Coville's title story. What makes it different from the others?

In "We Might as Well All Be Strangers" by M. E. Kerr, Alison's grandmother makes an interesting comparison of people who are anti-Semitic with those who are antihomosexual. Debate her views. How does Alison's mother react?

The book has been challenged for its sexual content. Discuss whether the parents who challenged the book might also challenge a book with heterosexual sexual content.

The publisher states that the intent of the book is to "dispel myths and provide needed information." Discuss whether the book accomplishes its purpose.

What might teens do to further dispel myths regarding homosexuality?

CHALLENGED FOR SIMILAR REASONS

Heron, Ann. *Two Teenagers in Twenty: Writings by Lesbian and Gay Youth*. New York: Alyson Publications, 1994.

This revision of *One in Ten* (1983) contains twenty-four short stories written by gay and lesbian teens about their personal journeys of coming out to family and friends and was removed from the Barron, Wisconsin, School District in 1998 because "it contains outdated information about AIDS." The Wisconsin American Civil Liberties Union filed a lawsuit to reinstate the book.

Levithan, David. *Boy Meets Boy*. New York: Knopf, an imprint of Penguin Random House, 2003.

This novel about a gay high school boy who finds and loses love was challenged in the West Bend, Wisconsin, public library in 2009–2010 after the library put it on a gay-themed reading list. The novel was retained.

Sedaris, David. *Naked*. New York: Back Bay Books, an imprint of Hachette Book Group, 1998.

"I Like Guys," a short story from this biographical collection about Sedaris's coming out as a gay man was banned from the Litchfield, New Hampshire, high school curriculum in 2009 because parents claimed a "political agenda." They objected to the subject matter, especially issues related to "abortion, cannibalism, homosexuality, and drug use." The controversy led to the resignation of the English curriculum advisor.

RESOURCES FOR RESPONDING TO CHALLENGES

What Reviewers Say

Publishers Weekly (May 2, 1994) praises the collection and calls it "honest, well-written and true to life." *Booklist* (May 1, 1994) gives the book a star and says that it is "wonderfully diverse in tone and setting." The reviewer for *Voice of Youth Advocates* (August 1, 1994) comments on the "high quality" of each story. *School Library Journal* (June 1, 1994) recommends the book for grades 7 and up and says the stories "speak of survival and hope." The *Horn Book Guide* (September 1, 1999) states that the collection is a "powerful commentary about our social and emotional responses to homosexuality." The *Kirkus* (May 15, 1994) starred review says that young people who are questioning their sexual orientation will "realize they are not alone, unique, or abnormal."

Other Justification for Inclusion in Curricula and Library Collections

❖ 1997 ALA/YALSA Popular Paperbacks for Young Adults
❖ 1995 Minnesota Book Awards: Young Adult Books
❖ 1995 Stone Wall Book Award
❖ 1994 Lambda Literary Awards: Young Adult–Children's

Sources of Information about Challenges to the Collection

Broz, William J. "Defending *Am I Blue*." *Journal of Adolescent & Adult Literacy* 45, issue 5 (February 2002): 340–350.

Sova, Dawn B. "*Am I Blue?*" *Literature Suppressed on Social Grounds*, volume 4, 17–19. New York: Facts on File, 2006.

INFORMATION ABOUT THE EDITOR

http://www.mariondanebauer.com (Bauer's official website)

Smith, Cynthia Leitich. "Author Feature: Marion Dane Bauer." *Cynsations* (blog), May 8, 2006. Accessed October 25, 2015. http://cynthialeitichsmith.blogspot.com/2006/05/author-feature-marion-dane-bauer.html.

FURTHER READING ABOUT THE COLLECTION

Ford, Michael Thomas. "*Am I Blue? Coming Out from the Silence*." *Lambda Book Report* 4, issue 2 (January/February 1994): 13.

Ford, Michael Thomas. "Gay Books for Young Readers: When Caution Calls the Shots." *Publishers Weekly* 241, issue 8 (February 21, 1994): 24–27.

"Homosexuality in Children's Literature." *Children's Literature Review* 119. Excerpts from *Reviews, Criticism, and Commentary on Books for Children and Young People*, edited by Tom Burns. Detroit: Gale, 2007.

Walker, K., and M. D. Bauer. "The Gay/Lesbian Connection: Two Authors Talk about Their Work." *Bookbird* 32 (Summer 1994): 25–30.

OTHER MEDIA SOURCES

https://www.youtube.com/watch?v=V2vyJx1OvzA. Posted May 27, 2013. Accessed October 25, 2015. This is a video adaptation of Bruce Coville's short story "Am I Blue?"

https://www.youtube.com/watch?v=Wtiahd143sM. Posted June 30, 2013. Accessed October 25, 2015. This is a book trailer for *Am I Blue? Coming Out from the Silence*.

4

❖ ❖ ❖

America

BY E. R. FRANK

New York: Simon & Schuster, 2002 (Op)
Simon & Schuster Pulse, 2003, 2015 (Reissue)
Lifetime Feature Film, 2009

> "I'm afraid to sleep because of the dreams, and I'm afraid to be awake because all these flashes keep squeezing through and I can't stuff them back the way I used to."

CHALLENGES: WHEN, WHY, AND WHERE

According to data collected by the American Library Association's Office for Intellectual Freedom, Frank's novel was #100 on the Top 100 Banned/Challenged Books List of 2000–2009.

2007–2008

The novel was challenged at Brown Middle School in Ravenna, Ohio, because of "profanity and sexual content." The outcome of the case is unknown.

2003–2004

Parents in a school in Twin Bridges, Montana, challenged the novel because of "inappropriate language and graphic sexual imagery." The school board voted to retain the book.

THE STORY

Life seems hopeless to fifteen-year-old America, a biracial boy who falls victim to a broken social services system. His mother is a drug addict, and he is sent to live with a wealthy white family. By the age of five his skin darkens, and the white family no longer wants him. The family's nanny, Mrs. Harper, takes him in as a foster child. America is in special education classes at school, and at home Mrs. Harper's half brother, Browning, is a bad influence on him. He tutors America in reading "pornographic" magazines, and eventually Browning starts molesting him. America suffers fits of anger and fear, and one night he sets Browning's mattress on fire. Browning dies, and America finds himself in court. Instead of jail, the judge sends America to a residential psychiatric facility where he meets Dr. B., who tries to help him deal with the issues of his past life. America is confused about many things, especially how to love and trust others. By the end of the novel, he feels forgiven for his "bad" behaviors, and he finally has a positive dream.

Themes
- ❖ Abandonment
- ❖ Anger
- ❖ Drugs and alcohol abuse
- ❖ Fear
- ❖ Foster families
- ❖ Love
- ❖ Racism and prejudice
- ❖ Sex abuse
- ❖ Social issues
- ❖ Special needs
- ❖ Suicide

TALKING WITH TEENS ABOUT THE ISSUES

How does the social service system fail America?

Explain how the white family that takes America betrays him. Why are they so bothered by the color of his skin?

Why is Mrs. Harper so willing to take America? Discuss what happens when she becomes too sick to watch out for him.

The novel has been challenged because of profanity. How is the use of profanity part of the street culture in which America lives?

The book has also been challenged because of graphic sexual imagery. Browning sexually molests America. Explain how the sexual imagery reveals the truth about America's situation. How might America's story alert teen readers to the realities of sex abuse? What should teens do if they fall victim to sex abuse?

CHALLENGED FOR SIMILAR REASONS

Frank, E. R. *Life Is Funny*. New York: Dorling Kindersley Publishing, 2000.

The first, and most volatile, challenge to this novel that deals with the daily struggles of eleven urban teens was banned in 2004–2005 at two middle school libraries in Merced, California, because of "an X-rated passage describing two teens' first experience with sexual intercourse." It was also challenged for "sexual content" in 2002–2003 at the junior high school in the Somerset, Texas, Independent School District. The resolution is unknown.

Rapp, Adam. *The Buffalo Tree*. Honesdale, Pennsylvania: Boyds Mills Press, 1997.

This novel about a young adolescent who is dealing with a past that sent him to a juvenile detention center was banned from the Muhlenberg High School in Pennsylvania because of "objectionable" content. The school board later reversed its decision to notify parents of reading material with troubling content.

RESOURCES FOR RESPONDING TO CHALLENGES

What Reviewers Say

Publishers Weekly (January 2, 2002) calls the novel "a powerful story of forgiveness." The reviewer for *Voice of Youth Advocates* (February 1, 2002) finds the plotline "tangled" and doesn't think most adolescent readers could benefit from more information at the beginning of the novel. *School Library Journal* (March 1, 2002) recommends it for grades 8 and up and says, "The author's control of this story is impressive." The *Booklist* (February 15, 2002) starred review states, "It is a piercing, unforgettable novel." They recommend it for grades 10–12. *Kliatt* (January 2002) says, "America is a true-to-life character whose trials will haunt readers."

Other Justification for Inclusion in Curricula and Library Collections

❖ 2005 ALA/YALSA Popular Paperback for Young Adults
❖ 2004 Tayshas High School Reading List, 2003–2004
❖ 2003 ALA/YALSA Best Books for Young Adults
❖ 2003 ALA/YALSA 100 Best of the Best for the 21st Century
❖ 2003 ALA/YALSA Quick Picks for Reluctant Readers: Fiction
❖ 2003 *Los Angeles Times* Book Award Finalist
❖ 2003 Thumbs Up! Award (Michigan)
❖ 2002 Junior Literary Guild Selection
❖ 2002 *New York Times* Notable Books: Children's Books
❖ 2002 *School Library Journal* Best Books of the Year

Sources of Information about Challenges to the Novel

Hinck, Debbie. "Banned Book Project: #100 *America*." *A Healthy Disregard for the Impossible* (blog). Posted November 23, 2013. Accessed September 17, 2015. https://debbiehinck.wordpress.com/tag/e-r-frank/.

"School Board Votes to Keep Book on Library Shelves." Associated Press Wire Report, June 16, 2004. Accessed June 8, 2015. http://www.firstamendmentcenter.org/school-board-votes-to-keep-book-on-library-shelves.

INFORMATION ABOUT THE AUTHOR

http://erfrank.com (Frank's official website)
Contemporary Authors Online, 2010. Books and Authors. Gale.

FURTHER READING ABOUT THE NOVEL

Atkins, Holly. "An Interview with E. R. Frank." *St. Petersburg Times Online*, February 16, 2004. Accessed June 8, 2015. http://www.sptimes.com/2004/02/16/Nie/An_Interview_with_ER_.shtml.

Russell, Mary Harris. "Lost Boy: The Hero of This Novel Has Been Abandoned, Abducted and Abused." *New York Times Book Review*, May 19, 2002.

OTHER MEDIA SOURCES

https://www.youtube.com/watch?v=R3-myivwc4I. Posted February 19, 2009. Accessed October 5, 2015. Rosie O'Donnell and the cast and crew of the movie *America* discuss the story.

5

❖ ❖ ❖

A Bad Boy Can Be Good for a Girl

BY TANYA LEE STONE

New York: Wendy Lamb Books, an imprint of Random House, 2006
Laurel-Leaf Paperback, 2007
Random House E-book, 2007

> "I'm such an idiot. And I'm so pissed at myself because when I get older and look back on my first time, I was really hoping it would be a nice memory."

CHALLENGES: WHEN, WHY, AND WHERE

According to data collected by the American Library Association's Office for Intellectual Freedom, the book was #6 on the Top Ten Most Frequently Challenged Books List in 2013–2014 because of "offensive language, sexual content, drugs and alcohol." The author cites additional challenges at a junior high school in Washington state, a high school in Kentucky, and a junior high school in Missouri.

2013–2014

The novel was challenged in the high school library in Currituck, North Carolina, because of "sexual content." The book was retained.

It was also challenged but retained at Elkhart High School in the Elkhart, Texas, Independent School District because of "profanity, sexual content or nudity, drugs or alcohol."

THE STORY

Josie, a high school freshman, has never really dated when she comes under the spell of a handsome senior jock. She is naive and surprised by his sexual advances and finally realizes that he is only interested in her for sex. She doesn't succumb to his desires and decides to issue a "warning" to other girls by writing about the "bad boy" on the end pages of the school library's copy of Judy Blume's *Forever*. She then spreads the word for girls to check out the book. Other girls write in the book, but Nicolette, a junior, dismisses the "warnings" and quickly comes under the spell of the "bad boy." He dumps her and focuses his attention on Aviva, a senior, who is completely caught off guard when the jock shows interest in her. He moves on to his next target immediately after she loses her virginity to him. Suffering from rejection, Nicolette writes her own message in *Forever*, but Aviva, who is an accomplished musician, elects to someday write a song about her experience. Each girl finds their own way to "warn" other girls to take control of their own bodies and not allow themselves to come under the spell of boys like this nameless super jock who is only interested in sex, not a relationship.

Themes
❖ Friendship
❖ Love
❖ Self-identity
❖ Sex

TALKING WITH TEENS ABOUT THE ISSUES

Describe the "bad boy" in the novel. Why do you think he isn't given a name? How does this contribute to his super jock, cool, "bad boy" status?

Why do you think Josie, Nicolette, and Aviva fall under the spell of the "bad boy"? What do they learn about themselves?

Explain the title of the novel. Debate whether a "bad boy" is really good for a girl.

Why is *Forever* by Judy Blume the appropriate novel to write "warnings" to other girls about the "bad boy"?

The novel has been challenged because of sexual content. How does the content in the novel reflect what many teenagers face in their high school years? What might girls learn from Josie, Nicolette, and Aviva?

It has also been challenged because of drugs and alcohol. Why is Josie so nervous when she goes to the party where there are older kids who are using drugs and alcohol? Discuss the safe thing to do when you find yourself at such a party.

CHALLENGED FOR SIMILAR REASONS

Blume, Judy. *Forever*. New York: Simon & Schuster, 2014. (Original copyright 1975.)

This novel about a girl's first sexual experience ranked #7 on the 100 Most Frequently Challenged Books of 1990–1999, and #16 on the Top 100 Banned/Challenged Books of 2000–2009.

Burgess, Melvin. *Doing It*. New York: Henry Holt, an imprint of Macmillan, 2004.

Three high school boys relate their sexual experiences with various girls in this novel that was challenged in 2005–2006 in a Fayetteville, Arkansas, high school library after a citizen determined it, along with fifty other books, was too "sexually explicit."

Sones, Sonya. *One of Those Hideous Books Where the Mother Dies*. New York: Simon & Schuster, 2004.

Ruby is in high school when her mother dies and she goes to live with the father she has never known. Both funny and painful, this novel was challenged at the Theisen Middle School in Fond du Lac, Wisconsin, in 2009–2010 because of "sexual content." It was retained.

RESOURCES FOR RESPONDING TO CHALLENGES

What Reviewers Say

In the starred review in *School Library Journal* (January 2006), the reviewer says the free verse has a "breathless, natural flow." They recommend it for grades 9 and up. *Kirkus* (January 1, 2006) doesn't review the book favorably and states that serious students will "find this shallow." *Booklist* (January 1, 2006) says the novel "packs a steamy, emotional wallop." *Kliatt* (January 2006) calls it an "amazing first novel." *Horn Book Magazine* (January/February 2006) comments that "the three girls are distinct characters."

Other Justification for Inclusion in Curricula and Library Collections

❖ 2007 ALA/YALSA Quick Picks for Reluctant Young Adult Readers: Fiction
❖ 2007 Texas Tayshas Reading Lists
❖ 2006 Maryland Great Books for Teens

Sources of Information about Challenges to the Novel

"*A Bad Boy Can Be Good for a Girl* Stays in NC Library." Comic Book Legal Defense Fund (blog), October 15, 2013. Accessed July 30, 2015. http://cbldf.org/2013/10/a-bad-boy-can-be-good-for-a-girl-stays-in-nc-library/.

Elrod, Christine. "Interview with Tanya Lee Stone." Vermont School Library Association. Accessed August 11, 2015. https://docs.google.com/document/d/155q3krp4ufZk8qAmP24YJdajriqsx83kkt8IwhnxGV0/edit?pli=1.

Hampton, Jeff. "Parent's Protest of Book Goes to Board of Education." *The Virginian-Pilot*, October 12, 2013. Accessed July 30, 2015. http://hamptonroads.com/2013/10/parents-protest-book-goes-board-education.

"Want to Get Involved in #BannedBooksWeek? Defend Books Being Challenged RIGHT NOW." National Coalition against Censorship (blog), September 26, 2013. Accessed August 17, 2015. http://ncac.org/blog/want-to-get-involved-in-bannedbooksweek-defend-books-being-challenged-right-now/.

INFORMATION ABOUT THE AUTHOR

http://www.tanyastone.com (Stone's official website)
https://twitter.com/tanyaleestone (Stone on Twitter)

FURTHER READING ABOUT THE NOVEL

Burns, Liz. "Interview with Tanya Lee Stone." *Pop Goes the Library* (blog), April 14, 2006. Accessed August 11, 2015. http://www.popgoesthelibrary.com/2006/04/interview-with-tanya-lee-stone.html.

Smith, Cynthia Leitich. "Author Interview: Tanya Lee Stone on *A Bad Boy Can Be Good for a Girl*." *Cynsations* (blog), February 14, 2006. Accessed August 11, 2015. http://cynthialeitichsmith.blogspot.com/2006/02/author-interview-tanya-lee-stone-on.html.

OTHER MEDIA SOURCES

https://www.youtube.com/watch?v=zW2PvJcImfU. Posted April 8, 2010. Accessed July 30, 2015. Tanya Lee Stone talks about *A Bad Boy Can Be Good for a Girl.*

https://www.youtube.com/watch?v=6lGUCatF3Y8. Posted by AdLit, January 24, 2011. Accessed July 30, 2015. Tanya Lee Stone talks about writing.

6

❖ ❖ ❖

Blood and Chocolate

BY ANNETTE CURTIS KLAUSE

New York: Delacorte, an imprint of Random House Children's Books, 1997
Recorded Books Audio, 2005
Laurel-Leaf Paperback, 2007 (Reissue)
Random House E-book, 2007

"I had the taste of blood and chocolate in my mouth, one as hated as the other."

CHALLENGES: WHEN, WHY, AND WHERE

According to data collected by the American Library Association's Office for Intellectual Freedom, the novel ranked #10 on the Top Ten Most Frequently Challenged Books List in 2001 because it was deemed "sexually explicit and unsuited to age group."

2008–2009

The Texas American Civil Liberties Union (Texas ACLU) reports that the book was banned at Cullen Middle School in the Corpus Christi Independent School District because of "profanity, sexual content, and violence."

2005–2006

According to the Texas ACLU, the novel was banned at the Ector Junior High School in the Ector Independent School District because of "sexual content and mysticism and paganism." It was recommended for high school students.

2001–2002

The novel was removed from the library shelves in La Porte, Texas, until a selection policy could be reviewed. The outcome of the challenge is unknown.

The novel was removed from all middle school libraries in the Greenville, South Carolina, School District because of "sexual content." The school board voted to retain it in high school libraries, but it was banned from use in the curriculum at any level.

THE STORY

Vivian Gandillon is a beautiful sixteen-year-old werewolf who is dealing with the death of her father, the former leader of the *loups-garoux*. Now the pack is struggling without a leader, and Vivian just wants a normal life. She attends a new high school in Maryland, where she meets and falls in love with Aiden, a human who does not know anything about her dual nature. Esme, her mother, is nervous about Vivian's new romance and wants her daughter to date only guys from the pack. But these guys are immature and out of control, and the longer they go without a leader, the worse the group dynamics become. Life becomes more complex and sad for Vivian when Aiden rejects her after she tells him the truth about her nature. In the meantime, the pack is in serious danger, and they resort to an old-fashioned ceremony called Ordeal and elect Gabriel the new leader. He has an interest in Vivian, but she rejects him until tragedy traps her in her half-form. It takes Gabriel sharing his own lost "human" love for the two to accept one another.

Themes
- ❖ Acceptance
- ❖ Chaos
- ❖ Fear
- ❖ Honesty
- ❖ Insecurity
- ❖ Love/Romance

TALKING WITH TEENS ABOUT THE ISSUES

Discuss the teenage angst in the novel. How is Vivian's desire for acceptance similar to that of most "human" teenagers? The novel has been challenged because of sexual content. How does the "sexual content" advance the teenage angst and the desire for love and romance?

Aiden rejects Vivian after she reveals her dual nature. How does she deal with his rejection? How does this rejection contribute to the overall message of the book?

Discuss why Vivian calls her human side "chocolate" and her wolf side "blood."

The novel has been challenged because of violence. Chart the violent content, and discuss why it is necessary to the plot.

The book has also been challenged because of mysticism and paganism. Debate whether these people object to the "werewolves" or fantasy in general. How might you defend the book to those who feel it threatens their religious beliefs?

CHALLENGED FOR SIMILAR REASONS

Bray, Libba. *A Great and Terrible Beauty.* New York: Delacorte, an imprint of Random House Children's Books, 2003.

In 2005–2006, this novel about a girl who suffers visions about secrets at her boarding school in England was banned from the high school in the Elkhart, Texas, Independent School District because of "sexual content and violence."

Cast, P. C., and Kristin Cast. House of Night Series. New York: St. Martin's Press, 2007–2014.

A local minister at the Austin Memorial Library in Cleveland, Texas, in 2014 challenged this series about a sixteen-year-old girl who is a new "vampyre" because of the "occult" and asked that taxpayers' money not be used to purchase such materials.

Jinks, Catherine. *The Reformed Vampire Support.* Boston: Houghton Mifflin Harcourt, 2010.

This witty novel about a group of vampires that forms a support group was banned in 2014 at the Vanguard Academy Charter School in Texas because of "violence and horror."

RESOURCES FOR RESPONDING TO CHALLENGES

What Reviewers Say

Booklist (June 15, 1997) recommends the novel for grades 11 and up and calls it "powerful and unforgettable." *School Library Journal* (August 1, 1997) says, "The book is well constructed with visual images and deft descriptions." They recommend it for grades 9 and up. *Publishers Weekly* (May 27, 1997) states that some readers will find the "sometimes bloody tale as addictive as chocolate." *Horn Book Magazine* (July/August 1997) calls it a "supernatural gothic romance." *Kirkus* (June 1, 1997) says the novel is a "suspenseful chiller." *Kliatt* (January 2000) calls the book "beautifully crafted."

Other Justification for Inclusion in Curricula and Library Collections

❖ 2008 ALA/YALSA Popular Paperbacks for Young Adults: Sex Is . . .
❖ 2000 Garden State Teen Book Award (New Jersey): Fiction: Grades 9–12
❖ 2000 South Carolina Book Award: Young Adult Category
❖ 1998 ALA/YALSA Best Books for Young Adults
❖ 1998 ALA/YALSA Quick Picks for Reluctant Young Adult Readers
❖ 1997 *Booklist* Editors' Choice: Books for Youth: Older Readers Category
❖ 1997 *School Library Journal* Best Books of the Year

Sources of Information about Challenges to the Novel

Ehrlich, Brenna. "What Did This YA Author Do to Get Banned from School Libraries?" MTV, September 26, 2014. Accessed August 12, 2015. http://www.mtv.com/news/1944296/banned-books-week-annette-curtis-klause/.

INFORMATION ABOUT THE AUTHOR

Contemporary Authors Online, 2007. Books and Authors. Gale.
Klause, Annette Curtis. "Growing Up to Be a Writer." *Voice of Youth Advocates* 14 (April 1991): 19.
Smith, Cynthia Leitich. "Author Update: Annette Curtis Klause." *Cynsations* (blog), January 14, 2006. Accessed October 12, 2015. http://cynthialeitichsmith.blogspot.com/2006/01/author-update-annette-curtis-klause.html.

FURTHER READING ABOUT THE NOVEL

Brachfeld, Melissa J. "Book Moves to the Silver Screen." Gazette.net (Maryland), January 31, 2007. Accessed August 12, 2015. http://www.gazette.net/stories/013107/rocknew222316_32321.shtml.
Klause, Annette Curtis. "A Young Adult Author Speaks Out: Why Vampites?" *Voice of Youth Advocates* 21, issue 1 (April 1998): 28–30.

OTHER MEDIA SOURCES

https://www.youtube.com/watch?v=5tt2uZSuQc0&index=27&list=PLa1SfOafpD61oKUt1u UZxb3Oc3RJDm50C. Posted September 23, 2011. Accessed October 12, 2015. A fan reads from the novel for the Banned Books Week Virtual Read-Out.

https://www.youtube.com/watch?v=UXvkHobfDdA. Posted December 7, 2013. Accessed August 12, 2015. A fan reviews *Blood and Chocolate*, her all-time favorite novel.

7

❖　❖　❖

A Child Called "It": One Child's Courage to Survive

BY DAVE PELZER

Deerfield Beach, Florida: Health Communications Inc., 1995
Health Communications Paperback, 1995
Health Communications E-book, 2000
Recorded Books Audio, 2006

> "Mother can beat me all she wants, but I haven't let her
> take my will to somehow survive."

CHALLENGES: WHEN, WHY, AND WHERE

2013–2014

The book was challenged at Housel Middle School in Prosser, Washington, because of "child abuse." Students are required to have parental permission to borrow the book.

2009–2010

A parent asked that the book be removed from the summer reading list for freshmen at a high school in South Hadley, Massachusetts. The review committee retained the book.

2001–2002

It was banned from the middle school in Sussex, Delaware, because of "profanity and violence." The resolution of the final review community is unknown.

THE STORY

Dave Pelzer lives in a normal family until the day his mother turns from Cub Scout leader to an alcoholic, deranged monster who takes out her anger on her son. He never knows what he does to enrage her, but she gains great pleasure in torturing him. She beats him, burns him, submerges him in freezing water, and makes him eat the contents of diapers and his own vomit. In her eyes he is not a person, but an "it." Pelzer is eventually placed in foster care, but his mother continues her attack on her son by attempting to have him committed to an institution. Yet she cannot break his enormous courage to survive. His journey is tough, but Pelzer grows up to become an emotionally healthy adult with a successful career. This is his memoir.

Themes

❖ Alcohol abuse
❖ Child abuse
❖ Resilience

TALKING WITH TEENS ABOUT THE ISSUES

Discuss the physical and emotional abuse that Pelzer suffers. Why does this brutal abuse cause some readers discomfort?

There are critics, and even some family members, who believe that Dave Pelzer's life was not as difficult as he presents it in his memoir. Discuss how these skeptics could possibly know this if they were not there.

The memoir has been challenged because of violence and profanity. This was Pelzer's childhood. Why is it important to know that such brutality exists?

What should a reader do if they find themselves too uncomfortable when reading the book?

How might teenagers who have been abused find hope in Pelzer's resilience?

Explain how writing a memoir like *A Child Called "It"* could be therapeutic for the writer.

CHALLENGED FOR SIMILAR REASONS

Atkins, Catherine. *When Jeff Came Home*. New York: Penguin, 1999.

In 2005–2006, this novel about a boy's struggle to adjust within his family after he was kidnapped and sexually abused was restricted to students with parental permission because of the "subject matter."

Dugard, Jaycee. *A Stolen Life*. New York: Simon & Schuster, 2011.

This memoir that chronicles life in captivity and sex abuse was banned from seventh-grade classroom libraries in Northview, Michigan, in 2014–2015 because of "sexual abuse and violence." This book may be used in the high schools.

RESOURCES FOR RESPONDING TO CHALLENGES

What Reviewers Say

School Library Journal (December 1, 1995) recommends the book for grades 9 and up and calls the book "unforgettable," but the reviewer thinks it does not provide an "understanding of extreme abuse." A reviewer on *Goodreads* (July 6, 2007) says, "A trainwreck of a book. I wanted to look aside, but just couldn't." She gave it one star.

Other Justification for Inclusion in Curricula and Library Collections

❖ 2010 ALA/YALSA Popular Paperbacks for Young Adults: Hard Knock Life
❖ 2005 Abraham Lincoln Illinois High School Book Award
❖ 2005 Western Australian Young Readers' Book Award: Older Readers
❖ 2000 Soaring Eagle Book Award (Wyoming)

Sources of Information about Challenges to the Novel

Constantine, Sandra. "Todd Sugrue Urges South Hadley School Committee to Drop *A Child Called 'It'* from Summer Reading List Because of Child Abuse." *Mass Live*, October 8, 2009. Accessed October 22, 2015. http://www.masslive.com/news/index.ssf/2009/10/todd_sugrue_urges_south_hadley.html.

Malmsheimer, Taylor. "Teacher in Prosser, WA, Asks School Board to Ban Two Books from School Libraries." *New York Daily News*, May 1, 2013. Accessed October 22, 2015. http://www.nydailynews.com/blogs/pageviews/teacher-prosser-wa-asks-school-board-ban-books-school-libraries-blog-entry-1.1640477.

INFORMATION ABOUT THE AUTHOR

http://www.davepelzer.com (Pelzer's official website)

Contemporary Authors Online, 2002. Books and Authors. Gale.

FURTHER READING ABOUT THE NOVEL

Bedell, Geraldine. "Child Abuse as Entertainment." *Guardian*, September 2, 2001. Accessed October 22, 2015. http://www.theguardian.com/books/2001/sep/02/biography.features.

Kellaway, Kate. "No Pain, No Gain." *Guardian*. Accessed November 19, 2015. http://www.theguardian.com/books/2004/feb/15/biography.features.

Plotz, David. "Dave Pelzer: The Child-Abuse Entrepreneur." Slate.com. Accessed October 22, 2015. http://www.slate.com/articles/news_and_politics/assessment/2000/09/dave_pelzer.html.

Stevens, Nancy L. "Parent Involvement in Reading." *Illinois Reading Council Journal* 43, issue 3 (Summer 2015): 39–42.

Waibel-Duncan, Mary Katherine, and Jennifer Whitehouse Yarnell. "The Challenge Mode: Examining Resilience in Pelzer's *A Child Called 'It.'*" *Journal of Child and Adolescent Psychiatric Nursing* 24, issue 2 (August 2011): 168–174.

OTHER MEDIA SOURCES

https://www.youtube.com/watch?v=RnSntzvGteI. Posted May 4, 2011. Accessed October 22, 2015. Dave Pelzer talks about his abusive childhood on *Larry King Live*.

https://www.youtube.com/watch?v=bIzM3EW2IUc. Posted September 25, 2014. Accessed October 22, 2015. A fan reads *A Child Called "It"* for the Banned Books Week Virtual Read-Out.

8

❖ ❖ ❖

The Chocolate War

BY ROBERT CORMIER

New York: Pantheon Books, 1974
Random House Paperback, 1993
Listening Library Audio, 2007

"There was nothing more beautiful in the world than the sight of seeing a teacher get upset."

CHALLENGES: WHEN, WHY, AND WHERE

According to data reported by the American Library Association's Office for Intellectual Freedom, the earliest reported challenge to the novel was in Lapeer, Michigan, in 1981 because the language was deemed too "offensive" and the "sexual content" too explicit for high school students. The book was temporarily removed from the English curriculum but later reinstated. Since that time, the novel was #10 on the Top Ten Most Frequently Challenged Books List in 2008–2009; #2 in 2007–2008; #10 in 2006–2007; #4 in 2005–2006; #1 in 2004–2005; #3 in 2002–2003; and #3 in 2001–2002. It ranked #4 on the 100 Most Frequently Challenged Books List of 1990–1999 and #3 on the Top 100 Banned/Challenged Books List of 2000–2009.

2014–2015

According to the National Council of Teachers of English, the novel was challenged in the ninth-grade curriculum at a school in Minnesota because of "profanity, racism, and sexual content."

2008–2009

According to the Texas American Civil Liberties Union (Texas ACLU), the novel was challenged at Hooks High School in the Hooks Independent School District because of "profanity and sexual content." An alternate book is allowed when used in the curriculum.

2007–2008

Parents of students at Lake Oswego Junior High School in Lake Oswego, Oregon, challenged the novel as "optional reading in a bullying unit" because of "profanity, violence, and derogatory slang terms for sexual intercourse."

It was also challenged in the school district in Johnstown, Ohio, because of the "R rated content."

In the same year, it was removed from the curriculum at the Harford County High School in Maryland because the administration felt the issues related to bullying were "overshadowed by vulgar language." The decision was later reversed, and teachers have the option to use the novel with parental permission.

Parents in the Coeur d'Alene school district in Idaho requested that parents must give permission for their students to read the novel.

It was also challenged as required reading by a parent of a seventh-grader at the John H. Kinzie Elementary School in Chicago, Illinois.

2006–2007

The novel was challenged but retained at the King Philip Middle School in West Hartford, Connecticut, because of "language, sexual content, and violence."

In the same academic year, it was challenged in the Wake County, North Carolina, School District because of "vulgar and sexually explicit language."

2004–2005

The Texas ACLU reports that the novel was challenged as part of the curriculum at the Idalou Middle School in the Idalou Independent School District because of "profanity and sexual content." The novel was restricted, though the conditions are unknown.

2002–2003

A group called Parents against Bad Books in Schools (PABBIS) in Fairfax County, Virginia, challenged the book because of "profanity, drug abuse, sexual content, and torture."

2001–2002

A group asked that the book be removed from the high school English curriculum in Lisbon, Ohio, claiming it was "pornographic."

It was challenged but retained at a middle school in St. Petersburg, Florida, because of "profanity, masturbation and sexual fantasy." It was also considered "denigrating to girls."

2000–2001

The novel was retained as optional reading at Rice Avenue Middle School in Girard, Pennsylvania, after a grandmother found the book "offensive."

It was challenged for "sexual content" in York County, Virginia. The outcome is unknown.

"The book teaches immorality" was the reason for a challenge at the Maple Heights School in Ohio. The outcome of the case is unknown.

The novel was challenged because of "language and content" as part of the eighth-grade reading list in the Lancaster, Massachusetts, School District.

It was also challenged at the Silverheels Middle School in Colorado because parents opposed the "sexually suggestive language."

THE STORY

Jerry Renault is a freshman at Trinity, an all-male Catholic prep school, where he comes face to face with the Vigils, a secret society that hazes students who are not part of their group. Brother

Leon is launching a school fundraiser and asks each boy to sell fifty boxes of chocolates. The Vigils tell Jerry that he must defy Brother Leon by refusing to sell the chocolates for ten days. After the ten days, Jerry continues to refuse to sell the chocolates, causing other boys to lose interest in the sale. Brother Leon is desperate and asks Archie, the leader of the Vigils, for help. Archie agrees and hints that Brother Leon must promise the Vigils certain privileges. They set out to make Jerry's life miserable in and outside of school. But he continues to stand by the message on the poster he placed in his locker at the beginning of the school year: "Do I Dare Disturb the Universe?" Life is tough at home as well. His mother died of cancer just before his freshman year, and his dad, who is still grieving, is working harder and is almost unresponsive to Jerry's needs. The final blow comes at the end of the novel when the Vigils stage a boxing match in the football stadium, where Jerry is so severely beaten that an ambulance takes him away. And on the hillside is Brother Leon watching the entire massacre with a bit of satisfaction. In *Beyond the Chocolate War* (1985), Jerry Renault no longer attends Trinity, but the Vigils continue to reign until someone finally gets the nerve to stand up to Archie Costello.

Themes
- Alienation
- Bullying
- Courage
- Father-son relationship
- Nonconformity
- Violence

TALKING WITH TEENS ABOUT THE ISSUES

Explain the meaning of Jerry Renault's poster "Do I Dare Disturb the Universe?" How does Jerry "Disturb the Universe"? Discuss how "nonconformity" takes courage.

Jerry is bullied when he refuses to sell the chocolates. Discuss how Trinity allows the bullying to happen. How is Brother Leon a bully? Jerry feels alone as he continues to defy Brother Leon. Where might kids like Jerry seek help?

Jerry cannot count on the support of his grieving father. How might the novel have a different message and outcome if Jerry's father had interfered?

The novel has been banned because of profanity and violence. How might the novel spark discussion about gangs and secret societies that create violence in schools?

To what scenes are censors referring when they oppose "sexual content"? Discuss how such sexual exploration is normal among adolescents.

School administrators have opposed the book because it describes "degradation of schools and teachers." Debate whether these administrators feel threatened by the book. Discuss whether some of the behaviors at Trinity are a reality in schools. How might student groups like student council help bring these issues to light?

The novel has also been banned because there is no happy ending. Create an ending that might satisfy these censors. Discuss how the new ending changes the novel. How does Cormier's ending create more "real" conversation about issues in the lives of teens?

CHALLENGED FOR SIMILAR REASONS

Avi. *Nothing but the Truth.* New York: Orchard Books, an imprint of Scholastic, 1991.

According to the Texas ACLU Banned Books Report in 2004–2005, this novel about a high school freshman who is rejected by his friends after he is disciplined for violating school policy was challenged at the Oak Run Middle School sixth-grade campus in the New Braunfels Independent School District because of "profanity." It was retained.

Cole, Brock. *The Goats.* New York: Farrar, Straus & Giroux, an imprint of Macmillan, 1987.

This novel about a girl and a boy who fall victim to a summer camp prank when older campers strip them of their clothing and label them "goats" has been challenged numerous times. It was removed from all Londonderry, New Hampshire, schools in 2000 because of "sexual content."

Cormier, Robert. *Beyond the Chocolate War.* New York: Knopf, an imprint of Random House, 1985.

This sequel to *The Chocolate War* set at Trinity School was challenged in 2000–2001 by a woman who did not want her granddaughters reading it in the eighth grade at the Rice Avenue Middle School in Girard, Pennsylvania, because she found it "offensive." It was retained as optional reading.

RESOURCES FOR RESPONDING TO CHALLENGES

What Reviewers Say

Kirkus (April 1, 1974) comments on the "strong, staccato scenes." *Booklist* (March 15, 1975) says the book is "cynical and undermining moral values." The *New York Times Book Review* (May 5, 1974) praises the "complex ideas." *School Library Journal* (November 1982) gives the novel a star and calls it "an uncompromising portrait of human cruelty and conformity."

Other Justification for Inclusion in Curricula and Library Collections

❖ 2000 ALA/YALSA 100 Best Books for Young Adults: 1950–2000
❖ 1974 ALA/YALSA Best Books for Young Adults
❖ 1974 ALA/YALSA The Best of the Best for Young Adults
❖ 1974 *Kirkus* Reviews Choice
❖ 1974 *New York Times* Notable Books of the Year
❖ 1974 *School Library Journal* Best Books of the Year

Sources of Information about Challenges to the Novel

Beckman, Wendy Hart. *Robert Cormier: Banned, Challenged, and Censored.* Authors of Banned Books Series. Berkeley Heights, New Jersey: Enslow Publishers, 2008.

Close, Elizabeth, and Katherine Ramsey. "Middle Talk." *English Journal* 90, issue 3 (January 2001): 126–130.

"Parents Pushing for Ban on *The Chocolate War* for Seventh Graders." *ILA Reporter* 25, issue 6 (December 2007): 25.

Pen America/Free Expression Literature. "On Robert Cormier's *The Chocolate War.*" Accessed July 7, 2015. http://www.pen.org/nonfiction/robert-cormier's-chocolate-war.

Tigner-Räsänen, Mary. "Meeting a Censorship Challenge." *English Journal* 90, issue 3 (January 2001): 126–129.

INFORMATION ABOUT THE AUTHOR

Contemporary Authors Online, 2003. Books and Authors. Gale.

Campbell, Patricia J. *Presenting Robert Cormier.* Twayne's United States Authors Series No. 496. Farmington Hills, MI: Twayne, 1989.

Campbell, Patty. *Robert Cormier: Daring to Disturb the Universe*. New York: Delacorte eBook, a division of Penguin Random House, 2012.

Hyde, Margaret O. *Robert Cormier*. Who Wrote That? Series. New York: Chelsea House, an imprint of Facts on File, 2005.

Thompson, Sarah L. *Robert Cormier*. The Library of Author Biography Series. New York: Rosen Reference Ebook, an imprint of Rosen Publishing Group, 2009.

FURTHER READING ABOUT THE NOVEL

Bryfonski, Dedria. *Peer Pressure in Robert Cormier's* The Chocolate War. Social Issues in Literature Series. Farmington Hills, MI: Cengage Gale, 2009.

Carter, Betty, and Karen Harris. "Realism in Adolescent Fiction: In Defense of *The Chocolate War*." *Top of the News* 36, issue 3 (Spring 1980): 283–285.

Keeling, Kara. "'The Misfortune of a Man Like Ourselves': Robert Cormier's *The Chocolate War*." *ALAN Review* 26, issue 2 (Winter 1999): 9–12.

Peters, Mike. "*The Chocolate War* and After: The Novels of Robert Cormier." *School Librarian* 40 (August 1992): 85–87.

Tarr, Anita C. "The Absence of Moral Agency in Robert Cormier's *The Chocolate War*." *Children's Literature* 30 (2002): 96–124.

OTHER MEDIA SOURCES

http://putlocker.is/hdstream/hdstream.php?movie=The%20Chocolate%20War%20(1988). Accessed July 13, 2015. This is a link to the full-length movie of *The Chocolate War*.

https://www.youtube.com/watch?v=mxrjkuPzKo8. Posted December 27, 2012. Accessed July 13, 2015. Robert Cormier talks about his father's influence on his career as a writer.

9

❖ ❖ ❖

The Contender

BY ROBERT LIPSYTE

New York: HarperCollins, 1967
HarperTeen Paperback, 2003 (Reissue)
Recorded Books Audio, 2007
HarperCollins E-book, 2010

> "It's the climbing that makes the man.
> Getting to the top is an extra reward."

CHALLENGES: WHEN, WHY, AND WHERE

2008–2009

According to the Texas American Civil Liberties Union (Texas ACLU), the novel was challenged at Roach Middle School in the Frisco Independent School District because it was deemed "politically, racially, or socially offensive." At the time of the report, the case was pending.

According to an editorial written by Robert Lipsyte (http://www.ncte.org/library/NCTEFiles/Involved/Action/censorship/Authors-Rationales/Lipsyte_Robert_OneFatSummer.pdf), *The Contender* was challenged in Washington state because it lacked "middle-class African American role models." Neither the institution nor the date of the actual challenge is documented.

THE STORY

Seventeen-year-old Alfred Brooks, a high-school dropout, lives with his widowed Aunt Pearl and her three daughters in Harlem. Alfred tries to avoid the bad influences of his environment by taking a job at the Epsteins' store. James, Alfred's best friend, needs money to feed his drug addiction and robs Mr. Epstein after Alfred shares that Mr. Epstein leaves money in the cash register. James is arrested, and Alfred worries that his boss will never trust him again. Wandering the streets trying to deal with his guilt, Alfred happens upon Donatelli's Boxing Gym, ascends the stairs and commits to being a "contender." While Alfred eventually learns that he doesn't have the "killer instinct" to make it as a boxer, his training does help him gain control of his life. During this time, he never gives up on James. Three companion novels deal with self-identity and survival: *The Brave* (1991), *The Chief* (1993), and *Warrior Angel* (2003).

Themes

- ❖ Courage
- ❖ Determination
- ❖ Guilt
- ❖ Manhood
- ❖ Self-identity
- ❖ Survival

TALKING WITH TEENS ABOUT THE ISSUES

Aunt Pearl says, "Oh Alfred, it's like you're my own son. I know you try so hard, you so good. I know it ain't easy living here." Discuss the difficult things about living with Aunt Pearl. What are the easy things? Describe the positive ways Alfred's environment contributes to his life.

Compare and contrast the differences in the way Alfred reacts to his inner-city environment with the way James responds.

Explain what Alfred means when he says, "The gym looked like Reverend Prince's hell."

In what ways, other than boxing, does Alfred show signs of being a "contender"? Discuss what Mr. Donatelli means when he says, "Anyone can be taught how to fight. A contender, that you have to do yourself." Define *contender* and discuss whether Alfred is successful.

The book was challenged because it "lacked middle-class African American role models." Discuss the importance of role models from all socioeconomic groups. Who are the role models in the novel? How do they influence Alfred? Discuss how Alfred is trying to be a role model to James.

Explain why the book is labeled "politically, racially, or socially offensive."

After the Epsteins' store is broken into, Alfred says, "They don't even trust me to go to the bank anymore." How does associating with the wrong crowd cause people to lose trust in someone? What should a person do to protect himself or herself when they feel pressured by a friend to do the wrong thing?

CHALLENGED FOR SIMILAR REASONS

Lynch, Chris. *Shadow Boxer.* Magnolia, MA: Peter Smith Publishers, 1996. New York: Simon & Schuster, 2013.

George is the man of the family and tries to stop his younger brother, Monty, from following his dream of becoming a boxer, a sport that killed their father. According to the Texas ACLU 2001–2002 Banned Books Report, the novel was placed on a restricted shelf at the middle school in the Anahuac Independent School District because of "profanity."

Myers, Walter Dean. *Hoops.* New York: Delacorte, an imprint of Penguin Random House, 1981.

In the 2008–2009 school year, a parent in the Council Bluffs Community School District in Iowa challenged this novel about a seventeen-year-old basketball player dealing with the social distractions of his Harlem community because of "racial slurs, violence, sexual content, and drugs." There are also two earlier recorded challenges.

RESOURCES FOR RESPONDING TO CHALLENGES

What Reviewers Say

Horn Book Magazine (December 1967) comments on the "warm relations with understanding adults and flashes of humor." *School Library Journal* (November 15, 1967) states, "As a sports story, this is a superior, engrossing, insider's book." The reviewer for *Kirkus* (October 1, 1967) gives the novel a star and says that it is "so honest and taut and incisive."

Other Justification for Inclusion in Curricula and Library Collections

❖ 1994 ALA/YALSA Silver Anniversary Best of the Best Books for Young Adults: "Top 100 Countdown"

Sources of Information about Challenges to the Novel

Simmons, John S. "Middle Schoolers and the Right to Read." *ALAN Review* 27, issue 3 (Spring 2000): 45–49.

INFORMATION ABOUT THE AUTHOR

http://www.robertlipsyte.com/index.htm (Lipsyte's official website)
Contemporary Authors Online, 2009. Books and Authors. Gale.
Cart, Michael. *Presenting Robert Lipsyte*. Young Adult Authors Series, Volume 649. Farmington Hills, MI: Cengage Gale, 1995.
Scales, Pat R. "Robert Lipsyte." *Book Links* 15, issue 6 (July 2006): 40–41.

FURTHER READING ABOUT THE NOVEL

Feldman, Sari. "Up the Stairs Alone: Robert Lipsyte on Writing for Young Adults." *Top of the News* 39, issue 2 (1983): 198–202.
Goering, Chris. "Interviewing the Interviewer: Talking with Robert Lipsyte." *ALAN Review* 34, issue 2 (Winter 2007): 52–58. Accessed July 7, 2015. http://scholar.lib.vt.edu/ejournals/ALAN/v34n2/goering.pdf.
Lipsyte, Robert. "The 2001 Margaret A. Edwards Acceptance Speech." *Journal of Youth Services in Libraries* 14, issue 4 (Summer 2001): 21–23.
Lipsyte, Robert. "Listening for the Footsteps: Books and Boys." *Horn Book Magazine* 68, issue 3 (May/June 1992): 290–296.
Myers, Walter Dean. "Pulling No Punches." *School Library Journal* 47, issue 6 (June 2001): 44–47.
Simmons, John S. "Lipsyte's *Contender*: Another Look at the Junior Novel." *Elementary English* 49, issue 1 (January 1972): 116–119.

OTHER MEDIA SOURCES

https://www.youtube.com/watch?v=oyUllzN3eXk. Posted September 5, 2013. Accessed July 20, 2015. A fan reviews *The Contender* and discusses its contribution to young adult literature.

10

❖ ❖ ❖

Crank

BY ELLEN HOPKINS

New York: Margaret K. McElderry Books, an imprint of Simon & Schuster, 2004
Highbridge Audio, 2008
Simon & Schuster E-book, 2012
Simon & Schuster Paperback, 2013 (Reissue)

> "Girls get screwed. Not that kind of screwed, what I mean is,
> they're always on the short end of things."

CHALLENGES: WHEN, WHY, AND WHERE

According to data collected by the American Library Association's Office for Intellectual Freedom, the novel was #4 on the Top Ten Most Frequently Challenged Books List in 2010 because of "drugs, language and sexual content."

2013–2014

A parent in the Panther Valley School District in Pennsylvania challenged the novel because of "drugs, masturbation, oral sex, and group sex" and asked that middle school students not be allowed to attend a planned author's visit. The school board voted to allow students with parental permission to attend.

2009–2010

Ellen Hopkins was uninvited to the TeenFest in Humble, Texas, after a middle school teacher disapproved of Hopkins's novels, including *Crank*, and rallied parents to complain to the superintendent. The TeenFest was canceled after a number of authors pulled out in protest.

The administration in the Norman, Oklahoma, public schools pulled *Crank* and *Glass* from the library at the Whittier Middle School for further review and subsequently said that Hopkins wouldn't be allowed to speak in any of the schools in the district. She went to Norman anyway and spoke at Hillsdale Free Will Baptist College, where 150 students, teachers, and parents showed up to hear her speak.

THE STORY

In the summer before her junior year in high school, Kristina goes to Albuquerque, New Mexico, to visit the dad she's never really known. She is left alone most of the time and learns that she cannot really count on her dad. Then she meets Adam, who introduces her to crank, "the monster," and she is quickly under the spell. When Kristina returns to Reno, her mother notices a big difference in her. But she rejects her mother's questions and continues the use of crank. She becomes so desperate for the drug that she falls into the hands of dealers. Before she realizes it, she is peddling as well. Then she gets pregnant after a guy she meets at the water park rapes her. She contemplates an abortion, but when she feels a slight flutter in her belly, she can't go through with it. Her life is in shambles when she gives birth to a baby boy at the age of seventeen. In *Glass* (2007), Kristina is a struggling young mother, and when she can't seem to lose her crank addiction, her mother has her declared an unfit mother. She gets pregnant again by a different guy, and the two take off for California. *Fallout* (2010) is the third book about Kristina Snow. This time, her five children, three of whom live with different guardians, share resentments toward their mother for never being there for them. They find one another and work to overcome the obstacles that life has handed them.

Themes
* ❖ Abandonment
* ❖ Betrayal
* ❖ Drug addiction
* ❖ Family
* ❖ Making choices
* ❖ Sex
* ❖ Teen parenting

TALKING WITH TEENS ABOUT THE ISSUES

Discuss why her mother has been reluctant to allow Kristina to visit her father in New Mexico. What are Kristina's expectations when she meets her father? What does she discover?

How is he partially responsible for her falling into the hands of Adam, and crank?

Kristina's mother notices a difference in her daughter when she returns home. How is Kristina so zoned out on crank to listen to her mother?

Discuss Kristina's decision to keep her baby. She has four more children in *Glass* and *Fallout*. How is she irresponsible to bring children into the world with the predisposition for addiction? Explain how crank clouds the mind and causes a person to make poor decisions.

The novel has been banned because of drugs and sexual content. How might Kristina's story serve as a warning to teens that drugs and promiscuous sex are addictive and harmful?

Ellen Hopkins has been uninvited to schools where she was scheduled to speak because of the content of her books. Why are school administrators so nervous about teens reading about these social issues?

Suggest ways parents might broach the conversation about drugs and sex with their teens so that they don't make the same mistake Kristina does.

CHALLENGED FOR SIMILAR REASONS

Friend, Natasha. *Lush*. New York: Scholastic, 2006.

According to the Texas American Civil Liberties Union, this novel about a teenage girl dealing with an alcoholic father and the cruelties of her peers at school was challenged in 2013–2014 at the middle school in the Overton Independent School District because of "profanity, sexual content, offens[e] to religious sensitivities, and drug and alcohol use." The novel has been restricted, but the conditions are unknown.

Hopkins, Ellen. *Tricks*. New York: Margaret K. McElderry Books, an imprint of Simon & Schuster, 2009.

Ellen Hopkins had a scheduled visit to Norman, Oklahoma, canceled in 2009 because of the subject matter of her books. *Tricks*, a novel that deals with teenage prostitution, homosexuality, and drug use, was one of the novels that gave the visit organizers pause.

Tyree, Omar. *Flyy Girl*. New York: Simon & Schuster, 1996. (Original copyright 1993.)

In 2001–2002, this novel about a girl who has sex with a variety of men, but who turns her life around after she observes the tragic life of a neighbor who is a "crack whore," was challenged at the high school in the Longview, Texas, Independent School District because of "profanity and sexual content." It was retained.

RESOURCES FOR RESPONDING TO CHALLENGES

What Reviewers Say

Publishers Weekly (November 1, 2004) comments on the "creative use of form." *Voice of Youth Advocates* (February 1, 2005) calls the novel "gritty and fast-paced." *School Library Journal* (November 1, 2004) recommends the book for grades 8 and up and says, "The poems are masterpieces of words, shapes and pacing." *Booklist* (November 15, 2004) calls it "wrenching and cautionary." They recommend it for grades 8–12.

Other Justification for Inclusion in Curricula and Library Collections

- ❖ 2010 Delaware Diamonds Book Award: High School
- ❖ 2009 Abraham Lincoln Illinois High School Book Award
- ❖ 2009 Soaring Eagle Book Award (Wyoming)
- ❖ 2007 Gateway Readers Award (Missouri)
- ❖ 2005 ALA/YALSA Quick Picks for Reluctant Young Adult Readers: Fiction

Sources of Information about Challenges to the Novel

Bildner, Phil. "Texas: If You Can't Ban Books, Ban Authors." Time.com, September 29, 2010. Accessed August 16, 2015. http://content.time.com/time/nation/article/0,8599,2022356,00.html.

Gower, Ron. "PV Parent Protests Controversial Author's Visit." *Times News* (Pennsylvania), February 28, 2014. Accessed August 16, 2015. http://www.tnonline.com/2014/feb/28/pv-parent-protests-controversial-authors-visit.

Hopkins, Ellen. "Banned Books Week 2010: An Anti-Censorship Manifesto." *HuffPost Books* (blog). Posted September 30, 2010. Accessed August 16, 2015. http://www.huffingtonpost.com/ellen-hopkins/banned-books-anticensorship-manifesto_b_744219.html.

Kendall, Jennifer. "Ellen Hopkins on Censorship." *About Entertainment*. Accessed August 16, 2015. http://childrensbooks.about.com/od/censorship/a/Teen-Author-Ellen-Hopkins-On-Censorship.htm.

INFORMATION ABOUT THE AUTHOR

http://www.ellenhopkins.com (Hopkins's official website)
Contemporary Authors Online, 2013. Books and Authors. Gale.

FURTHER READING ABOUT THE NOVEL

Hopkins, Ellen. *Flirtin' with the Monster: Your Favorite Authors on Ellen Hopkins'* Crank *and* Glass. Dallas, TX: BenBella Books, 2009.
Kadaba, Lini S. "Books about Dark Topics Written in Verse Are Page Turners Even outside the Young Readers They're Aimed At." *Philadelphia Inquirer*, September 8, 2010.

OTHER MEDIA SOURCES

https://www.youtube.com/watch?v=-tUACNTWAK8. Posted September 16, 2011. Accessed August 16, 2015. A fan reads from *Crank* for the Banned Books Week Virtual Read-Out.
https://www.youtube.com/watch?v=z3tiN9-jev8. Posted September 16, 2012. Accessed August 10, 2015. This is a video review of *Crank*.
https://www.youtube.com/watch?v=EIyGK9ZCa80. Posted September 16, 2012. Accessed August 10, 2015. This is a follow-up video discussion of *Crank*.

11

❖ ❖ ❖

Daughters of Eve

BY LOIS DUNCAN

New York: Little, Brown, 1979 (Op)
Little, Brown Paperback, 2011 (Reissue)
Little, Brown E-book, 2011
Hachette Audio, 2011

"You know Tammy's 'candle with the blood on it'? I don't want to be there to see it burn."

CHALLENGES: WHEN, WHY, AND WHERE

According to data collected by the American Library Association's Office for Intellectual Freedom, Duncan's novel was #51 on the Top 100 Banned/Challenged Books List of 2000–2009.

2006–2007

Though parents never filed a formal complaint, the superintendent of the Clovis, New Mexico, Municipal School removed the book from the elementary schools because of "profanity and suggestive actions."

2005–2006

The novel was challenged at the middle school in Lowell, Indiana, because of "profanity and sexual content."

2001–2002

The Texas American Civil Liberties Union was challenged at Travis Middle School in Port Lavaca, Texas, in the Calhoun County Independent School District because of "profanity and violence." It was retained without restriction.

It was also challenged at La Porte Junior High School in the La Porte, Texas, Independent School District because of "profanity, sexual content, and violence." It was placed on a restricted shelf in the school library.

2000–2001

It was banned in all middle schools in Fairfax County, Virginia, because "it promotes risky behavior and violence and seeks to prejudice young vulnerable minds on several issues." It is available in high school libraries.

1997–1998

The novel was banned from the Jackson County, West Virginia, school libraries, along with sixteen other titles. The reason is unknown.

THE STORY

Set in 1979, the women's movement has not yet hit the small town of Modesta, Michigan, where girls are expected to follow the conventional roles of their mothers and accept chauvinistic behavior from the men in their lives. Ruth Grange does not know to argue when she has to do all the work around the house while her brothers do nothing. Jane Reardon stands by while she watches her father abuse her mother. And Laura Snow endures constant teasing about her obesity and just wants a friend. The girls face big changes when they are invited to join the Daughters of Eve, an elite secret society. The sponsor is Irene Stark, the new art teacher at school, who comes with a number of progressive beliefs. She is a feminist and sets out to change the ideas of the girls regarding their traditional roles. For a while, this teacher and her "new ideas" mesmerize the girls, but when she begins to encourage them to take revenge for the way they have been treated, they are faced with a dilemma: Do they remain loyal to the Daughters of Eve? Are they brave enough to stop the vindictive acts that Ms. Stark encourages before real tragedy happens?

Themes
- Family
- Feminism
- Peer pressure
- Self-identity
- Women's rights

TALKING WITH TEENS ABOUT THE ISSUES

What is the purpose of the Daughters of Eve secret society? There are only ten members in the Daughters of Eve. Explain why the focus is on the three new girls. Why is Laura Snow especially happy to be in the club?

Describe Irene Stark. How does she captivate the girls? At what point is it obvious that she is an evil person?

One reviewer calls attention to the "troubled, angry characters." Identify these characters. What causes their anger? How does Tammy show courage to stand up to Ms. Stark? Discuss how the other girls respond to Tammy.

The novel has been challenged for sexual content. There are no graphic sex scenes. Cite the scenes that some may label "sexual content." Why are these scenes necessary in the story?

Explain how the "profanity" defines the culture of Modesta High School and the Daughters of Eve.

It has also been challenged for violence. What are the most violent scenes? How does Lois Duncan imply violence without offering gory details? Discuss how Ms. Stark is the root of the violence.

Explain how the novel is a cautionary tale.

CHALLENGED FOR SIMILAR REASONS

Draper, Sharon. *The Battle of Jericho.* New York: Simon & Schuster, 2003.

According to a database maintained by the University of Illinois, this novel is about a high school junior and his cousin who suffer consequences after joining what appears to be a "reputable" and exclusive school club. The details of the challenge are not charted, but various blogs indicate that the issue is "hazing" that goes wrong.

Koertge, Ronald. *The Brimstone Journals.* Somerville, MA: Candlewick, 2001.

In 2007–2008, this novel, narrated by fifteen teenagers, exposes the culture of a fictional suburban high school. It was challenged at the William Chrisman High School Library in Independence, Missouri, because of "profanity" and "violence."

RESOURCES FOR RESPONDING TO CHALLENGES

What Reviewers Say

Booklist (July 15, 1979) believes that Duncan is successful in writing "a disturbing climate of latent evil." The *New York Times* (January 27, 1980) calls it a "savage novel full of troubled, angry characters." *Kirkus* (September 1, 1979) calls the novel "manipulated melodrama." *Bulletin for the Center for Children's Books* (January 1980) says the "style and characterization are competent." *School Library Journal* (September 1979) calls it a "slick, scary occult novel." A reviewer on *Goodreads* (October 27, 2007) calls the novel "a commentary on radicalism gone out of control."

Other Justification for Inclusion in Curricula and Library Collections

❖ 2015 Mystery Writers of America Grand Master Award for Lifetime Achievement
❖ 2009 Catholic Library Association: St. Katharine Drexel Award for "outstanding contribution to the growth of high school and young adult librarians and literature"

Sources of Information about Challenges to the Novel

"The Negative Effects of Girl Power." *Reading on the Edge* (blog), October 29, 2014. Accessed September 30, 2015. https://readingontheedge.wordpress.com/author/hwalter1/.
Plesyk, Christine Anne. "Banned Books: Killing Mr. Griffin/Daughters of Eve." *Business & Heritage Clarksville* (Tennessee). Accessed October 2, 2015. http://businessclarksville.com/arts/banned-books-killing-mr-griffendaughters-of-eve/2010/09/18/15507.
Strauss, Valerie. "Fairfax County Schools Reject Book Challenges." *Washington Post*, February 2, 2010. Accessed October 2, 2015. http://voices.washingtonpost.com/answer-sheet/literature/fairfax-countys-school-distric.html.

INFORMATION ABOUT THE AUTHOR

http://loisduncan.arquettes.com (Duncan's official website)
https://twitter.com/duncanauthor (Duncan on Twitter)
Kies, Cosette N. *Presenting Lois Duncan.* Twayne's United States Authors Series No. 635. Farmington Hills, MI: Cengage Gale, 1994.

Stone, RoseEtta. "Interview with Lois Duncan." *Absolute Write* (blog), January 18, 2002. Accessed September 2, 2015. http://www.absolutewrite.com/specialty_writing/lois_duncan.htm.

Sutton, Roger. "A Conversation with Lois Duncan." *School Library Journal* 38 (June 1992): 20–24.

FURTHER READING ABOUT THE NOVEL

Atwell, Mary Stewart. "Feminism Turns Fatal in a 1970s Classic." NPR Books. Accessed September 1, 2015. http://www.npr.org/2012/12/05/162632367/feminism-turns-fatal-in-a-1970s-classic.

"*Daughters of Eve* by Lois Duncan." *Novel Concepts* (blog). Accessed September 20, 2015. http://novel--concepts.blogspot.com/2013/02/daughters-of-eve-by-lois-duncan.html.

Duncan, Lois. "1992 Margaret A. Edwards Award Acceptance Speech." *Journal of Youth Services in Libraries* 6 (Winter 1993): 108–112.

Gerlach, Jeanne. "Mother/Daughter Relationships in Lois Duncan's *Daughters of Eve*." *ALAN Review* 19, issue 1 (Fall 1991): 36–39.

Kaywell, Joan. "An Interview with Lois Duncan." *Journal of Adolescent & Adult Literacy* 52, issue 6 (March 2009): 545–547.

Roy, Leila. "Rewind: Lois Duncan's *Daughters of Eve*." *Kirkus*, October 13, 2010. Accessed October 2, 2015. https://www.kirkusreviews.com/features/Kirkus_YA/.

OTHER MEDIA SOURCES

https://www.youtube.com/watch?v=6XmuneJnTEo. Posted January 21, 2009. Accessed October 6, 2015. Lois Duncan talks about her writing career.

https://www.youtube.com/watch?v=2o6rgR_54n8. Posted April 7, 2013. Accessed September 30, 2015. A fan provides a video review of *Daughters of Eve*.

12

❖ ❖ ❖

A Day No Pigs Would Die

BY ROBERT NEWTON PECK

New York: Knopf, an imprint of Random House, 1972 (Op)
Laurel-Leaf Paperback, 1994
Recorded Books Audio, 1997
Penguin Random House E-book, 2014

"Come spring, you aren't the boy of the place. You're the man."

CHALLENGES: WHEN, WHY, AND WHERE

The earliest recorded challenge to the novel was in 1988 in Colorado. The novel has continued to be challenged, and according to the American Library Association's Office for Intellectual Freedom, it was #16 on the 100 Most Frequently Challenged Books List of 1990–1999 and #80 on the Top 100 Banned/Challenged Books List of 2000–2009.

2013–2014

According to the Oregon Intellectual Freedom Clearinghouse, a parent challenged the novel because of "offensive language, religious views and violence." No information was provided about which school or town the challenge occurred. It was retained.

2004–2005

According to the Texas American Civil Liberties Union (Texas ACLU), a parent of a ninth-grade student at Longview High School in the Longview Independent School District requested that the novel be removed from the reading list. The parent was informed that alternate titles are offered to students.

1996–1997

A teacher resigned her job after school officials banned the novel from the St. Lawrence School in Utica, Michigan. The controversy was over a passage about "pig breeding."

1994–1995

The "gory" details of "two pigs mating" and "a cow giving birth" caused school officials to pull the book from a middle school in Anderson, South Carolina.

It was also banned from the Pawhuska Middle School in Oklahoma because of "language" and because it "lacks religious values."

1993–1994

It was challenged but retained in the Waupaca, Wisconsin, school libraries after a parent complained about the "graphic passages dealing with sexuality."

In the same year, it was removed from the seventh-grade curriculum at the Payson Middle School in Utah after a number of complaints about the "language" and "animal breeding."

THE STORY

Set in the 1920s in the fictional town of Learning, Vermont, thirteen-year-old Robert Newton Peck tells the story of his journey to manhood on his father's pig farm. Haven Peck, Rob's illiterate father, is a simple man and rears his son by strict Shaker law. This makes Robert an outsider at school and causes him to be the target of teasing and taunts from his classmates. One day Rob has had enough teasing and decides to skip out on school. He takes a shortcut through Mr. Tanner's property and comes upon Apron, Mr. Tanner's prize cow, in the middle of a difficult birth. Rob knows exactly what to do to save Apron and her calf. As a thank-you, Mr. Tanner gives Rob a pig that he names Pinky. It turns out that Pinky is barren, and Rob must stand by as his father slaughters his pet for winter food. Rob eventually learns to forgive his father, but he faces another devastating loss when his father dies. It's tough becoming the man of the family at such a young age, but that's the world in which Rob was reared, and he can't let his mother down. In *A Part of the Sky* (Random House, 1994), the Great Depression is weighing heavy on the Peck family, and Rob is forced to make the difficult decision to sell the farm.

Themes
❖ Coming of age
❖ Death and grief
❖ Family
❖ Forgiveness
❖ Isolation

TALKING WITH TEENS ABOUT THE ISSUES

Discuss the qualities of a hero. Some critics believe that Robert's father is a "quiet hero." What is a "quiet hero"? Contrast the way Robert views his father at the beginning of the book and at the end. Cite scenes from the novel that reveal that Robert's father is a hero to him.

The novel has been challenged because of the "gory" details of the "pigs mating" and the "cow giving birth." How is this the reality of farm life? Discuss how omitting these scenes would "sugarcoat" the rural setting.

The book has also been challenged because of "religious views." Use knowledge gained from reading the novel and discuss the Shaker religion. Why are people so threatened by novels that depict religious views other than their own?

At least one challenge to the novel states that it "lacks religious values." Cite passages in the novel that show Robert's family lives and upholds the values of their religion.

The book has also been challenged because of language. What is Aunt Matty's role in helping Rob improve his language skills? How does Rob's hope of continuing his education die when his father dies?

Discuss the meaning of "coming of age." How does Rob come of age in the novel? Discuss his journey. Is it gradual or abrupt?

Discuss Robert's feelings of isolation. What is Mr. Tanner's role in broadening Robert's world? At what point does Robert finally become comfortable being an outsider?

Cite evidence that Haven Peck knew that he would soon die. How does Robert deal with his father's death? What is symbolic about the last scene when Robert returns to his father's grave? Explain the significance of the title of the book.

CHALLENGED FOR SIMILAR REASONS

Paulsen, Gary. *The Beet Fields: Memories of a Sixteenth Summer*. New York: Delacorte, an imprint of Random House, 2000.

According to the 2005–2006 Texas ACLU report, this autobiographical book was banned from West Sabine High School in the West Sabine Independent School District because of "sexual content."

Steinbeck, John. *The Red Pony*. New York: Penguin Classics, an imprint of Penguin, 1994.

Originally published in 1932, this story about a boy's experiences growing up on his father's ranch was challenged in 1997–1998 in the Attalla, Alabama, school system because of "profanity and violence." There are also recorded challenges to the book in New York, Georgia, and North Carolina.

RESOURCES FOR RESPONDING TO CHALLENGES

What Reviewers Say

Christian Science Monitor (January 17, 1973) says that the novel is "sometimes sickening, often entrancing." *Library Journal* (November 15, 1972) calls out the novel for its "dry wit." The reviewer for *School Library Journal* (March 1973) calls it "moving" and comments on the "clear, understated style." The journal recommends it for young adults. *Saturday Review of Education* (February 1973) says that readers will likely be "caught up in the novel's emotion" in the first scene. The *New York Times* (May 13, 1973) calls it "an honest, unpretentious" novel. *Kirkus* (January 1, 1972) states that it's "the kind of sentiment many people cotton to."

Other Justification for Inclusion in Curricula and Library Collections

❖ 2011 Learn.org ranked it #18 on the "25 Banned Books That Should Be Read Today"
❖ 1977 Colorado Children's Book Award
❖ 1975 *Media & Methods* Maxi Award
❖ 1973 ALA/YALSA Best Books for Young Adults

Sources of Information about Challenges to the Novel

McCracken, Nancy. "Reading and Responding to the Censors: Ground for Defense." *ALAN Review* 22, issue 2 (Winter 1995): 41–43.

Mulvey, Jim. "A Defense of *A Day No Pigs Would Die*." In *Censored Books II: Critical Viewpoints, 1985–2000*, edited by Nicholas J. Karolides, 152–158. Lanham, MD: Scarecrow Press, 2002.

INFORMATION ABOUT THE AUTHOR

http://www.blahnik.info/rnpeck/ (Peck's official website)
Contemporary Authors Online, 2004. Books and Authors. Gale.

FURTHER READING ABOUT THE NOVEL

Hartvigsen, M. Kip, and Christen Brog Hartvigsen. "Haven Peck's Legacy in *A Day No Pigs Would Die*." *English Journal* 74, issue 4 (April 1985): 41–45.

Lucie-Nietzke, Terese J. "As Simple as Shaker Life: Teaching Metaphor in *A Day No Pigs Would Die*." *Clearinghouse* 64, issue 6 (July/August 1991): 399–400.

Sullivan, Michael. "Robert Newton Peck and Shaker Beliefs: A Day the Truth Would Die." *ALAN Review* 25, issue 1 (Fall 1997): 13–17.

OTHER MEDIA SOURCES

https://www.youtube.com/watch?v=m5DBdDYV1Ug. Posted by Minute Book Reports, March 15, 2013. Accessed July 4, 2015. This is a quick review and analysis of the novel.

https://www.youtube.com/watch?v=aQ4oAOTjKtU. Posted September 26, 2013. Accessed June 14, 2015. The novel is read aloud for the Banned Books Week Virtual Read-Out.

13

❖ ❖ ❖

Deliver Us from Evie

BY M. E. KERR

New York: HarperCollins, 1994
HarperCollins Paperback, 1995
HarperCollins E-book, 2009
Open Road Media E-book, 2013

"Don't miss me Parr. Think of me, but don't miss me.
Get on with your life, and I'll get on with mine."

CHALLENGES: WHEN, WHY, AND WHERE

2006–2007

The book was among a long list of books challenged at the Webster School District in New York because of the "gay theme."

THE STORY

Set in a small conservative town in the Midwest at a time when being gay was taboo, Parr Burrman is aware of the whispers and jokes about his sister Evie. He realizes that she is masculine and likes helping out on the family farm, but he can't seem to deal with the idea that she might be lesbian. Then Evie falls in love with Patsy Duff, the daughter of a wealthy and influential man in town. The girls manage to keep their love affair a secret for a while, but when it becomes too difficult, they run away to New York City. Each member of the Burrman family deals with the news differently. Parr is focused on himself and wonders what it will do to his dreams of going away to college now that Evie isn't around to help his father on the farm. His father is concerned that Mr. Duff might renege on the loan that the Burrmans need for the farm. Each family member must find a way to come to terms with Evie's sexual orientation. Or, do they?

Themes
❖ Family
❖ Friendship
❖ Love
❖ Prejudices
❖ Sex and sexuality

TALKING WITH TEENS ABOUT THE ISSUES

Discuss how each member of the Burrman family reacts when they learn that Evie is lesbian. How does the Duff family react when they discover that Patsy is involved with Evie?

How is the news complicated by the conservative views of their small Missouri town?

What does "unconditional love" mean? Discuss which family, the Burrmans or the Duffs, best understands the term.

The novel has received several awards and accolades from well-known professional review journals. Yet, it has been challenged because of homosexual content. Discuss the novel's contribution to contemporary young adult literature, especially literature with gay and lesbian themes.

Engage in a conversation about the bullying that occurs in the novel. How are gay/lesbian teens often the target of bullies? Explain how this is a form of prejudice.

Some high schools have formed a Gay-Straight Alliance on their campuses. How is this a positive effort to promote tolerance? Discuss ways of using Kerr's novel to spark open and honest conversation about bullying, prejudices, and tolerance of all students, regardless of their sexuality.

CHALLENGED FOR SIMILAR REASONS

Garden, Nancy. *Annie on My Mind*. New York: Farrar, Straus & Giroux, an imprint of Macmillan, 1982.

This novel about a high school senior who is questioning her sexuality was removed from the Olathe East High School in Olathe, Kansas, in 1993. Students and their parents sued the school board, and the courts ordered the book back on the shelves.

Peters, Julie Ann. *Far from Xanadu*. New York: Little, Brown, 2005.

Life is already tough for Mike Szabo when she develops a crush on an exotic new girl in her small Kansas town. The novel was banned from the middle and high school in the Thorndale, Texas, Independent School District in 2009–2010 because of "profanity."

Scoppettone, Sandra. *Happy Endings Are All Alike*. New York: HarperCollins, 1978.

In 1983–1984, this novel about two girls who fall in love and are victim to small-town prejudices was banned from the Evergreen School District in Vancouver, Washington. The American Civil Liberties Union filed suit, but the results are unknown.

RESOURCES FOR RESPONDING TO CHALLENGES

What Reviewers Say

Voice of Youth Advocates (October 1994) says, "Unquestionably, this is the best Kerr in years, if not ever." In the starred review for *Booklist* (September 15, 1994), Hazel Rochman writes that the narrator's "voice is perfectly pitched between wit and melancholy." She recommends it for grades 7–12. *School Library Journal* (November 1, 1994) recommends it for grades 9 and up and says, "Kerr is in absolute control of the narrative." *Publishers Weekly* (October 3, 1994) calls it "thought-provoking."

Other Justification for Inclusion in Curricula and Library Collections

❖ 1999 National Council of Teachers of English Best Young Adult Novels of the '90s Pick
❖ 1997 California Young Reader Medal
❖ 1995 *Horn Book* Fanfare Honor Book
❖ 1994 *Booklist* Editors' Choice: Books for Youth: Older Readers Category
❖ 1994 Michigan Library Association: Best Book Honor Award

Sources of Information about Challenges to the Novel

Scales, Pat R. "Banned Books Week Common Teachers Guide." Open Road Media. Accessed August 21, 2015. http://www.openroadmedia.com/ebook/common-core-standards-and-banned-books-week/.

INFORMATION ABOUT THE AUTHOR

Contemporary Authors Online, 2008. Books and Authors. Gale.

FURTHER READING ABOUT THE NOVEL

Abate, Michelle Ann. "From Cold War Lesbian Pulp to Contemporary Young Adult Novels: Vin Packer's *Spring Fire*, M. E. Kerr's *Deliver Us from Evie*, and Marijane Meaker's *Fight against Fifties Homophobia*." *Children's Literature Association Quarterly* 32, issue 2 (Fall 2007): 231–251.

Cart, Michael. "Honoring Their Stories Too: Literature for Gay and Lesbian Teens. *ALAN Review* 25, issue 1 (Fall 1997). Accessed August 7, 2015. http://scholar.lib.vt.edu/ejournals/ALAN/fall97/cart.

Cockett, Lynn. "Entering the Mainstream: Fiction about Gay and Lesbian Teens." *School Library Journal* 41 (February 1995): 32–33.

Glasgow, Jacqueline N. "Teaching Social Justice through Young Adult Literature." *English Journal* 90, issue 6 (July 2001): 54–61.

Newman, Leslea. *"Deliver Us from Evie." Lambda Book Report* 4, issue 7 (November/December 1994): 36.

Zarr, Sara. "M. E. Kerr and *Deliver Us from Evie*." Posted May 12, 2015. Accessed August 1, 2015. http://www.gayya.org/?p=2460.

OTHER MEDIA SOURCES

https://www.youtube.com/watch?v=TQnWexvvkeQ. Posted October 5, 2014. Accessed August 21, 2015. High school students present a video review and discussion of *Deliver Us from Evie*.

https://www.youtube.com/watch?v=LyQu_vQ7vdk. Posted February 22, 2015. Accessed August 21, 2015. A book trailer created by a fan of *Deliver Us from Evie*.

14

❖ ❖ ❖

The Drowning of Stephan Jones

BY BETTE GREENE

New York: Delacorte, an imprint of Random House, 1991
New York: Open Road Media E-book, 2011

"Sadness that a sweet and gentle man lay in his grave, and in her own hometown, people who ought to know better acclaimed and applauded his murderers."

CHALLENGES: WHEN, WHY, AND WHERE

According to data collected by the American Library Association's Office for Intellectual Freedom, the novel ranked #96 on the 100 Most Frequently Challenged Books List of 1990–1999.

2004–2005

An organized group called Library Patrons of Texas challenged the novel at the Montgomery County Memorial Library System because of "gay-positive themes."

2002–2003

Parents were successful in getting the book banned in the Horry County School District in South Carolina because it is "educationally unsuitable and contains unacceptable language."

1998–1999

The novel was removed, and later reinstated by the courts, in the Barron School District in Wisconsin. The ban focused on the "homosexual themes."

1995–1996

The book was banned, and an English teacher fired, from the Mascenic Regional High School in New Ipswich, New Hampshire, because it is about "gays and lesbians." The teacher was later reinstated.

1993–1994

The novel was removed from the curriculum and the library shelves in Boling, Texas, because it "teaches anti-Christian beliefs and condones illegal activity."

3906513792
7669
Transited:
March 9,
2018 10:15
AM

Set i
sing
prej
to o
con
Mo
hoi
bee
Ste
An
en
th
th

w
se
S

]
‹
‹
.

and has always felt like an outsider. Her
ce and to speak up against any type of
:hool heartthrob Andy Harris causes her
hardware store. It's Christmas, and Carla
nd services at the church Andy attends.
wright preaches a sermon that condemns
' causes her to dismiss everything she has
begin harassing Frank Montgomery and
open an antique shop. Carla is aware that
>y making prank calls and sending threat-
rom date with Andy to bother herself with
ounter Frank and Stephan and they chase
iver and he drowns.
:ephan Jones, and Carla is called as a key
ivances toward him, the judge suspends the
much for Carla who knows the real truth.

TALKING WITH TEENS ABOUT THE ISSUES

Tolerance toward those who are different is a learned behavior. Explain how Carla's mother taught her tolerance. Where does Andy learn intolerance?

Discuss why Carla doesn't confront Andy when he and his friends begin harassing Frank and Stephan.

Why does Mr. Burwick tell Andy to testify that Stephan made sexual advances toward him? How does this make Mr. Burwick part of the crime? Who are the other guilty parties in the crime?

Discuss how Frank Montgomery discredits Andy in front of his family and the crowd of reporters.

One of the reasons that the book has been challenged and banned is profanity. Discuss how the profanity that Andy uses defines his character.

The novel has also been banned because of its gay-positive themes. Explain how the censors are missing the point of the story. How is censorship a form of intolerance?

At the end of the novel, Carla and her mother are moving to New Hampshire. How might the "gay bashing" in Rachetville and the murder of Stephan Jones cause Carla to choose her friends more closely in New Hampshire?

CHALLENGED FOR SIMILAR REASONS

Block, Francesca Lia. *Weetzie Bat*. New York: HarperCollins, 1989.

In 2010–2011, this novel that deals with gay marriage and the AIDS epidemic was banned at the Ehrhart Charter School in Beaumont, Texas, because of the "homosexual content."

Chambers, Aidan. *Dance on My Grave: A Life and Death in Four Parts*. New York: HarperCollins, 1986.

This novel about the love between two gay teens, and what happens when one dies, was challenged in 2004 at the Montgomery County Library System in Texas because of its "gay-positive" themes.

RESOURCES FOR RESPONDING TO CHALLENGES

What Reviewers Say

Publishers Weekly (November 8, 1991) calls the novel a "dramatic and graphic portrayal of persecution." *School Library Journal* (October 1, 1991) is lukewarm about the novel but does recognize that there are "powerful scenes of dialogue." They recommend the novel for grades 7–12. *The Horn Book Guide* (March 1, 1992) says, "The denouement is dramatic but unrealistic." *Kirkus* (November 15, 1991) recommends the book for ages fourteen and up but states that Greene has a "tendency to tell rather than show."

Other Justification for Inclusion in Curricula and Library Collections

❖ 1993 Lambda Literary Award: Children's and Young Adult Category

Sources of Information about Challenges to the Novel

"Banned Books Week Guest Post from Bette Greene: Author's Affidavit—the Murder of the Book *The Drowning of Stephan Jones*." *Write All the Words* (blog), September 18, 2012. Accessed June 9, 2015. http://www.ekristinanderson.com/?p=4215.

Greene, Bette. "An Author's Perspective on Censorship and Selection." *Library Talk* 14, issue 2 (March/April 2001): 12–14.

INFORMATION ABOUT THE AUTHOR

http://www.bettegreene.com (Greene's official website)

FURTHER READING ABOUT THE NOVEL

Alvine, Lynne. "Understanding Adolescent Homophobia: An Interview with Bette Greene." *ALAN Review* 21, issue 2 (Winter 1994): 5–9.

Campbell, Patty. "The Sand in the Oyster." *Horn Book Magazine* 69, issue 5 (September/October 1993): 568–572.

Finnessy, Patrick K. "Drowning in Dichotomy: Interpreting *The Drowning of Stephan Jones*." *ALAN Review* 25, issue 3 (Spring 1998): 24–27.

OTHER MEDIA SOURCES

http://media.openroadmedia.com/files/2011/10/24/BetteGreeneBullyingThread.mp4. Posted October 24, 2011. Accessed July 12, 2015. Bette Greene talks about bullying.

https://www.youtube.com/watch?v=oJ_iw9asPlI. Posted September 12, 2014. Accessed June 15, 2015. Bette Greene talks about the banning of *The Drowning of Stephan Jones.*

15

❖ ❖ ❖

The Earth, My Butt, and Other Big Round Things

BY CAROLYN MACKLER

Somerville, Massachusetts: Candlewick Press, 2003
Recorded Books Audio, 2004
Candlewick Paperback, 2005
Candlewick E-book, 2011

"Froggy Welsh the Fourth has made it up my shirt."

CHALLENGES: WHEN, WHY, AND WHERE

The American Library Association's Office for Intellectual Freedom recorded Mackler's novel as #34 on the Top 100 Banned/Challenged Books List of 2000–2009. It was #8 on the Top Ten Most Frequently Challenged Books List in 2009 and #4 in 2006. The reasons cited include "anti-family, offensive language, sexually explicit and unsuited to age group." In addition to the challenges listed below, there are others that are nonpublic.

2007–2008

A middle school librarian in Colorado Springs, Colorado, reported that the novel was removed from the library because of "profanity" and "sexual references."

It was challenged because of "sexual content" but retained at A.C. Middle School in the Mesquite, Texas, Independent School District.

2005–2006

The superintendent of schools in Westminster, Maryland, banned the novel because of "profanity" and "sexual references." After a protest from students and several free speech organizations, the book was retained in high school libraries, but not middle schools.

A parent verbally challenged the novel at the Travis Middle School in the Irving, Texas, Independent School District because of the "profanity" and "sexual content." The principal met with the parent, and a written complaint was never filed. The book was retained.

THE STORY

Virginia "Ginny" Shreves is fifteen years old and a sophomore at a private school in New York City, where she doesn't completely fit in. She is obese and dresses in oversized clothing in an attempt to disguise her weight. To make matters worse, she feels like an anomaly in a family that places value on appearance. Ginny's father is a business executive who eyes skinny girls, and her nagging mother, a psychologist for adolescents, is an exercise fanatic. Anais, her older sister, is thin and pretty, but she joined the Peace Corps to escape her mother. Her brother, Byron, the favored child, is good-looking and a rugby star at Columbia University until he is kicked out for date rape. Struggling to exist in such a dysfunctional family, Ginny makes friends with Froggy Welsh the Fourth who doesn't seem to care how large she is. As their relationship grows, Ginny's self-concept improves and she finds the courage to stand up to her mother. She purchases a plane ticket to visit her best friend who moved to Walla Walla, Washington, and when she returns, she takes up kickboxing. Her personal journey has just begun, but what she learns is that outward appearance is not nearly as important as what is on the inside.

Themes
❖ Family
❖ Friendship
❖ Self-concept
❖ Sibling relationships

TALKING WITH TEENS ABOUT THE ISSUES

Explain what Ginny means when she says she feels "un-Shreves like."

Ginny's mother is Dr. Phyllis Shreves, a psychologist for adolescents. Discuss why her mother is so unsuccessful in dealing with Ginny.

The novel has been challenged because of sexual content. What is Anais's role in Ginny's sex education? Anais tells Ginny that she got her information from *It's Perfectly Normal*. Discuss why it is so difficult for Dr. Shreves to talk with her children about sex.

Ginny's brother is kicked out of college for date rape. How might he have benefited from a sex talk?

The novel has also been challenged for profanity. Discuss whether the profanity defines the teenage culture at Ginny's posh school.

Chart Ginny's journey toward a more positive self-concept. What is Froggy Welsh the Fourth's role in her transformation?

Describe Ginny's relationship with her mother by the end of the novel. How might adults better understand the novel if they took the time to focus on the real conflict and the resolution?

CHALLENGED FOR SIMILAR REASONS

Atkins, Catherine. *Alt Ed*. New York: Putnam, an imprint of Penguin, 2003.

In 2007–2008, the novel about an overweight girl who is bullied was challenged at a junior high school in Lake Oswego, Oregon, after a parent objected to its use in a bullying unit because it is "peppered with profanities, sexual content and violence."

Kerr, M. E. *Dinky Hocker Shoots Smack*. New York: HarperCollins, 1972.

This novel about an overweight girl who is nagged by a mother too busy being a success to give her daughter the attention she needs was challenged but retained at the Merritt Brown Middle School in Panama City, Florida, in 1998 because of passages that are "sacrilegious and morally subversive."

RESOURCES FOR RESPONDING TO CHALLENGES

What Reviewers Say

Publishers Weekly (July 21, 2003) states that the main character is "believable and worthy of applause." The reviewer for *Horn Book Magazine* (September 1, 2003) recommends the book for middle and high school readers and praises Mackler for introducing readers to "a very cool chick with a little meat on her bones." *Voice of Youth Advocates* (October 3, 2003) notes "occasional use of strong language and mild sexual allusions are appropriate and well done." *Booklist* (September 1, 2003) applauds the novel for its hopeful ending. *Kirkus* (June 15, 2003) says the book has "substance and spirit."

Other Justification for Inclusion in Curricula and Library Collections

❖ 2010 ALA/YALSA Popular Paperbacks for Young Adults
❖ 2005 Amelia Bloomer Lists: Young Adult Fiction
❖ 2004 ALA/YALSA Best Books for Young Adults
❖ 2004 ALA/YALSA Michael L. Printz Honor Book

Sources of Information about Challenges to the Novel

"ACLU of Maryland Calls for Acclaimed Books to Be Returned to School Shelves." Posted December 8, 2005. Accessed August 7, 2015. https://www.aclu.org/news/aclu-maryland-calls-acclaimed -books-be-returned-school-shelves.

Goldberg, Beverly. "Banned Books Go Back to School." *American Libraries* 37, issue 2 (November 2006): 12.

INFORMATION ABOUT THE AUTHOR

http://carolynmackler.com (Mackler's official website)
https://twitter.com/carolynmackler (Mackler on Twitter)
Contemporary Authors Online, 2009. Books and Authors. Gale.

FURTHER READING ABOUT THE NOVEL

Coffey, Jesse. "Banned Books Week—*The Earth, My Butt, and Other Big Round Things*." *Lexington Literature Examiner*, October 1, 2010. Accessed May 23, 2015. http://www.examiner.com/ article/banned-book-week-the-earth-my-butt-and-other-big-round-things.

"An Interview with Carolyn Mackler." *Bookslut* (blog), December 2009. Accessed May 23, 2015. http://www.bookslut.com/features/2009_12_015466.php.

Karlin, Dorothy. "How to Be Yourself: Ideological Interpellation, Weight Control, and Young Adult Novels." *Jeunesse: Young People, Texts, Cultures* 6, issue 2 (Winter 2014): 72–89.

Lesesne, Teri S., and Don Gallo. "Bold Books for Innovative Teaching." *English Journal* 93, issue 4 (March 2004): 97–100.

Mackler, Carolyn. "Michael L. Printz Honor Speech." *Young Adult Library Services* 3, issue 1 (Fall 2004): 30–31.

OTHER MEDIA SOURCES

http://www.npr.org/2011/09/07/140256963/writers-reflect-on-childhood-torment-in-dear-bully. NPR Books, September 7, 2011. Accessed June 14, 2015. Neal Conan interviews Carolyn Mackler on *Talk of the Nation*.

https://www.youtube.com/watch?v=2eBCRyJ6YDY. Posted September 30, 2011. Accessed June 14, 2015. A passage from the novel is read aloud for the Banned Books Week Virtual Read-Out.

16

❖ ❖ ❖

Eleanor & Park

BY RAINBOW ROWELL

New York: St. Martin's Press, 2013
Listening Library Audio, 2013
St. Martin's Griffin Paperback, 2014

"He made her feel like more than the sum of her parts."

CHALLENGES: WHEN, WHY, AND WHERE

2013–2014

The Parents Action League in Minnesota filed a formal challenge and asked that the novel be removed from the Anoka-Hennepin School District libraries because of "profanity" and issues related to "sexuality." Rowell was scheduled to make an appearance in the schools, but her visit was canceled. A book review committee voted to retain the book, and Rowell was reissued an invitation to speak to students.

THE STORY

Set in Omaha, Nebraska, in the 1980s, fifteen-year-old Eleanor Douglas is a new girl at school. She is lonely and bullied because she is overweight and poor. The social culture on the school bus is well established, and Eleanor is not welcome. Then Park Sheridan, a half-Korean boy who is also an outsider, sits beside her and a friendship develops. Eleanor is as miserable at home as she is at school. She suffers abuse from Richie, her stepfather, and her mother is frightened and helpless. Eleanor finds solace with Park, but his mother does not approve. When Mrs. Sheridan sees Eleanor and her family in the grocery store on Christmas Eve, she changes her attitude toward the girl. Eleanor spends most of the remaining holiday break at Park's house, and his mother, a beautician, gives her a makeover. After another frightening outburst by Richie, Eleanor realizes that she is in danger and must leave. She goes to Park's house and tells him her situation. He borrows his father's truck and takes Eleanor to her uncle's house in Minnesota. Park misses Eleanor and writes her many letters, but she does not write back until six months later when she sends him a postcard with only three words.

Themes
❖ Abandonment
❖ Appearances
❖ Courage

❖ Family
❖ Gender roles
❖ Isolation
❖ Love
❖ Race

TALKING WITH TEENS ABOUT THE ISSUES

Trace the relationship that develops between Eleanor and Park from the beginning of the novel to the end. Why do you think Eleanor does not read Park's letters?

Describe Eleanor's home life. How does Eleanor's mother feel stuck in her relationship with Richie?

At first, Park's mother does not approve of Eleanor. Explain why seeing Eleanor and her family in the grocery store on Christmas Eve causes Mrs. Sheridan to change her view of Eleanor.

Park helps Eleanor by taking her to her uncle's house in Minnesota, where she is welcomed with open arms. Why do you think Eleanor didn't take her siblings with her?

There are objections to the novel because of sexual content. Eleanor and Park do make out several times, but it is only implied that they have sex in his father's truck. Debate whether their physical relationship means more to Park than to Eleanor. Why? Discuss what Eleanor might say to teenagers who are eager to engage in sex.

The novel has also been challenged because of profanity. How does the profanity reveal Eleanor's home life? Explain how softer language would change the story.

CHALLENGED FOR SIMILAR REASONS

Green, John. *Paper Towns.* New York: Dutton, an imprint of Penguin, 2008.

This 2009 Edgar Award winner about a high school boy who ditches his graduation ceremony and goes on a road trip in search of the missing girl he loves was removed from the eighth-grade reading list in 2013–2014 at the John Long Middle School in Pasco County, Florida, because of "profanity and teen sex." It was later placed back on the list.

Wittlinger, Ellen. *Hard Love.* New York: Simon & Schuster, 1999.

John and Marizol are mismatched teens, but a complicated relationship ensues when John finds himself falling for Marizol. According to a list of challenged books maintained by the University of Illinois, the novel has been challenged, though there is no specific reference to where and when. Sexual content is the likely reason.

RESOURCES FOR RESPONDING TO CHALLENGES

What Reviewers Say

Horn Book Magazine (May 7, 2013) calls the novel "an honest, heart-wrenching portrayal of imperfect but unforgettable love." *School Library Journal* (February 1, 2013) recommends the book for grades 9 and up and says it is "movingly believable." *Voice of Youth Advocates* (December 1, 2012) says the "bittersweet ending hits at hope for the two characters." *Publishers Weekly* (December 10,

2012) comments that the "solution—imperfect but believable—maintains the novel's delicate balance of light and dark." In the *Booklist* (January 1, 2013) starred review, it is noted that the relationship between Eleanor and Park is "urgent, moving, and of course, heartbreaking." *Christian Science Monitor* (December 9, 2013) comments, "Observant. Incisive. Tense, yet buoyant with hope."

Other Justification for Inclusion in Curricula and Library Collections

❖ 2015 Abraham Lincoln High School Book Award (Illinois)
❖ 2015 Florida Teens Read Award
❖ 2014 ABA Indies Choice Book Awards: Young Adult Book Award
❖ 2014 ALA/YALSA Top Ten Fiction for Young Adults
❖ 2014 Michael L. Printz Honor Book
❖ 2013 *Booklist* Top Ten Romance Fiction for Youth
❖ 2013 *Boston Globe–Horn Book* Award: Fiction
❖ 2013 *New York Times* Notable Children's Books

Sources of Information about Challenges to the Novel

Collins, Bob. "In Book Censorship, Anoka County Avoids Bullying Issue, Again." *NewsCut for MPR News* (blog). Accessed May 27, 2015. http://blogs.mprnews.org/newscut/2013/09/in-book-censorship-anoka-county-avoids-bullying-issue-again/.

Gilly, Casey. "Rainbow Rowell Talks to CBLDF about the Attack on *Eleanor & Park*." Comic Book Legal Defense Fund. Accessed May 27, 2015. http://cbldf.org/2013/09/rainbow-rowell-talks-to-cbldf-about-the-attack-on-eleanor-park/.

Holmes, Linda. "True Love, Book Fights and Why Ugly Stories Matter." NPR News, September 18, 2013. Accessed May 27, 2015. http://www.npr.org/sections/monkeysee/2013/09/18/223738674/true-love-book-fights-and-why-ugly-stories-matter.

Ortberg, Mallory. "A Chat with Rainbow Rowell about Love and Censorship." *The Toast*, September 17, 2013. Accessed May 27, 2015. http://the-toast.net/2013/09/17/chat-rainbow-rowell-love-censorship/.

Steinkellner, Kit. "Don't Ban Books Like *Eleanor and Park*, Teens Need Them." *BookRiot*, September 19, 2013. Accessed May 27, 2015. http://bookriot.com/2013/09/19/dont-ban-books-like-eleanor-park-teens-need/.

"Using 'R Rated' Book without Asking Parents Was Wrong, School Chair Says." *MPR News*, September 25, 2013. Accessed May 27, 2015. http://www.mprnews.org/story/2013/09/25/daily-circuit-eleanor-and-park-anoka-hennepin.

INFORMATION ABOUT THE AUTHOR

http://www.rainbowrowell.com (Rowell's official website)
Contemporary Authors Online, 2015. Books and Authors. Gale.

FURTHER READING ABOUT THE NOVEL

Bartel, Julie. "One Thing Leads to Another: An Interview with Rainbow Rowell." *YALSA The Hub* (blog), February 27, 2014. Accessed May 27, 2015. http://www.yalsa.ala.org/thehub/2014/02/27/one-thing-leads-to-another-an-interview-with-rainbow-rowell/.

Green, Amanda. "The Rumpus Interview with Rainbow Rowell." *The Rumpus*, October 17, 2014. Accessed May 27, 2015. http://therumpus.net/2014/10/the-rumpus-interview-with -rainbow-rowell/.

"Rainbow Rowell Interview: 'YA Books Teach You That Weird Stuff Is Normal.'" *Guardian*, August 7, 2014. Accessed May 27, 2015. http://www.theguardian.com/childrens-books-site/2014/ aug/07/rainbow-rowell-interview-young-adult-books.

Sutton, Roger. "Everybody Wants to Be a Teenager." *Horn Book Magazine* 89, issue 3 (May/June 2013): 7–8.

OTHER MEDIA SOURCES

https://www.youtube.com/watch?v=gR4gM_WXesQ. Posted by Minute Book Reports, October 13, 2014. Accessed July 4, 2015. This is a summary and analysis of the novel.

https://www.youtube.com/watch?v=sCYh886jcEY. Posted November 14, 2014. Accessed May 27, 2015. The Book Hoarder discusses the books of Rainbow Rowell.

17

❖ ❖ ❖

Fallen Angels

BY WALTER DEAN MYERS

New York: Scholastic, 1988
Scholastic Paperback, 2008
Recorded Books Audio, 2011
Zola Books E-book, 2013

"The little people you see running around here are not Mouseketeers.
Some of them are friendly, and some of them have a strong desire to kill you."

CHALLENGES: WHEN, WHY, AND WHERE

According to data collected by the American Library Association's Office for Intellectual Freedom, the novel ranked #11 on the Top 100 Banned/Challenged Books List of 2000–2009 and #36 on the 100 Most Frequently Challenged Books List of 1990–1999. It was #9 on the Top Ten Most Frequently Challenged Books List in 2001, #5 in 2003, and #2 in 2004.

2013–2014

The novel was challenged on the Danbury Middle School reading list in Toledo, Ohio, because of the gruesome details of the Vietnam War and the "foul language."

2008–2009

According to the Texas American Civil Liberties Union (Texas ACLU) the novel was challenged for use in all high schools in the Cypress-Fairbanks Independent School District because of "profanity, violence and drugs and alcohol use." If used in the curriculum, an alternate book must be offered. The same report records a challenge at Reagan County High School in the Reagan County Independent School District. No specific reason was given, and the outcome is unknown.

2007–2008

A parent in Duplin County, North Carolina, challenged the novel as part of the Accelerated Reading program list because the book is "littered with hundreds of expletives, including racial epithets and slang terms for homosexuals."

2006–2007

Parents in the Coeur d'Alene School District in Idaho challenged the novel and requested that students have parental permission to read it.

2005–2006

The book was challenged as part of a reading list at Northwest Suburban High School District 214 in Arlington Heights, Illinois. The novel was retained despite the promise of a school board member to bring "her Christian beliefs into all board decision-making."

The Texas ACLU reports that the novel was challenged at Llano High School in the Llano Independent School District because of "profanity." The use of the novel was restricted, though the report doesn't give the conditions. An alternate book was allowed.

2004–2005

In Overland Park, Kansas, the novel was banned from sophomore English classes in the Blue Valley, Kansas, School District.

It was banned as part of the sophomore English curriculum at Franklin Central High School in Indianapolis, Indiana, because of "profanity."

2001–2002

Parents against Bad Books in Schools (PABBIS) challenged the novel in Fairfax County, Virginia, elementary and secondary schools because of "profanity, drug abuse, sexually explicit conduct, and torture."

After expressed concerns about "profanity," the novel was banned from all George County Schools in Mississippi.

2000–2001

It was challenged but retained in the Arlington, Texas, junior high schools after a parent complained that the content was "too strong" for students.

1999–2000

The book was challenged by a parent of a junior high school student in the Arlington Independent School District in Texas because "the content was too strong for younger students." It was retained in all junior high school libraries.

1998–1999

After a complaint that the novel contains "too many swear words," it was banned in the Livonia, Michigan, public schools.

The Laton Unified School District in California banned the book because of "violence and profanity."

1996–1997

Parents challenged the novel because of "violence and vulgar language" at the Lakewood High School in Ohio. It was retained.

1994–1995

The novel, used in a twelfth-grade English class in Middleburg Heights, Ohio, was banned after a parent complained about the "sexually explicit language."

1991–1992

After complaints about the "undesirable language and sensitive material," the novel was restricted as supplemental classroom reading at the Jackson County High School in Georgia.

THE STORY

Seventeen-year-old Richie Perry is a good student, but he is from a poor, single-parent home in Harlem with no hope of attending college. He feels that his only option is to join the military, but he worries about himself and his family since the nation is at war in Vietnam. He leaves for basic training immediately after high school graduation and convinces himself that he will never see combat because of a knee injury. The injury is small in the eyes of the military, and Richie is deployed to the war zone, where he witnesses a buddy killed on the first day in the field. He longs to communicate his terror to his family, but he lacks the words to express his thoughts regarding the morality of the war, and why he is even there. He has a brief stay at a hospital due to a minor injury, and when he returns he comes face to face with a new sergeant who puts the black soldiers in the most dangerous spots. Unlike Myers's brother, who was killed in Vietnam, Richie escapes with enough battle wounds to send him home, but he is still in the army. On the return flight to the United States, along with caskets of dead soldiers, Richie has time to think about his role in the United States Army and gathers the courage to face new recruits with dignity.

Themes

❖ Family
❖ Friendship
❖ Heroism
❖ Race
❖ Realities of war
❖ Survival

TALKING WITH TEENS ABOUT THE ISSUES

Richie goes to war at a very young age. How does the reality of the battlefield cause him to question the morality of war? Cite passages from the novel to show that he also questions his reasons for enlisting.

Discuss the racial bigotry and the civil rights issues happening in the United States at the time of the Vietnam War. How do Richie and other black soldiers come face to face with the same type of racism in the United States Army?

Richie is terrified after he witnesses his buddy killed on the first day in the field. Why can't he share his thoughts with his family? Debate whether he is ashamed of his terror, or if he is protecting them.

The novel has been challenged in an elementary school program that was using it along with the Accelerated Reading program. Who is the novel's targeted audience? The novel was likely purchased for advanced readers. Discuss the difference between reading skill and reading maturity.

The novel has been challenged because of violence. How can there be war without violence?

The book has also been challenged because of foul language. Try substituting some of the profanity with language that censors might find more acceptable. How does it change the horror and devastation of the war?

Discuss how writers owe it to young readers to write the truth, even when that truth may be "tough, gritty and troublesome to some."

CHALLENGED FOR SIMILAR REASONS

Mazer, Harry. *The Last Mission*. New York: Laurel-Leaf, an imprint of Random House, 1981.

In 1995, this novel about an American Jewish boy who lies about his age to fight in World War II was banned in the Carroll Middle School library in Southlake, Texas, because of "excessive profanity." It was later returned to the collection.

O'Brien, Tim. *The Things They Carried*. Boston: Houghton Mifflin Harcourt, 1990.

This novel about fighting in the Vietnam conflict was challenged but retained in 2006 at the Northwest Suburban High School District 214 in Arlington Heights, Illinois, because of concerns based on "excerpts from the novel" that a school board member read on the Internet. It was banned in the George County, Mississippi, schools in 2002 because of "profanity."

RESOURCES FOR RESPONDING TO CHALLENGES

What Reviewers Say

School Library Journal (June/July 1988) recommends the book for grades 10 and up and calls it "riveting." The reviewer also states that the novel "neither condemns nor glorifies the war." The reviewer in the *Kirkus* (April 15, 1988) starred review calls the book "powerful" and "introspective." *Publishers Weekly* (May 7, 1988) states that the novel is "a worthy memorial" to Myers's brother. *Booklist* (April 15, 1988) acknowledges the political and social concerns related to the war and commends Myers for "blending them smoothly."

Other Justification for Inclusion in Curricula and Library Collections

- ❖ 2000 ALA/YALSA 100 Best Books for Young Adults: 1950–2000
- ❖ 1994 Keystone to Reading Book Award (Pennsylvania): Intermediate Category
- ❖ 1992 Charlotte Award (New York): Young Adult (Grades 6–12)
- ❖ 1991 South Carolina Young Adult Book Award
- ❖ 1989 Coretta Scott King Author Award
- ❖ 1988 ALA/YALSA Best Books for Young Adults
- ❖ 1988 ALA/YALSA Quick Picks for Reluctant Young Adult Readers
- ❖ 1988 *Horn Book* Fanfare Honor List
- ❖ 1988 National Council of Teachers of English/Children's Book Council "Notable Children's Trade Book in the Field of Social Studies"
- ❖ 1988 Parents' Choice Awards: Fiction
- ❖ 1988 *School Library Journal*'s Best Books of the Year

Sources of Information about Challenges to the Novel

Murray, Beth. "Defending *Fallen Angels* by Walter Dean Myers: Framing—Not Taming—Controversy." In *Censored Books II: Critical Viewpoints, 1985–2000*, edited by Nicholas J. Karolides, 167–172. Lanham, MD: Scarecrow Press, 2002.

Whelan, Debra Lau. "Walter Dean Myers Talks Book-Banning, Writing for Troubled Kids."
    National Coalition against Censorship (blog), August 9, 2013. Accessed June 11, 2015. https://
    ncacblog.wordpress.com/2013/08/09/walter-dean-myers-talks-book-banning-writing-for
    -troublemakers/.

INFORMATION ABOUT THE AUTHOR

http://walterdeanmyers.net/category/news/ (Myers's official website)
Jordan, Denise. *Walter Dean Myers: A Biography of an Award-Winning Urban Fiction Author.*
    African-American Icon Series. Berkeley Heights, NJ: Enslow Publishers, 2013.
Marler, Myrna Dee. *Walter Dean Myers.* Teen Reads: Student Companions to Young Adult
    Literature Series. Portsmouth, NH: Greenwood, 2008.

FURTHER READING ABOUT THE NOVEL

Chance, Rosemary, and Teri Lesesne. "And the Winner Is . . . : A Teleconference with Walter Dean
    Myers." *Journal of Reading* 94, issue 3 (November 1994): 246–249.
Hill, Rebecca A. "Sharing Stories, Exploring Issues." *Book Links* 20, issue 1 (October 2010): 23–25.
Kazemek, Francis E. "The Literature of Vietnam and Afghanistan: Exploring War and Peace with
    Adolescents." *ALAN Review* 23, issue 3 (Spring 1996): 6–9.
Myers, Walter Dean. "1994 Margaret A. Edwards Award Acceptance Speech." *Journal of Youth
    Services in Libraries* 8 (Winter 1995): 129–133.

OTHER MEDIA SOURCES

https://www.youtube.com/watch?v=EnYg6hYGU3w. Posted September 22, 2011. Accessed June
    11, 2015. A passage from *Fallen Angels* is read for the Banned Books Week Virtual Read-Out.
http://interviewly.com/i/walter-dean-myers-dec-2013-reddit. Posted December 2013. Accessed
    June 19, 2015. Walter Dean Myers takes calls from readers.
https://www.youtube.com/watch?v=oe6IyKM59Zw. Posted April 9, 2014. Accessed June 10,
    2015. Walter Dean Myers talks about writing *Fallen Angels.*

18

❖ ❖ ❖

The Fault in Our Stars

BY JOHN GREEN

New York: Dutton Books, an imprint of Penguin, 2012
Penguin E-book, 2012
Brilliance Audio, 2014
Penguin Paperback, 2014

"The world is not a wish-granting factory."

CHALLENGES: WHEN, WHY, AND WHERE

2014–2015

According to a report from the National Council of Teachers of English, the novel was removed from middle school libraries at the Riverside Unified School District in California because of "language and sexual content." It was later reinstated.

THE STORY

Seventeen-year-old Hazel Grace Lancaster has thyroid cancer and attends a support group for terminally ill teens, where she meets and falls in love with Augustus (Gus) Waters, who lost a leg to osteosarcoma. Hazel Grace asks Augustus to read *An Imperial Affliction* by Peter Van Houten, a novel about a girl stricken by cancer. The open ending troubles Gus, and Hazel Grace has a very specific question about the fate of one of the characters. Gus manages to locate Van Houten on the Internet and learns that the author lives in Amsterdam. He corresponds with Van Houten's assistant, but the author will only agree to answer their questions in person. Augustus surprises Hazel Grace with airline tickets to the Netherlands, but the Lancasters are nervous about their daughter traveling, especially since she had recently spent time in ICU. Hazel Grace's doctor agrees that she should go. It turns out that Van Houten is a jerk and a drunk. Augustus dies not too long after they return, and Hazel Grace is surprised when Van Houten shows up at the funeral. Hazel Grace wrote a eulogy to deliver at Gus's funeral, but at the last minute edits her words to comfort his parents. Then she learns from Isaac, another teen in the support group, that Gus had left special words for her—his eulogy to her.

Themes

❖ Death
❖ Family
❖ Friendship
❖ Love

TALKING WITH TEENS ABOUT THE ISSUES

Discuss how Hazel and Gus confront their illnesses. Debate whether the support group helps them face their mortality. Contrast their attitudes with that of Isaac.

Hazel Grace says, "Cancer books suck." Why do you think *An Imperial Affliction* by Peter Van Houten is her favorite book? Explain why she needs to know what happens in the book after the heroine dies. Gus uses his "wish" to take Hazel Grace to Amsterdam to meet Van Houten. Discuss why he is so mean to Hazel Grace and Gus.

What do Hazel Grace and Gus find in Amsterdam that they didn't fully understand prior to the trip? How does Hazel Grace's mother give them space?

Gus dies not too long after they return from Amsterdam. What does Hazel Grace learn about grief from observing Gus's family? Debate whether she better understands Van Houten when she learns that he had a daughter who died when she was eight. How does Gus's death help her better understand what her parents are facing?

The novel has been challenged because of "language and sexual content." How do the romance and the "sex" between these two terminally ill teenagers make their lives whole?

The novel was removed and later reinstated in a middle school in California. State reasons why the novel should be in middle and high school libraries.

CHALLENGED FOR SIMILAR REASONS

Crutcher, Chris. *Deadline.* New York: Greenwillow, an imprint of HarperCollins, 2007.

In 2009–2010, this novel about eighteen-year-old Ben who suffers a terminal illness was pulled, along with five other novels, from the approved curriculum at Montgomery County High School in Kentucky because of "sexual content, drug abuse, child abuse, and suicide."

Gunther, John. *Death Be Not Proud.* New York: Harper, 1949; Harper E-book, 2013.

This memoir about the death of the author's son from a brain tumor was retained in Edgecombe, North Carolina, in 1995 after complaints that the "book has words in it that even unsaved people would have spanked their children for saying."

RESOURCES FOR RESPONDING TO CHALLENGES

What Reviewers Say

Voice of Youth Advocates (April 1, 2012) says the novel alternates "between iridescent humor and raw tragedy." The *School Library Journal* (February 1, 2012) starred review recommends the novel for grades 9 and up and says that Green presents "a well-developed cast of characters." *Booklist* (January 1, 2012) gives the book a star and calls it Green's "best and most ambitious novel to date." *Horn Book Magazine* (February 22, 2012) says the main character is "the most multi-dimensional yet of John Green's Girls." The *Kirkus* (January 10, 2012) starred review calls the novel a "poignant journey." *Publishers Weekly* (January 9, 2012) also stars the book and calls it "smart, witty, profoundly sad."

Other Justification for Inclusion in Curricula and Library Collections

❖ 2015 ALA/YALSA Popular Paperback for Young Adults: Book to Movie: Ripped from the Pages
❖ 2015 California Young Reader Medal: Young Adult
❖ 2015 Garden State Teen Book Awards (New Jersey): Fiction (Grades 9–12)
❖ 2015 Golden Archer Awards (Wisconsin): Middle/Junior High School
❖ 2015 Sequoyah Book Awards (Oklahoma): High School Books
❖ 2015 Soaring Eagle Book Award (Wyoming)
❖ 2015 Young Reader's Choice Award (Pacific Northwest): Senior
❖ 2014 Abraham Lincoln Illinois High School Book Award
❖ 2014 Black-Eyed Susan Book Awards (Maryland): High School
❖ 2014 Blue Hen Book Award (Delaware): Teen Readers
❖ 2014 Georgia Peach Book Award for Teen Readers
❖ 2014 Rhode Island Teen Book Award
❖ 2014 Teen Buckeye Book Award (Ohio)
❖ 2014 Virginia Reader's Choice Award: High School (Grades 10–12)
❖ 2013 ALA/YALSA Best Fiction for Young Adults
❖ 2013 Indies' (Independent Book Sellers) Choice Awards: Young Adult Fiction
❖ 2013 Pennsylvania Young Reader's Choice Awards: Young Adult
❖ 2013 Westchester Fiction Award (California)
❖ 2012 *Booklist* Editors' Choice: Books for Youth: Older Readers Category
❖ 2012 *School Library Journal* Best Books of the Year
❖ 2012 Thumbs Up! Award (Michigan)

Sources of Information about Challenges to the Novel

Gibson, Megan. "John Green's Response to *The Fault in Our Stars* Being Banned Is Just Perfect." Time.com, September 29, 2014. Accessed August 19, 2015. http://time.com/3444896/john-green-fault-in-our-stars-banned/.

Herman, Barbara. "*The Fault in Our Stars* Author John Green Responds to California School Ban." *International Business Times* (New York), September 30, 2014. Accessed August 19, 2015. http://www.ibtimes.com/fault-our-stars-author-john-green-responds-california-school-ban-1697202.

Hurt, Suzanne. "Riverside: *Fault in Our Stars* Banned from Middle Schools." *The Press Enterprise* (Riverside, California), September 22, 2014; updated September 28, 2014. Accessed August 19, 2015. http://www.pe.com/articles/book-750585-school-committee.html.

Schaub, Michael. "John Green's *The Fault in Our Stars* Banned in Riverside." *Los Angeles Times*, August 19, 2015. Accessed August 19, 2015. http://www.latimes.com/books/jacketcopy/la-et-jc-john-green-the-fault-in-our-stars-banned-riverside-20140929-story.html.

INFORMATION ABOUT THE AUTHOR

http://johngreenbooks.com (Green's official website)
https://twitter.com/johngreen?lang=en (Green on Twitter)
Contemporary Authors Online, 2015. Books and Authors. Gale.

FURTHER READING ABOUT THE NOVEL

Grossman, Lev. "Being Green." *Time* 183, issue 22 (June 9, 2014): 48–50.

King, Helen. "Fighting through Fiction." *Culture, Medicine, and Psychiatry* 37, issue 4 (December 2013): 686–693.

Rosen, Rebecca J. "How John Green Wrote a Cancer Book but Not a 'Bullshit Cancer Book.'" *The Atlantic*, February 25, 2013. Accessed August 19, 2015. http://www.theatlantic.com/entertainment/archive/2013/02/how-john-green-wrote-a-cancer-book-but-not-a-bullshit-cancer-book/273441/.

Syme, Rachel. "*The Fault in Our Stars*: Love in a Time of Cancer." NPR Books, January 17, 2012. Accessed August 19, 2015. http://www.npr.org/2012/01/17/145343351/the-fault-in-our-stars-love-in-a-time-of-cancer.

OTHER MEDIA SOURCES

http://phusplay.com/stream/?movie=2582846&id=TOP. Accessed August 23, 2015. Access the full movie of *The Fault in Our Stars* on this website.

https://www.youtube.com/watch?v=n8EpX8UcDsk. Posted March 11, 2012. Accessed August 23, 2015. John Green discusses *The Fault in Our Stars*.

https://www.youtube.com/watch?v=9ItBvH5J6ss. Posted January 29, 2014. Accessed August 23, 2015. This is the official trailer for the 20th Century Fox film of *The Fault in Our Stars*.

19

❖ ❖ ❖

Feed

BY M. T. ANDERSON

Somerville, Massachusetts: Candlewick Press, 2002
Random House Audio, 2006
Candlewick E-book, 2010
Candlewick Paperback, 2012

"We went to the moon to have fun, but the moon turned out to completely suck."

CHALLENGES: WHEN, WHY, AND WHERE

2012–2013

The American Library Association's Office for Intellectual Freedom recorded a challenge at the William Monroe High School in Greene County, Virginia, because the book is "trash" and "covered with the F-word." A consent form was sent home before the novel was used in the curriculum, and a notice was posted on the teacher's website that the novel contained "mature content."

2010–2011

The school board of the Sedro-Woolley School District in Mt. Vernon, Washington, voted to restrict the use of the novel to optional reading in the eleventh- and twelfth-grade curriculum after parents of tenth-graders complained about the "language and sexual content."

2009–2010

The novel was challenged but retained at the Chisholm Trail Middle School in the Round Rock, Texas, Independent School District because of "profanity."

THE STORY

Titus is not a typical teenage boy. Like most babies in the future society where he lives, he was conceived by in vitro fertilization, and at birth his brain was implanted with a "feed," connecting him to a large computer network that controls his thoughts and behavior. During a spring-break trip to the moon, Titus and his friends go clubbing at the Ricochet Lounge, where a man hacks into their "feed." They land in the hospital to be repaired. At the same club, Titus meets Violet, an intriguing and strange girl, who is determined to fight the "feed" so that she might experience original and personal thoughts. She returns with Titus at the end of his vacation. They hang out at the mall and decide that it would be fun to try and fool their "feed" by looking at products that are the opposite of their "interests." Then Violet tells Titus that her "feed" has been hacked and she is dying. This is when Titus seems most human because he must learn to deal with the ultimate death of the one he loves. This satirical novel is a chilling reminder of the role of consumerism in our society, and the danger of power when it is allowed to control us.

Themes

- ❖ Consumerism
- ❖ Death
- ❖ Environment
- ❖ Friendship
- ❖ Identity
- ❖ Love
- ❖ Power

TALKING WITH TEENS ABOUT THE ISSUES

Explain why this is called a satirical novel. How is it both frightening and comical? What do you think Anderson wants young people to think about as they read this novel?

What are the ethical issues raised in the book?

Titus has a "feed" that controls his thoughts. Compare and contrast this concept to technology used by teens today.

Titus develops feelings for Violet. How does he deal with her impending death?

The novel was a finalist for the National Book Award for Young People. Discuss the complex literary elements and themes that qualified the novel for this honor.

The novel has been challenged because of language and sexual content. Debate whether the language is realistic to the characters. Cite scenes with sexual content. How are these scenes necessary to the novel?

Some critics feel it necessary to label the novel for "mature content." How might this label both restrict and entice readers?

CHALLENGED FOR SIMILAR REASONS

Doctorow, Cory. *Little Brother*. New York: Tor Teen, an imprint of Macmillan, 2008.

In 2014–2015, this novel about a group of teenagers who are under tight government surveillance after they hack into their high school computer system was pulled from the One Book/One School program at Booker T. Washington High School in Pensacola, Florida, because the book might encourage "hacking" and "questioning authority."

Philbrick, Rodman. *The Last Book in the Universe*. New York: Scholastic, 2002.

This dystopian novel where gangs rule and people use mind probes to temporarily forget their impoverished lives was banned in a middle school in Santa Rosa, California, because of "content about gangs."

RESOURCES FOR RESPONDING TO CHALLENGES

What Reviewers Say

Booklist (October 15, 2002) recommends the book for grades 9–12 and calls it "a cautionary tale." *Horn Book Magazine* (October 2002) recommends it for high schools and says it is "an ingenious satire." *Teacher Magazine* (March/April 2003) comments that the book will cause even "the most apathetic kid to think." *Kirkus* (September 1, 2002) comments that the novel has "obvious and enormous implications for today's readers." *Publishers Weekly* (July 22, 2002) calls the novel "thought-provoking." *School Library Journal* (September 1, 2002) recommends it for grades 8 and up and says it is a "gripping, intriguing, and unique cautionary novel."

Other Justification for Inclusion in Curricula and Library Collections

- ❖ 2010 ALA/YALSA Popular Paperbacks for Young Adults: Change Your World or Live to Regret It
- ❖ 2009 ALA/YALSA Outstanding Books for the College Bound: Science and Technology
- ❖ 2004 ALA/YALSA Outstanding Books for the College Bound: Literature and Language Arts
- ❖ 2003 ALA Best Books for Young Adults
- ❖ 2003 Book Sense Summer Pick for Teen Readers
- ❖ 2003 Boston Globe Horn Book Award for Fiction
- ❖ 2003 Golden Duck Awards: Hal Clement Award for Young Adults
- ❖ 2002 *Booklist* Editors' Choice: Books for Youth: Older Readers
- ❖ 2002 Finalist National Book Award
- ❖ 2002 *New York Times* Notable Books: Children's Books

Sources of Information about Challenges to the Novel

"Banned Books Week: Celebrating the Freedom to Read." *Creston News Advertiser* (Iowa), September 23, 2014.

Burkhalter, Aaron. "Brief. School Board Places Restriction on Use of Book." *Skagit Valley Herald* (Mt. Vernon, Washington), November 9, 2010.

INFORMATION ABOUT THE AUTHOR

http://www.mt-anderson.com (Anderson's official website)

https://twitter.com/_mtanderson (Anderson on Twitter)

Contemporary Authors Online, 2013. Books and Authors. Gale.

Thompson, Bob. "Profile: Author M. T. Anderson Challenges Young Adults with Complex Narratives." *Washington Post*, November 28, 2008. Accessed November 13, 2015. http://www.washingtonpost.com/wpdyn/content/article/2008/11/28/AR2008112802766.html.

FURTHER READING ABOUT THE NOVEL

Blasingame, James. "An Interview with M. T. Anderson." *Journal of Adolescent & Adult Literacy* 47, issue 1 (September 2003): 98.

Bullen, Elizabeth, and Elizabeth Parsons. "Dystopian Visions of Global Capitalism: Philip Reeve's *Mortal Engines* and M. T. Anderson's *Feed*." *Children's Literature in Education* 38, issue 2 (June 2007): 139–151.

Kramer, Melody Joy. "M. T. Anderson Eats Broccoli, Paces and Hums." NPR Books, November 24, 2006. Accessed April 29, 2015. http://www.npr.org/templates/story/story.php?storyId =6525913.

Tokuda-Hall, Maggie. "M. T. Anderson, Sci-fi Author, Accidental Prophet and Nice Guy." *BoingBoing* (blog), February 26, 2015. Accessed November 13, 2015. http://boingboing .net/2015/02/26/m-t-anderson-sci-fi-author.html.

Wilkinson, Rachel. "Teaching Dystopian Literature to a Consumer Class." *English Journal* 99, issue 3 (January 2010): 22–26.

OTHER MEDIA SOURCES

https://www.youtube.com/watch?v=n5IJ9fwepr0. Posted October 13, 2010. M. T. Anderson speaks at the 2010 National Book Award Festival.

https://www.youtube.com/watch?v=k5uE8YwNTnQ. Posted January 24, 2011. M. T. Anderson talks with AdLit.

20

❖ ❖ ❖

Forever

BY JUDY BLUME

New York: Bradbury Press, 1975
Simon & Schuster E-book, 2012
Simon & Schuster Hardback (Reissue), 2014
Simon & Schuster Paperback (Reissue), 2014

> "Sex is a commitment. . . . Once you're there
> you can't go back to holding hands."

CHALLENGES: WHEN, WHY, AND WHERE

The earliest recorded challenge to Blume's novel was in 1982 in Orlando, Florida. Throughout the 1980s, it was challenged in Missouri, Pennsylvania, Ohio, Wisconsin, Iowa, Nebraska, Virginia, Wyoming, California, and Maine. The 1990s brought challenges in Illinois, Wisconsin, Iowa, and Florida. Most of the challenges were due to "sexual content." According to data collected by the American Library Association's Office for Intellectual Freedom, *Forever* ranked #7 on the 100 Most Frequently Challenged Books List of 1990–1999; #16 on the Top 100 Banned/Challenged Books of 2000–2009. It was #2 on the Top Ten Most Frequently Challenged Books List of 2004–2005. The reasons cited are "profanity and sexual content."

2009–2010

A parent at the Sugarloaf School in Summerland Key, Florida, has requested that the novel be removed from the school because "it has a distorted view of sex, promiscuity, and is usurping parental control." The novel was retained.

2008–2009

The Texas American Civil Liberties Union (Texas ACLU) reports that the novel has been placed on a restricted list in all middle schools in the Alief Independent School District because of "profanity and sexual content." Classroom use requires that a letter be sent home to parents.

2005–2006

According to the Texas ACLU, the novel was banned at the Escontrias Elementary School in the Socorro Independent School District because of "sexual content."

2004–2005

According to the Texas ACLU, the novel was banned at the Chisum Middle School Library in the Chisum Independent School District and sent to the high school library. This yearly report also states that the novel was banned from all secondary school libraries in the Pasadena Independent School District because of "profanity and sexual content."

In Fayetteville, Arkansas, one woman led a crusade to ban *Forever* and more than fifty books from school libraries because they were "too sexually explicit" and some of them "promote homosexuality." A community group formed to pressure the school board to retain the books.

2001–2002

The school board in Elgin, Illinois, upheld the review committee's decision to allow the novel back into middle school libraries.

1997–1998

The novel was banned from middle school libraries in Elgin, Illinois, because of "sex scenes," but the decision was reversed in 2002.

1996–1997

The book was challenged in Wilton, Iowa, for junior and senior high school students. The outcome of the challenge wasn't reported.

1995–1996

The novel was challenged at the Delta High School in Muncie, Indiana. The novel was placed on a restricted shelf, and students must have parental permission to borrow it.

A science teacher objected to the "sexually explicit content" and a "reference to marijuana" at Fort Clarke Middle School in Gainesville, Florida. The book was removed from circulation.

1994–1995

The novel was challenged in the Mediapolis, Iowa, schools because it "does not promote abstinence and monogamous relationships and lacks any aesthetic, literary, or social value." It was removed but later returned to the high school libraries.

1993–1994

A high school counselor was fired after speaking out about the Rib Lake, Wisconsin, School District's materials review policy after *Forever* was placed on the "parental permission shelf."

The novel was removed from the Robert Frost Junior High School in Schaumburg, Illinois, because "it's basically a sexual 'how-to-do' book."

1992–1993

Students at Herrin Junior High School in Herrin, Illinois, must have parental permission to borrow the book.

THE STORY

Katherine Danziger is a senior in high school when she meets Michael Wagner at a New Year's Eve party. They are attracted to one another and gradually develop a steady relationship. Michael has had previous sexual partners, but Katherine is a virgin and isn't sure she is really ready to have sex. When Michael begins pressuring her, she seeks counsel from her best friend, Erica. The girls differ in their views. Erica believes that sex is merely a physical act, while Katherine thinks it should also be an emotional commitment. She thinks that she is ready for a commitment to Michael and goes to Planned Parenthood of New York for birth control. Katherine's parents become concerned when she begins to compromise her own hopes and dreams for those of Michael's. The two are separated when Katherine takes a summer job in New Hampshire and Michael in North Carolina. As the summer progresses, Katherine begins to see her parents' point of view. Most of all, she realizes that she isn't ready for a "forever" relationship.

Themes
❖ Family
❖ Friendship
❖ Goals
❖ Relationships
❖ Sex and sexuality

TALKING WITH TEENS ABOUT THE ISSUES

Katherine's mother and grandmother talk with her about sex. How is this type of open conversation necessary for teens to have a healthy attitude toward sex?

Compare and contrast Katherine and Erica's views toward sex. Why is Erica so determined to lose her virginity before going away to college?

Michael asks Katherine if she's a virgin. Why does he want to know? Katherine asks Michael if he's a virgin. Discuss his answer.

What might the reader learn from Sybil's mistake? Sybil gives her baby up for adoption. How is this a smart, but difficult, decision? This book was first published in 1975. Might Sybil's decision be different today?

Katherine's grandmother works for Planned Parenthood. How does this work give her a realistic view of teens and their sex lives? Katherine goes to Planned Parenthood of New York for birth control. How is this a responsible decision?

The novel is one of the most challenged books in America. Those who don't think teens should read the book say it presents "a distorted view of sex." Define the term *distorted*. Then debate whether the novel is distorted or realistic. Why do you think Judy Blume included "requirements for safe and responsible sex" in a later edition of the novel?

Some adults object to the novel because they believe it is a "sex manual" for teens. Discuss important lessons teens take away from the novel. How do these lessons explain the title of the novel?

At what age should a girl or a boy read the novel? Why does censoring the novel make it more enticing?

CHALLENGED FOR SIMILAR REASONS

Jahn-Clough, Lisa. *Me, Penelope*. Boston: Houghton Mifflin Harcourt, 2007.

This novel about a sixteen-year-old girl who wants to lose her virginity before she graduates high school was banned from two Tavares, Florida, middle schools and at Oak Park Middle School in Leesburg, Florida, because of "sexual content."

Klein, Norma. *It's Okay If You Don't Love Me*. New York: Knopf, an imprint of Penguin Random House, 1977.

This novel about a high school girl with a "liberated" view of sex was banned in California in 1981, Colorado in 1983, and in Washington in 1984 because of "sexually explicit passages" and "rough language."

Mazer, Norma Fox. *Up in Seth's Room*. New York: Delacorte, an imprint of Penguin Random House, 1979.

In 1982, this novel about a fifteen-year-old girl and her nineteen-year-old boyfriend who explore their thoughts about a developing sexual relationship was removed from the Campbell County School District libraries in Wyoming. It was later reinstated.

RESOURCES FOR RESPONDING TO CHALLENGES

What Reviewers Say

Kirkus (October 1, 1975) calls the novel "an updated *Seventeenth Summer*." *Booklist* (October 1975) says the "characters—including adults and friends of the protagonists—are well-developed and the dialogue is natural." A reviewer on *Goodreads* (May 31, 2011) says, "5 stars for the author telling a *realistic* story about a girl's first time with both falling in love and having sex."

Other Justification for Inclusion in Curricula and Library Collections

❖ 2012 NPR Your Favorites: 100 Best-Ever Teen Novels
❖ 2008 ALA/YALSA Popular Paperbacks for Young Adults
❖ 1996 ALA/YALSA Best of the Best Books for Young Adults: Top 100
❖ 1992 ALA/YALSA Best Books for Young Adults 1966–1992

Sources of Information about Challenges to the Novel

"Board Pulls Blume's *Forever*." *American Libraries* 25, issue 5 (May 1994): 390.
Flood, Alison. "Judy Blume: 'I Thought, This Is America. We Don't Ban Books. But We Did.'" *Guardian*, July 11, 2014. Accessed June 9, 2015. http://www.theguardian.com/books/2014/jul/11/judy-blume-interview-forever-writer-children-young-adults.
Forman, Jack. "Young Adult Books: 'Watch Out for #1.'" *Horn Book Magazine* 61, issue 1 (January/February 1985): 85.
Guerra, John L. "Parents: Book Too Racy for Youngsters." *Florida Keys and Key West Daily Online News*, January 16, 2010. Accessed June 9, 2015. http://keysnews.com/node/20059.
Margolis, Rick. "Illinois Librarian Fights On." *School Library Journal* 47, issue 11 (November 2001): 14.
Murray, Kate. "*Forever* a Forum That Talks to Teenagers." *Daily Telegraph* (Sydney, Australia), June 10, 2005.

INFORMATION ABOUT THE AUTHOR

http://www.judyblume.com (Blume's official website)

http://jwa.org/encyclopedia/article/blume-judy. Jewish Women's Archives offers biography of Blume.

Abrams, Dennis, and Elisa Ludwig. *Judy Blume*. Who Wrote That? Series. New York: Facts on File, 2009.

Tracy, Kathleen. *Judy Blume*. Greenwood Biographies Series. Santa Barbara, CA: ABC-CLIO.

FURTHER READING ABOUT THE NOVEL

Alter, Alexander, and Kathryn Shattuck. "What Judy Blume's Books Meant." *New York Times*, June 2, 2015. Accessed July 16, 2015. http://www.nytimes.com/2015/06/02/books/what -judy-blumes-books-meant.html.

Blume, Judy. "1996 Margaret A. Edwards Awards Acceptance Speech." *Journal of Youth Services in Libraries* 10 (Winter 1997): 148–156.

Crowe, E. V. "Why Judy Blume's *Forever* Is . . . For Ever." *Guardian*, June 14, 2013. Accessed June 6, 2015. http://www.theguardian.com/stage/2013/jun/14/judy-blume-forever-ev-crowe.

Crown, Sarah. "Teen Spirit." *Guardian*, June 8, 2005. Accessed June 6, 2015. http://www .theguardian.com/books/2005/jun/08/booksforchildrenandteenagers.sarahcrown.

Gough, John. "Reconsidering Judy Blume's Young Adult Novel *Forever . . .*" *Use of English* 36, issue 2 (Spring 1985): 29–36.

Kaplan, Jeffrey S. "Ted Hipple Was Right! How I Broke the Rules and Lived Happily Ever After." *English Journal* 83, issue 5 (September 1994): 25–28.

Kurtz, Jason, and Nicholle Schuelke. "Blume, Burgess, and Beyond: Sexuality and the Young Adult Novel." *Voice of Youth Advocates* 34, issue 3 (August 2011): 228–230.

Sutton, Roger. "An Interview with Judy Blume Forever . . . Yours." *School Library Journal* 42, issue 6 (June 1996): 24–26.

OTHER MEDIA SOURCES

https://www.youtube.com/watch?v=fuhp3VTQQ2Q. Accessed June 6, 2015. Judy Blume speaks about censorship for the American Library Association's Banned Books Week Virtual Read-Out in 2011.

https://www.youtube.com/watch?v=MxnfbKMrPXA&list=PLD88419A26ADC68B6. Accessed June 6, 2015. Judy Blume accepts the 2004 Distinguished Contribution to American Letters Award from the National Book Award Foundation.

Sullivan, J. Courtney. "Judy Blume Showed Innocence Isn't 'Forever,'" NPR Books, August 4, 2010. Accessed June 6, 2015. http://www.npr.org/templates/story/story.php?storyId=127482114. Judy Blume talks with *All Things Considered*, audio on the web.

21

❖ ❖ ❖

Geography Club

BY BRENT HARTINGER

New York: HarperCollins, 2003
HarperCollins Paperback, 2004
HarperCollins E-book, 2009

"The fact is, there's a difference between being alone and being lonely;
I may not have been completely alone in life, but I was definitely lonely."

CHALLENGES: WHEN, WHY, AND WHERE

2009–2010

The novel was challenged at the West Bend, Wisconsin, Community Memorial Library as being "obscene or child pornography." The board unanimously voted to retain the book in the young adult collection "without restriction or labels."

2005–2006

It was withdrawn from the junior and senior high schools in Curtis, Washington, after parents filed a complaint claiming the "casual and loose approach to sex" encourages use of Internet porn and the physical meeting of people through chat rooms.

THE STORY

The students at Robert L. Goodkind High School don't know that Russel Middlebrook is gay. For this reason, Russel feels lonely and isolated, and he is on guard about revealing his sexuality. Even Gunnar and Min, his best friends, don't know his sexual orientation. They simply view him an outsider, as they are. One night he is visiting a gay Internet chat room and engages in a conversation with another student from his high school. That student turns out to be super jock Kevin Land. The two boys form a friendship, and this gives Russel the courage to reveal his sexuality to Min. In their conversation, she tells Russel that she is bisexual and is currently in a lesbian relationship with Terese, a high school soccer player. They decide to start a club for LGBT students. They call it the Geography Club because they think the name is so boring that other students wouldn't want to join. But Belinda, another student who seriously wants to study geography, shows up and their cover is blown. After a teacher writes an article for the school newspaper about homophobia, the kids in the Geography Club decide it's time to form a "Gay Straight Alliance," and membership is open to all who want to join. Other novels in the Russel Middlebrook series include *The Order of the Poison Oak* (2005); *Double Feature* (originally released under the title *Split Screen* and divided into two parts), with part 1 titled *Attack of the Soul-Sucking Brain Zombies* and part 2 titled *Bride of the Soul-Sucking Brain Zombies* (2009); *The Elephant of Surprise* (2013); and *Two Thousand Pounds per Square Inch* (2014).

Themes
- ❖ Fear
- ❖ Isolation
- ❖ Loneliness
- ❖ Outsiders
- ❖ Sexual identity

TALKING WITH TEENS ABOUT THE ISSUES

Russel Middlebrook feels lonely and isolated. What other students at Robert L. Goodkind High School are outcasts? Discuss how the "popular" students make lives of the "outcasts" miserable at school.

Russel meets Kevin Land in a gay chat room. How is Kevin different at school than he is in the chat room? How does meeting Kevin give Russel the courage to reveal his sexual orientation to his friend Min?

Explain what happens with Russel and Kevin's relationship. Why does Kevin feel he has more to lose if his sexual orientation is revealed?

How is the Geography Club the first leg of a journey for the LGBT students? Discuss the courage of the teacher who wrote the article about homophobia for the school newspaper. How does this article take the LGBT students on the next leg of their journey?

Discuss why it is so difficult for gay students to reveal their sexual orientation at school. What should schools do to make these students feel safe and accepted?

The novel has been challenged because of child pornography. Define the term *child pornography*. How do people use the term loosely?

Book banners have said that the novel encourages students to enter Internet chat rooms. Discuss safety tips that students should follow when using the Internet and, specifically, chat rooms? Why is discussing Internet safety more important than forbidding Internet use?

CHALLENGED FOR SIMILAR REASONS

Howe, James. *Totally Joe*. New York: Simon & Schuster, 2005.
This novel about a thirteen-year-old boy who is bullied for being gay was to be pulled from schools in Davis, Utah, in 2012–2013 because of homosexuality.

Johnson, Maureen. *The Bermudez Triangle*. New York: Penguin, 2004.
In 2010–2011, this book about three girlfriends, where two of them become lovers, was challenged at the Leesburg, Florida, Public Library because of "sexual innuendo and adult topics." The novel was also challenged in the Bartlesville, Oklahoma, public schools because of the "gay-positive theme."

RESOURCES FOR RESPONDING TO CHALLENGES

What Reviewers Say

Hazel Rochman, reviewer for *Booklist* (April 1, 2003) recommends the novel for grades 7–10 and states it is "honest talk of love and cruelty, friendship and betrayal." *School Library Journal* (February 1, 2003) says, "Teens both gay and straight should find this novel intriguing." It recommends the book for grades 10 and up. *Voice of Youth Advocates* (April 1, 2003) commends Hartinger by saying that he "grasps the melodrama of high school well." *Horn Book Magazine* (March 1, 2003) calls the novel "an artful and authentic depiction of a gay teen." *Publishers Weekly* (February 3, 2003) reviews the book favorably and says that Hartinger "credibly captures high school pressure and intolerance."

Other Justification for Inclusion in Curricula and Library Collections

❖ 2005 ALA/ALSC-YALSA The Best, Notable and Recommended
❖ 2005 ALA/YALSA Popular Paperbacks for Young Adults
❖ 2003 Booklist Top Ten Youth First Novels

Sources of Information about Challenges to the Novel

"*Geography Club* Banned in Washington School District." *American Libraries*. Posted December 5, 2005. Accessed July 17, 2015. http://americanlibrariesmagazine.org/geography-club-banned-in-washington-school-system/.

Goldberg, Beverly. "Censorship Watch." *American Libraries* 37, issue 1 (January 2006): 18.

Mueller, Hannah. "Interview with Brent Hartinger, Author of Challenged Book, *Geography Club*." National Coalition against Censorship (blog), June 22, 2009. Accessed May 12, 2015. http://ncac.org/blog/interview-with-brent-hartinger-author-of-challenged-book-geography-club/.

"School District Bans Novel about Gay Teenagers." Associated Press, November 20, 2005. Accessed April 26, 2015. http://www.seattlepi.com/local/article/School-district-bans-novel-about-gay-teenagers-1187963.php.

Smith, Cynthia Leitich. "Author Interview: Brent Hartinger on the Banning of *Geography Club*." *Cynsations* (blog), November 23, 2005. Accessed April 25, 2015. http://cynthialeitichsmith.blogspot.com/2005/11/author-interview-brent-hartinger-on.html.

INFORMATION ABOUT THE AUTHOR

http://brenthartinger.com (Hartinger's official website)

Contemporary Authors Online, 2011. Books and Authors. Gale.

McCafferty, Dominique. "Geography of a Writer: An Interview with Brent Hartinger." *Public Libraries* 45, issue 4 (July/August 2006): 27–31.

FURTHER READING ABOUT THE NOVEL

Norton, Terry L., and Jonathan W. Vare. "Literature for Today's Gay and Lesbian Teens: Subverting the Culture of Silence." *English Journal* 94, issue 2 (November 2004): 65–69.

Pavao, Kate. "The Freedom of DIY: PW Talks with Brent Hartinger." *Publishers Weekly* 260, issue 27 (July 8, 2013): 31.

OTHER MEDIA SOURCES

http://geographyclub.com. Accessed July 17, 2015. This is the *Geography Club* official movie site from Huffington Pictures (2012).

https://www.youtube.com/watch?v=n3gn4k_PrMQ. Posted March 21, 2014. Accessed July 17, 2015. Brent Hartinger talks with WeStopHateUK about hate.

22

❖ ❖ ❖

Give a Boy a Gun

BY TODD STRASSER

New York: Simon & Schuster, 2000
Simon Pulse Paperback, 2002
Recorded Books Audio, 2002
Simon Pulse E-book, 2012

"Here's why you made my friggin' life miserable."

CHALLENGES: WHEN, WHY, AND WHERE

2009–2010

According to the Texas American Civil Liberties Union (Texas ACLU), the novel was challenged but retained at Chapa Middle School in the Hays Independent School District because of "profanity" and "violence"; it was also challenged for being "politically, racially or socially offensive."

2007–2008

The novel was challenged at a middle school in Bangor, Pennsylvania, because of "school violence." It was retained.

2004–2005

According to the Texas ACLU, the novel was banned from the Corsicana Residential Treatment Center Library at the Texas Youth Commission in Corsicana because it "could produce more violent and criminal behaviors."

THE STORY

Brendan Lawlor, a new kid in town, and Gary Searle are called "fags" and suffer other types of bullying from kids, especially the football players, at Middletown High School where they are students. The two boys attempt to drown their loneliness with drugs and alcohol. When things get worse at school, the boys steal a gun from a neighbor and make a plan for revenge. They attend a school dance, shoot out all the lights, tie up the students, and flash the gun around to terrorize the crowd. They end the quarterback's football career by shooting out his kneecaps. Gary commits suicide, but one of the football players beats Brendan into a coma. The players stand trial for attempted murder. Told from the viewpoint of the various survivors through a series of interviews, the person who vows to change the bullying culture at Middletown is Gary's stepsister. She is so troubled by the course of events that she leads a campaign that calls for respect toward all students. She also becomes a spokesperson for banning semiautomatic weapons.

Themes
- ❖ Bullying
- ❖ Competition
- ❖ Friendship
- ❖ Gun control
- ❖ Loneliness
- ❖ Revenge
- ❖ School violence
- ❖ Suicide

TALKING WITH TEENS ABOUT THE ISSUES

Describe Brendan and Gary. How do they become friends? Discuss which boy suffers the most from loneliness. Why?

How do drugs and alcohol make things worse for Brendan and Gary?

Why do the other students stand by and watch the bullying? What could they have done to make things different for Brendan and Gary?

Discuss the hints that Brendan and Gary are planning revenge.

The novel has been challenged because it might produce more violent and criminal behaviors. Consider Brendan's stepsister's vow to stop bullying and to speak out against gun violence. How is this the real message of the book?

Why is it more important to talk about violence than pretending it doesn't happen?

Make a plan to help students like Brendan and Gary in your school.

Debate issues related to gun violence in our society. What are the solutions?

CHALLENGED FOR SIMILAR REASONS

Giles, Gail. *Shattering Glass*. New York: Roaring Brook, an imprint of Macmillan, 2002.

This suspense novel about Simon Glass, the school misfit who is murdered by a classmate, was challenged as optional reading at the junior high school in Lake Oswego, Oregon, in 2007 because of "profanity and violence."

Picoult, Jodi. *Nineteen Minutes*. New York: Simon & Schuster, 2007.

In 2014–2015, this novel about a school shooting at a fictional high school was challenged at the Gilford, New Hampshire, high school and Kennett High School in Kennett Square, Pennsylvania, because of "violence." The novel was retained in both schools.

RESOURCES FOR RESPONDING TO CHALLENGES

What Reviewers Say

School Library Journal (September 1, 2000) recommends the book for grades 8 and up and says it may serve as a "springboard for a class discussion." *Booklist* (October 2, 2000) recommends it for grades 6–12 and calls it "powerful" and an "indictment of America's gun culture." *Kirkus* (July 1, 2000) says the novel is "vivid, distressing, and all too real." They recommend it for ages twelve–fourteen.

Other Justification for Inclusion in Curricula and Library Collections

❖ 2002 Charlotte Book Award (New York): Young Adult (Grades 6–12)
❖ 2001 Rhode Island Teen Book Award

Sources of Information about Challenges to the Novel

"Censorship Watch." *American Libraries* 39, issue 3 (March 2008): 24.
Strasser, Todd. "Dirty Minds? An Author Struggles to Make Sense of a Rating." *School Library Journal* 55, issue 11 (November 2010): 10.

INFORMATION ABOUT THE AUTHOR

http://www.toddstrasser.com (Strasser's official website)
https://twitter.com/toddstrasser (Strasser on Twitter)
Contemporary Authors Online, 2011. Books and Authors. Gale.
Lesesne, Teri S. "Surfing for Readers: An Interview with Todd Strasser." *Teacher Librarian* 30, issue 3 (February 2003): 48–49.

FURTHER READING ABOUT THE NOVEL

Langridge, Barb. "*Give a Boy a Gun.*" *A Book and a Hug* (blog), March 11, 2012. Accessed September 11, 2015. http://www.abookandahug.com/realistic-fiction-2/22154-giveaboyagun.
Sanner, Devon Clancy. "*Give a Boy a Gun.*" *Journal of Adolescent & Adult Literacy* 45, issue 6 (March 2002): 547–549.
Shoemaker, Joel. "Todd Strasser Takes Aim at School Shootings: An Interview." *Voice of Youth Advocates* 24, issue 2 (June 2001): 100–103.
Stan, Susan. "How Todd Strasser Became Morton Rhue." *ALAN Review* 35, issue 2 (Winter 2008). Accessed September 1, 2015. https://scholar.lib.vt.edu/ejournals/ALAN/v35n2/stan.html.

OTHER MEDIA SOURCES

https://www.youtube.com/watch?v=kUStJZKImno. Posted February 22, 2012. Accessed September 1, 2015. This is a student-created animation telling President Obama about *Give a Boy a Gun*.
https://www.youtube.com/watch?v=0hIfzREx9yk&list=PLK2qZSVMtqAi9qELCBwxjP9_Dw4hVH682. Posted March 2, 2014. Accessed September 1, 2015. A student gives a video review of *Give a Boy a Gun*.

23

❖ ❖ ❖

The Giver

BY LOIS LOWRY

Boston: Houghton Mifflin Harcourt, 1993
Houghton Mifflin Harcourt E-book, 1993
Listening Library Audio, 2001

"If everything's the same, then there aren't any choices!
I want to wake up in the morning and decide things!"

CHALLENGES: WHEN, WHY, AND WHERE

According to the American Library Association, the novel was #11 on the 100 Most Frequently Challenged Books List of 1990–1999. It ranked #23 on the Top 100 Banned/Challenged Books List of 2000–2009.

2007–2008

Appalled by descriptions of "adolescent pill-popping, suicide, and lethal injections given to babies and the elderly," two parents demanded that the Mt. Diablo Unified School District in Concord, California, eliminate the book from the school reading lists and libraries.

2006–2007

The novel was challenged but retained at the Seaman, Kansas, Unified School District 345 elementary school library. The result of the challenge is unknown.

2003–2004

The novel was challenged as suggested reading for eighth-grade students in Blue Springs, Missouri. Parents called the book "lewd" and "twisted" and pleaded for it to be tossed out of the district. The book was reviewed by two committees and recommended for retention, but the controversy continued in 2005.

2001–2002

The Pickens, South Carolina, school board voted to ban the novel in elementary classrooms after a parent complained that euthanasia isn't an appropriate topic for children. The book remained in school libraries.

1999–2000

A pastor objected to the book's "mature themes"—suicide, sexuality, and euthanasia—at Troy Intermediate School in Avon Lake, Ohio.

It was also challenged but retained at a Lake Butler, Florida, middle school because "issues of infanticide and sexual awakening" are discussed in the book.

Additional challenges recorded by Marshall University include Johnson County, Missouri, because it "desensitized children to euthanasia"; Sidney, New York, because of "mind control, selective breeding, and the eradication of the young when they are weak, feeble and of no more use"; and in Oklahoma because of the terms "clairvoyance," "transcendent," and "guided imagery."

1996–1997

A parent challenged the book at the Lakota High School in Cincinnati, Ohio. The result of the challenge is unknown.

1995–1996

The novel was restricted to students with parental permission in the Columbia Falls, Montana, school system because of the themes of infanticide and euthanasia.

A parent in Franklin County, Kansas, challenged the book, citing "degradation of motherhood and adolescence." The book was removed from the school libraries but available to teachers.

1994–1995

Four parents in the Bonita Unified School District in La Verne and San Dimas, California, challenged the novel soon after it won the Newbery Medal because of "violent and sexual passages."

THE STORY

Set in the future in a dystopian society, where all individuals practice Sameness and where everything is colorless and void of emotions, the twelve-year-olds are about to receive their assignments, or occupations, from the Committee of Elders. Assigned a number at birth, the children in the community are given a name in the Ceremony of One. At twelve, they are lined up by their original numbers and await their fate. Jonas, the main character, is apprehensive about the Ceremony of Twelve and is puzzled when they skip over him and move methodically through the group making assignments until they reach the last number. Then Jonas's number is called and he is given his life assignment: Receiver of Memory. When Jonas begins his training with the former Receiver, who is now known as the Giver, he receives pleasant memories—sunsets, sailing, holidays—that existed before Sameness. Eventually he is forced to experience unpleasant emotions—sadness, loneliness, and pain. His isolation grows as he begins to experience things his family and friends will never experience.

Jonas is forced to make a decision that will affect his future when he learns that Gabriel, a baby his family has been tending, is to be "released" for failing to thrive. Before becoming the Receiver, Jonas thought that being "released" meant going to Elsewhere. Now he understands that it means death. To make matters worse, Jonas's father, who is a Nurturer, is assigned to do the release.

At the end of *The Giver*, Jonas takes Gabriel and escapes to Elsewhere. The reader is left to wonder whether Jonas and Gabriel survive the journey. If so, where are they? There are now three other books that answer that question for readers: *Gathering Blue* (2000), *Messenger* (2004), and *Son* (2012).

Themes

❖ Conformity
❖ Euthanasia
❖ Family
❖ Friendship
❖ Home
❖ Memories

TALKING WITH TEENS ABOUT THE ISSUES

Jonas doesn't know Sameness until he becomes the Receiver of Memory. How does being the Receiver add conflict to his life?

How does Jonas's assignment change his relationship with friends and family?

What is Lowry's attitude about conformity?

Why do you think the Giver shows Jonas the videotape of his father's release of the baby twin? Debate whether this scene foreshadows Jonas's decision in the end.

The novel has been challenged for "desensitizing children to euthanasia." How does Jonas's decision to take Gabriel and leave the community make children more sensitive to issues of euthanasia?

Other complaints of the novel are related to sexuality and adolescence. What are the "stirrings"? How is this normal in adolescent development?

Why do adults get so nervous and hung up about sexual feelings in adolescents? Debate whether Jonas's community is suppressing development by dispensing pills for the "stirrings."

CHALLENGED FOR SIMILAR REASONS

Haddix, Margaret Peterson. *Among the Hidden.* New York: Paula Wiseman Books, an imprint of Simon & Schuster, 2005.

This first novel in the dystopian Shadow Children series, about a community that limits each family to two children and what happens when a third is born, was removed from several schools in Normal, Illinois, in 2011 because of "violence."

Nix, Garth. *Shade's Children*. New York: HarperCollins, 1997.

This dystopian novel where children are harvested on their fourteenth birthday to create a machine-like creature was on the American Library Association's 100 Most Frequently Banned/Challenged Books List of 2000–2009 because of "vulgarity and obscenity."

RESOURCES FOR RESPONDING TO CHALLENGES

What Reviewers Say

Horn Book Magazine (July 1993) says, "The story is skillfully written; the air of disquiet is delicately insinuated." *Voice of Youth Advocates* (August 1, 1993) calls it "a powerful story." They also say, "It should take its place with Orwell's *1984*." The reviewer for *School Library Journal* (May 1, 1993) recommends the book for grades 6–9 and says, "This tightly plotted story and its believable characters will stay with readers for a long time." *Publishers Weekly* (February 15, 1993) says that readers "will be easily seduced by the chimera of this ordered, pain-free society."

Other Justification for Inclusion in Curricula and Library Collections

- ❖ 2013 May Hill Arbuthnot Lecture
- ❖ 2007 Margaret A. Edwards Award
- ❖ 2006 Instructor Magazine Top 50 Kids Books Ever
- ❖ 1999 Virginia Reader's Choice Award: Middle School
- ❖ 1997 Buckeye Children's Book Award (Ohio)
- ❖ 1997 Land of Enchantment Book Award (New Mexico)
- ❖ 1996 Black-Eyed Susan Book Award (Maryland)
- ❖ 1996 Great Stone Face Children's Book Award (New Hampshire)
- ❖ 1996 Rebecca Caudill Young Readers Award (Illinois)
- ❖ 1996 Sequoyah Book Award (Oklahoma)
- ❖ 1996 William Allen White Award (Kansas)
- ❖ 1995 Grand Canyon Reader Award (Arizona)
- ❖ 1995 Maine Student Book Award
- ❖ 1995 Pennsylvania Young Reader's Choice Award
- ❖ 1994 ALA Notable Children's Books
- ❖ 1994 John Newbery Award

Sources of Information about Challenges to the Novel

Baldassarro, R. Wolf. "Banned Books Awareness: *The Giver* by Lois Lowry." Posted March 27, 2011. Accessed March 7, 2014. http://bannedbooks.world.edu/2011/03/27/banned-books-awareness -giver-lois-lowry/.

Bird, Betsy. "Top 100 Children's Novels #4: *The Giver* by Lois Lowry." *School Library Journal* (June 23, 2012). Accessed March 7, 2014. http://blogs.slj.com/afuse8production/2012/06/23/ top-100-childrens-novels-4-the-giver-by-lois-lowry/.

"*The Giver.*" *Newsletter on Intellectual Freedom* 50 (September 2001): 192–193.

"Suicide Book Challenged in Schools." *USA Today*, July 20, 2001. Accessed March 6, 2014. http:// usatoday30.usatoday.com/life/books/2001-07-20-the-giver.htm.

"2015 Celebration of Free Speech and Its Defenders." National Coalition against Censorship. Accessed November 7, 2015. http://ncac.org/2015-celebration-of-free-speech-its-defenders/.

INFORMATION ABOUT THE AUTHOR

http://www.loislowry.com/ (Lowry's official website)

Contemporary Authors Online, 2013. Books and Authors. Gale.

Albert, Lisa Rondinelli. *Lois Lowry: The Giver of Stories and Memories.* Authors Teens Love Series. Berkeley Heights, NJ: Enslow Publishers, 2007.

Lorraine, Walter. "Lois Lowry." *Horn Book Magazine* 70 (July/August 1994): 423–426.

FURTHER READING ABOUT THE NOVEL

Gann, Linda A., and Karen Gavigan. "The Other Side of Dark." *Voice of Youth Advocates* 35, issue 3 (August 2012): 234–238.

Lea, Susan G. "Seeing beyond Sameness: Using *The Giver* to Challenge Colorblind Ideology." *Children's Literature in Education* 37 (March 2006): 51–67.

Lowry, Lois. "Margaret A. Edwards Award Acceptance Speech: A Passionate Yearning." *Young Adult Library Services* 6, issue 1 (Fall 2007): 22–25.

Lowry, Lois. "The May Hill Arbuthnot Honor Lecture: 'Unleaving: The Staying Power of Gold.'" *Children and Libraries* 9, issue 2 (Summer 2011): 20–28.

Lowry, Lois. "1994 Newbery Acceptance Speech." *Journal of Youth Services in Libraries* 7 (Summer 1994): 361–367. Also appears in *Horn Book Magazine* 70 (July/August 1994): 414–422.

Silvey, Anita. "The Unpredictable Lois Lowry." *School Library Journal* 53, issue 6 (April 2007): 38–47.

Walters, Karla. "Other Voices: Pills against Sexual 'Stirrings' in Lowry's *The Giver*." *Bookbird* 32 (Summer 1994): 35–36.

OTHER MEDIA SOURCES

http://hdmovie14.net/watch/the-giver-2014/fullmovie-putlocker-megashare9. Accessed July 15, 2015. This is the full-length movie of *The Giver*.

http://www.youtube.com/watch?v=jvzsaK6z_WM. Speech, June 2, 2012. Accessed April 5, 2014. Lois Lowry speaks at the Children's Book and Author Breakfast at Book Expo 2012.

http://www.loc.gov/podcasts/bookfest12/podcast_lowry.html. September 7, 2012. Published May 9, 2013. Accessed April 5, 2014. This is a podcast of Lois Lowry from the 2012 National Book Festival in Washington, D.C.

https://www.youtube.com/watch?v=fkEurtMpQko. Posted September 24, 2014. Accessed July 12, 2015. Lois Lowry reads from *The Giver* for the Banned Books Week Virtual Read-Out.

24

❖ ❖ ❖

Go Ask Alice

BY ANONYMOUS

New York: Simon Pulse, an imprint of Simon & Schuster, 1971
Simon Pulse E-book, 1999
Recorded Books Audio, 2002
Simon Pulse Paperback, 2006

"I guess I'll never measure up to anyone's expectations.
I surely don't measure up to what I'd like to be."

CHALLENGES: WHEN, WHY, AND WHERE

According to data collected by the American Library Association's Office for Intellectual Freedom, this classic young adult novel ranked #25 on the 100 Most Frequently Challenged Books List of 1990–1999. It was #18 on the Top 100 Banned/Challenged Books List of 2000–2009. The earliest recorded challenge was in 1974 in Kalamazoo, Michigan. It was ultimately removed from all school libraries because of "objectionable language and explicit sexual scenes." The novel continued to be challenged throughout the 1970s and 1980s.

2008–2009

The novel was challenged in the language arts curriculum at Hanahan Middle School in Berkeley County, South Carolina, because of "explicit language using street terms for sex, talk of worms eating body parts, and blasphemy."

2000–2001

A grandmother in Girard, Pennsylvania, challenged the book when it was placed on the optional reading list for eighth-graders because she felt it contained too much "filth and smut." The novel was retained.

1998–1999

One middle school parent complained that the novel has too many "references to drug use, vulgar language, and descriptions of sex," and the Aledo, Texas, Independent School District removed the novel for all students. They also placed it on a restricted shelf in the high school library.

1997–1998

The principal at Tiverton Middle School in Rhode Island seized all copies of the book while students were engaged in a novel study. The school board later reinstated it.

1995–1996

In Plain City, Ohio, the novel was banned from the Jonathan Alder School District because of "objectionable" content.

It was also challenged at the Houston Junior and Senior High School in Wasilla, Arkansas, for similar reasons.

"Profanity and indecent situations" was the reason it was banned from a sophomore English supplemental reading list in Warm Springs, Virginia.

1994–1995

The novel was banned from a ninth-grade reading list at Shepherd Hill High School in Dudley, Massachusetts, because of "gross and vulgar language and graphic description of drug use and sexual conduct."

1993–1994

It was removed from the Wall Township Intermediate School in New Jersey after the superintendent denounced the "inappropriate language" and publicly stated that it "borders on pornography."

The novel was also removed from a high school English class in Buckhannon, Upshur County, West Virginia, because of "numerous obscenities."

THE STORY

An anonymous fifteen-year-old, who calls herself Alice, struggles to fit in. When her parents announce that her father, a college professor, is taking a position at another university, she sees the move as a chance to overcome her past social issues. She does make a new friend, but when summer comes, Alice returns to her old town to spend time with her grandmother. She goes to a party with some kids from her old high school, where she takes a wild ride on LSD and discovers she likes that "high" feeling. Back home at the end of the summer, Alice gets deeper into drugs after a doctor prescribes sleeping pills and tranquilizers because she cannot sleep. Then she meets Chris, a young woman who whisks her into the world of pot and speed. The two become frightened when boys they are dating want them to sell drugs to support their drug habit. At this point, Alice and Chris run away to San Francisco, but when the two return, life once again gets difficult for Alice. Finally her parents commit her to a mental hospital. She is released, but an editor's note at the end of the novel states that Alice died for unknown reasons.

Themes

❖ Drug abuse
❖ Loneliness
❖ Rebellion
❖ Self-identity
❖ Sex abuse

TALKING WITH TEENS ABOUT THE ISSUES

Explain why the author wrote the book as "anonymous." Why does the teenage main character use the name "Alice"? Explain why using an alias adds to the drama of the novel.

Describe Alice's social status in her "old" and "new" high school. How does her struggle to fit in contribute to the drug culture that overtakes her life?

Why do Alice and Chris become so frightened when the boys want them to sell drugs? Discuss an alternative to running away. Identify people and places in communities where teens like Alice might go for help.

Defend the claim that the novel is "an anti-drug testimonial." If it is indeed making a statement against drugs, then why do so many parents and school administrators object to the book?

The novel was first published in 1971. Why is it considered a groundbreaking book? The book is still challenged and banned in schools throughout the nation. Discuss the book's relevance to the teenage culture of the 21st century.

CHALLENGED FOR SIMILAR REASONS

Burgess, Melvin. *Smack*. New York: HarperCollins, 1999.

According to the Texas American Civil Liberties Union Banned Books Report in 2002–2003, the novel was banned in a school in Texas because of "drug use." The report does not indicate which school or school district. It is also targeted on the Parents against Banned Books in Schools (PABBIS) website in Virginia.

Hopkins, Ellen. *Glass*. New York: Margaret K. McElderry Books, an imprint of Simon & Schuster, 2007.

This companion novel to *Crank* by Ellen Hopkins deals with a girl who is unable to kick her drug habit. Parents in Humble, Texas, were successful in getting the school district to uninvite Hopkins to the TeenFest in 2009–2010. The festival was later canceled.

RESOURCES FOR RESPONDING TO CHALLENGES

What Reviewers Say

The reviewer for *Christian Science Monitor* (November 11, 1971) says the main character is a "compassionate and talented girl." *Library Journal* (March 15, 1972) calls it "an important book" and says it "deserves wide readership." *Kirkus* (September 14, 1971) says the novel is "a direct intercept of the youthful drug experience."

Other Justification for Inclusion in Curricula and Library Collections

❖ 2000 ALA/YALSA Popular Paperbacks for Young Adults
❖ 1983 ALA/YALSA Best of the Best Books for Young Adults: 1970–1983
❖ 1974 ALA/YALSA Still Alive: The Best of the Best Books for Young Adults, 1960–1974
❖ 1973 Media and Methods Maxi Award for Best Paperback
❖ 1972 Christopher Book Award

Sources of Information about Challenges to the Novel

Associated Press. "Librarians Say *Go Ask Alice* Is Censored Most in Schools." *New York Times*, November 28, 1982. Accessed September 26, 2015. http://www.nytimes.com/1982/11/28/us/librarians-say-go-ask-alice-is-censored-most-in-schools.html.

"Controversial Book Removed from Texas Middle School After One Parent Complains." Associated Press, November 28, 1982. First Amendment Center, June 22, 1999. Accessed September 29, 2015. http://www.nytimes.com/1982/11/28/us/librarians-say-go-ask-alice-is-censored-most-in-schools.html.

"*Go Ask Alice* Ban Draws Reaction." *Post and Courier* (Charleston, South Carolina), March 1, 2008. Accessed September 26, 2015. http://www.postandcourier.com/article/20080301/ARCHIVES/303019936.

"*Go Ask Alice Snatched from Students*." National Coalition against Censorship, Summer 1998. Accessed September 29, 2015. http://ncac.org/censorship-article/go-ask-alice-snatched-from-students/.

White, Caitlin. "*Go Ask Alice* Is Still Awash in Controversy, 43 Years after Publication." *Bustle* (blog), July 3, 2014. Accessed September 26, 2015. http://www.bustle.com/articles/29829-go-ask-alice-is-still-awash-in-controversy-43-years-after-publication.

Woods, L. B. "The Most Censored Materials in the U.S." *Library Journal* 103, issue 19 (November 1, 1978): 2170–2173.

INFORMATION ABOUT THE AUTHOR

Goldberg, Lina. "'Curiouser and Curiouser': Fact, Fiction, and the Anonymous Author of *Go Ask Alice*." Linagoldberg.com, October 2002. Accessed September 26, 2015. http://www.linagoldberg.com/goaskalice.html.

FURTHER READING ABOUT THE NOVEL

Adams, Lauren. "A Second Look: *Go Ask Alice*." *Horn Book Magazine* 74, issue 5 (September/October 1998): 587–592.

Bosmajian, Hamida. "Tricks of the Text and Acts of Reading by Censors and Adolescents." *Children's Literature in Education* 18, issue 2 (Summer 1987): 89–96.

Ellid. "Books So Bad They're Good: *Go Ask Alice* by Anonymous." DailyKos.com, February 8, 2014. Accessed September 29, 2015. http://www.dailykos.com/story/2014/02/09/1268810/-Books-So-Bad-They-re-Good-Go-Ask-Anonymous#.

Gershowitz, Elissa. "What Makes a Good 'Bad' Book?" *Horn Book Magazine* 89, issue 4 (July/August 2013): 84–90.

Isaacs, Kathleen T. "*Go Ask Alice*: What Middle Schoolers Choose to Read." *New Advocate* 5, issue 2 (Spring 1992): 129–143.

Nilsen, Alleen Pace. "The House That Alice Built." *School Library Journal* 26, issue 2 (October 1979): 109–112.

OTHER MEDIA SOURCES

https://www.youtube.com/watch?v=CBxT53r2AlU. Accessed September 26, 2015. This is the full movie of *Go Ask Alice* that was released in 1973.

https://www.youtube.com/watch?v=CBxT53r2AlU. Posted October 26, 2012. Accessed September 26, 2015. A fan reads from *Go Ask Alice* for the Banned Books Week Virtual Read-Out channel.

https://www.youtube.com/watch?v=CBxT53r2AlU. Posted November 1, 2013. Accessed September 26, 2015. A fan offers a video review of *Go Ask Alice*.

25

❖ ❖ ❖

Going Bovine

BY LIBBA BRAY

New York: Delacorte, an imprint of Random House, 2009
Delacorte E-book, 2009
Listening Library Audio, 2009
Laurel-Leaf Paperback, 2010

"So, now I've been to see a drug counselor who told me I needed to lay off the drugs and talk about my feelings, and a shrink who heard what I had to say and immediately put me on drugs."

CHALLENGES: WHEN, WHY, AND WHERE

2013–2014

The National Council of Teachers of English reports a challenge in the tenth-grade curriculum at a high school in Oregon because of "language, drug reference, sex, and mockery of religion." The result of the case is unknown.

2010–2011

According to the Texas American Civil Liberties Union, the novel was placed on a restricted shelf at the high school in the Union Hill Independent School District because of "profanity; sexual content or nudity." An additional note states: "Some profanity expected in YA books—this one went over the top with use."

THE STORY

Cameron Smith is a fifteen-year-old misfit in a family of overachievers. His sister is "perfect" in every way, and his parents are college professors. When Cameron begins experiencing hallucinations at school, he believes they may be caused from smoking pot. He winds up in drug counseling, but it turns out that he is suffering from mad cow disease. He is hospitalized where the hallucinations take him to a fantasy world that introduces him to Dulcie, who gives him a mission to save the world. She convinces Cameron that she can save his life if he locates a time-traveling physicist, Dr. X. Along the way, he comes in contact with some weird characters that could be a threat to his life. Dulcie issues a bracelet to Disney World that may keep the disease from spreading, or making him sicker. This all seems too close to his real life, and Cameron escapes the hospital with Gonzo, a videogame-playing classmate. They take off on a journey that takes them to New Orleans and, ultimately, to Disney World. There are various side adventures, and Cameron wakes up in the hospital where life-support machinery has been removed. He notes that his parents and sister are crying. The sky explodes, creating a dramatic and open ending.

Themes

- ❖ Coming of age
- ❖ Death
- ❖ Friendship
- ❖ Heroism
- ❖ Love
- ❖ Promises

TALKING WITH TEENS ABOUT THE ISSUES

Describe Cameron's status in his family. He thinks of himself as a misfit. Debate whether this causes him to succumb to drugs.

Cite scenes from the novel where Bray pokes fun at pop culture.

Bray says, "Comedy and tragedy are two sides of the same coin." Identify the comedic and tragic scenes in the novel.

The novel has been challenged because of language and drug references. Why is Cameron convinced that smoking pot causes the hallucinations? How does the ending leave the reader to decide the real cause of his hallucinations?

Explain the charge that the book "makes a mockery of religion." Discuss the thoughts of some that any fantasy is anti-religion.

CHALLENGED FOR SIMILAR REASONS

Adams, Douglas. *The Hitchhiker's Guide to the Galaxy*. London: Pan Books, an imprint of Macmillan, 1979.

In 2009, the National Coalition against Censorship reports that this comedy science fiction where two main characters are thrown into space was banned in some Catholic schools in the United States for being "anti-religion."

Jenkins, A. M. *Repossessed*. New York: HarperCollins, 2007.

This novel about a minion of the devil that enters the body of a slacker seventeen-year-old was challenged at Odem Junior High School in the Odem-Edroy, Texas, Independent School District in 2010–2011 because of "profanity" and "sexual content" and for being "offensive to religious sensitivities." It was moved to the high school and placed on a restricted shelf.

RESOURCES FOR RESPONDING TO CHALLENGES

What Reviewers Say

In the *Booklist* (August 1, 2009) starred review, Gillian Engberg praises the main character's "sardonic, believable voice." *Publishers Weekly* (August 3, 2009) recommends the novel for ages fourteen and up and comments on "Bray's surreal humor." *Voice of Youth Advocates* (October 1, 2009) says that the main character is "every teen struggling with his or her identity." *School Library Journal* (September 1, 2009) recommends the book for grades 8 and up and says that Bray "blends a hearty dose of satire." *Kirkus* (August 15, 2009) mentions the "zany details."

Other Justification for Inclusion in Curricula and Library Collections

❖ 2012 ALA/YALSA Popular Paperbacks for Young Adults: Adventure Seekers
❖ 2010 ALA/YALSA Best Books for Young Adults
❖ 2010 ALA/YALSA Michael L. Printz Award
❖ 2009 *Booklist* Editors' Choice: Books for Youth: Older Readers Category

Sources of Information about Challenges to the Novel

Bray, Libba. "Censorship Is Not Patriotic." Libba Bray's blog, August 13, 2007. Accessed October 27, 2015. https://libbabray.wordpress.com/2007/08/13/censorship-is-not-patriotic/.

Bright, Amy. Writing Bridges: How Writers Scaffold Mature Content in YA Literature." *ALAN Review*. Accessed October 27, 2015. https://scholar.lib.vt.edu/ejournals/ALAN/v40n2/pdf/bright.pdf.

INFORMATION ABOUT THE AUTHOR

http://libbabray.com (Bray's official website)
https://libbabray.wordpress.com (Bray's blog)
https://twitter.com/libbabray?lang=en (Bray on Twitter)
Contemporary Authors Online, 2013. Books and Authors. Gale.
Carter, Betty. "Born to Be Wild." *School Library Journal* 56, issue 7 (July 2010): 22–25.
White, Claire E. "A Conversation with Libba Bray." *Internet Writing Journal* (February 2004). Accessed September 17, 2015. http://www.writerswrite.com/journal/feb04/a-conversation-with-libba-bray-2042.

FURTHER READING ABOUT THE NOVEL

Engberg, Gillian. "The *Booklist* Printz Interview: Libba Bray." *Booklist* 106, issue 13 (March 1, 2010): 62.
Hayman, Stacey. "Wouldn't You Like to Know . . . Libba Bray." VOYA.com, December 8, 2012. Accessed October 27, 2015. http://www.voyamagazine.com/2012/12/08/wouldnt-you-like-to-know-libba-bray/.
Philpot, Chelsey G. H. "An Interview with Libba Bray." *Horn Book Magazine* 86, issue 4 (July/August 2010): 157.

OTHER MEDIA SOURCES

https://www.youtube.com/watch?v=KloEAoKvBqA. Posted August 24, 2009. Accessed September 17, 2015. Libba Bray talks about *Going Bovine*.
https://www.youtube.com/watch?v=5eNd6Hq0fig. Posted September 29, 2009. Accessed September 17, 2015. A young adult fan discusses *Going Bovine* for Banned Books Week.

26

❖ ❖ ❖

The Golden Compass

BY PHILIP PULLMAN

New York: Knopf, an imprint of Random House, 1996
Random House Children's Books, 2001
Yearling Paperback, 2001
Listening Library Audio, 2004

"We are all subject to the fates.
But we must act as if we are not, or die of despair."

CHALLENGES: WHEN, WHY, AND WHERE

According to data collected by the American Library Association's Office for Intellectual Freedom, *His Dark Materials* trilogy ranked #2 on the Top Ten Most Frequently Challenged Books List in 2008–2009; #4 in 2007–2008; and #8 on the Top 100 Banned/Challenged Books List of 2000–2009. The reason cited is that the books are "anti-Christian."

2008–2009

The novel was challenged but retained at the Dufferin-Peel Catholic District School Board in Mississauga, Ontario, Canada. The compromise for keeping the book included placing a disclaimer sticker inside the book: "representations of the church in this novel are purely fictional."

2007–2008

According to the Texas American Civil Liberties Union, the novel, along with *The Subtle Knife*, was challenged but retained at Cedar Valley Middle School in the Round Rock Independent School District because of "atheism and religious overtones."

It was placed on a restricted shelf at the intermediate school in the Shallowater Independent School District in Lubbock, Texas, because of "violence or horror, and mysticism or paganism."

The novel was challenged at Conkwright Middle School in Winchester, Kentucky, because it is "anti-Christian," and Lyra, the main character, "drinks wine and ingests poppy with her meals." The result of the challenge is unknown.

It was also banned at the St. John Neumann Middle School and Lourdes High School in Oshkosh, Wisconsin, because it is "anti-Christian."

The novel was banned but later returned to the shelves at the Ortega Middle School Library in Alamosa, Colorado, because of "anti-religious views."

THE STORY

In *The Golden Compass*, the first of the His Dark Materials trilogy, eleven-year-old Lyra Belacqua is an orphan living in Jordan College at Oxford, England, with her daemon Pantalaimon. Her uncle, Lord Asriel—the only relative she's ever known—is often away on secret explorations. When Lyra travels to the frozen North to save her best friend and other kidnapped children from terrible experiments by a board of scheming scientists, she encounters Gobblers, armored bears, witch clans, haunting secrets, and unspeakable dangers. Her guiding light is the alethiometer, the golden compass, a truth-telling device that helps her overcome the forces that threaten her safety as she maneuvers through different dimensions and unknown worlds. *The Subtle Knife* (1997) continues Lyra's search for her father and the dust phenomenon. Her adventures get more interesting when she meets Will Parry, a fatherless boy who is responsible for his ailing mother, when he is on the run for murdering an intruder. The two become allies and use the subtle knife to reclaim the alethiometer that was stolen from Lyra. The final novel is *The Amber Spyglass* (2000). Lyra and Will continue to encounter good and evil, and when their lives seem hopelessly in danger, the Armored Bear and Gallivespian Spies help them to travel to a place where no living creature has ever gone. In the end, the two return to Oxford because they cannot survive more than ten years in other worlds, and Lyra decides to follow John Parry's teachings and attempt to build the "Republic of Heaven" at home.

Themes
* Betrayal
* Courage
* Good vs. evil
* Innocence
* Power
* Survival

TALKING WITH TEENS ABOUT THE ISSUES

Pullman tells us that *The Golden Compass* takes place "in a universe like ours, but different in many ways." How do you think Lyra's universe relates to ours?

Power is an underlying theme in His Dark Materials trilogy. Which characters have the greatest power in the trilogy? Cite evidence that power is both good and evil in the novels.

The Golden Compass explores the idea of fate versus free will. Which characters embrace fate and which free will? Debate whether it's possible to have both.

How do the novels explore ideas of innocence versus experience? Explain how various characters have lost their innocence by the end of the trilogy.

Pullman is opposed to organized religion. How are his views revealed in the trilogy?

The novel has been challenged as "anti-Catholic." And the Catholic League called for a boycott of the movie. How might reading the book and seeing the movie actually strengthen individual religious beliefs?

Discuss why it's important to examine religion from various viewpoints.

CHALLENGED FOR SIMILAR REASONS

Barron, T. A. *Child of the Dark Prophecy*. New York: Philomel, an imprint of Penguin, 2004.

This work of fantasy about the seven roots of a great tree and the creatures that inhabit it was pulled from the middle school recommended reading list in Lackawanna, New York, in 2007–2008 because it deals with the "occult." After another group of parents charged the school board with censorship, the book was reinstated.

L'Engle, Madeleine. *A Wrinkle in Time*. New York: Farrar, Straus & Giroux, an imprint of Macmillan, 1962.

This 1963 Newbery Medal winner is a science fiction fantasy about a group of children that set out in search of Meg Murry's father, a scientist who goes missing while on a special mission. The novel has had numerous challenges, but the most recent recorded challenge by the American Library Association was in 1996 in Newton, North Carolina, because "it allegedly undermines religious beliefs."

RESOURCES FOR RESPONDING TO CHALLENGES

What Reviewers Say

Booklist (March 1, 1996) recommends the novel for grades 7–12 and calls it "a totally involving, intricately plotted fantasy." *School Library Journal* (April 1996) says there is "some fine descriptive writing." Roger Sutton, the reviewer for the *Bulletin for the Center of Children's Books* (April 1996) says that Pullman "blends not-quite science with not-quite magic." *Kirkus* (March 1, 1996) states that the main character is "thorough, intelligent, and charming." *Publishers Weekly* (February 19, 1996) comments that Pullman blends "impeccable characterization and seamless plotting."

Other Justification for Inclusion in Curricula and Library Collections

❖ 2004 ALA/YALSA Outstanding Books for the College Bound: Literature and Language Arts
❖ 2000 ALA/YALSA 100 Best Books: 1950–2000
❖ 1997 ALA/ALSC Notable Children's Books
❖ 1997 ALA/YALSA Best Books for Young Adults
❖ 1996 *Booklist* Editors' Choice: Books for Youth: Older Readers Category

Sources of Information about Challenges to the Novel

Elliott, Marissa. "Meeting the Challenge of His Dark Materials." *Kliatt* 42, issue 5 (September 2008): 3.
G. M. E. "The Golden Compass Accused of Anti-Catholic Bias." *American Libraries* 39, issue 1/2 (January/February 2008): 20.
Ryan, Erin. "A Furor over *The Golden Compass*." *National Catholic Reporter* 44, issue 6 (December 7, 2007): 20–21.

INFORMATION ABOUT THE AUTHOR

http://www.philip-pullman.com (Pullman's official website)

FURTHER READING ABOUT THE NOVEL

Chang, Margaret A. "Discovering *The Golden Compass*: A Guide to Philip Pullman's Dark Materials." *School Library Journal* 53, issue 10 (October 2007): 170.

Frost, Laurie. *The Elements of His Dark Materials: A Guide to Philip Pullman's Trilogy*. Buffalo, IL: Fell Press, 2006.

Lenz, Millicent, and Carole Scott. *His Dark Materials Illuminated: Critical Essays on Philip Pullman's Trilogy*. Detroit: Wayne State University Press, 2005.

Nicholson, Catriona, and Wendy Parsons. "Talking to Philip Pullman: An Interview." *Lion and the Unicorn* 23, issue 1 (January 1999): 116–134.

Stuttaford, Andrew. "Sunday School for Atheists." *National Review* 54, issue 5 (March 25, 2002): 56–58.

Townsend, John Rowe. "Paradise Reshaped." *Horn Book Magazine* 78, issue 4 (July/August 2002): 415–421.

OTHER MEDIA SOURCES

https://www.youtube.com/watch?v=WoclTyVgHzw. Posted December 8, 2007. Accessed July 10, 2015. Lizo Mzimba from the BBC interviews Philip Pullman about his books being made into movies.

https://www.youtube.com/watch?v=QKIh8wMgLxA. Posted January 14, 2008. Accessed July 10, 2015. Charlie Rose interviews Philip Pullman about *The Golden Compass* and his writing technique.

27

❖ ❖ ❖

How to Steal a Car

BY PETE HAUTMAN

New York: Scholastic Press, 2009
Scholastic E-book, 2010
Scholastic Paperback, 2011

"'I stole a couple cars,' I said. 'But it's not who I am. There's a difference.'"

CHALLENGES: WHEN, WHY, AND WHERE

2013–2014

According to the Texas American Civil Liberties Union, the novel was challenged at Truman Middle School in the Fort Worth Independent School District because of "profanity, sex, drugs and alcohol" and "the belief that anything is possible as long as you can get away with it." The case has not gone to committee and is pending.

THE STORY

Set in a Minneapolis suburb, fifteen-year-old Kelleigh Monahan and her best friend, Jen, are hanging out in a parking lot one summer night when Kelleigh sees a man drop his car keys. She picks them up, but instead of going after the man, Kelleigh decides to keep the keys. She finds out his address and begins taking his car out for joyrides, even though she is too young for a driver's license. She always brings the car back unharmed, but the shear act of taking the car leads to other car thefts. Her father, a successful attorney, is defending a man accused of a car theft in another state. And her mother is nursing her own brand of unhappiness with compulsive housekeeping and alcohol. Kelleigh's friends are nervous about her car-theft habit, and they move on with their own self-discoveries. One day Kelleigh sees the man of the first car she stole. She locates his car in the mall parking lot and discovers that the key she still has in the bottom of her purse works. She's off on another joyride.

Themes
❖ Alienation
❖ Anger
❖ Family
❖ Friendship
❖ Self-identity
❖ Values in conflict

TALKING WITH TEENS ABOUT THE ISSUES

Kelleigh and a friend steal a car one summer night for the joy of it. Why does Kelleigh continue stealing cars?

Describe Kelleigh's family. Discuss whether they are a happy family. How does her family contribute to her feelings of alienation? Explain the scene where Kelleigh confronts her father about his alleged affair. Identify the scene that reveals there is hope for her parents' marriage.

Discuss Kelleigh's anger. What is the source of her anger? Debate whether her anger adds to her compulsion to steal cars. Explain Deke's involvement.

Kelleigh has collected dolphin stuffed animals and figurines since she was a little girl. Explain the symbolism when she destroys her dolphin collection.

The novel has been challenged because of drugs, alcohol, and sex. How are these issues secondary to what the novel is really about?

Consider the ending of the book when Kelleigh finds the first car she stole and takes it on another joyride. Why does this ending trouble some people? How would it have been a different story if Kelleigh had simply quit stealing cars? What does this say about her feelings of alienation?

CHALLENGED FOR SIMILAR REASONS

Ferris, Jean. *Bad*. New York: Farrar, Straus & Giroux, 1999.

According to a database maintained by the University of Illinois, this novel about sixteen-year-old Dallas who gets a thrill from hot-wiring cars and other daring and illegal behaviors has been challenged. Details of the challenges are not published, but there is documentation on the Internet that the reason is "illegal behavior" and "dysfunctional family."

Zindel, Paul. *The Pigman*. New York: HarperCollins, 1968.

This novel, about two teens who engage in prank phone calls where they pretend they are collecting funds for a charity, which leads them to a lonely old man who is willing to donate, has been challenged numerous times. The first recorded challenge was in the Hillsboro, Missouri, School District in 1985 because it features "liars, cheaters and stealers."

RESOURCES FOR RESPONDING TO CHALLENGES

What Reviewers Say

School Library Journal (November 1, 2009) recommends the novel for grades 7 and up and states, "Kelleigh has just enough sarcasm and teen angst to be endearing." *Publishers Weekly* (September 14, 2009) describes Kelleigh as "an appealing wisecracker." The reviewer from *Booklist* (August 1, 2009) calls the novel "a moral briar patch," but believes most young adult readers will "identify Kelleigh's urge to break through life's suffocating safeguards." *Kirkus* recommends the book for ages thirteen and up and says it is "a sharply observed, subversive coming-of-age tale." *Horn Book Magazine* (November/December 2009) says the novel is for high school readers and calls the first-person narrator "charismatic."

Other Justification for Inclusion in Curricula and Library Collections

This novel has not received any awards and has not been selected as a notable or best book by any professional organization. It has received praise for its humor and teen angst on various teen blogs, such as TeenReads.

Sources of Information about Challenges

Articles related to the specific challenge to this novel cannot be located, but Pete Hautman canceled a planned appearance at the TeenFest in Humble, Texas, because of issues related to censorship. He weighs in on the following blog posts:

http://petehautman.blogspot.com/2010/08/nasty-thing-in-corner.html. Posted August 16, 2010. Accessed September 28, 2015.
http://petehautman.blogspot.com/2012/10/preemptive-censorship-bbw-post-3.html. Posted October 3, 2012. Accessed September 28, 2015.

INFORMATION ABOUT THE AUTHOR

http://www.petehautman.com (Hautman's official website)
http://petehautman.blogspot.com (Hautman's blog)
Contemporary Authors Online, 2013. Books and Authors. Gale.

FURTHER READING ABOUT THE NOVEL

Blasingame, James. "Interview with Pete Hautman." *Journal of Adolescent & Adult Literacy* 48, issue 5 (February 2005): 438–439.
"Interview with Pete Hautman." *Young Adult Review Network (YARN)*, November 5, 2010. Accessed May 22, 2015. http://yareview.net/2010/11/interview-with-pete-hautman/.
Kerr, Euan. "Author Pete Hautman on *How to Steal a Car*." MPR News, September 15, 2009. Accessed September 28, 2015. http://www.mprnews.org/story/2009/09/15/hautman.

OTHER MEDIA SOURCES

https://www.youtube.com/watch?v=1aXdZYFhSZU. Pete Hautman reads from *How to Steal a Car*. https://www.youtube.com/watch?v=zduQVBS3Vp0. This is a student-created video review of *How to Steal a Car*.

28

❖ ❖ ❖

The Hunger Games

BY SUZANNE COLLINS

New York: Scholastic, 2008
Scholastic Audio, 2008
Scholastic E-book, 2009
Scholastic Paperback, 2012

"You don't forget the face of the person who was your last hope."

CHALLENGES: WHEN, WHY, AND WHERE

According to data collected by the American Library Association's Office for Intellectual Freedom, the Hunger Games trilogy was #5 on the Top Ten Most Frequently Challenged Books List in 2013–2014, #3 in 2011–2012, and #5 in 2010–2011 because of its "graphic depiction of violence" and "religious viewpoint" and for being "unsuited to age group."

2012–2013

The Texas American Civil Liberties Union (Texas ACLU) recorded two challenges to Collins's work. It was challenged as part of the curriculum at Bartlett High School in the Bartlett Independent School District because the parent felt it "offensive to religious sensitivities." Teachers offered an alternative reading assignment.

The entire trilogy was challenged but retained at the Paint Rock School (K–12) in the Paint Rock Independent School District.

The Mapping Banned Books in Massachusetts blog post of October 25, 2013, reported a challenge in the Dighton Rehoboth Regional School District. The administration voted to remove *The Hunger Games* from the elementary school library but retain it in the middle and high school.

2010–2011

The entire trilogy was challenged but retained at the Mountain View Middle School in Goffstown, New Hampshire. The parent alleged "lack of morality, violent subject matter that could lead to school violence."

According to the Texas ACLU annual report, *The Hunger Games* was challenged but retained at the Kerr Middle School in the Burleson Independent School District in Texas. The book was part of the curriculum, and an alternate book was allowed.

THE STORY

Set in the post-apocalyptic nation of Panem where the Capitol establishes all rules, sixteen-year-old Katniss Everdeen is responsible for her family after the mining accident that killed her father left her mother in a deep depression and unable to cope. The Everdeens live in District 12, the poorest of all the districts, but Katniss learns hunting and survival skills from her best friend, Gale. Every year, Panem sponsors a ceremony called the Reaping, where the name of one boy and one girl from each of the twelve districts is drawn to become Tributes, those chosen to fight to the death in a televised battle called the Hunger Games. Katniss and Peeta Mellark represent District 12. The rules say there may be only one winner, but Katniss wants to protect Peeta and contrives a way to outwit the Capitol.

It turns out that President Snow doesn't like to be outwitted, and in *Catching Fire* (2009), the second book in the trilogy, he devises a plan for a second Hunger Games. Katniss and Peeta are once again named the Tributes from their district. This time Katniss finds herself in uncharted territory when she is deemed an enemy to the Capitol and faces an all-out rebellion that she may have helped create.

In the final book, *Mockingjay* (2010), the Districts have finally realized that they are victim of corruption and they plan an uprising against the Capitol. They learn that the Mockingjay is a spy weapon for the Capitol, but the Districts find a way to use the weapon to their advantage. Katniss turns out to be their best weapon with her strong fighting skills. The Capitol becomes enraged and destroys District 12, but Gale emerges the hero when he escorts the people to District 13, where they receive the help they need to survive.

Themes
* ❖ Control
* ❖ Family
* ❖ Friendship
* ❖ Identity
* ❖ Love
* ❖ Politics
* ❖ Power
* ❖ Sacrifice
* ❖ Survival

TALKING WITH TEENS ABOUT THE ISSUES

Describe life in District 12. How does the mining accident change Katniss's family? She volunteers to become a Tribute in place of her younger sister. How does she train for the Hunger Games?

Control and power are underlying themes in the Hunger Games. Discuss the power of those who rule Panem. How do they use their power to control the Districts? Explain why they plan a second games in *Catching Fire*. What does this have to do with power?

Discuss why the Hunger Games is televised. Debate whether this is one way the Capitol can maintain control over the people.

The Hunger Games trilogy has been challenged because of the graphic depiction of violence. Why is violence necessary to reveal the themes of the novels?

The trilogy has also been challenged because of sexual content. Cite and discuss the sexual scenes. How might you answer someone who claims the books are sexually explicit?

Draw a parallel between *The Hunger Games* and government corruption. How is this post-apocalyptic trilogy a cautionary story?

There have been challenges to the novels because elementary-age children are reading them. Debate whether the themes are too mature for younger readers.

CHALLENGED FOR SIMILAR REASONS

Card, Orson Scott. *Ender's Game*. New York: Tor Books, 1985.

A teacher was threatened with criminal charges in 2011–2012 after he read aloud this military science fiction novel at the Schofield Middle School in Aiken, South Carolina. A parent and a student claimed it was "pornographic."

Nelson, O. T. *The Girl Who Owned the City*. Minneapolis: Lerner Publishing Group, 1975.

In 2000, this science fiction novel where everyone over the age of twelve dies, leaving the city to be run by twelve-year-olds, was challenged in the Fort Fairfield, Maine, schools because the book promotes violence, including an explanation about how to make a Molotov cocktail.

RESOURCES FOR RESPONDING TO CHALLENGES

What Reviewers Say

Voice of Youth Advocates (October 1, 2008) calls *The Hunger Games* "a thrilling adventure." *School Library Journal* (September 1, 2008) recommends the novel for grades 7 and up and states, "Collins's characters are completely realistic," and comments that the tension is "dramatic, and engrossing." In the *Booklist* (September 1, 2008) starred review, Francisca Goldsmith says the novel is "a superb tale of physical adventure." *Publishers Weekly* (November 3, 2008) says, "Readers will wait eagerly to learn more."

Voice of Youth Advocates (December 1, 2009) in the review of *Catching Fire* comments that the characters are "more dimensional." In the starred review in *Booklist* (July 1, 2009), Ian Chipman praises Collins's "crystalline, unadorned prose." The reviewer for *School Library Journal* (September 1, 2009) feels that "Katniss also deepens as a character." *Publishers Weekly* (June 22, 2009) says that the novel has the "pulse-pounding action readers have come to expect."

School Library Journal (October 1, 2010) calls *Mockingjay* "a fitting end of the series." In the starred review in *Booklist* (September 1, 2010), Ilene Cooper finds the novel hopeful and states, "There is still a human spirit yearning for good." *Publishers Weekly* (August 30, 2010) says that this final book in the trilogy is "beautifully orchestrated."

Other Justification for Inclusion in Curricula and Library Collections

The Hunger Games

- ❖ 2014 Bilby Children's Choice Award (Queensland, Australia)
- ❖ 2012 Georgia Children's Book Award
- ❖ 2012 Nutmeg Children's Book Award: Teen Category (Connecticut)
- ❖ 2012 Sequoyah Book Award (Oklahoma)
- ❖ 2011 Abraham Lincoln High School Book Award (Illinois)

❖ 2011 ALA/YALSA Popular Paperbacks for Young Adults: What If . . .
❖ 2011 Black-Eyed Susan Book Award: High School (Maryland)
❖ 2011 California Young Reader Medal: Young Adult
❖ 2011 Garden State Teen Book Award (New Jersey)
❖ 2011 Gateway Readers Award (Missouri)
❖ 2011 Georgia Children's Book Award
❖ 2011 Golden Archer Awards: Middle/Junior High School (Wisconsin)
❖ 2011 Golden Sower Award (Nebraska)
❖ 2011 Grand Canyon Reader Award: Tween Book (Arizona)
❖ 2011 Land of Enchantment Book Award: Young Adult (New Mexico)
❖ 2011 Rebecca Caudill Young Readers' Book Award (Illinois)
❖ 2011 Sequoyah Book Award: Intermediate and High School (Oklahoma)
❖ 2011 South Carolina Book Award: Junior Books and Young Adult Category
❖ 2011 Truman Readers Award (Missouri)
❖ 2011 Virginia Reader's Choice Award: High School
❖ 2011 Young Hoosier Book Award: Middle Books (Indiana)
❖ 2010 Beehive Awards: Young Adult Books (Utah)
❖ 2010 Blue Hen Book Award: Teen Book (Delaware)
❖ 2010 Charlotte Award: Young Adult (New York)
❖ 2010 Colorado Blue Spruce Young Adult Book Award
❖ 2010 Georgia Peach Book Award for Teen Readers
❖ 2010 Isinglass Teen Read Award (New Hampshire)
❖ 2010 Kentucky Bluegrass Award: Grades 9–12
❖ 2010 Maine Student Book Award
❖ 2010 Pennsylvania Young Reader's Choice Award: Young Adult
❖ 2010 Rhode Island Teen Book Award
❖ 2009 ALA/ALSC Notable Children's Books: Older Readers
❖ 2009 ALA/YALSA Best Books for Young Adults
❖ 2009 ALA/YALSA Quick Picks for Reluctant Young Adult Readers: Fiction
❖ 2009 Amelia Bloomer Lists: Young Adult Fiction
❖ 2009 Teen Buckeye Award (Ohio)
❖ 2009 Thumbs Up! Award (Michigan)
❖ 2008 *Booklist* Editors' Choice: Books for Youth: Older Readers
❖ 2008 *New York Times* Notable Books: Children's Books
❖ 2008 *School Library Journal* Best Books

Catching Fire

❖ 2015 ALA/YALSA Popular Paperbacks for Young Adults: Book to Movie: Ripped from the Pages
❖ 2012 Golden Archer Awards: Middle/Junior High School (Wisconsin)
❖ 2012 Soaring Eagle Book Award (Wyoming)
❖ 2010 ALA/YALSA Best Books for Young Adults
❖ 2010 Indies' Choice Book Award
❖ 2009 *Booklist* Editor's Choice: Books for Youth: Older Readers

Mockingjay

❖ 2013 Golden Archer Awards: Middle/Junior High School (Wisconsin)
❖ 2012 *Booklist* Editor's Choice: Books for Youth: Older Readers

Sources of Information about Challenges to the Novels

Barack, Lauren. "New Hampshire Parent Challenges *The Hunger Games.*" *School Library Journal*, October 19, 2010. Accessed July 15, 2015. http://www.slj.com/2010/10/censorship/new-hampshire-parent-challenges-the-hunger-games/#_.

Hilden, Julie. "A Spate of Complaints Asking Libraries to Censor the Hunger Games Trilogy: Why We Should Keep the Books Accessible to Kids." *Verdict*, April 16, 2012. Accessed January 10, 2013. http://verdict.justia.com/2012/04/16/a-spate-of-complaints-asking-libraries-to-censor-the-hunger-games-trilogy.

INFORMATION ABOUT THE AUTHOR

http://www.suzannecollinsbooks.com/ (Collins's official website)

Contemporary Authors Online, 2014. Books and Authors. Gale.

Hudson, Hannah. "Sit Down with Suzanne Collins." *Instructor* 120 (Fall 2010): 51–53.

FURTHER READING ABOUT THE NOVELS

Cook, Kristin, Donna Keller, and Alyce Myers. "Bioethics in *The Hunger Games.*" *Science Teacher* 81, issue 1 (January 2014): 31–37.

Dreher, Kwakiuti L. "Of Bread, Blood and the Hunger Games: Critical Essays on the Suzanne Collins Trilogy." *Journal of Popular Culture* 47, issue 4 (August 2013): 909–912.

Gann, Linda A., and Karen Gavigan. "The Other Side of Dark." *Voice of Youth Advocates* 35, issue 3 (August 2012): 234–238.

Garrow, Hattie. "Don't Be Afraid of the Dark." *Library Media Connection* 31, issue 3 (November/December 2012): 40–41.

Margolis, Rick. "The Last Battle: Interview with Suzanne Collins." *School Library Journal* 56, issue 8 (August 2010): 23–27.

McGuire, Riley. "Queer Children, Queer Futures: Navigating *lifedeath* in *The Hunger Games.*" *Mosaic: A Journal for the Interdisciplinary Study of Literature* 48, issue 2 (June 2015): 63–76.

Miller, Laura. "Fresh Hell: What's behind the Boom in Dystopian Fiction for Young Readers?" *New Yorker*, June 14, 2010. Accessed January 10, 2013. http://www.newyorker.com/arts/critics/atlarge/2010/06/14/100614crat_atlarge_miller.

Pappas, Stephanie. "Hunger Games: How Controversial Books Build 'Empathy Muscles.'" LiveScience, April 13, 2012. Accessed June 15, 2015. http://www.livescience.com/19670-hunger-games-controversial-banned-books.html.

Skinner, Margaret, and Kailyn McCord. "*The Hunger Games*: A Conversation." *Jung Journal: Culture and Psyche* 6, issue 4 (Fall 2012): 106–113.

Taber, Nancy, Vera Woloshyn, and Laura Lane. "'She's More Like a Guy' and 'He's More Like a Teddy Bear': Girls' Perception of Violence and Gender." *Journal of Youth Studies* 16, issue 8 (December 2013): 1022–1037.

Tan, Susan. Review of *Of Bread, Blood and* The Hunger Games: *Critical Essays on the Suzanne Collins Trilogy*, edited by Mary F. Pharr and Leisa A. Clark. *Lion and the Unicorn* 37, issue 1 (January 2013): 102–105.

OTHER MEDIA SOURCES

http://www.youtube.com/watch?v=XEmJJIl7rp0 and http://www.youtube.com/watch?v=zUTPQCYVZEQ. Scholastic, August 18, 2009. Accessed April 4, 2014. In this two-part video, Suzanne Collins talks about the classical and contemporary inspiration for *The Hunger Games* trilogy.

http://www.youtube.com/watch?v=FH15DI8ZW14. Scholastic, September 2, 2010. Accessed April 4, 2014. In this video, Suzanne Collins speaks about her childhood and the books that she read.

http://megashare.sc/watch-the-hunger-games-online-TlRFek9RPT0. Accessed July 15, 2015. This is a free full-length movie of *The Hunger Games.*

http://megashare.sc/watch-the-hunger-games-catching-fire-online-TnpRMk13PT0. Accessed July 15, 2015. This is a free full-length movie of *Catching Fire.*

29

❖ ❖ ❖

I Am J

BY CRIS BEAM

New York: Little, Brown, 2011
Little, Brown E-book, 2011
Little, Brown Paperback, 2012

> "He never looked the way he felt inside, and he hated being watched."

CHALLENGES: WHEN, WHY, AND WHERE

2012–2013

According to the Texas American Civil Liberties Union (Texas ACLU), the novel was removed from the summer reading list at the Grapevine High School in the Grapevine Colleyville Independent School District. The novel has been placed on a restricted shelf in the library office.

THE STORY

Seventeen-year-old J Silver knew at an early age that he had a girl's body but a boy's mind. When he reaches puberty, he begins reading articles on the Internet about gender transformation; he discovers a technique of binding his chest to disguise his breasts and learns that testosterone injections will lower his voice and cause him to grow a beard. The problem is that he must have parental permission since he is underage. Then he gets an e-mail from his best friend, Melissa, who wants to take a break from their friendship so that she might focus on her dream of becoming a dancer. J feels abandoned and begins skipping school where he does not fit in anyway. His parents are angry that he is not focused on his schoolwork because they have hopes that he will go to college. After his father says "You will always be my baby girl," J realizes that his parents are not likely to accept that he is transgender and he runs away. He enrolls in a new school where he is accepted, and he embarks on the difficult journey of revealing his true identity to his parents. His mother signs the agreement for the treatments, but by this time J has turned eighteen and does not need her permission. He is an excellent photographer, and it is through photography that he finds a way to tell Melissa, who wants to rekindle their friendship, about his transition. And it is through photography that J gets accepted into the college of his dreams.

Themes

- ❖ Acceptance
- ❖ Bullying
- ❖ Family
- ❖ Friendship

❖ Self-acceptance
❖ Self-identity
❖ Sex and sexuality

TALKING WITH TEENS ABOUT THE ISSUES

Describe J's family. How do his parents' mistakes contribute to their hopes and dreams for J's future?

J makes the statement that he was born with a girl's body but has the mind of a boy. At what age was he first aware of this?

Trace J's relationship with Melissa from the beginning to the end of the novel. What causes Melissa to cool their friendship for a while? How does he use photography to communicate to Melissa what is happening with him? How does she react?

Discuss whether his relationship with Melissa has anything to do with his decision to change schools. What does he find at his new school that he would never find in his old high school?

Why is it easier for J to run away than admit to his parents that he is transgender? Contrast the way his mother and father react when he finally tells them.

J makes the decision to get testosterone treatments. How does this liberate him?

The novel has been challenged for unknown reasons. Why do you think it has been challenged?

How might J's story offer hope to transgender teens? Explain how the novel might help teens gain empathy for transgender friends and classmates.

CHALLENGED FOR SIMILAR REASONS

Kuklin, Susan. *Beyond Magenta: Transgender Teens Speak Out.* Somerville, MA: Candlewick, 2014.

In 2014–2015, this book was challenged but retained at MacArthur High School in the Irving, Texas, Independent School District because of "subject matter not appropriately presented."

Peters, Julie Anne. *Luna.* New York: Megan Tingley Books, an imprint of Little, Brown, 2004.

According to the Texas ACLU 2005–2006 report, this novel about a boy transitioning to a girl was placed on a restricted bookshelf at the Audie Murphy Middle School in the Killeen, Texas, Independent School District because of issues related to "transgender and gender identity."

RESOURCES FOR RESPONDING TO CHALLENGES

What Reviewers Say

In the starred review for *Booklist* (December 1, 2010), the reviewer comments on the "multilayered, absolutely believable character." *School Library Journal* (February 1, 2011) recommends the book for grades 9 and up and points out the "realistic language and convincing dialogue." *Publishers Weekly* (January 31, 2011) comments on "J's authentic voice." They recommend it for ages fifteen and up. *Voice of Youth Advocates* (April 1, 2011) calls it a "heartfelt story." *Horn Book Magazine* (March/April 2011) says, "The book is a gift to transgender teens." The starred review in *Kirkus* (February 1, 2011) states that "gender and transition matter, but do not define his existence."

Other Justification for Inclusion in Curricula and Library Collections

❖ 2012 ALA Rainbow Book List: GLBTQ Books for Children and Teens
❖ 2012 ALA/YALSA Best Books for Young Adults
❖ 2012 ALA/YALSA Quick Picks for Reluctant Young Adult Readers: Fiction
❖ 2012 Texas Tayshas High School Reading List
❖ 2011 *Booklist* Top Ten First Novels for Youth
❖ 2011 Junior Library Guild Selection
❖ 2011 *Kirkus* Best Books

Sources of Information about Challenges to the Novel

Jensen, Kelly. "3 on a YA Theme: Trans* Experiences and Identities." *BookRiot*, January 7, 2015. Accessed July 29, 2015. http://bookriot.com/2015/01/07/3-ya-theme-trans-experiences-identities/.

INFORMATION ABOUT THE AUTHOR

http://www.crisbeam.com (Beam's official website)
Contemporary Authors Online, 2013. Books and Authors. Gale.

FURTHER READING ABOUT THE NOVEL

Beam, Cris. "My Transgender Novel Is Too Personal to Be Propaganda." *Guardian*, April 2, 2013. Accessed July 29, 2015. http://www.theguardian.com/books/booksblog/2013/apr/02/novels-personal-propaganda-transgender.
Miller, Mary Catherine. "Identifying Effective Trans Novels for Adolescent Readers." *Bookbird: A Journal of International Children's Literature* 52, issue 1 (2014): 83–86.
Sager, Jeanne. "Mom of Transgender Daughter Shares Big Secret to Making It Work." The Stir/Cafemom.com, March 7, 2011. Accessed August 14, 2015. http://thestir.cafemom.com/teen/117129/mom_of_transgender_daughter_shares.
Wickens, Carrine M. "Codes, Silences, and Homophobia: Challenging Normative Assumptions about Gender and Sexuality in Contemporary LGBTQ Young Adult Literature." *Children's Literature in Education* 42, issue 2 (2011): 148–164.

OTHER MEDIA SOURCES

https://www.youtube.com/watch?v=hfb98Kym34Q. Book Talk with J. C. Brown. Posted by May 17, 2012. Accessed July 29, 2015. J. C. Brown, a student at the University of Iowa, discusses *I Am J.*
http://infoblog.infopeople.org/2014/08/23/michael-cart-talks-about-transgender-ya-lit/. Posted August 23, 2014. Accessed July 29, 2015. Michael Cart talks about transgender young adult literature in this podcast.

30

❖ ❖ ❖

Impulse

BY ELLEN HOPKINS

New York: Margaret K. McElderry, an imprint of Simon & Schuster, 2007
Simon Pulse Paperback, 2008
Simon & Schuster E-book, 2008
HighBridge Audio, 2009

> "One foot in front of the other, counting tiles on the floor so I don't
> have to focus the blur of painted smiles, fake faces."

CHALLENGES: WHEN, WHY, AND WHERE

2009–2010

The novel was restricted to the eleventh and twelfth grades in the Union Hill, Texas, Independent School District because of "profanity, sexual content, drugs and alcohol."

Ellen Hopkins was uninvited to the TeenFest in Humble, Texas, after parents objected to all of her books. The festival was canceled after a group of authors pulled out in protest.

2008–2009

According to the Texas American Civil Liberties Union, the novel was challenged because of "sexual content" but retained at Round Rock Opportunity Center in the Round Rock Independent School District.

Ellen Hopkins was uninvited to a middle school in Norman, Oklahoma, after a parent objected to the "inappropriate content" in the books. Ironically she was asked to speak at Hillsdale Free Will Baptist College for a community-wide event.

THE STORY

Conner, Tony, and Vanessa are patients at Aspen Springs Psychiatric Hospital because they each tried to escape their dysfunctional, but very different, families by attempting suicide. Conner is from an affluent family and feels the pressure to be like his "perfect" twin sister. He doesn't want to continue living after he is forced to end an affair with a female teacher. He is not a very good shooter and missed his heart when he pulled the trigger. Tony, who is homeless, was raped by his mother's boyfriend, became good friends with an older guy who died of AIDS, and begins questioning his sexuality. He was discovered and revived after he downed a handful of Valium. Vanessa is bipolar, a condition she inherited from her mother. She cuts herself on a regular basis as a means of coping with depression. She took a knife to her wrists but was found before she bled to death. Now the three form a special bond, and on a supervised wilderness trip, Vanessa and Tony are surprised and devastated when Conner takes his life by jumping off a cliff. *Perfect* (2011), a companion novel, is about Conner's twin sister's struggle to live up to her parents' expectations.

Themes
- ❖ Anger
- ❖ Depression
- ❖ Family
- ❖ Friendship
- ❖ Sex and sexuality
- ❖ Suicide

TALKING WITH TEENS ABOUT THE ISSUES

Conner, Vanessa, and Tony have very different life experiences. Compare and contrast their families. On the surface, it may seem that Conner has the most stable life. How is his dysfunctional life masked by affluence?

Conner has an affair with a teacher. Debate whether his affection for an older woman is in any way related to his need for a mother. How does he respond to his female counselor at Aspen Springs? Discuss how she reacts.

Tony's mother's boyfriend rapes him. He then becomes friends with Philip, who dies from AIDS. How does this cause Tony to question his sexuality? Explain his thoughts when he falls in love with Vanessa.

Conner and Tony are dealing with anger. What is the basis of their anger? Which boy struggles the most to conquer his anger?

Vanessa deals with the guilt of having an abortion. Why did she feel as though that was her only option when she got pregnant?

The novel has been challenged because of profanity, sexual content, drugs, and alcohol. Discuss the conditions under which the teens in the novel turn to sex, drugs, and alcohol. Who are their role models? Discuss how parents, not books, are role models.

How might books like *Impulse* cause readers to develop empathy for teens who are suffering emotional stress?

CHALLENGED FOR SIMILAR REASONS

Green, John. *An Abundance of Katherines*. New York: Dutton, an imprint of Penguin, 2006.

According to the National Council of Teachers of English, this novel about a seventeen-year-old boy who suffers depression because of the pressures of being a genius and being "dumped" by a number of girls named Katherine was challenged as part of recommended reading for high school English classes in the Highland Park, Texas, Independent School District in 2013–2014 because of "sex, profanity, and rape."

Kaysen, Susanna. *Girl, Interrupted*. New York: Random House, 1996.

In 2009–2010, this book about the seventeen months that Kaysen spent in a mental institution was challenged in the New Rochelle, New York, School District because of "sexual content and profanity." It was also temporarily removed from the curriculum at the high school in Orono, Maine, because of "strong language and vivid descriptions."

McCormick, Patricia. *Cut*. Honesdale, PA: Boyds Mills Press, 2000.

This novel about a girl in a "treatment facility" after her parents discover that she is cutting herself was #86 on the 100 Most Frequently Banned/Challenged Books List of 2000–2009 because of "graphic material about self-mutilation."

RESOURCES FOR RESPONDING TO CHALLENGES

What Reviewers Say

School Library Journal (February 1, 2007) recommends the novel for grades 9 and up and calls it a "hefty problem novel"; the reviewer also states that readers who like the "free verse" format will "devour" it. The review in *Voice of Youth Advocates* (February 1, 2007) isn't completely favorable, but the teen reviewer does say that the dark moments are handled with "warmth, humor, and gravity." *Publishers Weekly* (January 22, 2007) says that "readers will find themselves invested in the characters."

Other Justification for Inclusion in Curricula and Library Collections

- ❖ 2010 ALA/YALSA Popular Paperbacks for Young Adults: Hard Knock Life
- ❖ 2010 ALA/YALSA Quick Picks for Reluctant Young Adult Readers: Fiction
- ❖ 2009 Georgia Peach Book Award for Teen Readers
- ❖ 2008 ALA/YALSA Popular Paperbacks for Young Adult Readers: Hard Knock Life
- ❖ 2008 Kentucky Bluegrass Award: Grades 9–12

Sources of Information about Challenges to the Novel

Bildner, Phil. "Texas: If You Can't Ban Books, Ban Authors." Time.com, September 29, 2010. Accessed August 5, 2015. http://content.time.com/time/nation/article/0,8599,2022356,00 .html.

Hopkins, Ellen. "Banned Books Week 2010: An Anti-Censorship Manifesto." *HuffPost Books* (blog), September 30, 2010. Accessed August 9, 2015. http://www.huffingtonpost.com/ellen-hopkins/ banned-books-anticensorship-manifesto_b_744219.html.

Kendall, Jennifer. "Ellen Hopkins on Censorship: A Powerful Advocate for Teens and the Right to Read." *About Entertainment*. Accessed August 2, 2015. http://childrensbooks.about.com/od/ censorship/a/Teen-Author-Ellen-Hopkins-On-Censorship.htm.

INFORMATION ABOUT THE AUTHOR

http://ellenhopkins.com/YoungAdult/ (Hopkins's official website)
Contemporary Authors Online, 2013. Books and Authors. Gale.

FURTHER READING ABOUT THE NOVEL

Jacobstein, Karis. "Banned Book Author Showcase: Ellen Hopkins." *YA Litwit* (blog), September 26, 2011. Accessed August 9, 2015. http://yalitwit.blogspot.com/2011/09/banned-book-author -showcase-ellen.html.

Kadaba, Lini S. "Books about Dark Topics Written in Verse Are Page Turners Even outside the Young Readers They're Aimed At." *Philadelphia Inquirer*, September 8, 2010.

OTHER MEDIA SOURCES

https://www.youtube.com/watch?v=GLNwTHeZcoQ. Posted September 16, 2011. Accessed August 2, 2015. Ellen Hopkins talks about censorship for the Banned Books Week Virtual Read-Out.

http://ellenhopkins.com/YoungAdult/. Posted November 13, 2012. Accessed July 3, 2015. Ellen Hopkins speaks at the annual National Coalition against Censorship dinner.

31

❖ ❖ ❖

The Internet Girls Series

BY LAUREN MYRACLE

New York: Amulet Books, an imprint of Abrams, 2005–2014
Abrams Paperback, 2007–2014
Abrams E-book, 2014

CHALLENGES: WHEN, WHY, AND WHERE

According to data collected by the American Library Association's Office for Intellectual Freedom, *ttyl*; *ttfn*; and *l8r, g8r* (Internet Girls series) ranked #1 on the Top Ten Most Frequently Challenged Books List in 2001 and 2009, #3 in 2008, and #7 in 2007 because of "drugs, offensive language; religious viewpoint" and for being "sexually explicit."

2013–2014

The novels *ttyl*; *ttfn*; and *l8r, g8r* were banned at the middle school in Levelland, Texas, because of "sex and drugs" and "profanity."

2010–2011

A parent of a student at the John Muir Middle School in Wausau, Wisconsin, challenged *ttyl* because of "sexually explicit content." It was retained.

The novel *ttyl* was challenged but retained at the Ponus Ridge Middle School Library in Norwalk, Connecticut, because of "foul language and sexual content."

2009–2010

The novel *ttyl* was challenged but retained in middle school libraries in the Round Rock, Texas, Independent School District because of "sex, alcohol, and inappropriate teacher-student relationships." Some of the parents called the book "porn." The school district promised to police what the students borrow from the library if parents are concerned about what their adolescents are reading. The novel *ttfn* was removed from the middle school library in Marietta, Oklahoma, because of "descriptions of sex and drug use."

2008–2009

According to the Texas American Civil Liberties Union, *ttyl*; *ttfn*; and *l8r, g8r* were challenged at the Jim Barnes Middle School in the Seguin Independent School District because of "profanity and sexual content." The books were placed on a restricted shelf, but the conditions of the restriction are unknown. The book *ttyl* was challenged but retained at the West Ridge Middle School in the Eanes, Texas, Independent School District because of "sexual content and drug and alcohol use."

2007–2008

A parent challenged *ttyl* at the William Floyd Middle School Library in Mastic, New York, because of "curse words, crude references to the male and female anatomy, sex acts, alcohol use and flirtation with a teacher that almost goes too far." It was retained.

THE NOVELS

The novels *ttyl* (talk to you later, 2005), *ttfn* (ta ta for now, 2007), *l8r, g8r* (later, gator, 2008), and *yolo* (you only live once, 2014) follow three best friends, Angela, Zoe, and Madigan, beginning when they are in middle school in Atlanta and ending in their freshman year at college. The girls, who have very different personalities, communicate with one another through text messages. Angela is boy crazy, Zoe is a "goody two-shoes," and Madigan is the hotheaded one. They talk about typical teenager concerns: boys, alcohol and drugs, parties, and sex. As they mature, two of the girls find themselves in uncharted territory: one experiments with pot, and another goes to bed with a boy. When Madigan's father loses his job and moves the family to California, the girls feel as though their friendship is at risk. They continue to text one another their confusion about life and love and their nervousness about going away to different colleges. Madigan goes to college in California, Zoe in Ohio, and Angela in Georgia. Staying in touch is easy, but their lives are different once they move in different directions.

Themes

* Acceptance
* Alcohol and drug use
* Change
* Coming of age
* Dating and boys
* Family
* Friendship
* Sex

TALKING WITH TEENS ABOUT THE ISSUES

Compare and contrast the personalities of Angela, Zoe, and Madigan. How do their differences contribute to a strong friendship?

Cite times when their friendship appears in jeopardy.

How do their issues and concerns become more complex as they get older?

The novels have been challenged for profanity in a number of middle schools. Debate whether the profanity is more apparent because of the text-messaging format.

How might the format be explained to adults who do not understand it?

The novels have also been challenged because of sexual content and drug use. How does this reflect teen culture? Zoe is described as a "goody two-shoes." Write a text message that she might send to Angela and Madigan about some of their behaviors.

CHALLENGED FOR SIMILAR REASONS

Blume, Judy. *Tiger Eyes*. New York: Simon & Schuster, 1982.

After her father is murdered, Davey and her mother move to New Mexico where Davey meets a guy who helps her deal with her grief. In 1999–2000, the novel was banned from several junior high school libraries in Louisiana because of "alcohol, profanity, and sexual content."

Ockler, Sarah. *Twenty Boy Summer*. New York: Little, Brown, 2009.

Anna and Frankie are looking for a summer filled with romance, but Anna confesses that she already had a romance with Frankie's older brother in the days before he was tragically killed in an accident. The novel was removed from the high school in Republic, Missouri, in 2010–2011 because of "sexual promiscuity." The book was later reinstated, but it cannot be required reading.

Shepard, Sara. *Pretty Little Liars*. New York: HarperCollins, 2006.

Told in a series of e-mails, this first in a series of novels about a group of girlfriends whose lives are filled with teenage drama was banned from the Navarro Junior High School in the Navarro, Texas, Independent School District in 2008–2009 because of "profanity and sexual content."

RESOURCES FOR RESPONDING TO CHALLENGES

What Reviewers Say

School Library Journal (April 1, 2004) recommends *ttyl* for grades 8–10 and calls it "wonderfully realistic." *Booklist* (May 15, 2004) comments on the "rich characters" and recommends the book for grades 6–10. *Publishers Weekly* (March 1, 2004) says that "the style makes for an engaging, quick read." They recommend it for ages thirteen–seventeen. A teen reviewer for *Voice of Youth Advocates* (June 1, 2004) says the book offers a "voyeuristic view of high school life." *Kirkus* (March 1, 2004) calls it "a surprisingly poignant tale."

Booklist (April 1, 2006) calls *ttfn* "as satisfying as the first book." *School Library Journal* (March 1, 2006) praises the plot and character development. *Publishers Weekly* (February 20, 2006) comments on the author's "appreciation for online culture." *Kirkus* (February 15, 2006) says the novel is "well-crafted."

The reviewer for *Booklist* (March 15, 2007) comments on each character's "distinctive voice" in *l8r, g8r*. *School Library Journal* (June 1, 2007) calls the novel "well-written" and "thoughtful."

In the *Booklist* (August 1, 2014) starred review of *yolo*, the reviewer calls the novel "honest, nuanced, accessible, and credible." *Publishers Weekly* (August 18, 2014) states that the girls "remain highly relatable." *Kirkus* (July 15, 2014) calls the novel "funny, deceptively smart."

Other Justification for Inclusion in Curricula and Library Collections

❖ *ttyl* 2005 ALA/YALSA Quick Picks for Reluctant Young Adult Readers: Fiction

Sources of Information about Challenges to the Novels

Flood, Alison. "Author Lauren Myracle Calls on Overprotective Parents to Stop Banning Books." *Guardian*, September 25, 2015. Accessed November 7, 2015. http://www.theguardian.com/books/2015/sep/25/author-lauren-myracle-calls-on-overprotective-parents-to-stop-banning-books.

Myracle, Lauren. "And the Banned Played On." *HuffPost Books* (blog), April 16, 2012. Accessed November 7, 2015. http://www.huffingtonpost.com/laurenmyracle/post_3252_b_1428066.html.

Myracle, Lauren. "I'm with the Banned." *HuffPost Books* (blog), April 9, 2014. Accessed November 7, 2015. http://www.huffingtonpost.com/lauren-myracle/im-with-the-banned_b_5113407.html.

Pesta, Abigail. "Should This Woman's Books Be Banned?" *Daily Beast*, April 11, 2012. Accessed November 7, 2015. http://www.thedailybeast.com/articles/2012/04/11/lauren-myracle-on-why-her-books-top-list-that-america-wants-banned.html.

Saint Louis, Catherine. "Childhood, Uncensored." *New York Times*, December 30, 2012. Accessed November 7, 2015. http://www.nytimes.com/2012/12/30/fashion/lauren-myracle-calling-it-as-she-sees-it.html?_r=0.

INFORMATION ABOUT THE AUTHOR

http://www.laurenmyracle.com (Myracle's official website)
https://twitter.com/laurenmyracle (Myracle on Twitter)
Contemporary Authors Online, 2012. Books and Authors. Gale.

FURTHER READING ABOUT THE NOVELS

Corbett, Sue. "Lauren Myracle: 'This Generation's Judy Blume . . .'" *Publishers Weekly* 258, issue 8 (February 21, 2011): 31.

Driscoll, Molly. "Lauren Myracle's 'Internet Girls' Series Gets Revamped for a New Age." *Christian Science Monitor*, February 7, 2014. Accessed November 10, 2015. http://www.csmonitor.com/Books/chapter-and-verse/2014/0207/Lauren-Myracle-s-Internet-Girls-series-gets-revamped-for-a-new-age.

Hardwick, Mindy. "Twists and Changes in the Young-Adult Novel: Some Alternative Structures Offer Fresh Ways to Hold a Teenage Audience." *Writer* 119, issue 12 (December 2006): 42–43.

Smith, Cynthia Leitich. "Author Interview: Lauren Myracle on *ttyl* and *ttfn*." *Cynsations* (blog), January 26, 2007. Accessed November 10, 2015. http://cynthialeitichsmith.blogspot.com/2007/01/author-interview-lauren-myracle-on.html.

"*Ttyl* by Lauren Myracle." *Books and Chocolate* (blog), September 27, 2009. Accessed November 7, 2015. http://karensbooksandchocolate.blogspot.com/2009/09/ttyl-by-lauren-myracle.html.

"YA Author Apologizes to *Wall Street Journal* Critic." NPR, July 6, 2011. Accessed November 7, 2015. http://www.npr.org/2011/07/06/137651883/ya-author-apologizes-to-wall-street-journal-critic.

OTHER MEDIA SOURCES

https://www.youtube.com/watch?v=2GOJ7yGd8UQ. Posted May 17, 2010. Accessed November 10, 2015. Lauren Myracle talks with ABC News about censorship.

https://www.youtube.com/watch?v=HNU9oNapH9E. Posted October 2, 2012. Accessed November 7, 2015. A fan reads *ttyl* for the Banned Books Week Virtual Read-Out.

32

❖ ❖ ❖

Killing Mr. Griffin

BY LOIS DUNCAN

New York: Little, Brown, 1978 (Op)
Recorded Books Audio, 2002
Little, Brown Paperback, 2010 (Reissue)
Little, Brown E-book, 2010

> "Mr. Griffin lay silent. Only the straining of the tendons in his
> neck showed that he was conscious and listening."

CHALLENGES: WHEN, WHY, AND WHERE

According to data collected by the American Library Association's Office for Intellectual Freedom, the novel ranked #64 on the 100 Most Frequently Challenged Books List of 1990–1999. It was #25 on the Top 100 Banned/Challenged Books of 2000–2009. The earliest recorded challenge to the novel was in 1988 in an elementary school in Milpitas, California. The novel is recommended for older readers.

2002–2003

The novel was challenged at the Salem-Keizer School District in Oregon because of "violence." It was retained.

2001–2002

The Texas American Civil Liberties Union reports that the novel was placed on a restricted shelf at the middle school in the Anahuac Independent School District because of "violence."

It was also challenged at the middle school library in the Garland, Texas, Independent School District because of "violence." The decision was pending at the time of the report.

A parent in Florida challenged the book because of the "gruesome details."

It was removed from middle school classroom reading lists in Greenville, South Carolina, because of "violence" and "profanity." It remained available in the libraries.

2000–2001

It was challenged at the middle school in Bristol, Pennsylvania, because of "violence and profanity."

THE STORY

The students in Mr. Griffin's English class at Del Norte High School in Albuquerque, New Mexico, believe that he is too strict. The truth of the matter is that he demands excellence. When Mr. Griffin hands out Fs for late assignments, a group of five students join hands in kidnapping him. Mark Kinney is repeating English and already has a bad track record. He is the mastermind of the prank. David Ruggles, the president of the senior class, is not accustomed to Fs and is especially vindictive, while some of the others, like unpopular Susan McConnell, simply follow along to satisfy their distain for Mr. Griffin. The students do not intend to hurt him; they only want to scare him. They take him to an isolated spot in the mountains, tie him up, and instruct him to beg to be let go. They also destroy his nitroglycerin, which he needs for angina attacks. The students leave, but they intend to go back for him after he has had a good scare. When they return, they find their teacher dead. One crime leads to another, and after a harrowing few days, Mark is tried for three murders. Three of the other students face second-degree murder charges, but Susan can escape with only a manslaughter charge if she tells the truth about the events.

Themes

❖ Guilt
❖ Horror
❖ Peer pressure
❖ Violence

TALKING WITH TEENS ABOUT THE ISSUES

Describe the families of the guilty students. How do the family relationships contribute to the students' crimes?

The students did not actually kill Mr. Griffin, but they cause his death. How is this a really bad prank that turned tragic?

Discuss how Mr. Griffin's death leads the students to commit true crimes.

Debate the punishments for the crimes. Why does Susan escape with only a manslaughter charge?

The novel is classed as a mystery and a thriller, but parents have challenged it because of violence. Discuss whether the novel is too realistic for young adult readers. What might readers learn from the novel?

Some school administrators think the book may cause violent behavior among students. Explain how the book may be used as a springboard for conversation about consequences of pranks, lying, and crimes. Why is this an important conversation to have in the wake of school violence?

CHALLENGED FOR SIMILAR REASONS

Bennett, Jay. *To Be a Killer*. New York: Scholastic, 1985.

In 2001–2002, this novel about a high school student who plots to kill his science teacher because he thinks he is responsible for the death of a beloved coach was placed on a restricted shelf at the Bleyl Middle School in the Cypress-Fairbanks, Texas, Independent School District because it was deemed too "mature for sixth-graders."

Cooney, Caroline B. *The Face on the Milk Carton*. New York: Delacorte, an imprint of Random House Children's Books, 1990.

Janie Johnson is in high school when she sees her picture as a child on a milk carton, which means that she is a missing child. This novel about the events that follow when Janie attempts to solve her own mystery ranked #80 on the 100 Most Frequently Challenged Books List of 1990–1999 and #29 on the Top 100 Banned/Challenged Books List of 2000–2009 because of "sexual content," "challenge to authority," and for being "inappropriate for age group."

Duncan, Lois. *I Know What You Did Last Summer*. New York: Little, Brown, 1973.

This novel about four teens bound by a dark secret that someone has uncovered was challenged at the middle school in Charlestown, Indiana, in 1993 because of "graphic passages, sexual references, and alleged immorality."

RESOURCES FOR RESPONDING TO CHALLENGES

What Reviewers Say

Kirkus (April 1, 1978) calls the novel "another of Duncan's nonstop thrillers." *School Library Journal* (May 1978) praises Duncan for her "skillful plotting." *New York Times Book Review* (April 30, 1978) says the novel "breaks some new ground."

Other Justification for Inclusion in Curricula and Library Collections

* 1992 ALA/YALSA Here We Go Again: 25 Years of Best Books: Selections from 1967–1992
* 1988 *New York Times* Best Books for Children
* 1986 ALA/YALSA Nothin' but the Best: Best of the Best Books for Young Adults: 1966–1986
* 1983 ALA/YALSA Best of the Best Books for Young Adults: 1970–1983
* 1982 Massachusetts Children's Book Award
* 1978 ALA/YALSA Best Books for Young Adults

Sources of Information about Challenges to the Novel

Johnston, Susanne L. "In Defense of *Killing Mr. Griffin*." In *Censored Books II: Critical Viewpoints, 1985–2000*, edited by Nicholas J. Karolides, 285–289. Lanham, MD: Scarecrow Press, 2002.

Plesyk, Christine Anne. "Banned Books: Killing Mr. Griffin/Daughters of Eve." *Business & Heritage Clarksville* (Tennessee). Accessed October 2, 2015. http://businessclarksville.com/arts/banned-books-killing-mr-griffendaughters-of-eve/2010/09/18/15507.

INFORMATION ABOUT THE AUTHOR

http://loisduncan.arquettes.com (Duncan's official website)

Contemporary Authors Online, 2015. Books and Authors. Gale.

Kaywell, Joan. "An Interview with Lois Duncan." *Journal of Adolescent & Adult Literacy* 52, issue 6 (March 2009): 545.

Stone, RoseEtta. "Interview with Lois Duncan." *Absolute Write* (blog), January 18, 2002. Accessed October 2, 2015. http://www.absolutewrite.com/specialty_writing/lois_duncan.htm.

Sutton, Roger. "A Conversation with Lois Duncan." *School Library Journal* 38 (June 1992): 20–24.

FURTHER READING ABOUT THE NOVEL

Duncan, Lois. "1992 Margaret A. Edwards Award Acceptance Speech." *Journal of Youth Services in Libraries* 6 (Winter 1993): 108–112.

Lesesne, Teri S., Lois Buckman, and G. Kylene Beers. "Review of *Killing Mr. Griffin.*" *Journal of Adolescent & Adult Literacy* 40, issue 4 (December/January 1996): 316–317.

Overstreet, D. W. "Help, Help! An Analysis of Female Victims in the Novels of Lois Duncan." *ALAN Review* 21 (Spring 1994): 43–45.

OTHER MEDIA SOURCES

http://www.imdb.com/title/tt0119461/. Accessed October 2, 2015. This is a link to the 1997 television movie of *Killing Mr. Griffin.*

https://www.youtube.com/watch?v=6XmuneJnTEo. Posted January 21, 2009. Accessed October 8, 2015. This is a video visit with Lois Duncan.

33

❖ ❖ ❖

Looking for Alaska

BY JOHN GREEN

New York: Dutton, an imprint of Penguin, 2005
Penguin Paperback, 2006
Brilliance Audio, 2006
Penguin E-book, 2008

"I know so many last words. But I will never know hers."

CHALLENGES: WHEN, WHY, AND WHERE

According to data collected by the American Library Association's Office for Intellectual Freedom, the novel was #7 on the Top Ten Most Frequently Challenged Books List in 2013 and #7 in 2012. The reasons cited were "drugs/alcohol/smoking, nudity, offensive language and sexually explicit."

2014–2015

The National Coalition against Censorship reports a challenge by a parent in a high school in Waukesha, Wisconsin, because "it's not suitable for teenagers."

The novel was also banned, and then reinstated for seventh- and eighth-graders in the Lumberton, New Jersey, Township because of "sexual content."

2013–2014

The National Council of Teachers of English reports that the novel was challenged for "sexual content" in the tenth-grade curriculum in a high school in Wisconsin. The book was retained in the classrooms and libraries in the school district.

A parent challenged the novel at the Verona, New Jersey, high school because the "sexual content" seemed inappropriate for the curriculum. The outcome of the challenge is unknown.

The novel was challenged in a ninth-grade classroom at the Fort Lupton, Colorado, Middle and High School for "sexual content."

2011–2012

The novel was challenged as part of required outside reading in Honors and Advanced Placement classes at Karns High School in the Knox County, Tennessee, School District because of "inappropriate language." It was removed.

It was also banned from the curriculum in Sumner County, Tennessee, because of an "oral sex" scene.

2009–2010

According to the National Council of Teachers of English, the novel was challenged in a twelfth-grade general English class in Ohio. The result of the case is unknown.

2007–2008

Parents challenged the novel in English classes in Depew, New York, because of "graphic language and sexual content." The book was retained, but students may ask for an alternative reading assignment.

2006–2007

According to the Texas American Civil Liberties Union (Texas ACLU), the novel was removed from the Diboll High School Library in the Diboll Independent School District after a teacher filed a challenge because of the "sexual content."

THE STORY

Miles Halter is a rising junior in high school when he asks his parents if he can leave his school in Florida and attend Culver Creek boarding school in Birmingham, Alabama, to seek "the great perhaps." When he meets his new classmates, he quickly learns how sheltered his life has been. He loses his innocence when he meets his roommate Chip Martin, called the Colonel, and Alaska Young, a self-destructive and screwed-up girl, who lives on his hall in the dormitory. It isn't long before Alaska steals Miles's heart, but she is an experienced girl in matters of the heart, and Miles finds himself a little over his head. To top off this complicated relationship, Miles, Alaska, the Colonel, and a few other students are at war with the "Weekday Warriors," rich day students from the Birmingham area. The teens engage in a "Best Day/Worst Day" drinking game that results in a deadly accident. They each deal with guilt for not stopping Alaska from getting behind the wheel of her car while drunk, but they also contemplate whether her death was indeed an accident or suicide.

Themes
❖ Choices
❖ Death
❖ Friendship
❖ Guilt
❖ Home
❖ Love
❖ Self-discovery
❖ Sex and sexuality
❖ Trust

TALKING WITH TEENS ABOUT THE ISSUES

Explain why Miles Halter elects to go to boarding school. Debate whether he finds what he is searching for.

Discuss Miles and Alaska's relationship. How is she different from any girl he has ever known? What does she contribute to his "social" education at Culver Creek?

What is the purpose of the "Best Day/Worst Day" drinking game?

Contrast the way Miles and the Colonel deal with Alaska's death. Why do they think that her death may have been suicide?

Discuss the battle between the boarding students and the "Weekday Warriors." How do they unite in the end?

The novel has been challenged multiple times because of profanity. How does the language define the culture in most high schools? How might teenagers like Miles, the Colonel, Alaska, and other kids at Culver Creek know that the language they use with one another may not be appropriate in their families and extended social circles?

Other challenges deal with sexual content. Cite specific scenes where some adults may experience discomfort. Discuss whether this is an attempt to shelter teenagers. How might Miles and his classmates benefit from reading a novel like *Looking for Alaska*?

Discuss ways to communicate the importance of the novel to parents and school officials.

CHALLENGED FOR SIMILAR REASONS

Knowles, John. *A Separate Peace*. New York: Scribner Paperback, a division of Simon & Schuster, 2003.

Originally published in 1959, this classic coming-of-age novel about the loss of innocence in a New England boarding school is one of the most challenged novels in schools. Documented challenges have occurred in New York, Pennsylvania, Tennessee, Illinois, and North Carolina because it is a "filthy, trashy sex novel" and for "graphic language."

Sittenfeld, Curtis. *Prep*. New York: Random House, 2005.

According to the Texas ACLU Banned Books Report of 2008–2009, this book about a scholarship student at the prestigious Ault Prep School was challenged but retained at MacArthur High School in the Irving Independent School District because of "sexual content."

RESOURCES FOR RESPONDING TO CHALLENGES

What Reviewers Say

The starred review in *School Library Journal* (February 1, 2005) says that the language is "realistically drawn." The review recommends the novel for grades 9 and up. *Publishers Weekly* (February 7, 2005) calls it an "ambitious first novel." The starred review in *Kirkus* (March 1, 2005) says it is a "gorgeously told tale." *Horn Book Magazine* (March 1, 2006) comments on the "complex and realistically portrayed teenagers." *Voice of Youth Advocates* (April 1, 2005) calls the novel "provocative, moving, and sometimes hilarious."

Other Justification for Inclusion in Curricula and Library Collections

- ❖ 2009 ALA/YALSA Outstanding Books for College Bound: Literature and Language
- ❖ 2009 ALA/YALSA Popular Paperbacks for Young Adults: Death and Dying
- ❖ 2006 ALA/YALSA Best Books for Young Adults
- ❖ 2006 ALA/YALSA Michael L. Printz Award

❖ 2006 ALA/YALSA Quick Picks for Reluctant Young Adult Readers: Fiction
❖ 2006 Kentucky Bluegrass Award: Grades 9–12
❖ 2006 Top Ten Best Books for Young Adults
❖ 2005 *Booklist* Editors' Choice: Books for Youth: Older Readers Category
❖ 2005 *School Library Journal* Best Books

Sources of Information about Challenges to the Novel

Gomez, Betsy. "John Green's *Looking for Alaska* under Attack in Wisconsin." Comic Book Legal Defense Fund, July 11, 2014. Accessed August 7, 2015. http://cbldf.org/2014/07/john-greens-looking-for-alaska-under-attack-in-wisconsin/.

Hall, Wes. "Pornographic Required Reading in Knox Schools?" *Knoxville Journal*, March 9, 2012. Accessed July 30, 2015. http://theknoxvillejournal.com/pornographic-required-reading-in-knox-schools/.

Peterson, Karyn. "John Green Says *Looking for Alaska* Challenged by Colorado Parents." *School Library Journal*, October 2, 2013. Accessed July 30, 2015. http://www.slj.com/2013/10/censorship/john-green-says-looking-for-alaska-challenged-at-co-high-school/.

INFORMATION ABOUT THE AUTHOR

http://johngreenbooks.com (Green's official website)

https://twitter.com/johngreen?lang=en (Green on Twitter)

Contemporary Authors Online, 2015. Books and Authors. Gale.

Cooper, Ilene. "A Conversation with John Green and Ilene Cooper." *Booklist* 108, issue 9 (January 1, 2012): 106.

Cooper, Ilene. "Last Words from a First Novelist." *Booklist* 101, issue 13 (March 1, 2005): 1181.

FURTHER READING ABOUT THE NOVEL

Barkdoll, Jayme K., and Lisa Scheriff. "Literature Is Not a Cold, Dead Place: An Interview with John Green." *English Journal* 97, issue 3 (January 2008): 67–71.

Green, John. "Does YA Mean Anything Anymore? Genre in a Digitized World." *Horn Book Magazine* 90, issue 6 (November/December 2014): 15–25.

Green, John. "The Printz Award Acceptance Speech." *Young Adult Library Services* 6, issue 1 (Fall 2007): 14.

Hunt, Jonathan. "A Printz Retrospective." *Horn Book Magazine* 85, issue 4 (July/August 2009): 395–403.

Ross, Ashley. "John Green Takes Fans inside His Creative Process." Time.com, January 13, 2015. Accessed July 30, 2015. http://time.com/3664424/john-green-looking-for-alaska/.

OTHER MEDIA SOURCES

https://www.youtube.com/watch?v=fHMPtYvZ8tM. Posted by Vlogbrothers, January 30, 2008. Accessed July 30, 2015. In this video, titled *I Am Not a Pornographer*, John Green responds to those attempting to ban *Looking for Alaska*.

https://www.youtube.com/watch?v=LjcM7JEzZ28. Posted September 29, 2012. Accessed July 30, 2015. A bookstore owner reads *Looking for Alaska* for the Banned Books Week Virtual Read-Out.

34

❖ ❖ ❖

Mexican WhiteBoy

BY MATT DE LA PEÑA

New York: Delacorte, an imprint of Random House Children's Books, 2008
Dell E-book, 2008
Random House Paperback, 2010
Brilliance Audio, 2015

"I'm a white boy among Mexicans, and a Mexican among white boys."

CHALLENGES: WHEN, WHY, AND WHERE

2011–2012

The Tucson Unified School District in Arizona shut down the successful Mexican American studies program, and books and materials were boxed and marked "banned." *Mexican WhiteBoy* was one of the books. The school district labeled it "anti-American" and objected to a "fight scene." District authorities said that while the book had no place in the classroom, it was available in the school libraries.

THE STORY

Sixteen-year-old Danny Lopez has long arms that give him power on the pitcher's mound, and he knows that his ninety-five-mile-an-hour fastball could earn him scholarship offers to colleges he never dreamed of attending. The problem is that Danny isn't on the baseball team at the elite, all-white private school he attends. He suffered a bad case of nerves on the day of tryouts, and he threw balls far out of the strike zone. In his mind, that finished his baseball career. Because Danny is half Mexican, the kids at school ignore him, and Danny feels that he doesn't really fit in. Though his father hasn't been in his life for four years, Danny has a strong desire to connect with his Mexican heritage. He decides to spend the summer with his father's relatives in a poor, predominantly Mexican neighborhood in San Diego while his mother is off with her rich boyfriend. Things aren't always good there because Danny doesn't speak Spanish, and he feels that his whiteness interferes with forming a good relationship with his relatives and the neighborhood kids.

When Danny meets Uno, a half-black, half-white boy, whose father is also absent, the two form a friendship that sets them on a journey of self-discovery. Together they learn to confront the demons that are holding them back on the baseball field and in life.

Themes
❖ Belonging
❖ Family

❖ Friendship
❖ Racial and cultural prejudice
❖ Self-identity

TALKING WITH TEENS ABOUT THE ISSUES

Define the term *bigotry*. What is the difference between overt and covert racism? Which type of racism does Danny face?

Describe Danny's identity crisis. How is this related to a "label" placed on him by society?

What is symbolic about the scene where Danny and Uno go to the train bridge and await an on-coming train? Debate whether this begins his journey or completes it.

The state of Arizona shut down the Mexican American studies program in Tucson and banned *Mexican WhiteBoy*. Why do you think the politicians and school officials in Arizona feel threatened by the novel?

The Tucson Unified School District has a large Mexican American population. Discuss the message the school board sent the students in Tucson when they banned the book.

Some of the students spoke up and protested the politicians' actions. How would you respond if this type of censorship occurred in your school or school system?

What are proactive steps that teenagers can take to combat bigotry and racism in their school?

CHALLENGED FOR SIMILAR REASONS

Carlson, Lori Marie. *Red Hot Salsa: Bilingual Poems on Being Young and Latino in the United States.* New York: Henry Holt, an imprint of Macmillan, 2005.

This collection of poems about living Latino in the United States was banned in 2011–2012 from the Tucson, Arizona, Unified School District when the Mexican American studies program was shut down.

Cisneros, Sandra. *The House on Mango Street.* New York: Knopf, an imprint of Random House, 1994.

In 2011–2012, this novel about Esperanza who deals with oppression as she comes of age in her Chicago neighborhood was banned because it was deemed "anti-American" from the Tucson, Arizona, Unified School District when the Mexican American studies program was shut down.

RESOURCES FOR RESPONDING TO CHALLENGES

What Reviewers Say

Lynn Rutan, reviewer for *Booklist* (August 1, 2008) says, "The author juggles his many plotlines well." Madeline Walton-Hadlock states in *School Library Journal* (September 1, 2008), "As the characters develop, their language starts to feel familiar and warm." Matthew Weaver, the reviewer for *Voice of Youth Advocates* (October 1, 2008), focuses on the many obstacles that the characters face: "In a fantastic move by the author that is not cloying or obvious, they also have the temerity to overcome them." Safia Uddin, reviewer for *SIGNAL Journal* (Spring/Summer 2009), calls the novel "another engaging and perceptive read with realistic characters and authentic language." *Horn Book Magazine* (September/October 2008) calls the novel "unique in its gritty realism."

Other Justification for Inclusion in Curricula and Library Collections

❖ 2013 ALA/YALSA Popular Paperbacks for Young Adults: I'm New Here Myself
❖ 2009 American Library Association Best Book for Young Adults (Top Ten Pick)
❖ 2009 Notable Books for a Global Society
❖ 2009 Texas Tayshas Reading List
❖ 2008 Bulletin of the Center for Children's Books Ribbon List
❖ A Junior Library Guild Selection

Sources of Information about Challenges to the Novel

Winerip, Michael. "Racial Lens Used to Cull Curriculum in Arizona." *New York Times*, March 19, 2012. Accessed March 11, 2014. http://www.nytimes.com/2012/03/19/education/racial-lens -used-to-cull-curriculum-in-arizona.html?ref=education&_r=0.

INFORMATION ABOUT THE AUTHOR

http://mattdelapena.com (de la Peña's official website)
Contemporary Authors Online, 2014. Books and Authors. Gale.

FURTHER READING ABOUT THE NOVEL

Buehler, Jennifer. "Their Lives Are Beautiful, Too: How Matt de la Peña Illuminates the Lives of Urban Teens." *ALAN Review* 37 (Winter 2010). Accessed March 11, 2014. http://scholar.lib .vt.edu/ejournals/ALAN/v37n2/buehler.html.
Manfredi, Angi. "Talking about Your World." *Voice of Youth Advocates* 36, issue 3 (August 2013): 14–17.
Peña, Matt de la. "Sometimes the 'Tough Teen' Is Quietly Writing Stories." NPR, November 11, 2013. Accessed March 11, 2014. http://www.npr.org/blogs/codeswitch/2013/11/11/ 243960103/a-reluctant-reader-turns-ya-author-for-tough-teens.
Rudnicki, Alicia. "Longing to Belong: In *Mexican WhiteBoy* a Confused Teen Searches for Home Base." Examiner.com. Accessed March 11, 2014. http://www.examiner.com/article/ longing-to-belong-mexican-whiteboy-a-confused-teen-searches-for-home-base.

OTHER MEDIA SOURCES

http://www.teachingbooks.net/book_reading.cgi?id=3842&a=1. Accessed March 11, 2014. Matt de la Peña talks about writing *Mexican WhiteBoy* and reads an excerpt from the novel.
http://www.readwritethink.org/parent-afterschool-resources/podcast-episodes/conversation -with-matt-pena-30322.html. Accessed March 11, 2014. This podcast is a conversation be-tween Matt de la Peña and Professor Jennifer Buehler.
http://www.youtube.com/watch?v=2WkDD_IPaEs; http://www.youtube.com/watch?v=w_AgZ13 Sj0Q&feature=relmfu; http://www.youtube.com/watch?v=r-4d8s-1yg0&feature=relmfu; http:// www.youtube.com/watch?v=F-0X7lMd7JM&feature=relmfu. Accessed March 11, 2014. This four-part presentation by Matt de la Peña is sponsored by the Center for Fiction in New York.
http://www.youtube.com/watch?v=NWURx3aZjSY. New York City Educators, 2012. Accessed March 11, 2014. This video features Matt de la Peña at an author event in New York City.

35

❖ ❖ ❖

The Miseducation of Cameron Post

BY EMILY M. DANFORTH

New York: HarperCollins, 2012
HarperCollins E-book, 2012
HarperCollins Paperback, 2013

"You can't catch somebody doing something when they're not hiding."

CHALLENGES: WHEN, WHY, AND WHERE

2014–2015

The novel was removed from the summer reading list for ninth-graders at the Cape Henlopen School District in Delaware because of "profanity" and the "gay theme." The book was on the Blue Hen Book Award List for Teens, and ninth-graders were asked to read one book on the list. The school board ultimately dismissed the entire list.

THE STORY

Set in Miles City, Montana, twelve-year-old Cameron Post is orphaned when her parents are killed in a car accident. She lives with guilt that she may have been responsible for her parents' death because the day before the accident she stole her first kiss with her best friend, Irene. She knows that her parents would not approve, and part of her is relieved that her parents will never know about the kiss. As she moves through adolescence, Cameron realizes that she is a lesbian, and she is sure that Aunt Ruth, her ultraconservative legal guardian, thinks that homosexuality is a sin. She manages to keep her sexual orientation private until Coley Taylor, a beautiful bisexual girl, moves to town and shows up at the fundamentalist church Cameron attends. The two girls engage in an affair that becomes public, and Aunt Ruth ships Cameron off to God's Promise, a camp that practices "religious conversion therapy." Aunt Ruth is convinced that Cameron will return home "cured" of homosexuality. During her time at God's Promise, Cameron gets to know other kids who are on similar journeys, and she learns to be true to herself, regardless of who it offends.

Themes
- ❖ Betrayal
- ❖ Coming of age
- ❖ Guilt
- ❖ Self-acceptance
- ❖ Sex and sexuality

TALKING WITH TEENS ABOUT THE ISSUES

Explain why Cameron Post feels that she is responsible for her parents' accident. How does this guilt drive her into isolation?

Aunt Ruth is extremely conservative, and Cameron's grandmother is very conventional. How do their views regarding homosexuality reflect the views taught in the church they attend?

Cameron shoplifts, drinks, and smokes pot. She also has a heavy diet of "adult only" movies. Discuss whether these behaviors are Cameron's way of rebelling against her conservative upbringing.

Discuss the teachings of God's Promise. How do these teachings drive some of the young adults into self-mutilation and further guilt? Cameron makes a personal journey while at God's Promise. How does she grow to realize that "being true to self" is important? What is that truth for Cameron?

The novel has been challenged because of the gay theme. How might the people who challenge this novel be compared to Aunt Ruth and the views of the fundamentalist church in Miles City, Montana? Debate whether it is possible to change the views of these people.

Those who object to the novel miss the most important message of the book. Explain how the book is about tolerance and self-acceptance.

CHALLENGED FOR SIMILAR REASONS

Hautzig, Deborah. *Hey Dollface*. New York: Greenwillow, an imprint of HarperCollins, 1978.

In 2004–2005, this novel about two girls who are misfits at school and develop sexual feelings for one another was challenged at the Montgomery County Memorial Library in Texas because of the "gay positive" theme.

Knowles, Jo. *Lessons from a Dead Girl*. Somerville, MA: Candlewick Press, 2007.

This novel about the sexual experimentation between two girls was among five novels banned from the curriculum in Montgomery County, Kentucky, in 2010–2011 because of "homosexual content, language, and drug use."

Myracle, Lauren. *Kissing Kate*. New York: Dutton, an imprint of Penguin, 2003.

The Texas American Civil Liberties Union 2010–2011 annual report states that the novel about two girls who discover they have romantic feelings for one another and are concerned about their families' reaction was banned at Valley Mills Junior High and High School in the Valley Mills, Texas, Independent School District because of "profanity and sexual content."

RESOURCES FOR RESPONDING TO CHALLENGES

What Reviewers Say

Publishers Weekly (January 9, 2012) gives the book a star, calls it an "impressive debut," and recommends it for ages fourteen and up. The reviewer for *School Library Journal* (March 1, 2012) gives the novel a star and calls it a "sophisticated coming-of-age novel." The journal recommends it for grades 10 and up. *Voice of Youth Advocates* (December 15, 2011) calls it an "important book," especially for "a teen struggling with his or her own sexuality." In the starred *Booklist* (December 15,

2011) review, Michael Cart says, "There is nothing superficial or simplistic." *Kirkus* (February 7, 2012) stars the book and comments on the "carefully crafted symbols."

Other Justification for Inclusion in Curricula and Library Collections

❖ 2013 ALA/YALSA Best Fiction for Young Adults
❖ 2013 Rainbow List
❖ 2012 *Booklist* Editors' Choice: Books for Youth: Older Readers Category
❖ 2012 Montana Book Award
❖ 2012 *School Library Journal* Best Books of the Year

Sources of Information about Challenges to the Novel

Lo, Malinda. "*The Miseducation of Cameron Post* Removed from Delaware Summer Reading List: Update." *Diversity in YA* (blog), July 7, 2014. Accessed September 7, 2015. http://www.diversity inya.com/2014/07/the-miseducation-of-cameron-post-removed-from-delaware-summer -reading-list/.
"Read the Winning Cameron Post Essays." National Coalition against Censorship. Accessed September 7, 2015. http://ncac.org/campostheroes/.
"Who Should Decide What High School Kids Are Allowed to Read?" TheAtlantic.com, September 5, 2014. Accessed September 7, 2015. http://www.theatlantic.com/education/archive/2014/09/ who-should-decide-what-high-school-kids-read/379609/.
Wong, Curtis M. "Delaware School District Scraps Summer Reading after Lesbian-Themed Book Sparks Controversy." *Huffington Post*, August 12, 2014. Accessed September 7, 2015. http://www.huffingtonpost.com/2014/08/12/the-miseducation-of-cameron-post-reading -program-_n_5672411.html.

INFORMATION ABOUT THE AUTHOR

http://www.emdanforth.com (emily m. danforth's official website)
https://twitter.com/emdanforth (emily m. danforth on Twitter)
"The PEN Ten with emily m. danforth." PEN America. Accessed September 7, 2015. http://www .pen.org/interview/pen-ten-emily-m-danforth.

FURTHER READING ABOUT THE NOVEL

Bittner, Robert. "Hey, I Still Can't See Myself! The Difficult Positioning of Two-Spirit Identities in YA Literature." *Bookbird: A Journal of International Children's Literature* 52, issue 1 (2014): 11–22.
Bovberg, Jason. "An Interview with emily m. danforth." *Dark Highway Press* (blog), November 27, 2013. Accessed September 7, 2015. http://www.jasonbovberg.com/emily-danforth/.
Carpenter, Susan. "Not Just for Kids: *The Miseducation of Cameron Post*." *Los Angeles Times*, February 5, 2012. Accessed September 7, 2015. http://articles.latimes.com/2012/feb/05/entertainment/ la-ca-emily-danforth-20120205.
Lo, Malinda. "YA Pride: Interview with emily m. danforth." *YA Pride* (blog), June 13, 2012. Accessed September 7, 2015. http://www.malindalo.com/2012/06/ya-pride-interview-with-emily-m -danforth/.

Sittenfeld, Curtis. "The Best Novel about 'De-Gaying Camp' Ever Written." *Slate*, February 8, 2012. Accessed September 7, 2015. http://www.slate.com/articles/double_x/doublex/2012/02/ the_miseducation_of_cameron_post_by_emily_danforth_a_conversation_between_the_ writer_and_novelist_curtis_sittenfeld_.single.html.

OTHER MEDIA SOURCES

http://articles.latimes.com/2012/feb/05/entertainment/la-ca-emily-danforth-20120205. Posted January 4, 2012. Accessed September 7, 2015. Published by HarperTeen, this is a video book summary of *The Miseducation of Cameron Post*.

https://www.youtube.com/watch?v=ZizPIR2tHsU. Posted February 6, 2012. Accessed September 7, 2015. emily m. danforth talks about *The Miseducation of Cameron Post*.

https://www.youtube.com/watch?v=nwxiPgGcLmc. Posted July 28, 2015. Accessed September 7, 2015. A fan offers a video review of *The Miseducation of Cameron Post*.

36

❖ ❖ ❖

Monster

BY WALTER DEAN MYERS

New York: HarperCollins, 1999
HarperCollins Paperback, 2004
HarperCollins E-book, 2009

"The best time to cry is at night, when the lights are out and someone is being beaten up and screaming for help."

CHALLENGES: WHEN, WHY, AND WHERE

2012–2013

The novel was challenged in Oak Park, Illinois, by parents who didn't think the "explicit language" and "mature themes" were appropriate for a middle school language arts curriculum. A review committee retained the novel, and parents may request an alternative book for their child.

2006–2007

Some parents in the Blue Valley, Kansas, School District asked that the novel be removed from all high school classrooms because it is too "sexual[ly] explicit" and contains "vulgar language" and "violent imagery."

THE STORY

Born and reared in Harlem, Steve Harmon is sixteen years old when he is asked to be the "lookout" guy in a drugstore robbery that resulted in the murder of the storeowner. Two of the guilty escape prison by striking a plea bargain, but James King and Steve are sent to a detention facility to await trial. Steve admits to knowing the guys who committed the crime, but he swears he was not involved. His situation is almost more than he can handle, but he learns to cope by writing a movie script and daily diary entries about his life behind bars. His father visits, but only expresses his dream of his son attending Morehouse College, and Steve is unsure whether his father will really ever be a part of his life. Then he questions whether his defense attorney believes his innocence. There are a number of witnesses at the trial, but one of the most important is George Sawicki, Steve's film club advisor who speaks to Steve's moral character. James King is convicted and Steve is released, but he is riddled with scars of his ordeal.

Themes

- ❖ Crime
- ❖ Dehumanization
- ❖ Guilt/innocence
- ❖ Identity
- ❖ Peer pressure
- ❖ Prejudice
- ❖ Racism
- ❖ Truth

TALKING WITH TEENS ABOUT THE ISSUES

Explain what Steve means when he describes his first days in prison as a "grainy screen." The prosecutor labels him "Monster," and that is what he titles his movie. Why is this an unfortunate label, especially when he has not been found guilty of the crime?

Describe life in prison from Steve's point of view. What are his fears?

In this country, a person is considered innocent until proven guilty. Why does Steve question whether his defense attorney believes his innocence? Explain why she walks off when Steve attempts to hug her after he is found innocent.

The book has been challenged by parents who felt it was "too violent" to be included in a middle school language arts curriculum. Why is it important to talk about novels like *Monster*? What are the larger issues that should be addressed over the violent content?

The novel has also been challenged for language. How does the language define Steve's environment in and outside of prison?

What are the positive themes expressed in the novel? Discuss what readers might learn from Steve. How might you explain this to a parent who only focuses on the violence and language?

CHALLENGED FOR SIMILAR REASONS

Booth, Coe. *Tyrell*. New York: Scholastic, 2006.

The writer reports that she has actually seen her novel about an inner-city teen whose father is in jail and the influences of the street that threaten his existence placed in locked book shelves in libraries.

Rodriguez, Luis J. *Always Running*. Willimantic, CT: Curbstone Press, 1993.

Written for adults but adopted by young adults, this memoir focuses on the author's growing up as a young Chicano gang member in East Los Angeles. It has been challenged numerous times, but the latest recorded challenge, which resulted in banning the book, was in the Santa Barbara, California, schools in 2004 because a parent complained about "graphic passages depicting violence and sex."

RESOURCES FOR RESPONDING TO CHALLENGES

What Reviewers Say

School Library Journal (July 1, 1999) recommends the novel for grades 7 and up and says, "Many elements of this story are familiar, but Myers keeps it fresh." *Booklist* (May 1, 1999) believes the novel is more appropriate for grades 9–12 and states, "The tense drama of the courtroom scenes will enthrall readers." *Voice of Youth Advocates* (August 1, 1999) says that "the journal and the script techniques" set the pace of the novel.

Other Justification for Inclusion in Curricula and Library Collections

❖ 2004 ALA/YALSA Outstanding Books for the College Bound: Literature and Language Arts
❖ 2003 Isinglass Teen Read Award (New Hampshire)
❖ 2002 Kentucky Bluegrass Award: Grades 9–12
❖ 2000 ALA/YALSA Best Books for Young Adults
❖ 2000 ALA/YALSA Michael L. Printz Award
❖ 2000 ALA/YALSA Quick Picks for Reluctant Young Adult Readers
❖ 1999 *Booklist* Editors' Choice: Books for Youth: Older Readers Category
❖ 1999 *New York Times* Notable Books: Children's Books

Sources of Information about Challenges to the Novel

Dean, Terry. "District 97 Will Not Remove 'Controversial' Novel." OakPark.com, May 14, 2013. Accessed June 10, 2015. http://www.oakpark.com/News/Articles/5-14-2013/District-97-will -not-remove-'controversial'-novel/.

Whelan, Debra Lau. "Walter Dean Myers Talks Book-Banning, Writing for Troubled Kids." National Coalition against Censorship (blog), August 9, 2013. Accessed June 10, 2015. https://ncacblog .wordpress.com/2013/08/09/walter-dean-myers-talks-book-banning-writing-for-trouble makers/.

INFORMATION ABOUT THE AUTHOR

http://walterdeanmyers.net (Myers's official website)

Goodson, Lori Atkins, and Jennifer Funk. "Walter Dean Myers: A Monster of a Voice for Young Adults." *ALAN Review* 36, issue 1 (Fall 2008): 26–31.

Jordan, Denise. *Walter Dean Myers: A Biography of an Award-Winning Urban Fiction Author.* African-American Icon Series. Berkeley Heights, NJ: Enslow Publishers, E-book, 2013.

Marler, Myrna Dee. *Walter Dean Myers.* Teen Reads: Student Companions to Young Adult Literature Series. Portsmouth, NH: Greenwood, 2008.

McElmeel, Sharron L. "A Profile: Walter Dean Myers." *Book Report* 20, issue 2 (September/October 2001): 42–45.

FURTHER READING ABOUT THE NOVEL

Engles, Tim, and Fern Kory. "Incarceration, Identity Formation, and Race in Young Adult Literature: The Case of *Monster* versus *Hole in My Life.*" *English Journal* 102, issue 4 (March 2013): 53–58.

Gallo, Don. "A Man of Many Ideas: Walter Dean Myers." *Writing* 26, issue 5 (February/March 2004): 10–11.

Groenke, Susan Lee, and Michelle Youngquish. "Are We Postmodern Yet? Reading *Monster* with 21st-Century Ninth Graders." *Journal of Adolescent & Adult Literacy* 54, issue 7 (April 2011): 505–513.

Myers, Walter Dean. "Escalating Offenses." *Horn Book Magazine* 77, issue 6 (November/December 2001): 701–702.

Myers, Walter Dean. "The May Hill Arbuthnot Honor Lecture: The Geography of the Heart." *Children and Libraries: Journal of the Association for Library Service to Children* 7, issue 3 (Winter 2009): 8–26.

Rochman, Hazel. "The Booklist Interview: Walter Dean Myers." *Booklist* 96, issue 12 (February 15, 2000): 1101.

Schneider, Dean. "The Novel as Screenplay: *Monster* and *Riot* by Walter Dean Myers." *Book Links* 19, issue 2 (January 2010): 20–23.

OTHER MEDIA SOURCES

https://www.youtube.com/watch?v=soueMVStVzs. Posted January 22, 2012. Accessed June 10, 2015. Walter Dean Myers, 2012 National Ambassador for Young People's Literature, talks about writing.

https://www.youtube.com/watch?v=nUJ37nrfNV4. Posted July 31, 2012. Accessed June 10, 2015. Walter Dean Myers returns with talks about the importance of reading in his old Harlem neighborhood.

https://www.youtube.com/watch?v=QtlkXnf3-vY. Posted April 8, 2014. Accessed June 10, 2015. Walter Dean Myers discusses *Monster*.

37

❖ ❖ ❖

One Fat Summer

BY ROBERT LIPSYTE

New York: HarperCollins, 1977
HarperCollins Paperback, 2004
HarperCollins E-book, 2010

> "I was tall for my age and I had large, heavy bones,
> so I didn't look like a circus freak. Just like a very fat boy."

CHALLENGES: WHEN, WHY, AND WHERE

2004–2005

The novel was banned in the Ansonia, Connecticut, public library, middle schools, and from summer reading lists after a parent complained about the scene that describes the "masturbation fantasy of a teenage boy."

1999–2000

The novel was banned at the Rock Crusher Elementary School in Crystal River, Florida, after a parent complained about the "derogatory terms for African-Americans, Jews, and Italians" and because of the implied "masturbation" scene.

1996–1997

The superintendent removed the novel from the required reading list at the Jonas E. Salk Middle School in Levittown, New York, because it was "sexually explicit and full of violence."

It was also challenged but retained in a middle school in Greenville, South Carolina, because of the passage that implies "masturbation."

THE STORY

Bobby Marks, an overweight fourteen-year-old, spends the summers with his family at Rumson Lake, where many of the town residents resent the affluent summer folks. Bobby's only hope for enjoying the summer is working on a school project with his best friend, Joanie. When she returns to the city without a hint of an explanation, Bobby is at loose ends. His father thinks he should work at a local day camp, but Bobby has no interest in spending the summer with bratty kids or putting himself in the position of being teased about his weight. He secretly takes a job as Dr. Kahn's yard boy. It turns out that Dr. Kahn is difficult and bullies Bobby into working harder.

To Bobby's surprise, he begins losing weight and gains the self-confidence to face off with Willie Rumson, the town bully. Bobby's journey toward manhood continues in *Summer Rules* (1981) and *The Summerboy* (1982).

Themes
❖ Bullying
❖ Courage
❖ Family
❖ Friendship
❖ Secrets
❖ Self-discovery
❖ Sex and sexuality

TALKING WITH TEENS ABOUT THE ISSUES

Describe Bobby Marks. What do Bobby and Joanie have in common? Why is he devastated by her secret?

Explain why Bobby keeps his job a secret. Some adults may find this "secrecy" troubling. Why is it important for Bobby to have this experience without interference from his parents? How might they hamper his success?

Discuss why Bobby hates the idea of spending the summer at Rumson Lake. How does his view change by the end of the novel?

Identify the bullies in the novel. How do their ways of bullying differ? Discuss how Bobby learns to deal with each of the bullies.

The novel has been challenged because of violence. How does the underwater fight between Bobby and Willie Rumson contribute to Bobby's growth as a character? Discuss the best way to explain this scene to a person who only sees it as a "violent" act.

Discuss the racial and ethnic slurs in the novel. What do these slurs say about the characters who use them?

Identify the scene that some have called "too sexually explicit." The scene isn't graphic and simply implies masturbation. How is this a normal act for a fourteen-year-old boy?

The novel has been banned in an elementary school in Florida. Discuss why a coming-of-age novel is more appropriate for adolescents.

CHALLENGED FOR SIMILAR REASONS

Going, K. L. *Fat Kid Rules the World*. New York: Putnam, an imprint of Penguin, 2003.

In 2007–2008, this book about an extremely overweight seventeen-year-old who is contemplating suicide when he is asked to be the drummer in a band was banned from the Pickens County, South Carolina, middle and high schools because of "language, sexual references and drug use."

Lynch, Chris. *Extreme Elvin*. New York: HarperCollins, 1999.

In this sequel to *Slot Machine*, overweight Elvin Bishop is now in high school and worries about bullies, girls, and not fitting into the crowd. It was removed from the Crawford County, Georgia, middle school in 2003 because "it deals with complex issues teenagers confront."

RESOURCES FOR RESPONDING TO CHALLENGES

What Reviewers Say

Kirkus (April 1, 1977) says that readers are "bound to like this fat boy right from the start." *School Library Journal* (March 1977) is lukewarm about the novel and states, "Bobby's self-absorption grows tiresome." A young adult reader on *Goodreads* (January 30, 2015) gives the novel five stars and says, "Great characters, great scenarios, and a great back story." An adult reader on *Goodreads* (July 10, 2010) says, "Highly recommended for fat and skinny readers." *Booklist* (April 1977) says the book is "smoothly written." The *New York Times* (July 10, 1977) says, "Bobby's metamorphosis is effectively rendered." Zena Sutherland, the reviewer for *Bulletin for the Center of Children's Books* (July/August 1977), comments, "The plot elements are nicely balanced and paced."

Other Justification for Inclusion in Curricula and Library Collections

- 1977 ALA/YALSA Best Fiction for Young Adults
- 1977 *New York Times* Outstanding Children's Book of the Year Citation
- 1970–1987 ALA/YALSA Best of the Best Fiction for Young Adults

Sources of Information about Challenges to the Novel

Behrendt, Barbara. "Grade School Bans Books." *St. Petersburg Times*, October 26, 1999. Accessed June 17, 2015. http://www.sptimes.com/News/102699/Citrus/Grade_school_bans_boo.shtml.

Bertin, Joan. "Don't Cave in to the Book Banners." National Coalition against Censorship, June 13, 1997. Accessed June 17, 2015. http://ncac.org/censorship-article/dont-cave-in-to-the-book-banners/.

Vinciguerra, Thomas. "A 1977 Comes under Scrutiny." *New York Times*, June 8, 1997. Accessed June 16, 2015. http://www.nytimes.com/1997/06/08/nyregion/a-1977-comes-under-scrutiny.html.

INFORMATION ABOUT THE AUTHOR

http://www.robertlipsyte.com/index.htm (Lipsyte's official website)
Contemporary Authors Online, 2009. Books and Authors. Gale.
Cart, Michael. *Presenting Robert Lipsyte*. Young Adult Authors Series, Volume 649. Farmington Hills, MI: Cengage Gale, 1995.
Scales, Pat R. "Robert Lipsyte." *Book Links* 15, issue 6 (July 2006): 40–41.

FURTHER READING ABOUT THE NOVEL

Feldman, Sari. "Up the Stairs Alone: Robert Lipsyte on Writing for Young Adults." *Top of the News* 39, issue 2 (1983): 198–202.

Kenny, Kevin. "An Interview with Robert Lipsyte." *Voice of Youth Advocates* 8 (December 1985): 303–305.

Lipsyte, Robert. "The 2001 Margaret A. Edwards Award Acceptance Speech." *Journal of Youth Services in Libraries* 14, issue 4 (Summer 2001): 21–23.

"*One Fat Summer* by Robert Lipsyte." *Adolescent Literature* (blog), July 30, 2008. Accessed June 23, 2015. http://readingbloggingarithmetic.blogspot.com/2008/07/one-fat-summer-by-robert-lipsyte.html.

Scales, Pat. "Robert Lipsyte's Summer Trilogy." *Book Links* 8, issue 1 (September 1998): 30–33.

OTHER MEDIA SOURCES

https://www.youtube.com/watch?v=6TOqJK1tWGI. Posted July 18, 2010. Accessed July 2, 2015. This is a student-created animated video on *One Fat Summer*.

38

❖ ❖ ❖

The Perks of Being a Wallflower

BY STEPHEN CHBOSKY

New York: MTV, a division of Simon & Schuster, 1999
Simon & Schuster, Limited E-book, 2012
Recorded Books Audio, 2012

> "So, this is my life. And I want you to know that I am both happy and sad
> and I'm still trying to figure out how that could be."

CHALLENGES: WHEN, WHY, AND WHERE

According to data collected by the American Library Association's Office for Intellectual Freedom, the novel was #8 on the Top Ten Most Frequently Challenged Books List in 2013–2014; #8 in 2012–2013; #3 in 2008–2009; #6 in 2007–2008; #6 in 2006–2007; #8 in 2005–2006; and #5 in 2003–2004. It was #10 on the Top 100 Banned/Challenged Books List in the decade 2000–2009. The reasons cited include "drugs/alcohol/smoking; sexually explicit; offensive language; and unsuited to age group."

2014–2015

In Wallingford, Connecticut, a parent asked that the novel be removed from the freshman curriculum because of "glorification of alcohol use and drugs." The review committee voted to retain the book, but the superintendent of schools overrode the decision and banned its use.

2013–2014

The novel was challenged after it was placed on a summer reading list for freshmen at Wharton High School in Tampa, Florida, because of the "sexual content and drug use."

2012–2013

A long-term substitute teacher used the novel with freshmen at the Grandview Heights High School in Grandview Heights, Ohio, and sparked a volatile battle because of the "pornographic" content, which resulted in the superintendent of schools promising to "revamp" the way novels are selected for the classroom.

Parents of an eighth-grader at Hadley Junior High School in Glen Ellyn, Illinois, asked that the novel be removed from the classroom and the library because of "sexual content" and "inappropriate language." After students lobbied the school board, the book was reinstated.

2010–2011

A parent of a junior at Clarkstown North High School in New York challenged the novel because of "graphic teenage sex, homosexuality, and bestiality." They felt it inappropriate for the curriculum. The student was offered a substitute title.

2009–2010

The novel was challenged at the West Bend Community Memorial Library in West Bend, Wisconsin, because it was deemed too "obscene" for "Young Adults." The board voted to retain the book, ending a campaign by West Bend Citizens for Safe Libraries to move "sexually explicit" books to the adult section of the library.

Parents of a student at William Byrd High School in Roanoke County, Virginia, challenged the novel because of its "graphic" content. The committee voted to retain the book, but restricted it to juniors and seniors in all Roanoke County high schools. Freshmen and sophomores must have parental permission to borrow the book.

2008–2009

The novel was removed from classrooms at the Portage High School in Portage, Indiana, because of "homosexuality, drug use, and sexual behavior."

2007–2008

Parents challenged the choice to include the novel on the summer reading list at the Commack High School in New York because of a "two-page date rape scene."

2006–2007

According to the Texas American Civil Liberties Union, the novel was banned at the high school in the Woodville Independent School District after a parent requested a review because her daughter, a freshman, was offended by the "sexual content."

The novel was challenged but retained at the Northwest Suburban High School District in Illinois because of "references to masturbation, homosexuality, and bestiality."

2004–2005

After the book was challenged by the grandmother of an elementary school student in Apache Junction, Arizona, the Arizona superintendent of schools sent a letter advising that the book would no longer be available to any student in any Arizona public school because of "sexual references."

2003–2004

The novel was removed from the reading list of an elective sociology class at the Massapequa High School in New York because it's "offensive."

2002–2003

An organized group called Parents against Bad Books in Schools (PABBIS) in Fairfax County, Virginia, challenged the book because of "profanity and descriptions of drug abuse, sexually explicit conduct, and torture."

THE STORY

Written in a series of letters by fifteen-year-old Charlie to an unknown "friend" as he embarks on his freshman year in high school, this coming-of-age novel explores the angst of a teenage loner who does not fit the mold of a typical high school student. Then Charlie meets Sam and Patrick, two seniors who are stepsiblings, at a football game, and the three become friends. Charlie develops a crush on Sam, but he is inexperienced with issues related to first love. He is an excellent observer, and watches his sister fall for a boy who abuses her. He even looks on as they engage in sex. When she gets pregnant, it is Charlie who takes her to get an abortion. Charlie's social education continues when he attends a party where there are drugs and alcohol, loose sexual encounters between girls and boys, and Patrick and another boy. Though he continues to attend parties with Patrick, Sam, and Mary Elizabeth, his girlfriend for a short amount of time, he continues to appear lonely and out of touch with most of his classmates. He does receive encouragement from Bill, a first-year teacher who recognizes that Charlie is a gifted writer. He even learns from Bill that there are understanding adults who can be trusted. Still, Charlie is unstable and lands in the hospital for several months, where he finally reveals to a psychiatrist that his Aunt Helen, now deceased, had molested him for many years. The hospitalization helps him confront his "tomorrows" and gives him the courage to fully engage in his high school years going forward.

Themes
❖ Coming of age
❖ Depression
❖ Eating disorders
❖ Family
❖ Friendship
❖ Self-identity
❖ Sexuality
❖ Suicide

TALKING WITH TEENS ABOUT THE ISSUES

Define the term *wallflower*. How does *wallflower* connote "loneliness" and "awkwardness"? What might Charlie say are the perks of being a "wallflower"?

Describe the friendship that develops between Charlie, Sam, Patrick, and Mary Elizabeth. What is their influence on him? Why do you think they bring Charlie into their group?

Discuss the structure of the novel. How are the letters an effective way of peeling away Charlie's emotional issues?

The novel has been challenged and banned because of language and sexual content. How is this typical of the social scene in high schools? Explain why Charlie is happy to have a peer group but uncomfortable with some of the activities that he witnesses.

There are elements of hope in the novel. How is Bill a symbol of hope for Charlie?

Charlie is clearly suffering from trauma. The reader doesn't understand what that trauma is until the end of the novel. How does this early life trauma explain his awkwardness?

Charlie winds up in a psychiatric hospital, where he finally is able to talk about his Aunt Helen and the years that she molested him. How is his time in the hospital a symbol of hope? How might this hope be explained to those who want to censor the novel?

Why is this considered a coming-of-age novel? How does coming of age almost always involve a journey, often filled with positive and negative influences? Explain why adults are so uncomfortable with coming-of-age themes.

The book has been called "obscene" by parents who didn't want their teens to read it. Explain how the graphic content is necessary to Charlie's story. One parent who challenged the book objected to "bestiality." What scene is this parent referencing?

The book was challenged in an elementary school in Arizona. What is the appropriate age for the book? Why is it difficult to defend the book for elementary-age students? This challenge prompted the Arizona superintendent of schools to ban the book in all Arizona public schools. Make a case for including the book in high school libraries and the English curriculum.

CHALLENGED FOR SIMILAR REASONS

Korman, Gordon. *Jake Reinvented*. New York: Disney-Hyperion, 2005.

This novel about a mysterious jock who disrupts the social culture at his new high school when he eyes the girlfriend of a popular football player was challenged in 2007–2008 in the Higley Unified School District in Gilbert, Arizona, because of "teen drinking, sex, and violence."

Salinger, J. D. *The Catcher in the Rye*. New York: Little, Brown, 1951.

Though published as an adult book, this coming-of-age novel has been adopted by young adult readers and has been challenged in school and public libraries across the nation because it is deemed "filthy" and "undermines morality." The most recent recorded challenge was in 2009 at the Big Sky High School in Missoula, Montana.

RESOURCES FOR RESPONDING TO CHALLENGES

What Reviewers Say

School Library Journal (June 1, 1999) recommends the novel for grades 9 and up and says, "An epistolary narrative clearly places readers in the role of Charlie's unfolding story." The reviewer for *Booklist* (February 15, 1999) states that the author captures "adolescent angst, confusion, and joy." *Voice of Youth Advocates* (December 1, 1999) comments, "The novel has the disjointed and almost a dreamlike quality of a music video." *Kirkus* (January 15, 1999) says the novel has "an upbeat ending to a tale of teenaged angst."

Other Justification for Inclusion in Curricula and Library Collections

❖ 2000 ALA/YALSA Best Books for Young Adults
❖ 2000 ALA/YALSA Quick Picks for Reluctant Young Adult Readers

Sources of Information about Challenges to the Novel

Donato, Claire. "Wish You Were Here: The Perks of Being Banned." Pen America, August 25, 2013. Accessed June 6, 2015. http://www.pen.org/nonfiction/wish-you-were-here-perks-being-banned.

Gomez, Betsy. "Author Responds to Connecticut Ban of *The Perks of Being a Wallflower*." Comic Book Legal Defense Fund, April 3, 2015. Accessed June 6, 2015. http://cbldf.org/2015/04/author-responds-to-connecticut-ban-of/.

O'Connor, Acacia. "The Perks of Being a Reader: Kids Fight and Win Book Battle in Glen Ellyn." *ILA Reporter* 31, issue 4 (August 2013): 4–7.

Truong, Quan. "Glen Ellyn D41 Removes *Perks of Being a Wallflower* from School Shelves." *Chicago Tribune*, May 13, 2013. Accessed June 6, 2015. http://articles.chicagotribune.com/2013-05-13/news/ct-tl-glen-ellyn-d41-book-ban-20130510_1_reconsideration-committee-wallflower-stephen-chbosky.

Vo, Eric. "'Do I Want My Book Banned? No,' *Perks of Being a Wallflower* Author Says after Wallingford Book Controversy." Associated Press, April 12, 2015. Accessed June 6, 2015. http://www.nbcconnecticut.com/news/local/Do-I-Want-My-Book-Banned-No-Perks-of-Being-a-Wallflower-Author-Says-After-Wallingford-Book-Controversy-299494901.html.

INFORMATION ABOUT THE AUTHOR

https://twitter.com/stephenchbosky (Chobosky on Twitter)
Contemporary Authors Online, 2012. Books and Authors. Gale.

FURTHER READING ABOUT THE NOVEL

Beckerman, Marty. "An Interview with Stephen Chbosky." *Word Riot* (blog). Accessed June 6, 2015. http://www.wordriot.org/template.php?ID=552.

Beisch, Ann. "Interview with Stephen Chbosky, Author of *The Perks of Being a Wallflower*." *LA Youth* (November/December 2001). Accessed June 6, 2015. http://www.layouth.com/interview-with-stephen-chbosky-author-of-the-perks-of-being-a-wallflower/.

Matos, Angel Daniel. "Growth and Development in Stephen Chobsky's *The Perks of Being a Wallflower*." *The Ever and Ever That Fiction Allows* (blog), October 14, 2012. Accessed June 6, 2015. http://angelmatos.net/2012/10/14/stephen-chboskys-the-perks-of-being-a-wallflower/.

Thomas, P. L. "Challenging Texts." *English Journal* 99, issue 3 (January 2010): 76–79.

OTHER MEDIA SOURCES

https://www.youtube.com/watch?v=n5rh7O4IDc0. Posted June 4, 2012. Accessed August 21, 2015. This is the official movie trailer of the full-feature film based on the novel that was released in theaters in the United States in September 2012 by Summit Entertainment.

https://www.youtube.com/watch?v=dVL1zjzJatw. Posted September 29, 2012. Accessed June 6, 2015. Stephen Chbosky reads for the American Library Association's Banned Books Week Virtual Read-Out.

https://www.youtube.com/watch?v=3Vqkc5BPEMc. Posted October 16, 2012. Accessed June 6, 2015. Stephen Chbosky talks about his novel being banned.

39

❖ ❖ ❖

Persepolis: The Story of a Childhood

BY MARJANE SATRAPI

New York: Knopf Doubleday, an imprint of Random House, 2003
Knopf Doubleday Paperback, 2004

"You are a free woman. The Iran of today is not for you. I forbid you to come back."

CHALLENGES: WHEN, WHY, AND WHERE

This work of nonfiction was #2 on the American Library Association's Top Ten Most Frequently Challenged Books List in 2014–2015.

2014–2015

According to the National Council of Teachers of English, the novel was challenged in the tenth-grade curriculum in North Carolina. The outcome of the case is unknown.

It was also challenged in the Three Rivers School District in Murphy, Oregon, because of "objectionable language and torture."

It was challenged but retained on the reading list at Glenwood High School in Chatham, Illinois. A parent objected to "images of dismembered bodies and a guard using urine as torture."

The book was also challenged by a student enrolled in a graphic novel class at Crafton Hills College in Yucaipa, California. She labeled the book, along with four other titles, "pornography" and "garbage." A college administrator defended its use and academic freedom.

2013–2014

A parent requested that the book be removed from the high school curriculum in Smithville, Texas, because of the Islamic culture. The book was retained.

2012–2013

The novel was banned from classrooms and libraries in Chicago's public schools because of "graphic illustrations and language" and concerns about "developmental preparedness." The ban later only applied to "general use in the seventh-grade curriculum." Students protested the challenge on social media.

THE STORY

This autobiography chronicles Marji Satrapi's life in Iran during the Islamic revolution between Iran and Iraq. Her story begins in 1980 when she was only ten years old and required to wear a veil and attend schools that were segregated by gender. Flashbacks reveal that her family is a modern family, and Satrapi does not understand the "old" Islamic practices that she is required to follow. Even as young as six, she declared that she would become a prophet and change the inequities in her country, especially for girls and women. After the Ayatollah Khomeini became the leader of the Islamic Republic, life became even more difficult for Satrapi's family and friends, driving some to seek refuge in the United States and Europe. Her Uncle Anoosh tries to reassure them that things will get better, but he is soon arrested and executed as a Russian spy. There is destruction all around her family's home, and Marji is sickened when she learns of the demise of a neighbor's daughter. This political violence propels her to become more of a rebel, which frightens her family. In 1994, Marji's mother insists that her daughter go to Europe, where she can live as a free woman. In *Persepolis 2: The Story of a Return* (2004), Satrapi graduates school in Vienna and goes back to Iran, where she discovers just how much she has changed and wonders if she can ever live in the country of her birth.

Themes
- ❖ Censorship
- ❖ Coming of age
- ❖ Family
- ❖ Fear
- ❖ Freedom
- ❖ Gender inequality
- ❖ Religious practices
- ❖ Revolution

TALKING WITH TEENS ABOUT THE ISSUES

Contrast Satrapi's family with other Iranian families. How is Marji wise beyond her years? Discuss her family's role in shaping her views.

Explain the last quote in the book, "Freedom had a price." What was the price that Satrapi paid?

How is the book about censorship? Explain the irony in banning it from students.

Satrapi's story is autobiographical, but is in the format of a graphic novel. Why are images more troubling than text for some people?

The book has been challenged because of torture. Students in Chicago defended the book by saying the torture in the book is similar to other images they see while studying the Holocaust or slavery. Debate the students' defense.

Discuss whether censors are reacting to the book because of prejudices toward the Middle East and the Muslim culture. Why is it important that Americans understand the Islamic religion and culture?

CHALLENGED FOR SIMILAR REASONS

Hernandez, Gilbert. *Palomar: The Heartbreak Soup Stories.* Seattle, WA: Fantagraphics Books, 2003. In 2015, this graphic novel about the lives of the inhabitants of a small Central American town was challenged at the high school in Rio Rancho, New Mexico, because of "sexual and graphic passages." The review committee successfully defended the book, but there is indication that parental permission may be required for students under the age of eighteen.

Spiegelman, Art. *The Complete Maus.* New York: Knopf Doubleday, an imprint of Random House, 1996.

According to the Comic Book Legal Defense Fund, this graphic novel about Spiegelman's father, a Polish Holocaust survivor, was challenged at the Pasadena, California, Public Library because it made a Polish American patron uncomfortable.

RESOURCES FOR RESPONDING TO CHALLENGES

What Reviewers Say

School Library Journal (August 1, 2003) recommends the novel for adults and high school students and comments on its "immense power and importance for Westerners." *Publishers Weekly* (July 14, 2003) gives the novel a starred review and says, "Satrapi never lapses into sensationalism or sentimentality." *Library Journal* (May 1, 2003) stars the book and calls it an "extraordinary autobiography."

Other Justification for Inclusion in Curricula and Library Collections

Persepolis: The Story of a Childhood

- 2007 ALA/YALSA Popular Paperbacks for Young Adults: I'm Not Making This Up
- 2004 ALA/YALSA Best Books for Young Adults
- 2004 ALA/YALSA Outstanding Books for the College Bound: Literature and Language Arts
- 2004 Alex Award
- 2004 Amelia Bloomer Lists: Young Adult Nonfiction
- 2003 *Booklist* Editors' Choice: Adult Nonfiction for Young Adults
- 2003 *Library Journal* Best Books
- 2003 *New York Times* Notable Books: Nonfiction
- 2003 *School Library Journal's* Adult Books for High School Students
- 2003 *Time Magazine* Best Books of the Year

Persepolis 2: The Story of a Return

- 2013 ALA/YALSA Popular Paperbacks for Young Adults: I'm New Here Myself
- 2005 ALA/YALSA Best Books for Young Adults
- 2005 Ignatz Awards: Outstanding Graphic Novel
- 2004 *Library Journal's* Best Books
- 2004 *School Library Journal's* Adult Books for High School Students

Sources of Information about Challenges to the Novel

"Case Study: *Persepolis*." Comic Book Legal Defense Fund. Accessed October 13, 2015. http:// cbldf.org/banned-comic/banned-challenged-comics/case-study-persepolis/.

"CPS *Persepolis* Ban? Marjane Satrapi's Graphic Novel Inappropriate for 7th Graders, District Says." *Huffington Post*, March 15, 2013. Accessed October 15, 2015. http://www.huffington post.com/2013/03/15/cps-persepolis-ban_n_2883999.html.

Souppouris, Aaron. "Chicago Bans *Persepolis* Graphic Novel from Seventh-Grade Classroom." The Verge, March 25, 2013. Accessed October 13, 2015. http://www.theverge.com/2013/3/25/4144958/chicago-public-schools-bans-persepolis-graphic-novel-from-schools.

Williams, Maren. "Grad Student Uncovers Truth about *Persepolis* Ban in Chicago Public Schools." Comic Book Legal Defense Fund, February 19, 2015. Accessed September 11, 2015. http://cbldf.org/2015/02/grad-student-uncovers-truth-about-persepolis-ban-in-chicago-public-schools/.

INFORMATION ABOUT THE AUTHOR

Contemporary Authors Online, 2008. Books and Authors. Gale.

FURTHER READING ABOUT THE NOVEL

Botshon, Lisa, and Melinda Plastas. "Homeland In/Security: A Discussion and Workshop on Teaching Marjane Satrapi's *Persepolis*." *Feminist Teacher* 20, issue 1 (2009): 1–14.

Chute, Hillary. "The Texture of Retracing in Marjane Satrapi's *Persepolis*." *Women's Studies Quarterly* 36, issue 1–2 (2008): 92–110.

Darda, Joseph. "Graphic Ethics: Theorizing the Face in Marjane Satrapi's *Persepolis*." *College Literature* 40, issue 2 (Spring 2013): 31–51.

Kaplan, Arie. "Marjane Satrapi." In *Masters of the Comic Book Universe Revealed!* by Arie Kaplan, 235–252. Chicago: Chicago Review Press, 2006.

Lopamudra, Basu. "Crossing Cultures/Crossing Genres: The Re-invention of the Graphic Memoir in *Persepolis* and *Persepolis 2*." *Children's Literature Review* 4, issue 3 (September 2007): 1–19.

Malek, Amy. "Memoir as Iranian Exile Cultural Production: A Case Study of Marjane Satrapi's *Persepolis* Series." *Iranian Studies* 39, issue 3 (September 2006): 353–380.

Naghibi, Nima, and Andrew O'Malley. "Estranging the Familiar: 'East' and 'West' in Satrapi's *Persepolis*." *English Studies in Canada* 31, issue 2–3 (June 2005): 223–247.

Satrapi, Marjane. "Why I Wrote *Persepolis*." *Writing* 26, issue 3 (November/December 2003): 9–11.

OTHER MEDIA SOURCES

https://www.youtube.com/watch?v=v9onZpQix_w. Posted September 19, 2010. Accessed October 13, 2015. This is an interview with Marjane Satrapi.

https://www.youtube.com/watch?v=KNgLkDZVdOY. Posted March 29, 2013. Accessed October 13, 2015. This is a news story about the banning of *Persepolis* in the Chicago Public Schools.

https://www.youtube.com/watch?v=yN2EywlBHJE. Posted October 1, 2015. Accessed October 13, 2015. A reader shares her views of *Persepolis* for Banned Books Week.

40

❖ ❖ ❖

Push

BY SAPPHIRE (RAMONA LOFTON)

New York: Knopf, an imprint of Random House, 1996
Knopf Paperback, 1997

"How is something a memory if you never forget? But I push it to the corner of my brain."

CHALLENGES: WHEN, WHY, AND WHERE

2011–2012

The book was on the extracurricular reading list for middle school students in Horry County, South Carolina, and was banned after parents complained about the "sexual content."

2004–2005

A parent in Fayetteville, Arkansas, challenged the novel because of the "sexual content." She promised to challenge every book that she believes "could be pornographic."

THE STORY

Set in Harlem, sixteen-year-old Precious Jones is obese, illiterate, and brutally abused by her mother. She is repeatedly raped by her father, which results in two pregnancies. Her regular school thinks that she would be better off at an alternative school called Each One Teach One, but her mother only wants her to forget school and apply for welfare. Precious is reluctant about the new school, but once there she meets five other troubled girls and Ms. Blue Rain, an amazing pre-GED teacher who happens to be a lesbian. Ms. Rain believes in her students, and she instills a love of literature and writing in them. She encourages them to write every day, and then she collects their stories and creates a class anthology titled "Life Stories—Our Class Book." Things are going well at school for Precious, but life with her mother is tough. When her mother kicks her out of the house, Ms. Rain steps in and finds a shelter for Precious that has daycare for her two children. Then Precious learns that her father has died of AIDS, and she is HIV positive. She is relieved to learn that her children are not. Rita, one of her friends from school, convinces her that she needs to join support groups for HIV and incest victims.

Themes
❖ Abuse
❖ Coping
❖ Courage
❖ Racial prejudice

❖ Self-image
❖ Sex abuse
❖ Survival
❖ Value of education

TALKING WITH TEENS ABOUT THE ISSUES

Explain how Precious Jones's life seems hopeless. How does Ms. Rain give her hope?

Precious Jones writes her story in the first person. How does the writing improve as Precious becomes more literate? Discuss the open ending of the novel. How does this symbolize an unknown future for Precious?

Read a synopsis of *The Color Purple* by Alice Walker, and discuss why Precious is so moved by this novel.

Rita, a friend at school, encourages Precious to attend support groups for HIV positive and incest victims. Find out where in your community teens like Precious Jones could go for help.

The novel has been challenged because of sexual content. Explain why adults have such a problem with talking about these very real issues.

Not all readers relate to this novel. Discuss why it is important to read novels like *Push* to develop empathy. How might this be explained to those who want to censor the novel?

CHALLENGED FOR SIMILAR REASONS

Angelou, Maya. *I Know Why the Caged Bird Sings*. New York: Random House, 1969.

The first recorded challenge to this autobiography about a life of racism, rape, and homelessness was in Alabama in 1983. In 2009–2010, it was challenged in the Newman–Crows Landing Unified School District in California because a school board member questioned whether the English Department faculty at the high school was qualified to teach a book about "African American culture."

Hopkins, Ellen. *Identical*. New York: Margaret K. McElderry Books, an imprint of Simon & Schuster, 2008.

Sixteen-year-old Kaeleigh and her identical twin, Raeanne, struggle in a dysfunctional, affluent family, but Kaeleigh is sexually abused by her father. The sexual content caused a parent in Middletown, Delaware, to challenge the book in 2014–2015.

Mazer, Norma Fox. *Silver*. New York: William Morrow, an imprint of HarperCollins, 1988.

In 2001–2002, this novel about fourteen-year-old Sarabeth Silver, who learns that one girl in her affluent school is being sexually abused by her uncle, was restricted at the middle school in the Pleasant Grove, Texas, Independent School District because it was deemed "inappropriate for age group."

RESOURCES FOR RESPONDING TO CHALLENGES

What Reviewers Say

Publishers Weekly (April 22, 1996) states that Precious is a "remarkable heroine." *Library Journal* (June 1, 1996) calls the novel "compelling, graphic." *Booklist* (May 1, 1996) says, "*Push* is an intense work, both heartbreaking and frightening." *Kirkus* (May 15, 1996) says that the novel speaks to the "value of recovery groups."

Other Justification for Inclusion in Curricula and Library Collections

❖ 2010 ALA/YALSA Popular Paperbacks for Young Adults: Hard Knock Life
❖ 2004 ALA/YALSA Outstanding Books for the College Bound: Literature and Language Arts
❖ 1997 ALA/Black Caucus Award: First Novelist Category

Sources of Information about Challenges to the Novel

"*Push*, by Sapphire." *The "C" Word* (blog), March 2, 2011. Accessed November 23, 2015. http://censorshipdown.blogspot.com/2011/03/push-by-sapphire.html.

"School District Pulls Book from Schools after Parents Complain." WMBF News (Myrtle Beach, South Carolina). Posted February 28, 2011. Accessed November 23, 2015. http://www.wmbf news.com/story/14159491/school-district-pulls-book-from-schools-after-parent-complaints.

INFORMATION ABOUT THE AUTHOR

Contemporary Authors Online, 2011. Books and Authors. Gale.
Contemporary Black Biography. Volume 14, 1997. Gale.

FURTHER READING ABOUT THE NOVEL

Dagbovie-Mullins, Sika A. "From Living to Eat to Writing to Live: Metaphors of Consumption and Production in Sapphire's *Push*." *African American Review* 44, issue 3 (Fall 2011): 435–452.

Hester Williams, Kim D. "'Fix My Life': Oprah, Post-racial Economic Dispossession, and the Precious Transfiguration of *Push*." *Cultural Dynamics* 26, issue 1 (March 2014): 53–71.

Hillsburg, Heather. "Compassionate Readership: Anger and Suffering in Sapphire's *Push*." *Canadian Review of American Studies* 44, issue 1 (2014): 122–147.

Jarman, Michelle. "Cultural Consumption and Rejection of Precious Jones: Pushing Disability into the Discussion of Sapphire's *Push* and Lee Daniels's *Precious*." *Feminist Formations* 24, issue 2 (Summer 2012): 163–185.

Kokkola, Lydia. "Learning to Read Politically: Narratives of Hope and Narratives of Despair in *Push* by Sapphire." *Cambridge Journal of Education* 46, issue 1 (Spring 2013): 55–69.

Rountree, Wendy A. "Overcoming Violence: Blues Expression in Sapphire's *Push*." *Atenea* 24, issue 1 (June 2004): 133–143.

Wilson, Marq. "'A Push out of Chaos': An Interview with Sapphire." *MELUS* 37, issue 4 (Winter 2012): 31–39.

OTHER MEDIA SOURCES

https://www.youtube.com/watch?v=Hj5gbFecRFw. Posted November 9, 2009. Accessed November 24, 2015. Sapphire talks about writing *Push*.

https://www.youtube.com/watch?v=GkXb0ygjC_o. Posted November 24, 2015. Accessed November 24, 2015. This is a reading, summary, and discussion of *Push* at the Boston Public Library.

41

❖ ❖ ❖

Rainbow Boys

BY ALEX SANCHEZ

New York: Simon & Schuster, 2001
Simon & Schuster E-book, 2001
Simon & Schuster Paperback, 2003

"Not every gay teenager has a mom like mine.
Most teens don't. Most aren't even out to
their parents, or anyone else. There's a reason for that.
As you just heard, it's dangerous being gay."

CHALLENGES: WHEN, WHY, AND WHERE

According to data collected by the American Library Association's Office for Intellectual Freedom, the novel ranked #48 on the Top 100 Banned/Challenged Books List of 2000–2009.

2007–2008

The novel was removed from the high school summer reading list, but later reinstated, in the Webster, New York, School District.

The novel was challenged, along with other gay-themed titles, at the St. Louis County, Missouri, library. The outcome of the case is unknown.

2005–2006

The Texas American Civil Liberties Union reports that the parents of a seventh-grader challenged the novel at the IDEA College Prep School in IDEA Public Schools because of "sexual content." A committee reviewed the book and restricted the book to students below ninth grade.

The novel was challenged, along with fifty other books, in Fayetteville, Arkansas, because of "sexual content" and a "homosexual agenda."

2004–2005

The novel was challenged, along with fifteen other young adult novels, in the Montgomery County, Texas, Independent School District because of the "gay positive theme."

It was also challenged but retained in high school libraries in the Owen-Withee School District in Owen, Wisconsin, after a complaint about the "sexual content."

THE STORY

Jason Carrillo, a senior jock on the basketball team at Whitman High School, has a steady girl-friend, but he questions his sexuality and attends a support group for gay teens. He is surprised to see classmates Kyle Meeks and Nelson Glassman at the meeting. Kyle has slowly come to terms with his sexuality, but Nelson has been openly gay for a very long time. Kyle and Nelson are good friends and fall victim to name-calling and other forms of bullying from homophobic students. When they ask to start a Gay-Straight Alliance at Whitman, they face opposition from a number of people in the community. A school board meeting is held to address the issue, and Nelson's mother, who has always known that her son is gay, makes a passionate speech. The school board allows the alliance, but in the meantime, Nelson goes on a search for a boyfriend since Jason and Kyle have become a couple. He has unprotected sex and now must worry if has contracted AIDS. *Rainbow High* (2005) and *Rainbow Road* (2005) continue the boys' stories as they find love and position in life.

Themes
❖ Acceptance
❖ Bullying
❖ Family
❖ Friendship
❖ Sexual identity

TALKING WITH TEENS ABOUT THE ISSUES

Discuss Jason Carrillo's attitude toward Nelson Glassman at the beginning of the novel. Why do you think he turned away when other students bullied Nelson?

Nelson's mother is very accepting of her son's sexuality. How do Kyle's parents react when they learn that he is gay? Contrast the way Jason's mother and father deal with the news that he is gay.

Define homophobia. Discuss why the school administration allowed such homophobic bullying to take place.

What is the purpose of the Gay-Straight Alliance that Nelson and Kyle start? Why is it important for all high schools to consider such an organization?

The novel has been challenged because of the gay theme. How might Mrs. Glassman's speech before the school board resonate with adults who want to censor the book?

CHALLENGED FOR SIMILAR REASONS

Cart, Michael. *My Father's Scar*. New York: Simon & Schuster, 1996.

In 2004–2005, this novel about an adult who flashes back to his adolescence as he comes to terms with his homosexuality was challenged at the Montgomery County Memorial Library, along with fifteen other titles, because of "gay-positive themes."

Kerr, M. E. *"Hello," I Lied*. New York: HarperCollins, 1997. Open Road Media E-book, 2013.

This novel about a gay teenager was banned at the Brenham Middle School in the Brenham, Texas, Independent School District because of the "homosexual content."

RESOURCES FOR RESPONDING TO CHALLENGES

What Reviewers Say

Publishers Weekly (November 26, 2001) recommends the novel for ages twelve and up and calls it "believable and touching." *School Library Journal* (October 2001) recommends it for grades 9 and up and says it is a "gutsy, in-your-face debut novel." Michael Cart, the reviewer for *Booklist* (November 15, 2001), praises the "realistic, right-in dialogue." He recommends it for grades 9–12.

Other Justification for Inclusion in Curricula and Library Collections

* 2003 IRA Young Adult Choices
* 2002 ALA/YALSA Best Books for Young Adults
* 2001 *Bulletin for the Center for Children's Books* Blue Ribbon Winner

Sources of Information about Challenges to the Novel

Loudon, Bennett J. "Author Decries Removal of Gay-Themed Book." *Rochester Democrat and Chronicle*, August 29, 2006. Accessed July 31, 2015. http://www.alexsanchez.com/banned_books/banned_book_1.html.

INFORMATION ABOUT THE AUTHOR

http://www.alexsanchez.com (Sanchez's official website)
Contemporary Authors Online, 2008. Books and Authors. Gale.
McCafferty, Dominique. "Love and Accept Yourself for Who You Are: An Interview with Alex Sanchez. *Young Adult Services* 4, issue 4 (Summer 2006): 10–12.

FURTHER READING ABOUT THE NOVEL

Crisp, Thomas. "The Trouble with Rainbow Boys." *Children's Literature in Education* 39, issue 4 (December 2008): 237–261.
Emert, Toby. "An Interview with Alex Sanchez, Author of *Rainbow Boys*." *ALAN Review* 30, issue 1 (Fall 2002): 12–14.
Sanchez, Alex. "Open Eyes and Change Lives: Narrative Resources Addressing Gay-Straight Themes." *English Journal* 94, issue 3 (January 2005): 46–48.

OTHER MEDIA SOURCES

https://www.youtube.com/watch?v=7D5WGv4JQEs. Posted July 14, 2015. Accessed July 31, 2015. Alex Sanchez speaks at the Queer Young Adult Literature Conference in Boulder, Colorado.
https://www.youtube.com/watch?v=hX6o-73M5zM. Posted April 2, 2012. Accessed July 31, 2015. A library school student book talks *Rainbow Boys*.

42

❖ ❖ ❖

Speak

BY LAURIE HALSE ANDERSON

New York: Farrar, Straus & Giroux, an imprint of Macmillan, 1999
Listening Library Audio, 2006
Squarefish Paperback, 2011
Farrar, Straus & Giroux E-book, 2011

"Is there a chain saw of the soul, an ax I can take to my memories or fears?"

CHALLENGES: WHEN, WHY, AND WHERE

According to data collected by the American Library Association's Office for Intellectual Freedom, *Speak* was #60 on the Top 100 Banned/Challenged Books List of 2000–2009. The challenges below represent only those that are public. Institutions of other challenges have asked to remain anonymous.

2012–2013

A parent challenged the novel in the eighth-grade language arts curriculum at Laurel Nokomis Middle School in Sarasota, Florida, because it is "pornography" and promotes "theft" and "promiscuity." A review committee was convened, and the book was retained.

The novel was challenged at the Junction High School in Junction, Texas, because of "profanity and sexual content." An alternative book was offered.

2010–2011

The novel was challenged in the Republic, Missouri, School District because it is "soft-pornography" and "glorifies drinking, cursing, and premarital sex."

2008–2009

The novel was banned at the Windsor Village Elementary School in the Houston Independent School District because of "profanity."

2002–2003

The Texas American Civil Liberties Union reports that the novel was banned from the C. T. Eddins Elementary School Library in the McKinney Independent School District because of "sexual content."

THE STORY

In the summer before her freshman year, Melinda Sordino and some of her friends attend a party where there are much older teens. There is underage drinking, and Andy Evans, who is older, a hunk, and one of the most popular students at Merryweather High School, rapes Melinda. She calls the cops but runs away before they arrive. Her friends refuse to talk to her, and she spends her ninth-grade year friendless. She slips into a deep depression and begins skipping school. Finally David Petrakis, her lab partner, encourages her to speak up. Word spreads about what Andy did to Melinda, and Rachel, Melinda's best friend until the summer party, dumps Andy before their prom date. Andy is so angry that he attacks Melinda in the janitor's closet, her hiding place at school. Melinda does eventually confide in her art teacher, and by the end of the year, her friends begin to rally behind her.

Themes

- ❖ Cliques
- ❖ Courage
- ❖ Depression
- ❖ Friendship
- ❖ Guilt
- ❖ Isolation
- ❖ Peer pressure
- ❖ Sexual assault
- ❖ Survival

TALKING WITH TEENS ABOUT THE ISSUES

Compare and contrast Merryweather High School to most high schools. How is Melinda's description of cliques accurate?

Melinda is reading *I Know Why the Caged Bird Sings* by Maya Angelou and *The Scarlet Letter* by Nathaniel Hawthorne. Compare Melinda's trauma with that of Maya Angelou and Hester Prynne, the main character in Hawthorne's novel.

What is symbolic about the tree on the cover of the novel?

The novel was called "soft porn" in Missouri. How does this label denounce sexual violence that girls and women face?

The novel has also been challenged because it "glorifies drinking." How is underage drinking a social issue in most high schools? Discuss how *Speak* might give students the voice to discuss this issue.

Melinda clearly didn't think that she could talk with her parents. She finally confides in her art teacher. How is it sometimes easier to talk with an adult other than your parents?

Discuss why "speaking up" and "speaking out" is more important than silence.

CHALLENGED FOR SIMILAR REASONS

Peck, Richard. *Are You in the House Alone?* New York: Viking, an imprint of Penguin, 1976.

The American Library Association's Office for Intellectual Freedom records a challenge to this novel about a girl who is raped, because it is "sexually explicit" and "inappropriate for age group." The institution asked to remain anonymous.

Summers, Courtney. *Some Girls Are*. New York: St. Martin's Press, 2009.

In 2015–2016, this novel about a high school girl who falls from the social ladder because of rumors about her and her best friend's boyfriend was removed from the freshman summer reading list at West Ashley High School in Charleston, South Carolina, because of "bullying, rape, and teenage drug use."

RESOURCES FOR RESPONDING TO CHALLENGES

What Reviewers Say

Horn Book Magazine (August 1, 1999) says, "Melinda's distinctive narrative employs imagery that is as unexpected as it is acute." *Publishers Weekly* (September 13, 1999) calls the book "a stunning first novel." The reviewer for *Voice of Youth Advocates* (December 1, 1999) comments on the "current slang, accurate portrayal of high school life, and engaging characters." *School Library Journal* (October 1, 1999) recommends the novel for grades 8 and up and says it is "a compelling book, with sharp crisp writing." *Booklist* (September 15, 1999) says, "Anderson perfectly captures the harsh conformity of high-school cliques." They recommend it for grades 8–12. *Kirkus* (September 15, 1999) states, "The plot is gripping and the characters are powerfully drawn."

Other Justification for Inclusion in Curricula and Library Collections

* 2012 ALA/YALSA Quick Picks for Reluctant Young Adult Readers
* 2004 ALA/YALSA Outstanding Books for the College Bound: Literature and Language Arts
* 2002 Garden State Book Award (New Jersey): Fiction: Grades 9–12
* 2002 Sequoyah Book Award (Oklahoma): Young Adult
* 2002 South Carolina Book Award: Young Adult
* 2001 Kentucky Bluegrass Award: Grades 9–12
* 2000 ALA/YALSA Michael L. Printz Honor Book
* 2000 ALA/YALSA Top Ten Best Books for Young Adults
* 2000 Carolyn W. Field Award (Pennsylvania)
* 2000 Golden Kite Award for Fiction
* 2000 *Horn Book Magazine* Fanfare: Best Books of the Year
* 1999 *Booklist* Editor's Choice: Books for Youth: Older Readers Category
* 1999 *Bulletin of the Center of Children's Books* Blue Ribbons: Fiction
* 1999 Golden Kite Award: Society of Children's Book Writers and Illustrators
* 1999 National Book Award Finalist
* 1999 *School Library Journal*'s Best Books of the Year

Sources of Information about Challenges to the Novel

"Authors and Readers Rally to Defend Rape Novel from School Ban." *Guardian*, September 29, 2010. Accessed June 2, 2015. http://www.theguardian.com/books/2010/sep/29/defend-novel-school-ban.

Grinberg, Emanuella. "*Speak* Author: 'We as Adults Struggle to Talk to Kids Honestly about Sex.'" CNN, April 12, 2014. Accessed June 2, 2015. http://www.cnn.com/2014/04/12/living/laurie-halse-anderson-speak/.

Staino, Rocco. "Anderson's *Speak* under Attack, Again." *School Library Journal*, October 13, 2010. Accessed June 2, 2015. http://www.slj.com/2010/10/industry-news/andersons-speak-under-attack-again/#_.

Williams, Maren. "*Speak* at 15: Laurie Halse Anderson Talks Teen, Resilience Literature, and Censorship." Comic Book Legal Defense Fund (blog), April 16, 2014. Accessed June 2, 2015. http://cbldf.org/2014/04/speak-at-15-laurie-halse-anderson-talks-teens-resilience-literature-and-censorship/.

INFORMATION ABOUT THE AUTHOR

http://madwomanintheforest.com (Anderson's official website)

Contemporary Authors Online, 2013. Books and Authors. Gale.

Glenn, Wendy J. *Laurie Halse Anderson: Speaking in Tongues*. Lanham, MD: Rowman & Littlefield, 2009.

Lew, Kristi. *Laurie Halse Anderson*. New York: Rosen Publishing Group, 2013.

FURTHER READING ABOUT THE NOVEL

Alsup, Janet. "Politicizing Young Adult Literature: Reading Anderson's *Speak* as a Critical Text." *Journal of Adolescent & Adult Literacy* 42, issue 2 (October 2003): 158–166.

Anderson, Laurie Halse. "Speaking Out." *ALAN Review* 27, issue 3 (2000): 25–26.

Bott, C. J. "Why We Must Read Young Adult Books That Deal with Sexual Content." *ALAN Review* 33, issue 3 (Summer 2006): 26–29.

Charaipotra, Sonia. "12 Authors Share the Books They're Most Thankful For." *Aberdeen American News*, November 24, 2014.

Hill, Christine M. "Laurie Halse Anderson Speaks: An Interview." *Voice of Youth Advocates* 23, issue 23 (December 2000): 325–327.

Jackett, Mark. "Something to Speak About: Addressing Sensitive Issues through Literature." *English Journal* 96, issue 4 (March 2007): 102–105.

Latham, Don. "Melinda's Closet: Trauma and the Queer Subtext of Laurie Halse Anderson's *Speak*." *Children's Literature Association Quarterly* 31, issue 4 (Winter 2006): 369–382.

Malo-Juvera, Victor. "Speak: The Effect of Literary Instruction on Adolescents' Rape Myth Acceptance." *Research in the Teaching of English* 48, issue 4 (May 2014): 407–427.

McGee, Chris. "Why Won't Melinda Just Talk about What Happened? *Speak* and the Confessional Voice." *Children's Literature Association Quarterly* 34, issue 2 (Summer 2009): 172–187.

Miller, S. J. "'Speaking' the Walk, 'Speaking' the Talk: Embodying Critical Pedagogy to Teach Young Adult Literature." *English Education* 40, issue 2 (January 2008): 145–154.

O'Quinn, Elaine J. "'Between Voice and Voicelessness': Transacting Silence in Laurie Halse Anderson's *Speak*." *ALAN Review* 29, issue 1 (Fall 2001): 54–58. Accessed June 1, 2015. http://scholar.lib.vt.edu/ejournals/ALAN/v29n1/pdf/oquinn.pdf.

Tannert-Smith, Barbara. "'Like Falling Up into a Storybook': Trauma and Intertextual Repetition in Laurie Halse Anderson's *Speak*." *Children's Literature Association Quarterly* 25, issue 4 (Winter 2010): 395–414.

Verderame, Carla L. "Out of Silence into Speech: Two Perspectives of Growing Up Female." *ALAN Review* 28, issue 1 (Fall 2000): 42–49.

Wolf, Shelby Anne, and Leslie K. Maniotes. "Silenced by Sex: Hard Truths and Taboos in Teaching Literature." *New Advocate* 15, issue 3 (Summer 2002): 197–204.

OTHER MEDIA SOURCES

https://www.youtube.com/watch?v=ic1c_MaAMOI. Posted April 28, 2011. Accessed June 2, 2015. Laurie Halse Anderson reads a poem titled "Listen" that she wrote using words from letters she has received about *Speak*.

https://www.youtube.com/watch?v=MJU7b3C8QMk. Posted January 5, 2012. Accessed June 1, 2015. Laurie Halse Anderson talks about writing *Speak.*

https://www.youtube.com/watch?v=tyjMaSyQLE8. Posted May 21, 2013. Accessed June 2, 2015. Laurie Halse Anderson talks to the American Booksellers Foundation for Free Expression on censorship.

http://interviewly.com/i/laurie-halse-anderson-apr-2014-reddit. Posted April 2014. Accessed June 2, 2015. Laurie Halse Anderson takes calls from readers.

43

❖ ❖ ❖

Staying Fat for Sarah Byrnes

BY CHRIS CRUTCHER

New York: Greenwillow, an imprint of HarperCollins, 1993
HarperCollins Paperback, 2003
Recorded Books Audio, 2007
HarperCollins E-book, 2009

> "It's a scary thing; moving on. Part of me wishes life were more predictable
> and part of me is excited that it's not. I think it's impossible to tell the
> good things from the bad things while they're happening."

CHALLENGES: WHEN, WHY, AND WHERE

2010–2011

The novel was challenged as required reading for high school freshmen in the Belleville, Wisconsin, high school because the language was deemed "pervasively vulgar." The parent who challenged the book also called it "pornographic." The book was retained.

2005–2006

It was challenged as part of the ninth-grade curriculum because of "graphic language" in the high school curriculum in Westmoreland, New York. The school board voted to retain the book.

2001–2002

The book was removed from the ninth-grade reading list at Columbus Grove High School in Columbus Grove, Ohio, because of "negative views toward Christians." It was reinstated in 2007.

1995–1996

A parent in the Smithville, Missouri, School District was successful in getting the novel removed from the ninth-grade curriculum.

THE STORY

Sarah Byrnes and Eric Calhoune have a close bond that is centered on body issues. Her hands and face are severely scarred from burns she suffered as a child. He is extremely obese and eats to comfort himself. They are both outcasts and endure teasing and name calling because of their physical appearance. Eric, called Moby because of his weight, joins the swim team and starts to slim down, but he wants to stay fat because he fears he might otherwise lose his friendship with Sarah Byrnes. The two eighteen-year-olds are enrolled in Ms. Lemry's Contemporary American Thought class, where the students are expected to engage in discussion about various controversial issues. One day, for no obvious reason, Sarah Byrnes becomes mute and catatonic in class. She is hospitalized, and Eric learns that her father burned her as a child and that she fears he is planning to kill her. Ms. Lemry offers to help Sarah locate her mother, since she is the only person who can testify to the abuse. Virgil Byrnes stabs Eric, and Sarah tries to run away because she cannot bear to see others hurt in her behalf.

Themes
- Abuse
- Appearance
- Bullying
- Family
- Friendship
- Trust

TALKING WITH TEENS ABOUT THE ISSUES

The novel deals with serious issues, but there is also humor. Cite some of the most humorous scenes.

Describe the friendship between Eric and Sarah Byrnes. How do they support one another? Which other characters in the novel grow to support Eric and Sarah?

Discuss the bullying that Eric and Sarah endure because of their physical appearance. How do they deal with the bullying? Who is the biggest bully in Sarah's life? Debate whether the bullying is resolved at the end of the novel.

A parent in one high school called the novel "pornographic" and asked that it be removed from the freshman reading list. Define pornography. How is it a subjective term? What might students gain from discussing the novel?

Another parent challenged the book because of the negative views toward Christians. What is this parent referencing? Explain the following quote to a person who may challenge the book: "I figure if those things were in God's jurisdiction, he'd do something different about them. But they aren't. Those are in our jurisdiction."

CHALLENGED FOR SIMILAR REASONS

Crutcher, Chris. *Chinese Handcuffs*. New York: Greenwillow, an imprint of HarperCollins, 1989.

This novel about a boy who witnessed his brother's suicide and a girl who is sexually abused by her father and stepfather was challenged but retained in 2008–2009 at the high school in Delphi, Indiana, because of "graphic language" and "sexual content."

Hopkins, Ellen. *Burned*. New York: Margaret K. McElderry Books, an imprint of Simon & Schuster, 2006.

In a 2009 interview with the National Coalition against Censorship, Hopkins says that this novel about a teenage girl who witnesses her father abuse her mother was banned in Pocatello, Idaho, because of "abuse" and because "the girl questions her Mormon religion."

Limb, Sue. *Girl, 15, Charming but Insane*. New York: Delacorte, an imprint of Random House Children's Books, 2004.

In 2006–2007, this novel about fifteen-year-old Bridget Jones who suffers body issues was banned from Kingwood Middle School in the Humble, Texas, Independent School District because of "profanity and sexual content."

RESOURCES FOR RESPONDING TO CHALLENGES

What Reviewers Say

Booklist (March 15, 1993) recommends the book for grades 7–12 and says it is "strong on relationship, long on plot." The starred review in *Kirkus* (March 15, 1993) says, "Pulse-pounding, on both visceral and intellectual levels." *Publishers Weekly* (March 29, 1993) calls it "riveting" and "powerful." *Horn Book Magazine* (May/June 1993) comments on the strong characterization and says, "The author has created one of his strongest female characters to date." They recommend it for ages twelve and up.

Other Justification for Inclusion in Curricula and Library Collections

❖ 2010 ALA/YALSA Popular Paperbacks for Young Adults: Bodies
❖ 2000 ALA/YALSA 100 Best Books (1950–2000)
❖ 1997 California Young Reader Medal: Young Adult
❖ 1994 South Dakota Library Association Young Adult Reading Program Best Books
❖ 1993 *School Library Journal* Best Books

Sources of Information about Challenges to the Novel

Adams, Helen R. "The American Civil Liberties Union: Another Ally for School Librarians." *School Library Monthly* 28, issue 4 (January 2012): 27–28.

Bittner, Rob. *"Staying Fat for Sarah Byrnes."* The "C" Word (blog), January 25, 2011. Accessed September 12, 2015. http://censorshipdown.blogspot.com/2011/01/staying-fat-for-sarah -byrnes.html.

Lamberson, Carolyn. "Book Notes: Spotlight on Crutcher during Banned Books Week." *Spokesman-Review* (Spokane, Washington), September 22, 2013.

INFORMATION ABOUT THE AUTHOR

http://www.chriscrutcher.com. (Crutcher's official website)

Contemporary Authors Online, 2014. Books and Authors. Gale.

Chance, Rosemary. "The King of Teen Psychology." *Teacher Librarian* 31, issue 1 (October 2003): 36.

Davis, Terry. *Presenting Chris Crutcher*. Twayne's United States Authors Series. Farmington Hills, MI: Cengage Gale, 1997.

Gillis, Bryan, and Pam B. Cole. *Chris Crutcher: A Stotan for Young Adults*. Lanham, MD: Rowman & Littlefield, 2012.

FURTHER READING ABOUT THE NOVEL

Daley, Patricia A. "Iser, Crutcher, and the Reader: Creating the World of Sarah Byrnes." *Journal of Children's Literature* 28, issue 1 (Spring 2002): 32–38.

Elish-Piper, Laurie, Linda S. Wold, and Kathy Schwingendorf. "Scaffolding High School Students' Reading of Complex Texts Using Linked Text Sets." *Journal of Adolescent & Adult Literacy* 57, issue 7 (April 2014): 565–574.

Jensen, Karen. "That Time I Met Chris Crutcher and Sobbed Like a Teenage Girl Who Had Just Met R Patz." *School Library Journal*, October 12, 2012. Accessed October 8, 2015. http://www.teenlibrariantoolbox.com/2012/10/that-time-i-met-chris-crutcher-and-sobbed-like-a-teenage-girl-who-had-just-met-r-patz/.

Sheffer, Susannah. "An Adult Reads Chris Crutcher." *ALAN Review* 24, issue 3 (Spring 1997): 10–11.

Soublis, Theoni, and Erik Winkler. "Transcending Bias through Reader-Response Theory." *English Journal* 94, issue 2 (November 2004): 12–14.

OTHER MEDIA SOURCES

https://www.youtube.com/watch?v=cKo16t-BX2Y. Posted March 17, 2009. Accessed September 12, 2015. Chris Crutcher talks about writing for young adults and where he gets his inspiration.

https://www.youtube.com/watch?v=NwjAQytPeqk. Posted July 8, 2012. Accessed September 12, 2015. This is a video review of *Staying Fat for Sarah Byrnes* by a young adult reader.

44

❖ ❖ ❖

Stuck in Neutral

BY TERRY TRUEMAN

New York: HarperCollins, 2001
Recorded Books Audio, 2005
HarperCollins Paperback, 2012
HarperCollins E-book, 2012

"I do sometimes wonder what life would be like if people, even one person, knew that
I was smart and that there is an actual person hidden inside my useless body."

CHALLENGES: WHEN, WHY, AND WHERE

2012–2013

The novel was challenged as "an inappropriate reading assignment" because of "obscene" language and the discussion of "euthanasia" at Creekwood Middle School in Humble, Texas.

2002–2003

According to a report of the Texas American Civil Liberties Union, the novel was challenged but retained at Franklin Middle School in Abilene, Texas, for "profanity/language and sexual content."

The book was also challenged at Crawford Middle School in Crawford, Texas, for "profanity or inappropriate language, sexual content, violence or horror."

It was also challenged but retained on the reading list for eighth-graders at the Evansville High School in Wisconsin despite concerns about profanity, sexual imagery, and violence.

THE STORY

Shawn McDaniel was born with cerebral palsy and has been locked inside his head for his entire life. Though he cannot communicate, he has similar thoughts of most fourteen-year-old boys. According to Shawn, and unknown to those around him, he has a "special ability" to recall every conversation that he has heard. He enjoys watching and listening to his older brother and sister and their friends, and he credits them with teaching him about matters of life.

Shawn's parents divorced when he was four years old, and he believes that he is the cause. His father, a journalist and Pulitzer Prize–winning poet, simply couldn't deal with his son's condition. Though his father visits the family, Shawn has counted the number of times that he and his father have been alone together—"six times in fourteen years." During one visit, Shawn's father says, "Maybe I should just end your pain," and Shawn thinks that this means his father is planning to kill him. The open ending leaves readers wondering if Shawn's father follows through.

Life Happens Next (2012) is the sequel to *Stuck in Neutral* and answers the questions raised by those troubled by the open ending of Trueman's first novel.

Themes
- ❖ Adolescent sexuality
- ❖ Dealing with disabilities
- ❖ Divorce
- ❖ Family
- ❖ Isolation
- ❖ Suffering

TALKING WITH TEENS ABOUT THE ISSUES

How is the entire McDaniel family affected by Shawn's condition?

Discuss how Cindy and Paul's friends react to Shawn. How is Shawn a victim of discrimination from those around him?

Some adults don't think the novel is appropriate for teens because of sexual content. Shawn is locked inside his own mind because he can't communicate. How are his thoughts and sexual fantasies similar to most adolescents?

Shawn's father wins a Pulitzer Prize for a poem that he wrote about his son. Discuss whether his father's poem is an effort to come to terms with his son's condition. Shawn's father appears on TV talk shows. How might audiences think that he is exploiting his son?

The novel has been challenged because of issues related to euthanasia. What is euthanasia? Why is Shawn so convinced that his father is trying to kill him?

The book has also been challenged for violence and horror. What is the difference between violence and horror? What scenes might a censor label "violent"?

The novel has an open ending, leaving Shawn's fate to the reader. What do you think happens? How might this open ending be troubling to some readers? Discuss the reason for the open ending.

Discuss how Shawn's story may cause readers to become more sensitive to people with disabilities.

CHALLENGED FOR SIMILAR REASONS

Tada, Joni Eareckson. *When Is It Right to Die? Suicide, Euthanasia, Suffering, Mercy.* Grand Rapids, MI: Zondervan, 1992.

This book about suicide and euthanasia was banned on "religious grounds" at the Travis Middle School in Port Lavaca, Texas, in 2011–2012.

Wittlinger, Ellen. *Hard Love.* New York: Simon & Schuster, 1999.

In 2009, this Printz Honor book (2000) about a boy from a broken home whose father doesn't want to be around him was challenged in West Bend, Wisconsin, along with numerous children's and young adult titles because "the books are obscene and the sexual content inappropriate for young readers."

RESOURCES FOR RESPONDING TO CHALLENGES

What Reviewers Say

Reviewers have praised the book for its unusual point of view and tone. *Publishers Weekly* (July 11, 2000) states, "The strength of the novel lies in the father-son dynamic." *School Library Journal* (July 1, 2000) calls the book an "intriguing premise" and states that it will challenge readers to "look beyond people's surfaces." They recommend it for grades 5–9. *Voice of Youth Advocates* (December 1, 2000) says, "Trueman explores the what-ifs, creating a compelling teenage character." The *Kirkus* (June 30, 2000) reviewer writes, "Shawn will stay with readers." Finally, Ilene Cooper states in *Booklist* (July 27, 2000), "Readers spend the entire book inside Shawn's head, a place so vivid, so unique they will be hard pressed to forget its mix of heaven and hell." She recommends the novel for grades 6–10.

Other Justification for Inclusion in Curricula and Library Collections

❖ 2010 ALA/YALSA Popular Paperbacks for Young Adults: Bodies
❖ 2005 Books Change Lives Award, California Center for the Book
❖ 2002 Kentucky Bluegrass Award
❖ 2001 ALA/YALSA Best Books for Young Adults
❖ 2001 ALA/YALSA Quick Pick for Reluctant Young Adult Readers
❖ 2001 Children's Book Council Not Just for Children Anymore List
❖ 2001 Michael L. Printz Honor Book
❖ 2001 New York Public Library Best Read for Teens
❖ 2000 *Booklist* Editor's Choice: Books for Youth: Older Readers Category
❖ 2000 *Booklist* Top 10 Youth First Novels
❖ 2000 *Parent's Guide to Children's Media*'s Outstanding Achievement in Fiction

Sources of Information about Challenges to the Novel

"Blogging Censorship: Talking 'Dark' YA Lit with Terry Trueman." National Coalition against Censorship, May 30, 2012. Accessed July 11, 2015. http://ncacblog.wordpress.com/tag/stuck-in-neutral/.

"Censorship Dateline." *Newsletter on Intellectual Freedom* 61 (July 2012): 153–184.

Janacek, Rick. "Changes Expected after Outcry over Book Selection." *Tribune* (Humble, Texas), May 14, 2012. Accessed July 11, 2015. http://ourtribune.com/article.php?id=13614.

Kirk, Bryan. "District Plans to Screen Books Closer." *Houston Chronicle*, May 22, 2012. Accessed July 11, 2015. http://www.chron.com/neighborhood/katy-news/article/District-plans-to-screen-books-closer-3577407.php.

INFORMATION ABOUT THE AUTHOR

http://www.terrytrueman.com/ (Trueman's official website)

Arth, Joan. "Author Profile: Terry Trueman." *Library Media Collection* 27, issue 1 (August/September 2008): 36–37.

Halls, Kelly Milner. "The Truth about Trueman: An Interview with Terry Trueman." *Voice of Youth Advocates* 25, issue 5 (December 2002): 346–347.

FURTHER READING ABOUT THE NOVEL

Jensen, Karen. "The Power of Reading *Stuck in Neutral*." *Teen Librarian Toolbox* (blog), August 9, 2012. Accessed December 5, 2012. http://www.teenlibrariantoolbox.com/2012/08/the-power -of-reading-stuck-in-neutral-by-terry-trueman/.

Roth, Marci. "Stuck in Neutral." *Scholastic Scope* 49, issue 16 (April 23, 2001): 11–14.

Squicciarini, Stephanie A. "The Worst Day Writing Is Better Than the Best Day at Work." *Public Libraries* 44, issue 4 (July/August 2005): 205–207.

OTHER MEDIA SOURCES

http://www.youtube.com/watch?v=uBrLtIlFvSQ and http://www.youtube.com/watch?v=AzjhEZ AE0dk. Posted September 11, 2007. Accessed July 11, 2015. A teen patron at the North Central Regional Library in Wenatchee, Washington, conducts this two-part interview with Terry Trueman.

http://www.youtube.com/watch?v=8nNKJnDnZrk. Posted April 12, 2009. Accessed July 11, 2015. Terry Trueman talks with Ed Spicer about *Stuck in Neutral* and his entire body of work.

https://www.youtube.com/watch?v=dS8PUsRjeQo. Posted April 1, 2012. Accessed July 11, 2015. A student portrays Shawn McDaniel, the main character in *Stuck in Neutral*.

45

❖ ❖ ❖

Thirteen Reasons Why

BY JAY ASHER

New York: Razorbill, an imprint of Penguin, 2007
Listening Library Audio, 2007
Penguin Paperback, 2011

"A lot of you cared, just not enough."

CHALLENGES: WHEN, WHY, AND WHERE

According to the American Library Association's Office for Intellectual Freedom, the novel was #3 on the Top Ten Most Frequently Challenged Books List of 2012 because of "drugs/alcohol/smoking, suicide, sexually explicit and unsuited for age group."

2014–2015

The novel was challenged at the Lee-Davis High School in the Hanover County Public Schools in Ashland, Virginia, because of "sexual activity and violence." The school board voted to retain the book.

2012–2013

According to data collected by the National Council of Teachers of English, the novel was challenged in the ninth-grade curriculum in Michigan because of "obscene language" and "sexual content." The novel was returned to the curriculum and the library shelves.

It was also challenged in an eighth-grade classroom library in Pennsylvania because of the topic of "suicide." The outcome of the case is unknown.

2009–2010

According to the Texas American Civil Liberties Union, the novel was challenged but retained in the Round Rock Independent School District because of "profanity or horror."

THE STORY

Clay Jenson, the teen narrator, arrives home from school one afternoon and discovers a shoe box of seven tapes on his front porch. He searches for a cassette player so that he might listen to the tapes and is disturbed when he hears Hannah Baker's voice, a classmate who committed suicide two weeks earlier. She offers thirteen reasons why she took her life and names twelve people who contributed to her decision. She names Clay, but doesn't implicate him as she does eleven others. Among them are Justin, who started a nasty rumor about Hannah; Alex, who told others that Hannah had the "best ass" in town; and Jessica and Courtney, who only used Hannah while making her think she was a friend. Ryan steals Hannah's poem titled "Soul Alone" and publishes it in the school newspaper, but the most disturbing of all is Mr. Bryce, the guidance counselor, who does nothing to get help for Hannah when he knows she is in emotional distress. Feeling guilty that he could have done more to help Hannah, Clay grows personally from his exposure to Hannah's audio suicide note and reaches out to another classmate who he believes is suicidal.

Themes
❖ Bullying
❖ Death and dying
❖ Substance abuse
❖ Suicide

TALKING WITH TEENS ABOUT THE ISSUES

Explain why Hannah included Clay in her audio suicide message. Debate whether she expected him to react the way he did. How do Hannah's tapes give Clay the courage to help Skye, another classmate contemplating suicide?

Jay Asher has made a fifty-state tour talking about bullying. Explain the difference between overt and covert bullying. Which type of bullying is most prevalent in the novel? How are these bullying issues the reality of high school culture? Discuss ways to combat bullying in schools.

Why is the map significant to the story? Explain how Clay's personal journey began by following the map. Debate whether the other names on the tape are as affected by Hannah's words as Clay is.

Document the warning signs that Hannah is suicidal. What might you do if you discover that a friend has suicidal thoughts?

How could Mr. Bryce, the counselor, have done more to help Hannah? Debate the ethics of placing responsibility for the rape on Hannah, rather than reporting it after she shared it with him.

Discuss why Sherman Alexie calls the novel "a mystery, eulogy, and ceremony."

The novel has been challenged because of language, sexual content, and violence. Explain how these issues represent the actualities of teenage life. Discuss how acknowledging that these things exist is healthier than denying them. How does awareness create safety?

CHALLENGED FOR SIMILAR REASONS

Guest, Judith. *Ordinary People*. New York: Viking, an imprint of Penguin, 1976.

This novel about a boy who attempts suicide after his brother's accidental death was challenged at Lancaster High School in New York because of "foul language, graphic references to sex, and inappropriate handling of the subject of suicide." The novel was reinstated.

LaCour, Nina. *Hold Still*. New York: Dutton, an imprint of Random House, 2009.

This novel about Caitlin, a high school girl who is struggling with her friend Ingrid's suicide, was banned from the Blue Springs, Missouri, School District libraries and classrooms in 2012–2013 because it is "riddled with obscenities."

Runyon, Brent. *The Burn Journals*. New York: Knopf, an imprint of Random House, 2004.

In 2008–2009, this memoir about a depressed fourteen-year-old who tries to commit suicide was removed from middle and high schools in Catoosa County, Georgia, because of "foul language, sexual content and ways to commit suicide."

RESOURCES FOR RESPONDING TO CHALLENGES

What Reviewers Say

Kirkus (September 1, 2007) gives the novel a starred review and comments on its "delicate—and artfully wrought—treatment of suicide." *Publishers Weekly* (November 8, 2007) recommends it for ages thirteen and up and says that Asher "gets all the characters right." *Booklist* (September 1, 2007) calls it "compelling reading" and recommends it for grades 8–11. *School Library Journal* (November 1, 2007) recommends it for grades 7 and up and compliments the "complex and soulful characters."

Other Justification for Inclusion in Curricula and Library Collections

❖ 2013 Abraham Lincoln High School Book Award (Illinois)
❖ 2012 ALA/YALSA Popular Paperbacks for Young Adults: Sticks and Stones
❖ 2012 Iowa High School Book Award
❖ 2011 Delaware Diamonds: High School Category
❖ 2010 Garden State Teen Book Award (New Jersey): Fiction (Grades 9–12)
❖ 2010 Gateway Readers Award (Missouri): High School
❖ 2010 Georgia Peach Honor Award for Teen Readers
❖ 2010 Sequoyah Book Awards (Oklahoma): High School Books
❖ 2010 South Carolina Book Awards: Young Adult Books
❖ 2009 Kentucky Bluegrass Award: Grades 9–12
❖ 2009 Texas Tayshas Reading Lists
❖ 2008 ALA/YALSA Best Books for Young Adults
❖ 2008 ALA/YALSA Quick Picks for Reluctant Young Adult Readers

Sources of Information about Challenges to the Novel

Miller, Suzanne. "Banned Books Week 2013: Information You May Not Have Known." Examiner. com, September 26, 2013. Accessed July 23, 2015. http://www.examiner.com/article/ banned-book-week-2013-information-you-might-not-have-known.

Ridolphi, Jim. "School Officials Reject Issues with Book." *Richmond Times Dispatch* (Virginia), February 24, 2015. Accessed July 23, 2015. http://www.richmond.com/news/local/hanover/ mechanicsville-local/article_c0e13cb0-bc46-11e4-9c50-73739457d9df.html.

"Thirteen Reasons Why." Banned Books Awareness, January 26, 2014. Accessed June 5, 2015. http://bannedbooks.world.edu/2014/01/26/banned-books-awareness-thirteen-reasons-why/.

INFORMATION ABOUT THE AUTHOR

http://jayasher.blogspot.com (Asher's blog)

https://twitter.com/jayasherguy (Asher on Twitter)

http://www.thirteenreasonswhy.com (official website for the novel and teen involvement about issues of bullying)

Contemporary Authors Online, 2013. Books and Authors. Gale.

FURTHER READING ABOUT THE NOVEL

Biedenharn, Isabella. "Q&A: *Thirteen Reasons Why* Author Jay Asher on Bullies and Teen Suicide Prevention." *Entertainment Weekly*, April 22, 2015. Accessed June 4, 2015. http://www.ew.com/article/2015/04/21/thirteen-reasons-why-jay-asher-bullying-suicide.

Brunner, Rob. "How This Guy's Mystery Novel Is Saving Teen Lives." *Entertainment Weekly*, June 10, 2011. Accessed July 23, 2015. http://www.ew.com/article/2011/06/10/how-this-guys-mystery-novel-saving-teen-lives.

Brunner, Rob. "*Thirteen Reasons Why* Author Jay Asher Responds to Anti-YA Article: 'I Got Very Upset.'" *Entertainment Weekly*, June 15, 2011. Accessed June 4, 2015. http://www.ew.com/article/2011/06/15/jay-asher-wsj-ya.

Chisholm, James S., and Brandie Trent. "'Everything . . . Affects Everything': Promoting Critical Perspectives toward Bullying with *Thirteen Reasons Why*." *English Journal* 101, issue 6 (July 2012): 75–80.

Diaz, Shelley. "Raw Honesty: Author Jay Asher Talks to *SLJ* about *Thirteen Reasons Why*." *School Library Journal*, February 27, 2014. Accessed June 4, 2015. http://www.slj.com/2014/02/interviews/raw-honesty-author-jay-asher-talks-to-slj-about-thirteen-reasons-why/.

Gillis, Bryan. "*Thirteen Reasons Why*." *Journal of Adolescent & Adult Literacy* 54, issue 7 (April 2011): 542–545.

Rich, Motoko. "A Story of a Teenager's Suicide Quietly Becomes a Best Seller." *New York Times*, March 10, 2009. Accessed June 4, 2015. http://www.nytimes.com/2009/03/10/books/10why.html?_r=0.

Smith, Cynthia Leitich. "Author Interview: Jay Asher on *Thirteen Reasons Why*." *Cynsations* (blog), February 5, 2008. Accessed June 4, 2015. http://cynthialeitichsmith.blogspot.com/2008/02/author-interview-jay-asher-on-thirteen.html.

OTHER MEDIA SOURCES

https://www.youtube.com/watch?v=5w6N9qaZ5cc. Posted by Barnes & Noble Studio, August 3, 2009. Accessed July 23, 2015. Jay Asher talks about *Thirteen Reasons Why*.

https://www.youtube.com/watch?v=YeVJkE2pAl8. Posted by Pequin Teen, March 17, 2014. Accessed July 23, 2015. Jay Asher discusses his 50 States Bullying Tour.

46

❖ ❖ ❖

This One Summer

BY JILLIAN TAMAKI AND MARIKO TAMAKI

New York: First Second Books, an imprint of Macmillan, 2014

"So. Last summer she stopped. Trying or whatever . . ."

CHALLENGES: WHEN, WHY, AND WHERE

2014–2015

The National Council of Teachers of English reports a challenge in the eighth-grade curriculum at a school district in Texas because of "profanity and obscenities to discuss sensitive topics." The graphic novel was retained in the library.

A school administrator in Berkeley, California, called the graphic novel "inappropriate" and asked that it be banned. The outcome of the challenge is unknown.

The Comic Book Legal Defense Fund reports several confidential challenges because the novel is considered "unsuited for age group."

THE STORY

It's a Wallace family tradition to spend every summer at their cottage on Lake Awago, where Rose looks forward to time with her slightly younger friend, Windy. They have always played in the sand and collected items from the beach, but this summer things are a little different. Rose is caught between childhood and adolescence, and she is not sure what that means. At times she finds Windy silly, and she becomes enamored with local teens who drink and use slang words like "slut." Rose is not ready to join these teens, but she merely observes as a way of understanding the next stage in her life. This confusion is topped off by her mother's sadness. She overhears her mother talking about a miscarriage she had earlier in the year and her infertility problems. This explains her mother's depression and why her parents fight so much. The summer progresses with Rose dealing with all her family issues, and she begins taking baby steps toward adolescence by watching horror movies, reading fashion magazines, and participating in the bullying of a teenage girl who is in a poor situation. She is sometimes mean to Windy and leaves the summer maybe "wiser," but maybe not.

Themes
❖ Bullying
❖ Coming of age
❖ Depression
❖ Family
❖ Friendship

TALKING WITH TEENS ABOUT THE ISSUES

Explain Rose's confusion about growing up. How is this confusion difficult for Windy to understand?

What is Rose's view of adolescence? Discuss why she is so interested in the activities of the older teens. Why does she think bullying a teenager in a difficult situation is okay?

Rose's parents are facing challenges of their own. Discuss whether Rose might have understood the fights if her parents had explained the root of her mother's sadness.

The novel has been challenged because of "obscenities to discuss sensitive topics." Discuss the "sensitive topics." How are such topics pertinent to teenage life?

The book won the Caldecott Medal for illustration, which includes books for children up to age fourteen. It has been challenged because it is deemed "inappropriate for age group." To what age group does the book target? How appropriate is it for this age group? Prepare a defense of this graphic novel to parents and teachers who assume the Caldecott Medal is for younger children.

CHALLENGED FOR SIMILAR REASONS

Schrag, Ariel. *Stuck in the Middle: 17 Comics from an Unpleasant Age*. New York: Viking, an imprint of Penguin, 2007.

This graphic novel about the angst of early adolescence was challenged in 2011 in three middle school libraries in Maine because of "objectionable sexual content and language." It was retained but placed in the professional collections.

Thompson, Craig. *Blankets*. New York: Public Square Books, 2006.

This memoir about the author's coming of age and questions about religion was challenged in 2008 at the Marshall, Missouri, Public Library because it was deemed "pornographic." The book was moved from the teen section to the adult collection.

RESOURCES FOR RESPONDING TO CHALLENGES

What Reviewers Say

In the starred review for *Kirkus* (May 1, 2014), the reviewer comments that the novel "skillfully portrays ups and downs" of an adolescent girl. *Publishers Weekly* (March 17, 2014) gives the book a star and praises the "fine characterization." They recommend it for ages twelve and up. In the starred *Booklist* (April 15, 2014) review, Sarah Hunter calls the novel "wistful, touching, and perfectly bittersweet." *School Library Journal* (May 1, 2014) recommends the book for grades 8 and up and comments, "Layers of story unfurl gradually." *Horn Book Magazine* (August 7, 2014) calls it a "poignant drama." *Voice of Youth Advocates* (June 1, 2014) praises the "tweens' frank and often humorous conversations." *Quill & Quire* (May 1, 2014) says the book is "timeless." The *New York Times* (June 13, 2014) calls it a "moving, evocative book."

Other Justification for Inclusion in Curricula and Library Collections

❖ 2015 ALA/ALSC Notable Children's Books: Older Reader Category
❖ 2015 ALA/ALSC Randolph Caldecott Honor Book
❖ 2015 ALA/YALSA Michael L. Printz Honor Book Award

❖ 2015 Young Adult Canadian Book Award
❖ 2014 *Booklist* Editors' Choice
❖ 2014 *Booklist* Top Ten Graphic Novels for Youth
❖ 2014 Governor General's Award for Children's Illustration (Canadian Council for the Arts)
❖ 2014 *Horn Book Magazine* Fanfare Title
❖ 2014 Ignatz Awards: Outstanding Graphic Novel
❖ 2014 *Kirkus* Best of the Year
❖ 2014 *New York Times* Notable Books

Sources of Information about Challenges to the Novel

Gomez, Betsy. "Adding *This One Summer* to Your Library or Classroom Collection." Comic Book Legal Defense Fund, February 20, 2015. Accessed October 8, 2015. http://cbldf.org/2015/02/adding-this-one-summer-to-your-libary-or-classroom-collection/.

McCabe, Caitlin. "The Tweeks Tackle the Controversy around *This One Summer*." Comic Book Legal Defense Fund, July 28, 2015. Accessed August 11, 2015. http://cbldf.org/2015/07/the-tweeks-tackle-the-controversy-about-this-one-summer/.

Scales, Pat. "Library Police: Who Determines What Is 'Appropriate'?" Scales on Censorship. *School Library Journal* (April 22, 2015). Accessed July 30, 2015. http://www.slj.com/2015/04/opinion/scales-on-censorship/library-police-who-determines-what-is-appropriate-scales-on-censorship/.

INFORMATION ABOUT THE AUTHOR AND ILLUSTRATOR

http://jilliantamaki.com/illustration/ (Jillian Tamaki's official website)
http://marikotamaki.blogspot.ca (Mariko Tamaki's blog)

FURTHER READING ABOUT THE NOVEL

Goellner, Caleb. "Jillian Tamaki and Mariko Tamaki Talk *This One Summer*." Comics Alliance, April 22, 2014. Accessed August 11, 2015. http://comicsalliance.com/jillian-tamaki-and-markiko-tamaki-this-one-summer-interview/.

Jaffe, Meryl. "Using Graphic Novels in Education: *This One Summer*." Comic Book Legal Defense Fund, February 19, 2015. Accessed August 11, 2015. http://cbldf.org/2015/02/using-graphic-novels-in-education-this-one-summer/.

"Mariko and Jillian Tamaki on Their Multiple Award-Winning *This One Summer*." *Paste Magazine*. Accessed August 11, 2015. http://www.pastemagazine.com/articles/2015/02/mariko-and-jillian-tamaki-on-creating-the-first-gr.htm.

"*This One Summer*: Mariko and Jillian Tamaki Bottle Up Adolescence." *Los Angeles Times*, October 22, 2013. Accessed August 11, 2015. http://herocomplex.latimes.com/comics/this-one-summer-mariko-and-jillian-tamaki-bottle-up-adolescence/#/0.

OTHER MEDIA SOURCES

https://www.youtube.com/watch?v=ODS7znhendE. Posted May 1, 2015. Accessed August 11, 2015. Jillian and Mariko Tamaki talk about *This One Summer* at the Los Angeles Festival of Books.

https://www.youtube.com/watch?v=9fykDYVT3JU. Posted July 27, 2015. Accessed October 8, 2015. Young adult fans offer a video review of *This One Summer* and give reasons it has been challenged.

47

❖ ❖ ❖

Twisted

BY LAURIE HALSE ANDERSON

New York: Viking, an imprint of Penguin, 2007
Random House Audio, 2007
Speak Paperback, Reprint Edition, 2008

> "I looked in the mirror and realized that I was already dead.
> I let you kill me one piece at a time, starting when I was, what?
> Eight years old? Nine? You killed yourself and then you came after us."

CHALLENGES: WHEN, WHY, AND WHERE

2009–2010

The novel, along with four other novels, was removed from the curriculum at Montgomery High School in Mt. Sterling, Kentucky, because of "foul language, sexual content, child abuse, and suicide and drug abuse." The parent also complained that the novel is not intellectually challenging for college-bound students. The superintendent removed the book because it was not on the "pre-approved" reading list.

A parent of a student at South Central Junior and Senior High School in Harrison County, Indiana, challenged the book because of "bad language." The mother stated, "[K]ids can't cuss at school, yet they are allowed to read a book with such bad words." The student was offered an alternative book.

THE STORY

Tyler Miller has always been a nerdy kid who was unnoticed by his peers, except for his best friend Yoda. In the summer between his junior and senior year, he gains plenty of notoriety after he spray paints graffiti on the walls of the school. He is sentenced to a summer of community service. To make matters worse, he suffers severe emotional abuse from his father at home. In his senior year, Tyler finds himself in unchartered territory when he lets his grades drop, and Bethany Milbury, the daughter of his father's boss, comes on to him. She wants a sexual relationship, but he does not. Then he is accused of posting pictures of a nude and drunk Bethany on the Internet. Life seems to be crashing down on him, and his parents make plans to send him away to military school. In a well-thought-out plan to commit suicide, he takes his father's handgun and places the barrel in his mouth and his finger on the trigger, but he cannot bring himself to go through with it. He spends that night at Yoda's house and returns the next day where he admits to his father that he contemplated suicide. Tyler's future is unknown; however, he drops his AP courses and continues his senior year a different guy, but he remains in the same school and at home with his family.

Themes
* ❖ Becoming a man
* ❖ Emotional abuse
* ❖ Family
* ❖ Friendship
* ❖ Suicide

TALKING WITH TEENS ABOUT THE ISSUES

Describe Tyler's family. What is the source of his rocky relationship with his father?

What is Tyler's motive when he spray paints graffiti on the school walls? Debate whether he expected to get so much attention for his crime. How does this act make him vulnerable to false accusations of other "crimes"? Explain his reaction when he is accused of posting the nude pictures of Bethany on the Internet.

The novel has been challenged because of "child abuse." Discuss what Tyler means when he says to his father, "You killed yourself and then you came after us." Mr. Miller defends himself when he tells Tyler that he had never hit him because his own father had beaten him. How is emotional abuse as bad as physical abuse?

Tyler takes his father's gun with the intention of killing himself. What stops him? Discuss his father's reaction when Tyler tells him that he contemplated suicide. Debate whether this changes the father-and-son relationship.

The novel has been challenged because of profanity. Discuss the argument that reading foul language sets a double standard when "kids aren't allowed to cuss at school."

CHALLENGED FOR SIMILAR REASONS

Dessen, Sarah. *Just Listen.* New York: Viking, an imprint of Penguin, 2006.

This novel about a teenage girl who feels lonely and isolated was challenged in 2008 at the Armwood High School in Hillsborough County, Florida, because the "sexual themes and profanity" make it "too intense" for teens. The book was retained.

Going, K. L. *Fat Kid Rules the World.* New York: Putnam, an imprint of Penguin, 2003.

This 2004 Michael L. Printz Honor Book about a seventeen-year-old fat boy who is about to commit suicide when a homeless guy intervenes was removed from the Pickens County, South Carolina, middle and high school in 2007–2008 because of "language, sexual references and drug use."

RESOURCES FOR RESPONDING TO CHALLENGES

What Reviewers Say

Kirkus (February 15, 2007) gives the novel a starred review and states that Anderson "stretches her wings by offering up a male protagonist." *Booklist* (January 1, 2007) comments on the "frank, on-target humor." *School Library Journal* (May 1, 2007) recommends the books for grades 9 and up and comments on the "gripping scenes and a rousing ending." *Publishers Weekly* (January 15, 2007) calls the novel "humorous" and praises the "compelling first-person narrative." *Voice of*

Youth Advocates (April 1, 2007) says it is "a compelling novel of growth and maturity." *Horn Book Magazine* (March 1, 2007) comments on the complexity of the supporting characters and believes they add "dimension to Tyler's journey."

Other Justification for Inclusion in Curricula and Library Collections

- ❖ 2012 ALA/YALSA Popular Paperbacks for Young Adults: Get Your Geek On
- ❖ 2009 Rosie Award: Eliot Rosewater Indiana High School Book Award
- ❖ 2008 ALA/YALSA Best Books for Young Adults
- ❖ 2008 ALA/YALSA Quick Picks for Reluctant Young Adult Readers: Fiction
- ❖ 2008 Texas Tayshas Reading Lists
- ❖ 2007 IRA Top Ten Books

Sources of Information about Challenges to the Novel

Anderson, Laurie Halse. "Censorship Themes in Young Adult Literature." Weebly.com. Accessed October 5, 2015. http://censorshipthemes.weebly.com/laurie-halse-anderson.html.

"Kids' Right to Read Protests Efforts to Remove *Twisted* by Laurie Halse Anderson." National Coalition against Censorship (blog), September 24, 2009. Accessed October 5, 2015. http://ncac .org/incident/kids-right-to-read-protests-efforts-to-remove-twisted-by-laurie-halse-anderson/.

Tobin, Dave. "Laurie Halse Anderson Reflects on Challenges to Her Books for Teens." *Post Standard* (Syracuse, NY), December 13, 2009. Accessed July 20, 2015. http://blog.syracuse.com/entertain ment/2009/12/laurie_halse_anderson_reflects.html.

INFORMATION ABOUT THE AUTHOR

http://madwomanintheforest.com (Anderson's official website)

Contemporary Authors Online, 2013. Books and Authors. Gale.

Glenn, Wendy J. *Laurie Halse Anderson: Speaking in Tongues.* Lanham, MD: Rowman & Littlefield, 2009.

Lew, Kristi. *Laurie Halse Anderson.* New York: Rosen Publishing Group, 2013.

FURTHER READING ABOUT THE NOVEL

Burner, Joyce Adams. "Keeping It Real." *School Library Journal* 53 (Fall 2007): 12–15.

Clarkin, Mary. "With Writer on Skype, HHS Class Gets Insight into Book." *Hutchinson News* (Kansas), April 2, 2015.

"A Conversation with Laurie Halse Anderson." *Journal of Adolescent & Adult Literacy* 52, issue 1 (September 2008): 78–83.

OTHER MEDIA SOURCES

http://madwomanintheforest.com. Posted November 10, 2007. Accessed October 6, 2015. Ed Spicer talks with Laurie Halse Anderson about *Twisted*.

https://www.youtube.com/watch?v=SdOhcZh79wA. Posted July 16, 2015. Accessed October 6, 2015. A teen gives a video review of *Twisted*.

48

❖ ❖ ❖

Two Boys Kissing

BY DAVID LEVITHAN

New York: Knopf, an imprint of Penguin Random House, 2013
Penguin Random House Audio, 2013
Random House E-book, 2013
Random House Paperback, 2015

"There is no reason that we should ever be ashamed
of our bodies or ashamed of our love."

CHALLENGES: WHEN, WHY, AND WHERE

2014–2015

A parent challenged the novel because of the "gay theme" in the high school in Fauquier County, Virginia.

THE STORY

In this sequel to *Every Day*, voices of gay men who died of AIDS tell the story of seventeen-year-old Harry and Craig, two friends who want to set a kissing record and get their names in the *Guinness Book of World Records*. They enter a 32-hour kissing marathon and gain the attention via the Internet of teen boys around the world who are dealing with their own issues of coming out to family and friends. Some of the boys face disapproving parents, and others have loving and understanding families. Many feel alone and lonely. They all fear the AIDS epidemic that has threatened gay communities worldwide. Harry and Craig enter the kissing contest with applause from many, but they also meet with disapproval, especially since the event takes place right in front of the high school.

Themes
❖ Acceptance
❖ Equality
❖ Family
❖ Friendship
❖ Loneliness
❖ Love
❖ Tolerance

TALKING WITH TEENS ABOUT THE ISSUES

Compare and contrast how each of the seven characters deals with his homosexuality.

How do the ghost narrators contribute to a deeper understanding of the struggles of the characters?

The novel appeared on the long list for the 2013 National Book Award for Young People's Literature. Discuss the literary elements that qualified this book for consideration.

The book has been challenged because of the "gay theme." What might gay and straight teens learn from the book?

The cover of the novel is a photograph of two boys actually kissing. How likely is it that the book was challenged because of the cover and not for the story?

CHALLENGED FOR SIMILAR REASONS

Crutcher, Chris. *Athletic Shorts*. New York: Greenwillow Books, an imprint of HarperCollins, 1991.

The six short stories in this book are about teens who deal with major issues in their lives, from bullying to violence and homosexuality and AIDS. It was among the Top 100 Most Frequently Challenged Books List of 1990–1999 because of "homosexuality" and "profanity."

Ferris, Jean. *Eight Seconds*. Boston: Houghton Mifflin Harcourt, 2000.

In 2005–2006, this novel about an eighteen-year-old boy who is dealing with his growing attraction to another boy on the same rodeo circuit was challenged in the Montgomery County, Texas, Memorial Library System because of the "gay positive" themes.

RESOURCES FOR RESPONDING TO CHALLENGES

What Reviewers Say

Booklist (August 1, 2014) says the book is for grades 9–12 and praises its "literary quality" and its contribution to LGBTQ literature. *School Library Journal* (September 1, 2013) believes the book is "didactic" but "the characters are likeable." *Publishers Weekly* (June 30, 2013) gives the book a starred review and calls it "a landmark achievement." They recommend it for ages twelve and up. *Kirkus* (July 15, 2013) says, "The novel has genuine moments of insight and wisdom." They recommend it for ages fourteen and up.

Other Justification for Inclusion in Curricula and Library Collections

- ❖ 2014 ALA Rainbow List
- ❖ 2014 ALA/YALSA Best Fiction for Young Adults
- ❖ 2014 Lawrence L. Winship/PEN New England Award
- ❖ 2013 Lambda Literary Awards: Young Adult/Children's
- ❖ 2013 *Library Journal* Best YA Literature for Adults

Sources of Information about Challenges to the Novel

"Censorship Dateline: Libraries." *Newsletter on Intellectual Freedom* 63, issue 3 (May 2014): 79–80.

Chung, Sandy. "Request to Ban *Two Boys Kissing* from Virginia High School Library Denied." *School Library Journal*, April 29, 2014. Accessed October 16, 2015. http://www.slj.com/2014/04/censorship/request-to-ban-two-boys-kissing-from-virginia-high-school-library-denied/.

Emerson, Lawrence. "*Two Boys Kissing* Remains in Fauquier High Library." *Fauquier Now* (Virginia), April 24, 2014. Accessed October 16, 2015. http://www.fauquiernow.com/index.php/fauquier_news/article/two-boys-kissing-remains-in-fauquier-high-library.

Grandstaff, Mark. "Fauquier Parent Demands Removal of *Two Boys Kissing* Book from High School Library." *Fauquier Now* (Virginia), April 4, 2015. Accessed October 16, 2015. http://www.fauquier.com/news/article/fauquier_parent_demands_removal_of_two_boys_kissing_book_from_high_school_l.

"NCAC to Fauquier Schools: Don't Ban *Two Boys Kissing* from the Shelves." National Coalition against Censorship. Accessed October 16, 2015. http://ncac.org/update/ncac-to-fauquier-schools-dont-ban-two-boys-kissing-from-the-shelves/.

INFORMATION ABOUT THE AUTHOR

http://davidlevithan.com (Levithan's official website)

https://twitter.com/loversdiction?ref_src=twsrc%5Egoogle%7Ctwcamp%5Eserp%7Ctwgr%5Eauthor (Levithan on Twitter)

Contemporary Authors Online, 2014. Books and Authors. Gale.

"One Thing Leads to Another: An Interview with David Levithan." *The Hub* (blog), August 29, 2013. Accessed October 16, 2015. http://www.yalsa.ala.org/thehub/2013/08/29/one-thing-leads-to-another-an-interview-with-david-levithan/.

FURTHER READING ABOUT THE NOVEL

Matos, Angel Daniel. "Queer Times: An Analysis of David Levithan's *Two Boys Kissing*." *The Ever and Ever That Fiction Allows* (blog), September 21, 2013. Accessed October 16, 2015. http://angelmatos.net/2013/09/21/david-levithans-two-boys-kissing/.

Piehl, Norah. "David Levithan: Inhabiting the Voice of a Generation." BookPage. Accessed October 16, 2015. http://bookpage.com/interviews/15521-david-levithan#.ViGE09ayhlI.

West, Gordon. "Ten Years Later, the Noted Teen Writer's View of Gay Life Is More Pragmatic." *Kirkus* 82, issue 17 (September 1, 2013): 92–93.

Zhu, Jasmine. "David Levithan's *Two Boys Kissing*: A Simple Premise, Complicated Story." *Everyday E Book* (blog). Accessed October 16, 2015. http://www.everydayebook.com/2013/10/david-levithans-two-boys-kissing-a-simple-premise-complicated-story/.

OTHER MEDIA SOURCES

https://www.youtube.com/watch?v=alKH5CqJ7nc. Posted July 26, 2012. Accessed October 16, 2015. Levithan talks about *Every Day*, the prequel to *Two Boys Kissing*.

https://www.youtube.com/watch?v=-xMeJqirQSc. Posted December 10, 2014. Accessed October 16, 2015. Levithan reads from *Two Boys Kissing*.

49

❖   ❖   ❖

Unwind

BY NEAL SHUSTERMAN

New York: Simon & Schuster, 2007
Simon & Schuster Paperback, 2009
Simon & Schuster E-book, 2009

"We have a right to our lives. . . . We have a right to choose what happens to our bodies."

CHALLENGES: WHEN, WHY, AND WHERE

2009–2010

The superintendent pulled the novel from classroom use at the Mt. Sterling High School in Montgomery County, Kentucky, because it wasn't on the "pre-approved list." Parents felt the book was unsuited to be taught in a coeducational classroom because of "foul language, drug abuse and sex." The novel remained available in the library.

THE STORY

Set in the near future, after a civil war over abortion, the government reaches a compromise and allows parents other options if they cannot tend for their babies or wish to rid themselves of their adolescents. Families struggling to care for young babies can "stork" them, which means they simply place the baby on the doorstep to become someone else's responsibility. Those burdened by their adolescents (ages thirteen–eighteen) may ship them off to "harvest camps" and have them "unwound," which means their body parts are harvested for later use. They justify this action by claiming that their children will eventually live on in the bodies of others. Connor is sixteen when his parents send him to be unwound because he is in so many fights; Risa is at risk because the state can no longer care for her due to budget cuts; and Lev, the tenth child of a wealthy couple, was conceived with the idea of having him unwound as a religious offering. The three adolescents meet and begin a journey of survival. Along the way, they pick up a "storked" baby and eventually find him a home. In *UnWholly*, book two of the Unwind Dystology series, Connor, Risa, and Lev lodge a revolt at Happy Jack Harvest Camp and cause some people to question the government's compromise. *UnSouled* is book three and continues the efforts of the AWOL adolescents to shut down the unwinding practice.

Themes

❖ Dealing with adversity
❖ Ethical issues
❖ Power
❖ Pro-choice vs. pro-life
❖ Survival

TALKING WITH TEENS ABOUT THE ISSUES

Discuss the reason for the civil war in the novel. Explain the government's compromise. How does this create a unique social issue?

Connor, Risa, and Lev are scheduled to be unwound. Trace their journey of survival. Identify their allies and their enemies.

Why does Connor pick up the "storked" baby?

The novel was challenged after some parents did not think the novel was appropriate to be taught in a coeducational classroom. Do you think these parents have read the book? Cite the scenes that these parents might find troubling. How would you defend the book to them?

What is the message of the book? How might discussing the book bring healthy debate about issues related to pro-choice/pro-life?

CHALLENGED FOR SIMILAR REASONS

Anderson, M. T. *Feed*. Somerville, MA: Candlewick Press, 2002.

This science fiction novel about young adults who are connected to one another through brain implants called the "feed" was challenged at the William Monroe High School in Greene County, Virginia, because it is "trash" and "covered with the F-word."

Darnton, John. *The Experiment*. New York: Dutton, an imprint of Penguin, 1999.

In 2001–2002, this novel about a colony of clones raised for organ replacement was restricted at Memorial High School in the Victoria, Texas, Independent School District because of "profanity and sexual content."

RESOURCES FOR RESPONDING TO CHALLENGES

What Reviewers Say

School Library Journal (January 1, 2008) recommends the book for grades 9 and up and calls it a "thought-provoking, well-paced read." *Voice of Youth Advocates* (October 1, 2007) says the novel is "poignant, compelling, and ultimately terrifying." *Publishers Weekly* (November 26, 2007) recommends the book for ages thirteen and up and says it is a "gripping, brilliantly imagined futuristic thriller." The reviewer for *Horn Book* (January 1, 2008) states the book is for high school readers and calls it "a nail-biting, character-driven thriller." *Booklist* (October 15, 2007) says the book is a "page-turner." *Kliatt* (November 2007) praises the novel's "provocative ideas about the meaning of life."

Other Justification for Inclusion in Curricula and Library Collections

❖ 2011 ALA/YALSA Popular Paperbacks for Young Adults: What If . . .
❖ 2011 Nutmeg Children's Book Award (Connecticut): Teen Category
❖ 2010 Black-Eyed Susan Award (Maryland): High School Category
❖ 2010 Rosie Award: Eliot Rosewater Indiana High School Award
❖ 2010 Sequoyah Book Award (Oklahoma): Intermediate Books
❖ 2010 Virginia Reader's Choice Award: High School (Grades 10–12)
❖ 2009 ALA/YALSA Quick Picks for Reluctant Young Adult Readers: Fiction: Top Ten

❖ 2009 Texas Lone Star Reading Lists
❖ 2009 Texas Tayshas Reading Lists
❖ 2008 ALA/YALSA Best Books for Young Adults
❖ 2008 ALA/YALSA Quick Picks for Reluctant Young Adult Readers: Fiction

Sources of Information about Challenges to the Novel

Bertin, Joan. "Kids' Right to Read Objects to Censorship in Kentucky High School." National Coalition against Censorship, September 24, 2009. Accessed June 13, 2015. http://ncac.org/update/kids-right-to-read-objects-to-censorship-in-kentucky-high-school/.

INFORMATION ABOUT THE AUTHOR

http://www.storyman.com (Shusterman's official website)
https://nstoryman.wordpress.com (Shusterman's blog)
https://twitter.com/nealshusterman (Shusterman on Twitter)
Contemporary Authors Online, 2012. Books and Authors. Gale.

FURTHER READING ABOUT THE NOVEL

"Dystopian Novels: Have You Read One Lately?" *Library Media Connection* 31, issue 1 (August/September 2012): 28–29.

Henry, Robin. "Meet the Storyman: Neal Shusterman." *Library Media Connection* 26, issue 2 (October 2007): 40–42.

Howard, Agnes R. "Hating the Teens We Indulge." *First Things: A Monthly Journal of Religion and Public Life*, issue 220 (February 2012): 23–24.

Moen, Christine Boardman. "Neal Shusterman." *Book Links* 18, issue 1 (September 2008): 37–39.

Streetman, Jonathan. "Author Neal Shusterman Visits Tuttle." *Journal Review Online*, October 24, 2013. Accessed June 13, 2015. http://www.journalreview.com/news/local/article_3b71d8e8-3c43-11e3-89af-001a4bcf887a.html.

OTHER MEDIA SOURCES

https://www.youtube.com/watch?v=bATROQuo1cQ. Posted May 15, 2009. Accessed June 11, 2015. Neal Shusterman gives a tour of his home.

https://www.youtube.com/watch?v=i3fe1WgwR8E. Posted January 24, 2011. Accessed June 11, 2015. Neal Shusterman talks about writing on this AdLit production.

https://www.youtube.com/watch?v=j_2yxLhS2jg. Posted September 25, 2012. Accessed June 11, 2015. A fan reads a passage from *Unwind* for the Banned Books Week Virtual Read-Out.

50

❖ ❖ ❖

Vegan Virgin Valentine

BY CAROLYN MACKLER

Somerville, Massachusetts: Candlewick Press, 2004
Candlewick Paperback, 2006
Recorded Books Audio, 2006
Candlewick E-book, 2011

> "I don't regret kissing James last weekend. It was oh-so-very wrong.
> But at the same time, nothing has ever felt more right."

CHALLENGES: WHEN, WHY, AND WHERE

2010–2011

The novel was challenged in a middle school library in Quitman, Texas, by a parent for being "on the verge of pornography."

2007–2008

The book was banned from Gonzales High School in the Gonzales Independent School District in Texas because of "language." The parent offered no specifics.

2006–2007

The novel was challenged in the Mandarin High School Library in Jacksonville, Florida, because of "inappropriate language."

THE STORY

Mara Valentine is seventeen years old and in the race for valedictorian at Brockport High School. She has already been accepted at Yale, has a part-time job at a local café, and concentrates on her new status as a proclaimed vegan. Travis Hart, her ex-boyfriend, is her biggest competition for the top academic spot, but Mara feels in control and looks forward to the time when he surrenders to salutatorian. Everything seems to be going according to plan when Vivienne Vail Valentine, the daughter of Mara's thirty-five-year-old sister, comes to live with them. Vivienne, called V, is totally different from Mara. She is into sex and drugs, while Mara guards her virginity. Things begin to change for both girls when V lands a spot in the school play, and Mara falls in love with her twenty-two-year-old boss. The girls change one another in some very positive ways and along the way become very close. When Mara almost ditches graduation, it is V who talks her into going. *Guyaholic* (2007) takes up V's story during her senior year at Brockport.

Themes

❖ Acceptance
❖ Achievement
❖ Family
❖ Independence
❖ Love

TALKING WITH TEENS ABOUT THE ISSUES

Contrast Mara and V's lives. Each girl is on a journey of self-discovery. How do they help one another?

Mara's competition for valedictorian is Travis Hart, her ex-boyfriend. Why is she so upset when V fools around with Travis?

Mara's parents put a lot of pressure on her to achieve. Discuss whether this pressure is a result of the failure of their older daughter.

V is suspended for smoking pot at school. How is this a turning point for V and Mara?

The novel has been challenged for "language." How do V's language and loose morals reveal her upbringing? Cite passages from the book that V is slowly changing her ways. Discuss how her grandparents handle her.

One challenge report states that the book is on "the verge of pornography." Define the term *pornography*. What scenes in the novel might this challenge target? How would you defend the novel to someone who takes language and specific scenes out of context and calls it "pornography"?

CHALLENGED FOR SIMILAR REASONS

Dessen, Sarah. *Keeping the Moon.* New York: Viking, an imprint of Penguin, 1999.

In 2001–2002, this novel about a girl who struggles with past weight issues was challenged at the League City Intermediate School Library in the Clear Creek, Texas, Independent School District because of "profanity." The resolution of the case is unknown.

Moore, Peter. *Blind Sighted.* New York: Viking, an imprint of Penguin, 2004.

This novel about a brilliant honors student who is struggling with self-identity as he experiences first love was challenged at the junior high school in the Red Oak, Texas, Independent School District in 2005–2006 because of "profanity." The decision was pending at the time of the Texas American Civil Liberties Union report.

RESOURCES FOR RESPONDING TO CHALLENGES

What Reviewers Say

Publishers Weekly (June 21, 2004) recommends the novel for ages fourteen and up and states, "Readers won't find anything groundbreaking here, but they will likely be entertained along the way." The reviewer for *School Library Journal* (August 1, 2004) says, "This is a fast, often humorous read with some meat but with no bite." They recommend it for grades 8 and up. Ilene Cooper, the reviewer for *Booklist* (June 1, 2004), recommends the novel for grades 8–12 and calls Mara's transformation by the end of the novel "credible." *Voice of Youth Advocates* (October 1, 2004) says the novel is "charged with sarcasm, angst, honesty and hope."

Other Justification for Inclusion in Curricula and Library Collections

❖ 2011 ALA/YALSA Popular Paperbacks for Young Adults: What's Cooking?
❖ 2005 ALA/YALSA Quick Picks for Reluctant Young Adult Readers: Fiction

Sources of Information about Challenges to the Novel

"Joint Letter to Mandarin High School Principal Regarding *Vegan Virgin Valentine*." National Coalition against Censorship. Posted March 16, 2007. Accessed August 8, 2015. http://ncac.org/update/joint-letter-to-mandarin-high-school-principal-regarding-vegan-virgin-valentine/.
Livingston, Layron. "Book Controversy in Quitman." KLTV. Posted November 16, 2010. Accessed August 8, 2015. http://www.kltv.com/Global/story.asp?S=13515676.

INFORMATION ABOUT THE AUTHOR

http://carolynmackler.com (Mackler's official website)
https://twitter.com/carolynmackler (Mackler on Twitter)
Contemporary Authors Online, 2009. Books and Authors. Gale.

FURTHER READING ABOUT THE NOVEL

Carlson, Christine. "Vegetarian Teens in YA Literature." *Voice of Youth Advocates* 37, issue 6 (February 2015): 26–29.
Castellitto, Linda. M. "Carolyn Mackler: Mastering the Mysteries of Teen-Speak." BookPage.com. Posted August 2004. Accessed August 8, 2015. http://bookpage.com/interviews/8265-carolyn-mackler#.VfhjELSyhlK.
Horn, Carolyn. "Novels for Testing Readers: Carolyn Mackler Tells Carolyn Horn Why She Enjoys Writing for Teenagers." *The Bookseller* 5120 (March 19, 2004): 30.

OTHER MEDIA SOURCES

http://www.npr.org/2011/09/07/140256963/writers-reflect-on-childhood-torment-in-dear-bully. NPR Books, September 7, 2011. Accessed June 14, 2015. Neal Conan interviews Carolyn Mackler on *Talk of the Nation*.
https://www.youtube.com/watch?v=GBh9P-E8Dqs. Posted March 26, 2015. Accessed August 7, 2015. A young reader offers a video review of the novel.

51

❖ ❖ ❖

We All Fall Down

BY ROBERT CORMIER

New York: Doubleday, an imprint of Random House Children's Books, 1991
Laurel-Leaf Paperback, 1993
Recorded Books Audio, 2003
Random House E-book, 2013

> "They left behind twenty-three beer cans, two empty vodka bottles,
> and damage later estimated at twenty thousand dollars, and, worst of all,
> Karen Jerome, bruised and broken where she lay sprawled on the cellar floor."

CHALLENGES: WHEN, WHY, AND WHERE

According to data collected by the American Library Association's Office for Intellectual Freedom, the novel ranked #8 on the Top Ten Most Frequently Challenged Books List of 2003–2004 because of "offensive language and sexual content." The earliest reported challenge was in 1994 when the book, targeted to teens, was pulled from elementary and junior high school libraries in Stockton, California, because it "glorifies alcoholism and violence."

2005–2006

The novel was challenged but retained in the teen collection at the Cherry Hill Public Library in New Jersey. The parent challenging the book called it "deplorable" and "unfit for young minds."

2003–2004

It was banned from the ninth-grade curriculum in Baldwin, Kansas, after the superintendent declared the book unfit "for his own daughter or granddaughter." The initial challenge cited over fifty objectionable passages that contained "profanity" and "sexual content." The book was reinstated after students distributed copies of the book at a football game.

2001–2002

It was challenged in the Tamaqua Area School District in Pennsylvania because "it might not be appropriate for younger schoolmates." The school district was considering a restricted books policy in the middle schools, but the outcome is unknown.

2000–2001

The novel was placed on a restricted books list in all middle and high schools in the Arlington, Texas, Independent School District because of "violent content."

It was banned from the Caver Middle School Library in Leesburg, Florida, after a parent complained about the novel's "content and language."

1994–1995

Parents in Stockton, California, challenged the novel because "it glorifies alcoholism and violence, and profanity." It was pulled from the elementary and junior high school libraries.

THE STORY

Set in the small town of Burnside, three characters and three story lines set up this thriller told in the third person. Jane Jerome is sixteen years old and attends the local high school. Early in the novel, the Jerome house is trashed by teenage vandals in what appears to be an April Fools prank. Karen, Jane's younger sister, suffers head injuries at the hands of one of the vandals and is in a coma. Sixteen-year-old Buddy Walker is struggling with his own demons and begins to abuse alcohol. His father walked out on the family, and Buddy craves companionship. He finds it in Jane Jerome, but he cannot find the words to tell Jane that he is one of the vandals who trashed her house. Mickey "Looney" Stallings, a middle-aged schizophrenic man who calls himself "The Avenger," was only eleven years old when he committed murder. Now thirty years later, he witnesses the crime against the Jerome family. He plans to search out those involved, but he also sets out to kill Jane Jerome because she is dating Buddy. He commits suicide before he carries out the plot.

Themes
- ❖ Abandonment
- ❖ Alcohol abuse
- ❖ Betrayal
- ❖ Family
- ❖ Fear
- ❖ Friendship
- ❖ Suicide
- ❖ Violence

TALKING WITH TEENS ABOUT THE ISSUES

Describe the boys who vandalize the Jerome home. Buddy is one of the vandals but is not the boy who pushed Karen Jerome down the stairs. Why does he stand by and let it happen?

Discuss Buddy's family. Why does his father leave? Buddy struggles with feelings of abandonment and succumbs to heavy alcohol use. Where could Buddy have sought help in dealing with his anger toward his father?

How does the vandalism affect the Jerome family? Explain the changes in Jane. Discuss her reaction when she finds out that Buddy was one of the vandals.

Interpret the title of the book. How do all of the characters "fall down" in some way?

The novel has been challenged because of language and violence. How does profanity define the character of the four vandals? Debate whether reading about violence causes violence.

Discuss why some who wish to ban the book call it "unfit for young minds." All of Cormier's works are "tough," "violent," and may seem hopeless to some people. Debate whether there is hope in *We All Fall Down*.

CHALLENGED FOR SIMILAR REASONS

Cormier, Robert. *After the First Death*. New York: Pantheon, 1979.

In 2000–2001, this novel about four foreign terrorists who hijack a busload of children on the way to a summer camp was challenged but retained on the ninth-grade reading list at Liberty High School in Fauquier, Virginia, because of "violence, suicide, and sexual content or gender stereotyping."

Cormier, Robert. *Tenderness*. New York: Bantam Doubleday, an imprint of Random House Children's Books, 1997.

This thriller about a fifteen-year-old girl and a teenage serial killer whose lives collide was challenged in the Fairfax County, Virginia, schools in 2002–2003 by a group called Parents against Bad Books in Schools (PABBIS) because of "profanity and descriptions of drug abuse, sexually explicit conduct and torture."

RESOURCES FOR RESPONDING TO CHALLENGES

What Reviewers Say

Michael Cart, the reviewer for *School Library Journal* (September 1, 1991), says, "Cormier is gingerly exploring some new terrain here, both literally and figuratively." He recommends the novel for grades 8 and up. *Publishers Weekly* (October 25, 1991) calls it "an unapologetically severe story." *Booklist* (September 15, 1991) recommends it for grades 8–12 and says "the elements of surprise" will appeal to teens. *Book Report* (March/April 1992) comments on the "sympathetic characters and suspenseful plot." They recommend it for grades 9–12.

Other Justification for Inclusion in Curricula and Library Collections

❖ 1994 California Young Reader Medal: Young Adult

Sources of Information about Challenges to the Novel

Beckman, Wendy Hart. *Robert Cormier: Banned, Challenged, and Censored*. New York: Enslow Publishers, 2008.

"Schools: Lawrence, Kansas." *Newsletter on Intellectual Freedom* 53, issue 1 (January 2004): 12.

INFORMATION ABOUT THE AUTHOR

Contemporary Authors Online, 2003. Books and Authors. Gale.

Campbell, Patricia. "Hangin' Out with Bob." *Top of the News* 42 (Winter 1986): 135–142.

Silvey, Anita. "An Interview with Robert Cormier." *Horn Book Magazine* 61 (March/April 1985): 145–155.

FURTHER READING ABOUT THE NOVEL

Campbell, Patty. *Robert Cormier: Daring to Disturb the Universe*. New York: Delacorte, an imprint of Penguin Random House, 2006 (E-book, 2012).

Shen, Fu-Yuan. "Narrative Strategies in Robert Cormier's Young Adult Novels." PhD diss., Ohio State University, 2006.

OTHER MEDIA SOURCES

https://www.youtube.com/watch?v=0xKkZkCUWJg. Posted December 27, 2012. Accessed August 16, 2015. Robert Cormier's son presents a video tribute to his father.

https://www.youtube.com/watch?v=0xKkZkCUWJg. Posted February 27, 2013. Accessed August 16, 2015. Robert Cormier talks about writing for teenagers today.

52

❖ ❖ ❖

Whale Talk

BY CHRIS CRUTCHER

New York: Greenwillow Books, an imprint of HarperCollins, 2001
Listening Library Audio, 2004
HarperCollins E-book, 2009
HarperCollins Paperback, 2009

> "He knew that we take what the universe gives us, and we either get the most
> out of it or we don't, but in the end we all go out the same way."

CHALLENGES: WHEN, WHY, AND WHERE

According to data collected by the American Library Association's Office for Intellectual Freedom, Crutcher's novel ranked #5 on the Top Ten Most Frequently Challenged Books List of 2005–2006.

2014–2015

According to data collected by the National Council of Teachers of English, the novel was challenged in the ninth-grade curriculum at a school district in Minnesota because of the "obscene amount of profanity, racism, and sexual content."

2008–2009

The Texas American Civil Liberties Union (Texas ACLU) reports that the novel was challenged but retained at Klein Oak High School in the Klein Independent School District because it is "politically, racially, or socially offensive."

2007–2008

The novel was challenged at the high school in Missouri Valley, Iowa, because of "racial slurs" and "profanity."

It was also challenged at the junior high school in Lake Oswego, Oregon, because it is "peppered with profanities, ranging from derogatory slang terms to sexual encounters and violence."

2005–2006

The novel was removed from the libraries in all five Limestone County, Alabama, high schools because of "profanity."

There is also a reported challenge at the Grand Ledge High School in Michigan because the book doesn't support "moral values." It was retained.

The South Carolina superintendent of education removed it from the suggested reading list for a pilot English literature curriculum. Her reason was "profanity" and "racial slurs."

2004–2005

The novel was challenged at Carver Bay High School in Georgetown, South Carolina. The challenger stated, "We're Christians and it's time that Christians take a stand."

According to the Texas ACLU, the novel was challenged in the curriculum at Ellison High School in the Killeen Independent School District because of "profanity." The use of the novel was restricted, though the conditions are unknown.

2003–2004

A parent of a student at Fowlerville High School in Michigan challenged the book and called it "vile, un-Godly, profane." It was retained but later removed from the curriculum.

It was also challenged at the Robert Gray Middle School in Portland, Oregon. The results of the challenge are unknown.

2001–2002

A parent in Missouri, Oregon, called the book "offensive."

THE STORY

Tao Jones, known as T.J., lives with his adoptive parents in the all-white town of Cutter, Washington. The jocks rule Cutter High School, but T.J. refuses to engage in sports because of anger issues that plagued him when he was younger. T.J. becomes captain of a newly formed swim team that includes an odd assortment of six students: intellectually slow Chris Coughlin; one-legged Andy Mott; and overweight Simon DeLong. The school does not have a pool, so the team trains at a local gym under the coaching leadership of a homeless man affectionately known as I.C.O. (interim coach Oliver). T.J.'s goal is to embarrass the jocks by having each guy on his swim team meet letterman requirements. When that happens, they meet with opposition from Coach Benson and his star athlete Mike Barbour. Coach Benson accepts the challenge to swim against Chris with the understanding that a victory for him will cause the swim team to relinquish their letters. Chris easily outswims the coach to great celebration. T.J. deals with racism, overt acts of bullying, a family tragedy, and a secret his father has harbored for a long time. He is a survivor, and through all his challenges he comes out stronger.

Themes
❖ Bullying
❖ Child abuse
❖ Discrimination
❖ Domestic abuse
❖ Family
❖ Forgiveness
❖ Violence

TALKING WITH TEENS ABOUT THE ISSUES

Describe the town of Cutter, Washington. Why is T.J. a "misfit" in town? How does he become a leader among other "misfits"? Discuss why Coach Benson and jocks like Mike Barbour are embarrassed by the success of the swim team.

T.J. has a chance encounter with Heidi, a biracial illegitimate child who is abused by her stepfather, Rich Marshall. Discuss why T.J.'s family invites Heidi and her mother to live with them. How does this lead to the tragic death of T.J.'s dad?

The novel has been challenged because of profanity and lack of moral values. Discuss how the term *moral values* is subjective. What is the moral of the story? Explain how T.J.'s values are to be admired.

Profanity out of context may offend many people. Why is it important to understand that profanity defines character? Heidi uses language that she has heard from her racist stepfather. What does this language say about Rich Marshall?

There are parents who object to the child abuse and violence in the novel. Discuss the realities of child abuse in our society. Find out what agencies in your community deal with issues related to child abuse.

Debate whether there is hope at the end of the novel. What does the ending say about the kind of man T.J. becomes?

CHALLENGED FOR SIMILAR REASONS

Childress, Alice. *Rainbow Jordan.* New York: Putnam, an imprint of Penguin, 1981.

This novel about fourteen-year-old Rainbow, who suffers abandonment, was challenged in the public schools in Gwinnett County, Georgia, because of "foul language and sexual references."

Cormier, Robert. *The Rag and Bone Shop.* New York: Delacorte, an imprint of Random House, 2001.

Twelve-year-old Jason Dorrant is lonely and bullied, but his life becomes even more complicated when a seven-year-old girl who lives next door is murdered. According to the 2003–2004 report of the Texas ACLU, the novel was banned from the Lueders Elementary Library in the Lueders-Avoca Independent School District because of "sexual content."

RESOURCES FOR RESPONDING TO CHALLENGES

What Reviewers Say

Booklist (April 1, 2001) praises the book for "quick pacing" and "well-constructed characters." They recommend it for grades 8–12. *School Library Journal* (May 1, 2001) calls the novel "undeniably robust." *Publishers Weekly* (March 12, 2001) says, "Crutcher delivers a frank, powerful message." The reviewer for *Horn Book Magazine* (May 1, 2001) calls the novel "melodramatic" but doesn't see that as a fault. *Kliatt* (March 2001) says that the book is told with "passion and humor."

Other Justification for Inclusion in Curricula and Library Collections

- ❖ 2005 ALA/YALSA Popular Paperbacks for Young Adults
- ❖ 2004 ALA/YALSA Outstanding Books for the College Bound: Humanities

❖ 2002 ABC Children's Booksellers Choices
❖ 2002 ALA/YALSA Best Books for Young Adults
❖ 2002 Pacific Northwest Booksellers Award
❖ 2002 Washington State Book Award

Sources of Information about Challenges to the Novel

"Alabama School Bans Children's Book, *Whale Talk*." First Amendment Center, March 11, 2005. Accessed July 21, 2015. http://www.firstamendmentcenter.org/alabama-school-bans-childrens -book-whale-talk.

Crutcher, Chris. "How They Do It." *Huffington Post*, August 2, 2011. Accessed July 21, 2015. http://www.huffingtonpost.com/chris-crutcher/how-they-do-it_b_915605.html.

"Pastor's Complaint Prompts District to Pull Book from Classroom." First Amendment Center, February 26, 2007. Accessed August 23, 2015. http://www.firstamendmentcenter.org/pastors -complaint-prompts-district-to-pull-book-from-classroom.

Stancil, Clyde L. "Banned Author Coming Here to Defend His Work." *Decatur Daily News* (Alabama), September 22, 2005. Accessed August 23, 2015. http://legacy.decaturdaily.com/ decaturdaily/news/050922/banned.shtml.

INFORMATION ABOUT THE AUTHOR

http://www.chriscrutcher.com (Crutcher's official website)

Contemporary Authors Online, 2014. Books and Authors. Gale.

Chance, Rosemary. "The King of Teen Psychology." *Teacher Librarian* 31, issue 1 (October 2003): 36.

Davis, Terry. *Presenting Chris Crutcher*. Twayne's United States Authors Series. Farmington Hills, MI: Cengage Gale, 1997.

Gillis, Bryan, and Pam B. Cole. *Chris Crutcher: A Stotan for Young Adults*. Lanham, MD: Rowman & Littlefield, 2012.

FURTHER READING ABOUT THE NOVEL

Brown, Jennifer M. "*PW* Talks with Chris Crutcher." *Publishers Weekly* 248, issue 11 (March 12, 2001): 92.

Halls, Kelly Milner. "Story behind the Story: Crutcher's People." *Booklist* 97, issue 15 (April 1, 2001).

Herald, Diana Tixier. "Adults as Good Guys in YA Novels." *Voice of Youth Advocates* 33, issue 2 (June 2010): 108–109.

OTHER MEDIA SOURCES

https://www.youtube.com/watch?v=2Xeeq4mv3JM. Posted September 25, 2009. Accessed August 23, 2015. A librarian from Missoula Public Library in Missoula, Montana, reviews *Whale Talk* for Banned Books Week.

https://www.youtube.com/watch?v=2kccTXaLyi8. Posted August 11, 2010. Accessed July 21, 2015. Chris Crutcher talks about censorship.

53

❖ ❖ ❖

What My Mother Doesn't Know

BY SONYA SONES

New York: Simon & Schuster, 2001
Simon & Schuster Paperback, 2003
Brilliance Audio, 2008
Simon Pulse E-book, 2010

> "'I love you,' Robin says.
> I feel my cheeks
> Turn the color of the sky.
> 'I love you, too,' I say."

CHALLENGES: WHEN, WHY, AND WHERE

According to data collected by the American Library Association's Office for Intellectual Freedom, Sones's novel was #5 on the Top 100 Banned/Challenged Books List of 2000–2009. It was ranked #6 on the Top Ten Most Frequently Challenged Books List in 2004–2005; #7 in 2005–2006; #7 in 2010–2011; and #8 in 2011–2012. The reasons cited include "profanity, sexual content and unsuited for age group."

2010–2011

A parent of a student at Theisen Middle School in Fond du Lac, Wisconsin, challenged the novel because of "sexual content." The school board voted to retain the book.

The Texas American Civil Liberties Union (Texas ACLU) reports that the book was placed on a restricted shelf at the Cesar E. Chavez Middle School in the La Joya Independent School District because of "sexual content and nudity."

2007–2008

According to the Texas ACLU the novel was challenged but retained at Keefer Crossing Middle School in the New Caney Independent School District because of "profanity and sexual content."

2006–2007

The novel was restricted to seventh- and eighth-graders at the middle school in Spring Hill, Wisconsin, after a parent of a sixth-grader called it "soft porn" because of "groping, masturbation and sexual fantasies."

2005–2006

The Texas ACLU reports that the novel was challenged at the Kitty Hawk Middle School in the Judson Independent School District because of "sexual content." It was restricted to an "eighth-grade reading section."

It was banned at the Hempstead Middle School in the Hempstead Independent School District because of "profanity."

2004–2005

The novel was challenged at Bonnette Junior High School in Deer Park, Texas, because of "foul language and references to masturbation."

2003–2004

It was removed from the library shelves at schools in the Rosedale Union School District in Bakersfield, California, because the narrator talks about how her "breasts react to cold."

It was challenged but retained at the Franklin Middle School Library in the Abilene, Texas, Independent School District because of "sexual content."

It was also challenged at the Hildebrandt Intermediate School in the Klein, Texas, Independent School District because of "profanity and sexual content." The result of the challenge is unknown.

THE STORY

Written in verse, fifteen-year-old Sophie Stein relates her interest in boys but reveals that her inexperience with matters of the heart complicates relationships during her freshman year. She has a brief fling with Lou, but after he dumps her, she falls for Dylan, a boy her friends find extremely "hot." The two date for a while, but he pressures her to have sex, and she is reluctant. She begins to realize that she does not love Dylan, and truth be known she does not even like him. As she deals with these thoughts, she enters an Internet chat room and meets a boy who calls himself Chaz. They agree to talk every night at ten, but he says things that cause her to suspect that he is a pervert. She leaves the relationship before she ever meets him in person. One day she visits an art museum and runs into Robin Murphy, a classmate who is not like the other guys she has known. He is not physically attractive or popular. And he is the target of bullies at school. She is surprised when she falls in love with him. Her friends do not understand, but Sophie and Robin respect one another for who they are, and that is the basis of their emerging relationship. *What My Girlfriend Doesn't Know* (2007) is a companion novel told from Robin Murphy's point of view.

Themes
❖ Family
❖ Friendship
❖ Love
❖ Lust

TALKING WITH TEENS ABOUT THE ISSUES

Describe Sophie's family. How are they present without presence?

Explain what the students in Sophie's school mean when they say, "Stop being such a Murphy."

Why does Sophie keep her relationship with Robin Murphy a secret? At the end of the novel, she sits with him at lunch. What does this gesture symbolize?

Discuss the difference between love and lust. Then trace Sophie's romantic journey. Which of her relationships are more about lust? How does she grow to understand what matters most in a relationship?

The novel has been challenged for sexual content. What might Sophie say to those who want to challenge her journey?

The novel was placed on a restricted shelf because some parents felt it was "soft porn." Define the term *soft porn*. To what scenes are they referring? How do these scenes make Sophie realize that she is dealing with a pervert?

Discuss the dangers of Internet chat rooms. Explain what readers might learn from Sophie's experience with Chaz.

Explain the title of the novel. Discuss what Sophie might want her mother to know should they have a real conversation.

CHALLENGED FOR SIMILAR REASONS

Naylor, Phyllis Reynolds. *Alice Alone*. New York: Atheneum, an imprint of Simon & Schuster, 2001.

In 2006, this novel about ninth-grader Alice McKinley who worries about losing her boyfriend to a new girl at school was banned from the junior high school library in the Katy, Texas, Independent School District because of "profanity and sexual content."

Wittlinger, Ellen. *Sandpiper*. New York: Simon & Schuster, 2007.

Sandpiper is a high school girl who uses guys, and they use her, for sex, until she meets kind and gentle Walker and then everything changes. The novel was challenged in 2007–2008 at the high school in Brookwood, Alabama, because of "sexual content and language." After much consideration, the board eventually retained the book.

RESOURCES FOR RESPONDING TO CHALLENGES

What Reviewers Say

Booklist (November 1, 2001) calls the novel "funny" and "touching." They recommend it for grades 6–10. *Publishers Weekly* (October 15, 2001) gives the book a star and calls the poems "fluid" and says there is a "satisfying ending." *School Library Journal* (October 1, 2001) says the novel is a "peep hole" into the lives of teenagers. They recommend it for grades 6–8. *Voice of Youth Advocates* (October 1, 2001) calls it "humorous and bittersweet." The starred review for *Kirkus* (September 15, 2001) comments, "Romantic and sexy, with a happy ending."

Other Justification for Inclusion in Curricula and Library Collections

- ❖ 2006 Iowa Teen Book Award
- ❖ 2003 IRA Young Adult Choices
- ❖ 2003 *VOYA* Top Shelf for Middle School Readers

❖ 2002 ALA/YALSA Best Books for Young Adults
❖ 2002 ALA/YALSA Quick Picks for Reluctant Young Adult Readers: Fiction
❖ 2002 Michigan Thumbs Up! Honor Book
❖ 2001 *Booklist* Editors' Choice
❖ 2001 Teenreads.com Editor's Choice

Sources of Information about Challenges to the Novel

Sones, Sonya. "Banned in Bakersfield." *Los Angeles Times*, September 27, 2011. Accessed August 5, 2015. http://articles.latimes.com/2011/sep/27/opinion/la-oe-sones-censorship-20110927.
"Wisconsin School Restricts Sones Book." *American Libraries* 38, issue 6 (June/July 2007): 33–34.

INFORMATION ABOUT THE AUTHOR

http://www.sonyasones.com (Sones's official website)
Contemporary Authors Online, 2012. Books and Authors. Gale.

FURTHER READING ABOUT THE NOVEL

Lesesne, Teri. "Gaining Power through Poetry: An Interview with Sonya Sones." *Teacher Librarian* 29, issue 3 (February 2002): 51–53.
Sones, Sonya. "Confessions of a Verse Novelist." *Voice of Youth Advocates* 33, issue 4 (October 2010): 314–315.

OTHER MEDIA SOURCES

https://www.youtube.com/watch?v=fP7q6n9Rr9c. Posted October 8, 2012. Accessed August 5, 2015. A fan reads from *What My Mother Doesn't Know* for the Banned Books Week Virtual Read-Out.
https://www.youtube.com/watch?v=d41CkggqvD8. Posted January 2, 2014. Accessed August 5, 2015. Sonya Sones speaks at the 2013 National Book Festival.

54

❖ ❖ ❖

Wintergirls

BY LAURIE HALSE ANDERSON

New York: Viking, an imprint of Penguin, 2009
Brilliance Audio, 2009
Penguin Paperback, 2010

> "Eating was hard. Breathing was hard.
> Living was hardest."

CHALLENGES: WHEN, WHY, AND WHERE

2008–2009

Williamson County school officials in Franklin, Tennessee, removed the book from one school website after parents complained that it was "extraordinarily salacious, sensual, and sensationalistic."

THE STORY

Cassie and Lia were friends in elementary school, but at eighteen they have grown apart. Both have deep emotional issues that cause severe eating disorders—one suffers from anorexia and the other bulimia. They once even engaged in a competition to see who could lose the most weight, and they both landed in the hospital. Much later, Cassie dies from a ruptured esophagus caused by her bulimic condition, and Lia is riddled with guilt because she refused to answer the telephone when Cassie called her thirty-three times on the day of her death. Cassie's mother is struggling to deal with her daughter's senseless death, and she appeals to Lia to answer questions regarding all that was going on with Cassie and why the eating disorder went too far. But Lia is dealing with her own issues at home, where she receives mixed messages about her health from her mother, stepmother, and father. Lia's problems become so complex that she lapses into a deep depression.

Themes
❖ Death
❖ Dysfunctional family
❖ Eating disorders
❖ Friendship
❖ Guilt
❖ Self-identity

TALKING WITH TEENS ABOUT THE ISSUES

Lia and Cassie engage in a competition about who can lose the most weight. Discuss the dangers of such a competition. What is the root of Lia and Cassie's eating disorders?

The girls had been best friends since elementary school. What caused their breakup? Cassie calls Lia thirty-three times on the night of her death. Why does Lia ignore the calls? Explain the guilt Lia suffers after Cassie dies.

Why does Cassie's mother have a need to speak with Lia after Cassie's death?

Describe Lia's family. Discuss Lia's relationship with her mother, father, and stepmother. How does she receive mixed messages from them about her weight?

The novel was banned in Tennessee after a parent called it "extraordinarily salacious, sensual, and sensationalistic." What is sensual about the novel?

One blogger believes that the book may serve as a manual for teens with eating disorders (http://well.blogs.nytimes.com/2009/05/11/the-troubling-allure-of-eating-disorder-books/?_r=0). Others argue that no books lead teens to eating disorders. Debate both sides of the issue. What might teens and their families gain from reading *Wintergirls*?

Laurie Halse Anderson says that she is told that many librarians are afraid to buy the book for their school libraries because they are afraid of challenges. How is this a type of censorship? Make a case for purchasing the book for high school libraries.

CHALLENGED FOR SIMILAR REASONS

Dessen, Sarah. *Just Listen.* New York: Penguin, 2006.

This novel about sisters who are teenage models, one with an eating disorder, was challenged in 2007 at Armwood High School in Tampa, Florida, because of "language and sexual content."

Halpern, Julie. *Get Well Soon.* New York: Feiwel & Friends, an imprint of Macmillan, 2007.

This novel about a teenage girl who is committed to a mental hospital for depression was challenged in 2009–2010 at Theisen Middle School in Fond du Lac, Wisconsin, because of "inappropriate content."

RESOURCES FOR RESPONDING TO CHALLENGES

What Reviewers Say

School Library Journal's (February 1, 2009) starred review highlights the "crisp and pitch-perfect first-person narrative" and recommends the novel for grades 8 and up. *Kirkus* (February 1, 2009) also gives the novel a star and says it "rises far above the standard problem novel." The reviewer for *Booklist* (December 15, 2008) gives the novel a star and states, "Anderson illuminates a dark but utterly realistic world." *Voice of Youth Advocates* (April 1, 2009) says the "style, language and topic are spot on." *Publishers Weekly* (January 26, 2009) gives the novel a star and says, "The author sets up Lia's history convincingly and with enviable economy."

Other Justification for Inclusion in Curricula and Library Collections
- 2010 ALA/YALSA Best Books for Young Adults
- 2010 ALA/YALSA Quick Picks for Reluctant Young Adult Readers: Fiction

- ❖ 2010 Amelia Bloomer Lists: Young Adult Fiction
- ❖ 2010 New York Public Library's Stuff for the Teen Age
- ❖ 2010 Pennsylvania School Library Association's Young Adult Top 40 Reading List
- ❖ 2009 *Booklist* Editors' Choice: Books for Youth: Older Readers Category
- ❖ 2009 *New York Times* Editors' Choice
- ❖ 2009 *Publishers Weekly* Best Children's Books
- ❖ 2009 Tayshas High School Reading List (Texas)

Sources of Information about Challenges to the Novel

"Reading about It Will Make You Do It?" National Coalition against Censorship (blog). Posted May 27, 2009. Accessed June 14, 2015. https://ncacblog.wordpress.com/2009/05/27/reading-about-it-will-make-you-do-it/.

Scales, Pat. "Mobilizing the Effort." *School Library Journal* 60, issue 4 (April 2014): 19.

INFORMATION ABOUT THE AUTHOR

http://madwomanintheforest.com (Anderson's official website)

Contemporary Authors Online, 2013. Books and Authors. Gale.

Glenn, Wendy J. *Laurie Halse Anderson: Speaking in Tongues*. Lanham, MD: Rowman & Littlefield, 2009.

Lew, Kristi. *Laurie Halse Anderson*. New York: Rosen Publishing Group, 2013.

FURTHER READING ABOUT THE NOVEL

Folios, Alison M. G. "What Does Normal Look Like?" *School Library Journal* 61, issue 5 (May 2015): 53.

Hill, Rebecca A. "The Weight of It." *Voice of Youth Advocates* 37, issue 2 (June 2014): 32–35.

Hsin, Chun (Jamie) Tsai. "The Girls Who Do Not Eat: Food, Hunger, and Thinness in Meg Rosoff's *How I Live Now* and Laurie Halse Anderson's *Wintergirls*." *Jeunesse: Young People, Texts, Cultures* 6, issue 1 (Summer 2014): 36–55.

Karlin, Dorothy. "How to Be Yourself: Ideological Interpellation, Weight Control, and Young Adult Novels." *Jeunesse: Young People, Texts, Cultures* 6, issue 2 (Winter 2014): 72–89.

North, Anna. "*Wintergirls*: Possibly Triggering, Definitely Thought-Provoking." *Jezebel* (blog), May 19, 2009. Accessed June 14, 2015. http://jezebel.com/5261055/wintergirls-possibly-triggering-definitely-thought-provoking.

Thayer, Kelly. "A Multigenre Approach to Reading Laurie Halse Anderson's *Wintergirls*: Converging Text, Constructing Meaning." *Signal* 35, issue 2 (Spring/Summer 2012): 7–11.

OTHER MEDIA SOURCES

https://www.youtube.com/watch?v=xdbe2gbMjcE. Posted September 30, 2011. Accessed June 14, 2015. Kristin Pekoll from the American Library Association's Office for Intellectual Freedom reads from *Wintergirls* for the Banned Books Week Virtual Read-Out.

https://www.youtube.com/watch?v=tyjMaSyQLE8. Posted May 21, 2013. Accessed June 2, 2015. Laurie Halse Anderson talks to the American Booksellers Foundation for Free Expression (ABFFE) about censorship.

APPENDIX A

❖ ❖ ❖

Adult Books That Have Been Challenged or Banned in the High School Curriculum

Adventures of Huckleberry Finn by Mark Twain, for "racial slurs"

Animal Farm by George Orwell, because "Orwell was a communist"

Anne Frank: The Diary of a Young Girl by Anne Frank, because it was "sexually offensive"

Around the World in Eighty Days by Jules Verne, because it was "very unfavorable to Mormons"

The Art of Racing in the Rain by Garth Stein, for "sexual content and bestiality"

As I Lay Dying by William Faulkner, for "language" and because it was "anti-Christian"

The Awakening by Kate Chopin, because it "shows a painting of a woman's bare breast"

Bastard out of Carolina by Dorothy Allison, because the "characters [are] not positive role models"

Beach Music by Pat Conroy, for "sexual assault, suicide, and violence"

The Bean Trees by Barbara Kingsolver, for "sexual content and vulgar language"

Beloved by Toni Morrison, for "bestiality, racism, and sex"

Black Boy by Richard Wright, for "profanity" and because it "may spark hard feelings between students of different races"

Bless Me Ultima by Rudolfo Anaya, for "profanity," "vulgar Spanish words," "sexual content," and because it "glorifies witchcraft and death" and was "offensive to religious sensitivities"

The Bluest Eye by Toni Morrison, for "sexual and violent content"

Brave New World by Aldous Huxley, for "language and moral content"

Catch-22 by Joseph Heller, for "references to women as whores"

The Catcher in the Rye by J. D. Salinger, for its "dreadful, dreary recital of sickness, sordidness, and sadism"

A Clockwork Orange by Anthony Burgess, for "objectionable language"

The Color Purple by Alice Walker, for "language and sexuality or 'obscenity'" and "racism, violence against women and rape"

Crime and Punishment by Fyodor Dostoyevsky

The Curious Incident of the Dog in the Nighttime by Mark Haddon, for "profanity" and using the "Lord's name in vain"

Ellen Foster by Kaye Gibbons, because it was "politically, racially, or socially offensive"

Extremely Loud and Incredibly Close by Jonathan Foer, for "profanity, sex, and violence"

Fahrenheit 451 by Ray Bradbury, for "alcohol," "violence," "dirty talk," and "using God's name in vain"

A Farewell to Arms by Ernest Hemingway, for "sex"

Flowers for Algernon by Daniel Keyes, for "sexual content and nudity"

The Glass Castle by Jeannette Walls, for "alcoholism and homelessness"

Go Tell It on the Mountain by James Baldwin, for "profanity and sex"

The Grapes of Wrath by John Steinbeck, for "language" and "sexual content"

The Great Gatsby by F. Scott Fitzgerald, for "language and sex"

The Great Santini by Pat Conroy, because it was "obscene and pornographic"

The Handmaid's Tale by Margaret Atwood, for "grossly inappropriate content" and because it was "sexually explicit, violently graphic and morally corrupt"

I Know Why the Caged Bird Sings by Maya Angelou, for the "graphic depiction of molestation and rape" and "sexual content"

The Immortal Life of Henrietta Lacks by Rebecca Skloot, for "explicit content—physical and sexual abuse"

The Invisible Man by Ralph Ellison, for "strong language" and "social and intellectual issues facing African Americans"

Jubilee by Margaret Walker, because it was "offensive and trashy"

The Jungle by Upton Sinclair, for "socialist views"

The Kite Runner by Khaled Hosseini, for "language, violence, homosexual rape, pedophilia, and pornography"

A Lesson before Dying by Ernest J. Gaines, for "sex, violence, and profanity"

Like Water for Chocolate by Laura Esquivel, for "profanity and sexual content"

The Lord of the Flies by William Golding

The Lords of Discipline by Pat Conroy, for "profanity and sadomasochistic acts" and "language, sexual content, and hazing"

Macbeth by William Shakespeare, because it was "too violent"

Moby Dick by Herman Melville, because it "contains homosexuality"

Native Son by Richard Wright, because it was "violent and sexually graphic"

Nickel and Dimed: On (Not) Getting By in America by Barbara Ehrenreich, for "economic fallacies and socialist ideas"

1984 by George Orwell, because it "promotes communism"

Of Mice and Men by John Steinbeck, because it was "politically, racially, or socially offensive"

One Flew over the Cuckoo's Nest by Ken Kesey

The Pillars of the Earth by Ken Follett, for "inappropriate sexual content"

A Prayer for Owen Meany by John Irving, for "profanity and sexual content"

The Prince of Tides by Pat Conroy, for "sexual content, suicide, and violence"

Running with Scissors by Augusten Burroughs, for "alcohol, profanity, and sexual content" and "explicit homosexual and heterosexual situations, profanity, moral shortcomings"

The Scarlet Letter by Nathaniel Hawthorne, because it was "a filthy book"

The Secret Life of Bees by Sue Monk Kidd, for "profanity and sexual content"

Silas Marner by George Eliot, because "you can't prove what that dirty old man is doing with that child between chapters"

Slaughterhouse Five by Kurt Vonnegut, because it was "obscene and immoral"

Snow Falling on Cedars by David Guterson, for "sexual content"

Song of Solomon by Toni Morrison, for "sexual imagery, profanity, and [an] incestuous relationship"

The Sun Also Rises by Ernest Hemingway, for "profanity, promiscuity and the overall decadence of its characters"

Their Eyes Were Watching God by Zora Neale Hurston, for "profanity and sexual explicitness"

To Kill a Mockingbird by Harper Lee, for "rape and racism"

Water for Elephants by Sara Gruen, for "sexual content"

The Water Is Wide by Pat Conroy, for "sexual references and use of God and Jesus in a vain and profane manner"

The Working Poor by David K. Shipler, for "sex abuse and abortion" and "sex, profanity, and rape"

APPENDIX B

❖ ❖ ❖

Rankings of Young Adult Books on the Top 100 Banned/Challenged Books List of 2000–2009

#2	*The Alice Series* by Phyllis Reynolds Naylor
#3	*The Chocolate War* by Robert Cormier
#6	*I Know Why the Caged Bird Sings* by Maya Angelou
#8	*His Dark Materials Trilogy* by Philip Pullman
#9	*The Internet Girls Series* (*ttyl*; *ttfn*; *18r, g8r*) by Lauren Myracle
#10	*The Perks of Being a Wallflower* by Stephen Chbosky
#11	*Fallen Angels* by Walter Dean Myers
#16	*Forever* by Judy Blume
#18	*Go Ask Alice* by Anonymous
#19	*The Catcher in the Rye* by J. D. Salinger
#22	*Gossip Girl Series* by Cecily von Ziegesar
#23	*The Giver* by Lois Lowry
#25	*Killing Mr. Griffin* by Lois Duncan
#29	*The Face on the Milk Carton* by Caroline B. Cooney
#30	*We All Fall Down* by Robert Cormier
#31	*What My Mother Doesn't Know* by Sonya Sones
#34	*The Earth, My Butt, and Other Big Round Things* by Carolyn Mackler
#39	*Kaffir Boy* by Mark Mathabane
#40	*Life Is Funny* by E. R. Frank
#41	*Whale Talk* by Chris Crutcher
#44	*Athletic Shorts* by Chris Crutcher
#48	*Rainbow Boys* by Alex Sanchez
#51	*Daughters of Eve* by Lois Duncan
#54	*The Facts Speak for Themselves* by Brock Cole
#56	*When Dad Killed Mom* by Julius Lester
#57	*Blood and Chocolate* by Annette Curtis Klause
#58	*Fat Kid Rules the World* by K. L. Going
#60	*Speak* by Laurie Halse Anderson
#63	*The Terrorist* by Caroline B. Cooney

(continued)

#79	*The Upstairs Room* by Johanna Reiss
#80	*A Day No Pigs Would Die* by Robert Newton Peck
#82	*Deal with It!* by Esther Drill
#83	*Detour for Emmy* by Marilyn Reynolds
#84	*So Far from the Bamboo Grove* by Yoko Watkins
#85	*Staying Fat for Sarah Byrnes* by Chris Crutcher
#86	*Cut* by Patricia McCormick
#87	*Tiger Eyes* by Judy Blume
#100	*America* by E. R. Frank

APPENDIX C

❖ ❖ ❖

Rankings of Young Adult Books on the Top 100 Most Frequently Challenged Books List of 1990–1999

#3	*I Know Why the Caged Bird Sings* by Maya Angelou
#4	*The Chocolate War* by Robert Cormier
#7	*Forever* by Judy Blume
#10	*The Catcher in the Rye* by J. D. Salinger
#11	*The Giver* by Lois Lowry
#14	*The Alice Series* by Phyllis Reynolds Naylor
#16	*A Day No Pigs Would Die* by Robert Newton Peck
#25	*Go Ask Alice* by Anonymous
#33	*Kaffir Boy* by Mark Mathabane
#35	*What's Happening to My Body? Book for Girls: A Growing-Up Guide for Parents and Daughters* by Lynda Madaras
#36	*Fallen Angels* by Walter Dean Myers
#38	*The Outsiders* by S. E. Hinton
#39	*The Pigman* by Paul Zindel
#41	*We All Fall Down* by Robert Cormier
#44	*Annie on My Mind* by Nancy Garden
#59	*The Anarchist Cookbook* by William Powell
#63	*Athletic Shorts* by Chris Crutcher
#64	*Killing Mr. Griffin* by Lois Duncan
#65	*Fade* by Robert Cormier
#75	*Arizona Kid* by Ron Koertge
#76	*Family Secrets* by Norma Klein
#80	*The Face on the Milk Carton* by Caroline B. Cooney
#89	*Tiger Eyes* by Judy Blume
#92	*Running Loose* by Chris Crutcher
#96	*The Drowning of Stephan Jones* by Bette Greene
#97	*That Was Then, This Is Now* by S. E. Hinton

APPENDIX D

❖ ❖ ❖

Resources for Teaching Young Adults about the Freedom to Read

FICTION

Blume, Judy, ed. *Places I Never Meant to Be.* New York: Simon Pulse, an imprint of Simon & Schuster, 2001. Twelve writers whose works have been banned or challenged contribute original short stories that have a central theme: the main characters are in places they never meant to find themselves. At the end of their story, the authors write about their experiences with censorship.

Brande, Robin. *Me, Evolution and Other Freaks of Nature.* New York: Knopf, an imprint of Random House Children's Books, 2009. Mena Reese, a high school freshman, knows firsthand that it's lonely to stick up for one's rights, but when a favorite science teacher faces off with censors over a unit on evolution, she finds a few open-minded friends who are willing to join forces to stand by their teacher.

Bryant, Jen. *Ringside 1925.* New York: Yearling Paperback, an imprint of Random House Children's Books, 2009. The trial of John T. Scope for teaching evolution, forbidden by Tennessee law, relates in free verse how the entire town was affected by the media frenzy.

Crutcher, Chris. *The Sledding Hill.* New York: Greenwillow Books, an imprint of HarperCollins, 2005. Fourteen-year-old Eddie takes direction from a ghost of a deceased friend as he battles a conservative minister who is leading a censorship war at his school.

Facklam, Margery. *The Trouble with Mothers.* New York: Clarion, an imprint of Harcourt Houghton Mifflin, 1989. Eighth-grader Luke Troy is devastated when his mother, a teacher, writes a historical novel that is considered pornography by some people in the community where they live.

Greene, Bette. *The Drowning of Stephan Jones.* New York: Open Road Media, 2011. Carla Wayland's mother is a public librarian in Rachetville, Arkansas, when members of a very conservative church attempt to remove books that offend them from the library's collection.

Hentoff, Nat. *The Day They Came to Arrest the Book.* New York: Delacorte, an imprint of Random House, 1982. Students in a high school English class protest the study of *Huckleberry Finn* until the editor of the school newspaper uncovers other cases of censorship and conducts a public hearing about the truth behind the mysterious disappearance of certain library books and the resignation of the school librarian.

Lasky, Kathryn. *Memoirs of a Bookbat.* Boston: Houghton Mifflin Harcourt Paperback, 1996. Fourteen-year-old Harper Jessup, an avid reader, runs away because she feels that her individual rights are threatened when her parents, born-again fundamentalist Christians, lodge a public promotion of book censorship.

Peck, Richard. *The Last Safe Place on Earth.* New York: Delacorte, an imprint of Random House Children's Books, 1995. The Tobin family is satisfied that Walden Woods is a quiet, safe community to rear their three children. Then, seven-year-old Marnie begins having nightmares after a babysitter tells her that Halloween is "evil." And Todd and Diana, sophomores in high school, witness an organized group's attempt to censor books in their school library.

Reed, M. K. *Americus*. Illustrated by Jonathan David Hill. New York: First Second Books, an imprint of Macmillan, 2011. Americus public library is under attack by a right-wing religious group, and ninth-grader Neal Barton, who is by nature quiet and reserved, finds himself in uncharted territory when he is thrust into an all-out defense of his favorite fantasy series.

NONFICTION

Barbour, Scott. *Censorship*. Opposing Viewpoint Series. Farmington Hills, MI: Greenhaven Press, an imprint of Cengage Gale, 2010. Both sides of issues related to censorship are presented to guide students toward forming their own opinions.

Bily, Cynthia A. *Banned Books*. Introducing Issues with Opposing Viewpoints Series. Farmington Hills, MI: Greenhaven Press, an imprint of Cengage Gale, 2012. Inspired by the Opposing Viewpoints Series, this work gives information about current issues related to book censorship.

Green, Jonathan, and Nicholas J. Karolides. *The Encyclopedia of Censorship*. New York: Facts on File, 2005. This reference work is well researched and broader in scope than the 1990 edition and covers all types of censorship in countries throughout the world.

Egendorf, Laura K., ed. *Censorship*. Examining Issues through Political Cartoons Series. Farmington Hills, MI: Greenhaven Press, an imprint of Cengage Gale, 2003. Illustrated with political cartoons, this collection of articles by various people of authority discusses freedom of speech in our democracy, censorship issues in schools, whether pornography should be censored, and whether the government should regulate art and pop art.

Gottfried, Ted. *Censorship*. Open for Debate Series. Tarrytown, NY: Benchmark Books, 2005. Case studies explain current and often volatile issues related to the Internet, book censorship, hate speech, and motion-picture ratings. A center section called "You Be the Judge" asks readers to debate specific real-life scenarios.

APPENDIX E

❖ ❖ ❖

Professional Resources for Book Censorship and the Freedom to Read

Abel, Richard L. *Speaking Respect, Respecting Speech*. Chicago: University of Chicago Press, 1998.

Adams, Helen R. *Ensuring Intellectual Freedom and Access to Information in the School Library Media Program*. Westport, CT: Libraries Unlimited, Inc., 2008.

Adams, Thelma, ed. *Censorship and First Amendment Rights: A Primer*. New York: American Booksellers Foundation for Free Expression, 1991.

Atkins, Robert, and Svetlana Mintcheva, eds. *Censoring Culture: Contemporary Threats to Free Expression*. New York: The New Press, 2006.

Bald, Margaret. *Literature Suppressed on Religious Grounds*. New York: Facts on File, 2011.

Boyer, Paul S. *Purity in Print: Book Censorship in America from the Gilded Age to the Computer Age*. Print Culture History in Modern America Series. Madison: University of Wisconsin Press, 2002.

Brown, Jean E. *Preserving Intellectual Freedom: Fighting Censorship in Our Schools*. Urbana, IL: National Council of Teachers of English, 1994.

Burress, Lee, and Edward Jenkinson. *The Students' Right to Know*. Urbana, IL: National Council of Teachers of English, 1982.

Coetzee, J. M. *Giving Offense: On Censorship*. Chicago: University of Chicago Press, 1997.

Dell, Pamela. *You Can't Read This: Why Books Get Banned*. Mankato, MN: Compass Point Books, 2010.

Doyle, Robert P. *Banned Books: Challenging Our Freedom to Read*. Chicago: American Library Association, 2014.

Foerstel, Herbert N. *Banned in the U.S.A.: A Reference Guide to Book Censorship in Schools and Public Libraries*. Portsmouth, NH: Greenwood, 2002.

Hull, Mary. *Censorship in America: A Reference Handbook*. Santa Barbara, CA: ABC-CLIO, 1999.

Johnson, Claudia. *Stifled Laughter: One Woman's Fight against Censorship*. Golden, CO: Fulcrum Publishing, 1994.

Karolides, Nicholas J. *Literature Suppressed on Political Grounds*. New York: Facts on File, 2011.

Karolides, Nicholas J., and Margaret Bald. *120 Banned Books: Censorship Histories of World Literature*. New York: Facts on File, 2005.

Karolides, Nicholas J., Lee Burress, and John M. Kean, eds. *Censored Books: Critical Viewpoints*. Lanham, MD: Scarecrow Press, 2001.

Kennedy, Sheila Suess, ed. *Free Expression in America: A Documentary History*. Portsmouth, NH: Greenwood, 1999.

Knox, Emily J. M. *Book Banning in 21st-Century America*. Lanham, MD: Rowman & Littlefield, 2015.

Knuth, Rebecca. *Burning Books and Leveling Libraries: Extremist Violence and Cultural Destruction*. Portsmouth, NH: Greenwood, 2006.

Lent, ReLeah Cossett, and Gloria Pipkin. *Keep Them Reading: An Anti-Censorship Handbook for Educators*. Language and Literacy Series. New York: Teachers College Press, Columbia University, 2012.

Lewis, Anthony. *Freedom for the Thought That We Hate: A Biography of the First Amendment*. New York: Basic Books, 2007.

Lusted, Marcia Amidon. *Banned Books*. Edina, MN: ABDO Publishing, 2013.

McNicol, Sarah, ed. *Forbidden Fruit: The Censorship of Literature and Information for Young People*. Boca Raton, FL: Brown Walker Press, 2008.

Morrison, Toni, ed. *Burn This Book: PEN Writers Speak Out on the Power of the Word*. New York: HarperStudio, 2009.

Noble, William. *Bookbanning in America: Who Bans Books? And Why* Forest Dale, VT: Paul S. Eriksson, 1990.

Office for Intellectual Freedom. *Intellectual Freedom Manual*. Chicago: American Library Association, 2010.

Reichman, Henry. *Censorship and Selection: Issues and Answers for Schools*. Chicago: American Library Association, 2001.

Scales, Pat R. *Books under Fire: A Hit List of Banned and Challenged Children's Books*. Chicago: American Library Association, 2014.

Scales, Pat R. *Scales on Censorship: Real Life Lessons from* School Library Journal. Lanham, MD: Rowman & Littlefield, 2015.

Scales, Pat R. *Teaching Banned Books: 12 Guides for Young Readers*. Chicago: American Library Association, 2001.

Sova, Dawn B. *Literature Suppressed on Sexual Grounds*. New York: Facts on File, 2011.

Sova, Dawn B. *Literature Suppressed on Social Grounds*. New York: Facts on File, 2011.

Thomas, R. Murray. *What Schools Ban and Why*. Westport, CT: Praeger, 2008.

APPENDIX F

❖ ❖ ❖

Censorship and Teaching Ideas about the First Amendment

Congress shall make no law respecting an establishment of religion, or prohibiting the free exercise thereof; or abridging the freedom of speech, or of the press; or the right of people peaceably to assemble, and to petition the Government for a redress of grievances.

CLASSROOM DISCUSSION

❖ One argument used by some people who wish to ban books is that the First Amendment doesn't specifically address the freedom to read. Read the First Amendment aloud to the class and ask them to discuss how this amendment applies to their lives. How would our nation be different if we didn't have free speech? Engage the class in a discussion about the relationship between free speech and the freedom to read.

❖ Conduct a classroom discussion about the difference between a book challenge and censorship. How might a book challenge cause school officials to ultimately censor a book? Most school districts have policies that outline the procedures for dealing with challenges. Make available your school district's Board Policy Manual to students. Ask them to find out what the school district's policy is regarding issues related to questionable books and materials. Invite a school board member or a district official to speak to the class about local challenges.

❖ Justice William Brennan, a free speech advocate who died in 1997, issued the following statement: "Schools cannot expect their students to learn the lessons of good citizenship when the school authorities themselves disregard the fundamental principles underpinning our constitutional freedoms." To what fundamental principles is Brennan referring? Ask the class to discuss the relationship between the Constitution and good citizenship. How does freedom require responsibility?

❖ Many free speech advocates blame right-wing political and religious groups (such as the Christian Coalition) for the censorship problems in the United States. While this group brings many book challenges, there are challenges brought by the politically left as well. Ask the class to compare and contrast the types of things that these two groups might challenge (e.g., the far right might challenge witchcraft, violence, and language; and the left is more likely to be offended by the negative portrayal of an ethnic group or the omission of information regarding sex and other sensitive topics). Have students consider books in this volume, and ask them to discuss which group is most likely to challenge these titles.

❖ It was reported to the American Library Association's Office for Intellectual Freedom that in 1997 a school superintendent in Marysville, California, removed *The Catcher in the Rye* by J. D. Salinger to "get it out of the way so that we didn't have that polarization over a book." Discuss how polarization can lead to healthy discussion. How does listening to all opinions promote the principles of intellectual freedom?

WRITING TOPICS

❖ Ask students to write an interpretation of one of the following quotes:
 "Every burned book enlightens the world."—Ralph Waldo Emerson
 "The books that the world calls immoral are the books that show the world its
   own shame."—Oscar Wilde
 "Fear of ideas makes us impotent and ineffective."—William O. Douglas
 "You have not converted a man because you have silenced him."—John Morley
 "Only the suppressed word is dangerous."—Ludwig Byrne
 "Free speech is life itself."—Salman Rushdie

❖ Ask students to research the life and works of Socrates. Then have them write and illustrate
 a comic book (in the style of a classic comic) that communicates Socrates's beliefs regarding
 free speech.

❖ *I Know Why the Caged Bird Sings* by Maya Angelou is one of the most censored books in
 America. Parents who don't want their teenagers to read the book object to the realistic images,
 specifically the rape scene. Literary critics feel that the book is an extremely moral book. Ask
 students to write an essay defending the novel based on the moral issues and themes in the book.

❖ Robert Cormier's books have been under attack by censors for his "negative portrayal of human
 nature" and because the endings appear hopeless since the good guys don't always win. Cormier
 responded to this criticism by stating that he was simply writing realistically. Read one of
 Cormier's works and write a rebuttal to the censors. What is the responsibility of the writer to
 present life as it is?

❖ React to the following words of Jamaica Kincaid: "No word can hurt you. . . . No idea can hurt
 you. Not being able to express an idea or a word will hurt you much more. As much as a bullet."

THINKING BEYOND

❖ Ask students to read about Justice Hugo L. Black and Justice William O. Douglas, two former
 Supreme Court justices who are considered the strongest champions of the Bill of Rights in
 the history of the Supreme Court. Then have them research the nine current Supreme Court
 justices and their record on free speech issues (https://www.law.cornell.edu/supct/justices/
 fullcourt.html). Which of the current justices is most likely to follow in the footsteps of Black
 and Douglas?

❖ Send students to the Thomas Jefferson Center for the Protection of Free Expression (http://
 tjcenter.org) and ask them to read about the recipients of the Jefferson Muzzles. These people
 or organizations are named Muzzles because they have forgotten or violated Thomas Jefferson's
 belief that "freedom of speech cannot be limited without being lost." Encourage students to
 read the newspaper and news magazines and identify people who might be candidates for the
 Jefferson Muzzles.

Note: Information in this appendix used by permission of Random House. A complete teacher's
guide for teaching the first amendment is available at http://www.randomhouse.com/highschool/
resources/guides3/censorship.html.

APPENDIX G

❖ ❖ ❖

Free Speech Organizations

American Booksellers for Free Expression: http://www.bookweb.org/advocacy/free-expression
American Civil Liberties Union: https://www.aclu.org
American Library Association/Office for Intellectual Freedom: http://www.ala.org/offices/oif
Association of American Publishers: http://publishers.org/priorities-positions/celebrating-freedom
    -expression
Comic Book Legal Defense Fund: http://cbldf.org
First Amendment Center: http://www.firstamendmentcenter.org
First Amendment Lawyers Association: http://www.firstamendmentlawyers.org
Freedom to Read Foundation: http://www.ftrf.org
National Coalition against Censorship: http://ncac.org
National Council of Teachers of English: http://www.ncte.org/action/anti-censorship
PEN American Center: https://www.pen.org
People for the American Way: http://www.pfaw.org
Project Censored: http://www.projectcensored.org

Index

About the Author

Pat R. Scales is a retired middle and high school librarian whose program Communicate Through Literature was featured on the *Today Show* and in various professional journals. She received the ALA/Grolier Award in 1997 and was featured in *Library Journal's* first Movers and Shakers in Libraries issue: People Who Are Shaping the Future of Libraries. Ms. Scales has served as chair of the prestigious Newbery, Caldecott, and Wilder Award committees. She is a past president of the Association of Library Service for Children, a division of the American Library Association. She has been actively involved with ALA's Intellectual Freedom Committee for a number of years, is a member of the Freedom to Read Foundation, serves on the Council of Advisers of the National Coalition against Censorship, and acts as a spokesperson for first amendment issues as they relate to children and young adults.